BITTERSWEET Addiction

Q.B. TYLER

CW01558537

Copyright © 2018 by Q.B. Tyler

All rights reserved.

No part of this publication may be reproduced, distributed, or transmitted in any form or by any means, including photocopying, recording, or other electronic or mechanical methods, without the prior written permission of the publisher, except in the case of brief quotations embodied in critical reviews and certain other noncommercial uses permitted by copyright law.

This is a work of fiction. Names, characters, businesses, places, events, and incidents are either the products of the author's imagination and used in a fictitious manner Any resemblance to actual persons, living or dead, or actual events is purely coincidental.

Cover Design: Design Honey
Editing: Kristen—Your Editing Lounge
Proofreading: Amy Halter
Interior Formatting: Champagne Book Design

BITTERSWEET
Addiction

Prologue

I AM SO FUCKED.

My feet are pounding the pavement, the sweat pouring out of me as I run the familiar trail at the ungodly hour of four am. I couldn't sleep, my mind racing a mile a minute at what I did yesterday.

What I did with Charlotte Pierce.

I kissed her.

Touched her.

Fucked her.

After three hours of tossing and turning, I threw the covers off me and decided to go for a run, hoping that the stress over sleeping with my married patient would melt away.

It is not working.

I knew I should have just made a drink.

I push myself well into mile four, my lungs on fire with the speed at which I'm flying through the park and yet, I can't stop.

If I don't stop, it didn't happen. If I don't stop, it didn't happen.

Focus on the pain, Will. Focus on trying to get the air into your lungs and not the ache in your dick that comes every time you think about Charlotte.

Her sweet smile.

Her sweet…cunt.

I close my eyes. *FUCK.* She tastes like sin. Pure sex wrapped in a white satin bow that I'd had the great pleasure of unwrapping with my teeth. I worshipped at the altar of Charlotte Pierce's body for hours in my office yesterday. No inch of skin was left unkissed, untouched, un*fucked*.

I knew it. I knew I should have turned Charlotte and her husband away. Refused to counsel them, made up some reason why I wasn't the right fit, then recommended someone else. The second I saw those eyes and she shot me that smile, I should have walked away. The second that she began to speak and I felt my heart breaking out of the block of ice that had been surrounding it for years, I should have told them I couldn't ethically be their counselor.

I had compassion for people, and the empathy that was required in my line of work. But that only went so far. I never let anyone in, due to things I learned as a marriage counselor: people are selfish and I wasn't willing to put my heart out there just to have it eviscerated.

I'd done that for years and it almost killed me.

Enter Charlotte Pierce; she has the warmest disposition, the sweetest heart, and is one of the most insanely gorgeous women I've ever met. I let her in. Somewhere between her mouth on my balls and her ass in my hands as I fucked her on the leather sofa where she sat with her husband twice a week, I had let her in.

And now, *I am fucked.*

I mean it wasn't completely my fault. I grit my teeth, angry at myself for trying to rationalize the choices I've made.

It's true, her husband is a dick, without a doubt. To be honest, I don't know why she puts up with his shit. I've counseled women that would have left his inconsiderate ass years ago. *And they were married to men that were much richer.*

They don't have kids. What exactly is keeping her in this unhappy marriage? *It can't be the sex.* They probably fuck face to face every time. Missionary style. Four polite minutes of sex and then they roll to their other sides of the bed.

There's no way he fucked her the way he needed to. *Certainly not the way I do,* which had her coming all over my cock…and my fingers…and my tongue.

Fuck, now I am thinking about her coming. I am thinking about making her come. I am thinking about her taste.

I stop running. The conclusion as blatant and obvious as the "Stop" sign in front of me.

I fucked Charlotte Pierce and I was going to do it again.

CHAPTER
One

Will

I RUB A HAND OVER MY JAW AS I RECALL HOW I GOT HERE IN THE first place. The steps I took and the decisions I made that have all led me to this moment—the woman I love is crying so hard she's shaking in my arms. She's in my lap, clinging to me as if I'm a life raft in the midst of the treacherous waters of her life. "Charley, sweetheart, we should get up." I pull her face out of my neck, stroking the skin just below her eyes before placing a kiss on her lips. "Come on, we're going to go home."

"Home?" she squeaks, her eyes large and full of wonder, and I realize she's probably not sure where that is exactly.

"My house." I rub my nose against hers. "You need to be with me."

Charlotte is silent the entire way home, her eyes never leaving the passenger side window. I drive her car, leaving mine at work in case Matt has some retaliatory idea of having her car towed from the premises. I grab her hand from her lap, lacing our fingers, and bring it to my mouth, rubbing my lips over her soft skin. I squeeze her hand gently and she looks at me, offering me a small smile before she returns her gaze back to the window, watching the tall buildings of the city turn to trees as we make our way into suburbia.

I pull into the garage and turn the car off, the sound of our unclicking seatbelts piercing the silence. "Charlotte," I say softly.

She looks at me, her brown eyes shimmering with unshed tears. "Baby, please don't cry. I promise everything will be okay."

She swallows and shuts her eyes, squeezing her lids together, and when she opens them a lone tear trickles down her cheek. "You can't promise me that." Her voice wobbles, alerting me that she's on the edge of a breakdown and that I need her in my arms. I'm out of the car in seconds, pulling her from her seat, and cradling her in my arms as I carry her through my house. I set her on the bed, pulling her shoes from her feet. I plant a kiss to both ankles and nod towards the head of the bed, telling her to move. She obeys and I wrap her in the blanket, pulling the covers up to her chin and kissing her cheek. "Get some rest, baby." She doesn't respond as she simply shuts her eyes, her lashes fanning out over her skin, worry etched across her features. I kiss her forehead, in hopes that the frown lines will soften, but the harshness of the 'V' between her eyebrows doesn't fade. I run my knuckles down her cheek before I slip out of the room, in preparation of making the phone call I desperately do not want to make.

My hand shakes as I pour the tumbler of scotch almost to the brim and down the whole thing like a shot while my thumb hovers over the contact. I put the phone to my ear, fearing condemnation, yet expecting something even worse.

I suddenly feel like I'm twelve years old again. *Get yourself together, Will. You're a grown man.*

"J.R. Montgomery," his greeting is barked into the phone and I shake my head. It isn't as if he hasn't looked at the phone. He knows who's on the other end.

But that was J.R.. Jack Robert Montgomery, the typical hardass father that resulted in his kids calling him by his first name and not "Dad." As a matter of fact, the only time I really acknowledge my father in that capacity was on the designated day in June when we have to.

The only time my father could truly be counted on to show

up was for my older brother or when my mother was hosting a dinner where she demanded his presence. I remember watching through the balusters of our staircase in equal parts fascination and disgust as my parents pretended to be the perfect couple in front of all the other WASPs in Georgia.

"J.R...Dad..." I rub my hand over my eyes, willing the strength from every deity there ever was. "Everything is...fucked."

"Go on," he says, his voice is even, with only a hint of condescension.

"Charley's husband knows."

It's quiet, and for a second, I think he hung up, but then I hear his judgment. "How could you let that happen, William?" My fingers tighten around the glass upon hearing my full name. "How did *it* even happen?"

"I don't know." I'm already exhausted from this conversation as the initial shock of the last few hours begins to wear off. *I should have just slept this off with Charlotte. I should be wrapped up in her right now.* I feel that familiar tingle in my fingers; they're desperate to touch her smooth skin, to hold her warm body.

"Try again."

My phone vibrates alerting me that I've received an email. For now, I ignore it, knowing J.R. rarely waited longer than a few seconds when he asked a question. "He showed up at my office. J.R... I don't —" I sigh. "I think I need a lawyer." *That was about as close to "I need you" as I was willing to go. So, he better not be a dick about it.*

I hear the slam of a door, and then his voice resounding through the phone. "Forward my calls, I'll be gone for the rest of the day." I can just picture him barking orders to his new assistant I met last week. A young, red-haired woman, fresh-faced out of law school, unknowing of what her life is about to become while working for the tyrannical J.R. Montgomery. I wince, feeling for her. I wonder how long it will take until she goes home in tears, having just been verbally ripped apart at the hands of my father. *How long 'till she feels she isn't good enough?* There's a reason why there is such a high turnover rate of women working for my father. He has unreasonable expectations, demanding perfection, and doling out harsh consequences to anyone that falls short.

I know that all too well.

Unless, of course, he's sleeping with this one. I wince, thinking about my formative years, watching as my mom made dinners where my father was frequently absent. The nights he wasn't home because he was "working late." I didn't understand until much later, in adolescence, that my father had strayed from my mother on more than one occasion.

My mother simply turned a blind eye.

"I'll be there in twenty, William. Is Charlotte there?"

"Yes." I sigh, hoping to the heavens that she can just stay asleep until after hurricane J.R. whips through my house.

"Good, I'll need to speak with you both."

"Is that really necessary? She's already a little skittish around you. I don't need you exploding all over her."

"What reason does she have to be skittish?"

"Don't bullshit me. You used your position as my father to try and intimidate the shit out of her, knowing you could."

"Watch your language, William." I hear his car start—a brand new black on black Maserati that no doubt cost more than a year of my salary.

"Keep your attitude in check towards her, J.R., I mean it." Charley is already on edge; her nerves are wound so tight she may snap at any second.

"You think I'm bad, you just wait until your mother gets wind of this. She's even less of a fan of your…girlfriend than I am."

Rubbing my eyes with the heel of my palm, I think about my mother. I groan inwardly. "Do not tell her to come here."

"No, I'm leaving her in the dark for now. We are going to get this under control."

"Great." I sigh.

"I'll be there in twenty."

"Fine." I hang up without another word. I expect a series of "I told you so's" and some hard truths, but I'm sure it's a sugar-coated glimpse of what my future looks like once the ethics board gets wind of this.

Fuck. The ethics board. Did Matt go to them already? Does his PI have pictures? Pictures of us together at the house?

I remember the email alert and half of me wonders if it's already the Director of the Board, requesting a meeting. I prepare myself for the worst but what I see shocks me instead.

From: Matthew Wells
Subject: No Subject
To: Dr. William Montgomery
Leave her and you can keep your practice.
MW

I sit on the edge of the bed, rage still coursing through me and I pull at my hair in frustration. I turn to look at the woman who's still sleeping in my bed and notice she's grabbed my pillow, submerging her face in it, and it makes me wonder if she is seeking comfort in my scent even in her slumber. My hand finds her hair, stroking her long tresses and a sigh escapes her lips.

My thoughts begin to race as I think about the events of the past twenty-four hours. Matt is spiraling. He's backed into a corner and he's self-destructing. *Does his email mean he hasn't told his lawyer? Hasn't reported me? What's his game?* I shake my head. *You already know what his game is: he wants to take power over you —and Charley. Well, fuck that. I'll turn myself in before I let him blackmail us.*

My mind drifts back to a different time. A time when Charlotte Pierce didn't consume my every waking thought. If I were stronger, I would have turned her and her husband away the second I laid eyes on her in that strapless mid-length dress looking like trouble with legs.

I move back into the living room, a fresh drink in my hand as I attempt to calm my nerves. I drop to the couch with a sigh, remembering the crossroads I came to seven months ago. I had called Charley to my office early, before her session, so that we could talk about what happened. I'd had the speech worked out perfectly. "What we did was unethical. We can't do this again." I'd repeated on a loop in my mind all morning. That all went to shit when she walked in wearing a dress that made her legs look a mile long. I knew in that moment that there was no way she was getting out of that room without my dick inside of her *again*.

I had never been attracted to a patient before, and I thought I could put my hormones aside to counsel them. Help them.

Instead I helped myself to his wife, then everything became a disaster.

———

"Ms. Pierce," I say as she closes the door behind her. The ball is in her court; if she wants it, she needs to let me know now. I know I want her again, but does she feel the same? My questions are answered when she locks the door, never taking her eyes off of me, and the sound of the click resounds off the walls of my office.

"Dr. Montgomery," she whispers as she stands by the door, not moving towards me. I think she's waiting for my move so I get up and make my way towards her, each step feeling like an eternity.

"Charlotte."

"William."

"Charley."

"Will."

I smile, already turned on by this flirtatious back and forth. "How are you?" I ask.

"The best I've felt in months," she answers, and I wonder if that has to do with me.

"Is that so?" I ask. The tension is crackling between us. I can almost taste her arousal, it surrounds me so completely. I know just by looking at her that her panties are completely flooded. "Why is that?"

"Because of you." She bites her lip and I have to reign in my hormones until I can get some clarity on this whole situation."

"Charlotte, what happened…"

"Was amazing," she finishes. "But I understand if…if it can't happen again," she says the words but her body language doesn't match them. She stares me square in the eye, daring me to challenge her.. But more importantly, as she shifts back and forth between left and right, I gather that she's turned on. She wants me. Now.

"Is that what you want?"

"I want whatever you think is best."

"This isn't what's best," I tell her honestly. But I know my body betrays my words as well.

"I see." Her eyes find the floor again, and I take a step towards her, extending my hand to move underneath her chin. "Doesn't mean I don't want it."

She takes a step forward reaching her hand out to me. I know this is the moment that will seal my fate but I let her wrap her arms around me, drawing them up around my neck and press her lips to mine, pouring herself into a kiss. "I need this, it's not a matter of want." She leans against me, and before I realize what's happened her tiny dress has been thrown across the room and I'm sucking her breast as if I'm trying to swallow it whole.

We finish defiling my office once more, and then we are breathing as if we have just run a marathon, a mess of limbs on my couch. She drags her lips over my chest and finds my mouth, kissing me with an aggression that I've never experienced. It's almost as if I've set a fire in her that she's never known and she's relishing in the sexy creature that she's become.

"Charley, we should talk about this," I say against her mouth, and I want to kick myself for interrupting her when I feel her lips leave mine. She sits up and nods once before her eyes find her hands that are fidgeting in her naked lap. "Don't be nervous," I whisper in her ear as I sit up and pepper kisses along her shoulder.

"You're going to say we shouldn't do this again," she whispers and to be honest, I was going to, until I saw that look in her eyes. Until I raked my gaze over the most gorgeous woman I've ever met, over the most delectable body I've ever kissed, the most perfect pink pussy I've ever had in my mouth, and all of those rational thoughts go out the window.

"We shouldn't do this. That much is obvious."

"I'm sensing a 'but'," she says with a wicked gleam in her eye.

"I was just going to suggest some ground rules."

"Ground rules?"

"Yes. To protect us both. I think we both know how damaging it will be on both sides if this gets out."

She nods. "Matt can't know."

"I agree." I fight the urge to tell her I don't want other men touching her. Even her husband. I can't tell her that for the past two months, I've had pangs of jealousy every time I think about her sleeping with her husband. No. That possessive caveman needs to stay locked up.

"Are you doing this with other women? Other patients?" she asks, and I can hear the apprehension in her voice.

"No," I answer immediately. Does she think my moral compass is that skewed? That I just go fucking any woman with a pulse without regard for the consequences? Can't she see that she's different? I don't think she does so I opt to tell her. "You're different, Charley."

"Why? I mean…why me?"

"I'm drawn to you in a way that I've never been drawn to

anyone. Frankly, I think whatever this is—is bigger than us both."
And I believe that. The universe wasn't going to let me leave this
earth without having a taste of Charlotte Pierce, and I was happy
to oblige that cosmic irony.

———

"What are you doing out here all by yourself?" Charley's voice
brings me back into the present as she appears in the living room
and immediately plants herself in my lap, wrapping a blanket completely around her. "I figured you were eventually coming to bed."

"I'm sorry, baby. My dad is on his way over, and I needed
something to take the edge off."

She whimpers and buries her face in my chest, pulling the
blanket completely over her head. "I'll be hiding in your room."

I pull the blanket down and kiss her before, shaking my head
slowly. "We can't hide from this. Any of it."

"Your parents hate me," she groans. "And this is only going to
make things worse." I hear my front door opening and my brother's voice rings through the air. Charley climbs out of my lap to
sit next to me when Andrew comes into view.

"What are you doing here, Drew?" I ask, wondering why he's
showing up unannounced. *Didn't he learn his lesson the last time?*

"J.R. called me."

Of course, he did.

"Why?"

"He thought you might need me." He looks at the woman sitting next to me and I immediately go on the defense. "I know we
didn't get off on the best foot." He smiles. "I'm Andrew, this asshole's big brother," he smiles the smile that's worked on a million
women and I wonder if mine will be as easily charmed.

She gives a polite nod. "I'm Charlotte."

He reaches a hand towards her and when she takes it he yanks
her to her feet causing her to squeal, and pulls her into a bear hug.

When he releases her, he rests his hands on her shoulders to steady her. "I was a dick that day. I didn't know how crazy my brother was about you…How much he loves you. How much you love him."

She starts to say something before she shakes her head. "What are you talking about? This is the first time we've met," she says giving him a knowing smile and he gives her one back. *I'm in awe of how Charley is reacting to this, her willingness to start over so easily with my brother despite their first interactions.*

"Well, alright then," he looks at me. "So, what's the next step?"

"I don't know, wait for J.R.…see what he thinks?" I rub my eyes, willing the headache away that comes whenever I'm preparing to be in the presence of either of my parents. I down the rest of my drink and Andrew raises an eyebrow at me.

"Alright, I'll pour us a round," he says pulling the glass from me and moving towards the kitchen.

CHAPTER
Two

Will

"I KNEW THIS WAS GOING TO HAPPEN. HOW COULD YOU NOT be more careful? You're telling me you couldn't have kept it in your pants until her divorce was finalized?" J.R. asks, the judgment dripping from his voice as he paces the length of my living room. Charley and I are seated on the couch like children in trouble as my father reads us the riot act.

I rub a hand over my forehead, recalling a time where I'd sat on the custom-made, leather couch that my mother had flown in from Italy. I was nine years old, trying to hold back my tears of embarrassment, as I hid the pain of my father's disapproval over not making the soccer team.

"We practiced for hours yesterday. What happened?" He shook his head, the disappointment all over his face.

"I don't know how you missed the athletic gene. It looks as if your brother got them all." He throws his hands up in defeat.

I look down, humiliated and unable to meet his gaze.

"J.R., lay off. Yelling at them now isn't helping," my brother interjects. My eyes shoot up, finding my brother, and I can't keep my fist from flexing slightly as I'm pulled out of the final moments of my trip down memory lane. "It's done, it's over with. Her husband knows."

"I'm shocked we haven't yet heard from Stein. Do we think that there's any chance he hasn't told his lawyers?" my father asks, his question geared more towards Charlotte—she does know him better than anyone else in the room.

I don't want to discuss the matter of the email in front of Charley because I haven't told her yet, but I shake my head anyway, answering the question for her. "I mean there's a chance. The fact that I haven't heard anything means he hasn't. The second the board gets wind of this, trust me, I'll know." I haven't given much thought to what I will do if the board finds out about my indiscretions. If I were no longer able to practice…if they revoke my license.

Where do I go from here?

I look over at Charley and notice her fidgeting, her hands rubbing her thighs nervously. I take one of her hands in mine and bring it to my lips.

Wherever I go, this woman will be by my side.

"I want to know why Matt just arbitrarily showed up," J.R. questions.

"Apparently, he was having Charlotte followed," I answer.

My father crosses his arms and stares down at us." Apparently?"

"He knows about the house. Evidently, his PI followed us there." I sigh, leaning back against the couch as the energy slowly leaves my body. I had a slight buzz earlier, but now it is wearing off and the exhaustion of the day and this conversation with my father is weighing on me.

My father looks back and forth between us, and even at my brother, as if he has the answer to the question written all over his face. He takes a step closer, towering over us. "House?"

"I bought a house."

"For what reason?" my father asks.

I resist the snort at his ridiculous question. My father drilled the importance of the real estate business into both me and my brother as we left college and entered the "real world."

I cock my head to the side, raising an eyebrow. "For Charlotte and me to live, J.R., why the hell do you think?"

"And his guy followed you to your future love nest," he shakes his head. "Fucking fantastic. I've really got my work cut out for me." He pulls his jacket off and fiddles with his cufflinks in the way that all pretentious assholes do. "Tell me you have something over Macallan twelve." He crosses the room like he owns it, and I happen to catch Charley's look of indignation as she follows him with her eyes.

That is one of the few things J.R. and I have in common. Our taste in Scotch.

That taste that almost ruined my future.

Ruined me.

I clear my throat. "I opened a bottle of eighteen earlier." He seems pleased with my answer and opens the bottle, pouring himself a glass. "I think we need to meet with him." My father suggests.

"Are you sure that's a good idea?" Charley's sweet voice floods the room. "I just…he's unreasonable right now. And unstable, and I just…worry…" She trails off and I can already hear where her mind is going. *She's worried about me.*

I smile at her and give her a kiss on her temple. "Don't worry." *I know the perfect way to get Matt alone based on his most recent communication.* I pull her into a hug, shielding her from J.R. when I shoot him a look and point to him and then my office. He nods in understanding.

"Charlotte, I think it would be best if I had some words with my son alone. Do you mind?"

Charley's warm, brown eyes find mine before looking toward my father. "Yes…I mean no, I don't mind," she stumbles, scrunching her eyes together. I can feel her nerves and all I want to do is take her upstairs and fuck them out of her. "I can go," she looks at me. "Should I go?"

"No," I say, shaking my head, my thoughts a mix of confusion and horror that she even considered it. "You're right where you belong…with me."

"Okay."

"I'll be ten minutes," I say brushing my lips against hers. "Drew, keep her company." I point at him and he nods.

"Absolutely, want to take some shots?" he says, shooting me a grin, and I shake my head as I follow my father back to my office.

———

He looks at my phone, staring hard at it before I see him forward the email to himself. "He just sent this?"

"Yeah, like an hour ago." I'm suddenly irrationally agitated. Despite the fact that we were in *my* house, in *my* office, I find myself searching the space wondering what my father can possibly make a comment about.

Who gives a fuck what he has to say?

That's what J.R. will say. He doesn't give a fuck about anyone's opinion and lets people know it —*often*.

The thing is, I give a fuck what people think.

I give a fuck what J.R. Montgomery thinks.

And he is ruthless with his thoughts.

He brings the glass to his lips, taking a healthy sip before he points at me, his eyes never leaving my phone. "This is what happens when you stick your dick somewhere it doesn't belong." He shakes his head. "I figured you would have gotten all of the inappropriate pussy out of your system in college or, I don't know, grad school? Who does this shit at thirty? Who throws a wrench in their life for a piece of ass?"

My blood begins to boil. I expected this. I was prepared for this. I repeated over and over the words *"do not engage,"* and yet I still can't stop the words as they flow from my mouth. "Oh, that is really rich coming from you. How many twenty something assistants have you slept with?"

"You watch your mouth, William. None of them were *married.*"

"No…just you. You were only risking *your* marriage." I cross my arms, narrowing my eyes at him. "I'm fairly certain there was a woman across town, that stuck by you and raised your sons while you were out philandering your way through Atlanta's slut-tiest," I snarl.

"Well, maybe you're better than me!" he yells. "Maybe I don't want you to be like me." The room becomes so silent, all you can hear is J.R.'s heavy breathing. I don't know what to say. His words hit me harder than I'd imagined, having never heard him say anything like that. "I was never going to sacrifice anything for them. And you're willing to give up everything for her. This is different. *You and I* are different."

Well, thank fuck for that. "You're right, I'd never hurt the woman I love."

"So easy to say that at thirty. Come talk to me in twenty years. You think you've got all the answers figured out? You don't. Love is fleeting, William."

"That's bullshit."

"You know what's not fleeting? Hard work that leads to a life-time of power and prestige. I'm leaving you and Drew the keys to the kingdom. A legacy you can count on. What will your legacy be if everything you've ever worked for is about to go up in flames for a whirlwind romance?"

"It's not a whirlwind, J.R."

"You've known her less than a year and you've already bought her a house? Are you insane? This all may be fun and romantic and exciting now, but what happens in a few years, William? I've seen this happen too, you know. You may know love, but I know divorce."

"So, do I. I'm a marriage counselor."

"Which is why I'm so astounded that you allowed yourself to

get into this position! You of all people should know that love is just as much about being smart and protecting your assets as it is about emotions."

"Look, I'm not here to argue the details of my relationship with Charley. I called you here to help me. So, either you can do that or you can leave."

He looks at me, those cold, blue eyes that are almost an exact replica of mine boring into me like they had so many times growing up. I am almost the spitting image of my father, something that to this day pisses me off. I hate that when I look in the mirror every day, I see *him*.

The devil in disguise.

People see a good-looking face. Women stop on the street, their eyes raking over me lasciviously, at times even in front of their husbands. They see something different than what I see.

It's why I've worked twice as hard to be *nothing* like him.

Drew looked like my mother, light colored hair, fairer skin, and freckles that dot across their faces, always growing darker under the blazing Atlanta sun. On our family vacations they huddled under umbrellas, or stayed indoors, hiding out from the UV rays and avoiding the sunburn, while my father forced me onto every golf course in a thirty-mile radius. Barking orders about what I was doing wrong and how I'd never amount to anything.

Because I was really interested in being the next Tiger Woods…

Well, I guess I'm about to have a sex scandal under my belt.

He finally speaks. "This email means he thinks he can get you to walk away. Are you—"

"I'm not walking," I interrupt, and he looks at me. For the first time since I told him about this predicament, he chuckles.

"You know, I was really looking forward to a light caseload this month. I'm supposed to be vacationing in St. Barths this time next week."

"I'm sorry for the inconvenience." I roll my eyes.

"I'll send you the bill."

"Take it out of my trust fund," I grumble, thinking about the hundreds of thousands of dollars I've refused to touch.

Long ago, I decided I didn't want it. I didn't want the "sorry for making your childhood shitty, here's a quarter of a million, I hope that makes up for it." Even when I was drowning in debt from getting my masters, I refused.

"You're so stubborn you know that?" *I am fully aware.* "Alright, speaking like a lawyer and not your father," he starts.

Thank God. Lawyer J.R. Montgomery is someone I can handle. It is his dad persona that has me wanting to step out into oncoming traffic.

"You really love this girl?"

I nod. "More than anything. She means more to me than my practice. I bought her a house last month. I know the timing and the circumstances could literally not be worse. But...*she's* all that matters. If I have to sacrifice my practice to do it, then so be it," I see the look he gives me. "I'm not going to regret it."

"And she's just as invested?"

"Absolutely."

He nods in understanding. "Call him."

"Call...Wells?"

"Yes, tell him you want to discuss the email in person and not over the phone. I have a plan but we have to move quickly."

J.R. may be the devil, but he is one hell of a lawyer. And though I do not trust my father, I trust J.R. Montgomery Esquire with my life and my career that was currently hanging in the balance.

I take a deep breath as I dial the man who is the only thing standing in the way of me and the woman I love. "Matthew Wells," he says tersely into the phone and I roll my eyes.

You know who this is, dick.

"It's Dr. Montgomery."

"I think we're past the formalities, don't you, *Will?*"

"Fine. I didn't call to discuss semantics. I want to discuss your email."

"I'm sure you do," he chuckles. "I knew you were so full of it with that 'I'm so in love with her' shit. Give me a break, Montgomery," he jokes. I clench my fists as I hear him disrespect my relationship with Charley. My father shakes his head at me, sensing my agitation and mouths at me to *calm down*.

"Would you meet me in my office? In say thirty minutes?"

"In person conversation, huh? That serious?"

"This doesn't really seem like the conversation I want to have on the phone, given that I don't trust you."

"*You* don't trust *me*? That's rich, you've been screwing my wife for how many months now?"

"LOOK," I growl and my father shakes his head and spins his finger in a circle signaling that I need to wrap up this conversation. "Thirty minutes, Wells."

"I'll see you then. Is *my wife* joining us?" he asks and I can sense the hostility through the phone.

"No," I say succinctly.

I don't want her anywhere near you, asshole. I'm ending this shit once and for all. And then Charley is mine.

I end the phone call with Matt and walk into my living room to see my brother and Charley playing what looks like…poker? "Got yourself a badass poker player here, little bro. Take this lady to Vegas."

"This is big," I say, kissing the top of her head. "No one beats my brother at poker." Something I've learned the hard way—many times.

She giggles before her smile turns to a frown. "Where are you going?" she asks, seeing my jacket pulled tight around me.

"J.R. and I are going into my office for a little while."

She furrows her brow and I know she has a million questions running through her brain. "Why?"

I kiss her forehead. "We'll talk when I get back, okay? Bro, stay here?" I give him a look that says *look out for my girl.*

"But—" she says, pulling my attention back to her. She gets up on her knees so that she's closer to eye level. "What happened to doing things together? Facing this together?" she whispers.

"We are…I just have to do one thing first, okay? Do you trust me?" I ask her.

"Yes." She nods. "Of course, I do." I lower my face to hers and she takes my lips immediately. Despite my father and brother in the room, I slide my tongue through her lips quickly. She responds to the kiss just as quick and it's amazing that a kiss that brief can arouse me instantly. "I love you," she says as my lips leave hers, our bodies still breathing the same air.

"I love you too. I won't be long," She nods and as I walk away from her, I notice something in her eyes.

Understanding.

CHAPTER
Three

WILL

MATT WALKS INTO MY OFFICE AS IF HE OWNS IT, ARROGANCE radiating from him with every step. He stops in his tracks as he crosses the threshold, and I think he's stunned that there will be another person present in the room. "What is this? I wasn't aware that I needed legal representation for this meeting."

"Have a seat, Mr. Wells," my father says, going into lawyer mode immediately.

Matt straightens his tie before he takes a seat across from me, only my desk separating myself and the husband of the woman I love. He crosses one leg over the other, his eyes narrowing and a smirk playing at his lips.

He thinks he's won.

"And here I thought you had come to your senses."

"Oh, we have, Mr. Wells. The question is, have you?" My father leans forward slightly, resting his hands on my desk, looking down at Matt.

"I want my lawyer."

"Go ahead…call him. My guess is you don't want to divulge though, that you tried to blackmail my client…and you put it in writing?" He rolls his eyes. "Your lawyer will be about ready to strangle you."

"What the fuck is this about? Get to the point," Matt snarls. His eyes narrow angrily, but I detect an uneasiness behind them.

"First, I just want to make sure I'm understanding your motives. You believe that your wife is a lying, manipulative, deceitful cheater and you don't want her to get away with that, correct?"

"I don't believe it…I know it."

"How can you be so sure?"

"I have proof!"

"Proof of what exactly?" J.R. clasps his hands, steepling his index fingers, and points at Matt. "So, you have a couple pics from a PI? Doctored probably." He shrugs. "That's all you've got?" He narrows his eyes at him and I have to admit I'm stunned. *Pictures were worth a thousand words.*

"They say more than enough. And they admitted it."

"No, they didn't." My father shrugs.

"Yes, they did!"

"It's your word against theirs, Mr. Wells." He moves around the desk and stands to the right of him, looking down at him, the same way he used to do to me when he was preparing to scold me. "Think about it, an ex-husband grasping at the straws of a failed marriage, but it's obvious it's over. Your wife doesn't want you." He shrugs again, his body language showing his indifference. He bends slightly, putting his hands on his knees so that he's at eye level with Matt. "So, in true lover's scorned fashion, you make up this whole story about an affair, and these so called illicit pictures which are merely my client helping his patient pick up the pieces of her life by finding a new home. A new home since *you* so selfishly sold the only one she's ever known."

"That's bullshit!" Matt slams his fist on my desk and I try my best to appear unphased as my father continues to belittle him.

"Let me guess, these pictures may show that they are *close.* But what else do they show?" I run through my brain wondering if Charley and I have ever been in any type of intimate embrace in public. The timeline is so hazy, and I don't know when exactly someone had started following her. *My father's gambling here. Typical lawyer trick.*

"They were having an affair."

"Maybe." My father shrugs. He walks to my window, staring out of it for a second before turning back to Matt with a sinister grin playing on his lips. "But can you prove it?" He doesn't wait for him to reply before he continues. "See, no. You can't. But *we* can prove that you tried to blackmail my client. You tried to blackmail a very well-respected and renowned *Doctor*. My client has received accolades for his service to the community, *you*, on the other hand, Mr. Wells, rip apart companies of hard working people and sell the parts off to the highest bidders. A profitable, smart business. But a selfish one."

"I am *not* the bad guy here. Charlotte cheated on *me*. With him!" His eyes shoot daggers at me. I can sense Matt is getting anxious as his hands begin to fidget with his tie and he sends a hand through his hair every few seconds. "My job has nothing to do with that."

"That's where you're wrong, Matthew. Because if you go after my son, I will go after everything you've worked your life to build." J.R. moves closer, almost in Matt's face at this point. "The career you chose over your marriage? I'll take that from you too." My eyes widen as I hear my father's fierce defense of me. I suppose if it came down to it, I expected this level of loyalty, but seeing it in action has rendered me speechless.

"I have them on tape!" Matt blurts out, and my father and I both freeze. "That's right. A tape. Of your son and my wife, *fucking*."

My father's eyes land on him and shoot back to me for a brief second. "Excuse me?"

What? How? And WHAT? My blood runs cold, knowing that I won't be able to deny anything if there are *visuals* of Charlotte and me.

Not to mention, that would destroy her.

"I wanted to know." He shrugs as if the answer to my questions and my father's need for clarification is that simple. He pulls out a small recorder, before rising from the chair. He kneels next to my couch pulling another small device from under it. "I needed to know, once and for all. And sure enough, a day after that bullshit post-marital session I had to sit through, just so I could plant this shit, you're in here on top of my wife." He points to the couch where just earlier today I'd made Charlotte come with my tongue.

Matt had all but begged me to set up a session and I'd obliged knowing that meant I'd also be able to have one with Charlotte.

Fuck.

"I knew you'd be meeting with my *wife* soon after you met with me." I hear the beep of the recorder, and I assume he's just shut it off.

"It's been going that entire time?" I ask. "Since you left here yesterday?" *Wait… so that means he has access to the very private information of every session I had between his and Charlotte's? Fuck.* I run through the last twenty-four hours.

Four couples.

Eight people.

"Indeed, Doc."

"So, let me see if I understand this correctly, you illegally planted a tape in my client's office, which by the way is inadmissible in any court of law or your divorce proceedings." He doesn't answer. "A tape, mind you, that is purely audio. Surely you can see the gaping holes in your story. Again, you're a man getting divorced and all of a sudden, shortly before you finalize your settlement, there's a mysterious tape that surfaces of your wife having sex with another man. I'm sure someone—me, for instance—will call bullshit."

I see him shift nervously in his seat and my father continues, knowing that he's got him where he wants him. "Let me ask you something: when you intentionally planted this listening device in my client's office, were you aware that you would be in violation of federal HIPAA laws as well as the privacy of any patients that you have inadvertently recorded in your quest for evidence? Each of whom could press charges against you, once they were informed?"

Again, he's silent, and I'll bet regretting not pushing harder to have his lawyer present, because this is a bloodshed. "All in all, Mr. Wells, it seems that the person who has the most to lose in all of this is you. Mrs. Pierce, is still entitled to half, and while my client may lose his practice due to the scandal this may cause, *you'll* be in prison. Can you imagine what the DA will do to you when he finds out that not only did you bring on potential malpractice suits but you blackmailed my client as well? You want to see how this all plays out in court? On top of ALL of that, do you think that we won't hesitate to bring up the fact that you manipulated Ms. Pierce into believing that her step-father who physically and mentally abused and tortured her for years was still out there looking for her, a year after he was dead? And you want to call Ms. Pierce a liar and claim that she's manipulative? I can assure you that the only person who will come out looking manipulative and deceitful is you, Mr. Wells. So, I guess my question for you is, what's your endgame here? You want my client to leave Ms. Pierce or else, what? You'll go to his board? Your lawyers?"

Matt's eyes narrow and his breathing has begun to accelerate, his chest moving up and down rapidly as if he's just run a marathon. "So, nothing happens? You just get to keep everything, after you ruined my marriage?" He raises his voice.

"I didn't ruin shit, Matt," I say.

You want to talk about who ruined your marriage? Are you kidding me? Your wife was drowning in misery before I even met with you.

Is he fucking delusional?

I'm snapped from my thoughts when I hear my father

continue nailing Matt to the wall. "The law doesn't give a shit about your hurt feelings or pride, Matt. Georgia law couldn't give a damn if Charlotte fucked everyone in Atlanta. Now, my client's ethics board, on the other hand, would have cared to know that he had an inappropriate relationship with his patient, and if you wanted a prayer at bringing charges over that, you should have gone about this completely differently. And to be perfectly honest, given Charley being of a consenting age, and the fact that she has asked for a divorce prior to the affair are both mitigating circumstances. So essentially, if my team played our cards right, we may be able to get him out of this with his medical license still intact. You, however, will be brought up on some pretty significant charges. At this point, the list is endless of what we can nail you with. Do you want to risk it?" my dad asks, the look on his face is one of a smug, arrogant lawyer who knows he's won his case.

J.R. Montgomery is fucking ruthless.

"Let me be clear, Mr. Wells, you do not want to go up against me in court. And neither does your spineless lawyer. I will bury you." His eyes are fixated on Matt, cold and angry; ones I've been on the receiving end of on more than one occasion while growing up. "You try and take my son down, Mr. Wells. I can promise you, as his lawyer and his father, I am taking you down too."

———

Matt leaves my office with his tail between his legs. I'm not sure if my Matthew Wells problem has completely disappeared but I can say for sure he won't be going to my ethics board...*at least not today*. My father drops me back off at my house, tells me he will be in touch, and to let him know the second I hear from Matt going forward. I enter my house, my mind still racing from the revelations of the past hour. I hear a noise in my living room and I make my way towards it to find Andrew on my couch watching television. My eyes sweep the length of the room in search of

Charley. "She's in your room. She wanted to lay down," he says as he bites into pizza that I assume he'd had delivered.

I nod and make my way to my room to find her lying in my bed, curled into fetal position. I climb into bed behind her and wrap my arms around her. She turns in my arms and I feel my heart breaking when I see the look in her eyes. "What's wrong?" I brush my knuckles down her face and I relish in the softness of her skin. "I'm sorry I took so long."

She shakes her head before she looks down, drawing circles in my chest. "What were you doing at your office?" she asks quietly. I sigh, wondering how I'm going to tell her about this recent development. I don't even have a chance to respond when she continues. "You went to see Matt…" Her eyes avoid mine as she sits up and plays with her hands nervously. "To discuss the email he sent?"

My heart plummets. *Wait, how did she know about the email? Did that asshole forward it to her?* "How—"

"He texted me. Showed me the email," she says as she hands me her phone. On the screen is a screenshot of the email followed by a message from Matt.

Matt: Sent this to OUR beloved marriage counselor. Within minutes he was calling me, telling me to meet him at his office. Probably didn't want to leave a paper trail that he was willing to trade you to save himself. I wouldn't be so sure that he'd never give you up, my darling wife. Maybe the pussy wasn't worth his practice? Gotta love the irony, after all of the lies, you'll be left without anyone to take care of you. Which is all you really wanted, right?

I am fuming. I want nothing more than to find him and rip him limb from limb. I do not need a reason to be angry with him, having spent the better part of the last hour resisting the urge not to lunge across my desk for his throat.

I note the timestamp on his text message. *This was before we met at my office. Smug bastard actually thought I was going to give in to his bullshit?*

"You didn't believe this, did you? Did you really think I was going there to give you up?"

"No." She shakes her head. "But I just wish you would have told me."

"I'm sorry. I should have told you. I just didn't want you to worry." I stroke the hair from her face. "There is something else…"

Her brows furrow slightly and her teeth find her bottom lip. My cock tries to respond, but I will it down. *Not the fucking time.*

"There's a tape…" I trail off. "Matt bugged my office."

Her eyes widen to the size of saucers and her hand covers her mouth in horror. "Bugged as in…" She looks away from me in confusion. "But…when? How? You mean like…he heard us?"

"Yesterday during his session. And yes, that would mean he heard us this afternoon."

"We…I…" She lets out a breath, and the tears well up in her eyes instantly.

"My father handled it, baby. Everything is okay."

"How!? Between that and whatever his private investigator has, he has a strong case against us, against you. I'll hate myself if he makes trouble for you. *Legal* trouble."

I pull her into my lap and stroke her back. "No hating yourself. It's taken care of. My father's a dick, but he's a great lawyer." I shake my head. "Him planting that bug was the worst thing he could have ever done. It's a federal offense, Charlotte. He tampered with people's privacy. Yours included."

"Oh…he has other people on tape, too?"

"I saw four couples in between your sessions."

"And he heard…" She blows out a breath.

"J.R. knows what he's doing. He's handling this. Your soon to be ex-husband doesn't want to risk incarceration, Charley. Nor does he want this in the public affecting his reputation."

"Can you get in trouble for your patients that were compromised?" It's all I've been able to think about since I heard Matt's revelation. I have a responsibility to my patients and due to my actions, I've betrayed them. As a consequence of my behaviors, their privacy had been violated. They trust me with their secrets…their skeletons, and my sins have allowed them to be brought to light.

"If we were to proceed with prosecuting Matt, then I would need to inform everyone whose privacy was violated. My guess is it won't come to that. But…I still have the responsibility to tell my patients, Charley. I may not have done right by you and Matt, but I've tried to do right by all of my patients."

"You did right by me," she says, and I have to resist the urge to snort.

"I think you're a bit biased. An unbiased party would say I had a large hand in bringing chaos to your life."

"I welcomed it."

"I was your counselor…they would say I took advantage of the situation."

"You may have been a counselor, but you are a man first. An unbelievably gorgeous man." She smiles. "And I'm a woman who was attracted to you. Things happened. I don't think you manipulated me or used your position to influence me. You weren't telling me in between thrusts that I was making the right decisions for my life. That your dick was the road to enlightenment or whatever psychobabble shit you used to spew at Matt and me before I called you on it." She giggles and I pinch her sides at her smartass mouth.

"Watch it, woman."

She giggles, but just as fast as her laughter comes, it's replaced by a frown. "So, what happens if you tell them and…they go to the board?"

"Then I deal with it. Ethically it's the right thing to do, Charley. I took an oath," I tell her honestly.

As unfortunate as it is, especially if Matt never breathes a word of what he knows, I've come to the startling realization that I still need to turn myself in. Maybe if I throw myself at the mercy of the board, they will only suspend me temporarily.

"I guess I was just hoping you could get out of this without losing anything."

"I'm not doing anything tomorrow, Charley, but it is a very real thing I'll be needing to take care of. I promise I'll discuss it with you first, okay?"

"Okay…"

I can tell something else is on her mind. Talk to me, baby.

"What are you thinking?"

"Well…" She chews on the inside of her cheek and looks at me. "Why didn't you tell me about the email? Is it because you weren't sure what you were going to do?"

"What?" I say my eyebrows furrowing together. "Charley, of course not."

"It's okay, I'm not mad. I don't blame you for wanting to think it over."

Is she insane? Does she really think I could ever give her up?

"There's nothing to think over. I want to be with you. End of story."

"You say that now…" she whispers.

"Forever." I pull her hands to my mouth.

"I know that you say that you're okay with losing your practice, that you won't resent me, but…you don't know what the future will hold. You don't know how you'll feel in ten years if this is still being held over your head."

"Charley, I mean in the same respect, you don't know how you are going to feel in ten years. No one knows what the future holds, that's not a reason to turn your back on something great or to be afraid to pursue something. I know that you are worried about the future but…we love each other." I brush my knuckles down her cheek. "I love you."

"I love you too. I'm just ready for next week," she adds.

"When you're a free woman," I tell her, picking up her left hand and pressing a kiss on her ring finger. "I can't wait 'till this holds the ring I give you." The tears are rolling down her face rapidly and I narrow my eyes curiously. "What's wrong, baby? Why are you crying?"

"I just can't believe that this is happening. Finally, we can be together and for the first time in…years. I'm happy," she whispers.

Happy.

Maybe my counseling did some good after all. All I ever wanted was for her to be happy. And now she is.

Finally.

CHAPTER
Four

Charlotte

FINALLY, I'M FREE.

I finish signing my name on the documents officially granting me my divorce. I've just dotted the last "I" and crossed the last "T", literally and figuratively. I set my pen down and look up at the judge who's sitting at the head of the table in the conference room of my lawyer's office. I pull the two small boxes out of my purse that hold my wedding ring and my engagement ring and set them on top of the papers. The red Cartier boxes are a stark contrast to the sea of black words on the crisp white paper. I chance a glance at Matt and he's staring at me as if he's ready to rip me apart. I swallow nervously, wondering if he's going to bring up my infidelity as I slide the papers to my lawyer and he passes them to his lawyer. Matt's eyes never leave mine as he glides his pen across the page, signing his name before he slams the pen down. His eyes are cold and dark, but what's scarier is that they appear almost empty. *Lifeless.*

And just like that, I'm divorced.

You could cut the tension with a knife, it's so thick. I hate that things ended like this, that Matt hates me, that I hate him. That the good times we had are so overshadowed by the last two years and even more specifically the last month.

How do people that get divorced remain friends with their ex? Right now, the thought is unfathomable.

Matt doesn't wait long before he leaves the room without so much as a *goodbye* or *have a nice life* or *fuck off*. I wasn't expecting to feel such a wide range of emotions. A part of me grieves for the woman that was so madly in love with Matthew Wells, but for the most part I feel relief. Relief to be free from such an unhappy marriage. The shackles removed. The tears flow down my cheeks before I can even convince myself that now is not the place to cry when I hear my lawyer's voice.

"We did it."

I sniffle and I'm happy to see that the room has cleared out. "Cromack…John…thank you," I whisper. "For everything," and before I know it I am hugging my divorce lawyer in a way that I assume most young women hug their fathers. So tightly that they never want to let go and Cromack has been more of a father to me than anyone I've ever known.

I don't think I want to let go.

He pulls away and stares me down, his hands on my shoulders. "You take care of yourself, okay? As fond as I am of you kid, I never want to see you in my office again, you hear me?"

I nod. "Yes, sir."

"Good." He smiles at me before he pulls me into another hug, and I wonder if he's ever hugged any of his clients. "I'm going to miss you, Charley."

"Because I made you a shit ton of money?" He pulls back again and I shoot him a knowing grin.

He chuckles. "Well, it didn't hurt," he nudges me before standing and pulling me to my feet, "but no. Because although I'm a lawyer and I sold my soul a long time ago, representing you made me remember all of the good that I wanted to do once upon a time. You're a good kid, Charley. Representing you made me feel less like the asshole lawyer that's going to hell and more like the lawyer I wanted to be in law school. The one for the people. The people that need me. That are hurting. That feel that they have no hope. You gave me back a little bit of my humanity, Charley. And I'll never forget that."

The tears that I was hoping would stop, are now in full force hearing Cromack's words, and I nod. "Stay in touch, okay? Keep me informed about Beth." I giggle as I mention his fifteen-going-on-twenty-five year old daughter.

He groans. "She's grounded for the rest of her life."

"Take it easy on her, being a teenage girl is hard. Hell being a twenty-nine year old girl is hard."

He rolls his eyes but I see the understanding behind them. The eyes that tell me, he gets it. "You're living breathing proof that tough times don't last. Tough *people* do." The words resonate with me and I find myself in his arms again. "I'll be on the lookout for your 'Save the Date.'"

I gasp as I pull away from him. "John!"

He raises an eyebrow at me. "Oh, I'm sorry, are we being diplomatic *now*?" He goes back to his seat and begins to pull out a folder assuredly for his next big case. "Go find that boy of yours and tell him the good news," he says, putting on his glasses. "Go start the rest of your life, you deserve it."

———

I'm barely through Will's front door before I'm sprinting, dropping my purse, kicking off my shoes, and tearing through the house, moving up the stairs two at a time. We had agreed that I would come back here after, Will having cleared his entire day so we could *celebrate* properly. I pass a bottle of champagne chilling in a bucket of ice as I make my way to his office. I open the door and his head snaps up, a smile crossing his face instantly.

"You're early," he says getting up out of his seat and making his way across the room towards me. I take a few steps, closing the gap between him and then I'm in his arms my legs immediately wrapping around his waist. And I *lose* it. I'm squeezing him so hard, in hopes that he'll tether me to the ground as the end of the storm finishes around me. I can barely hear his words over my sobs but I feel him stroking my back and the soothing sounds of his voice in my ear.

"Will," my voice breaks as I cry into his neck, "I'm…free," I sniffle and I almost can't breathe at how vulnerable I feel in this moment. *Will is the only man I can show this to. The only one that I can let my guard completely down with and still feel safe, protected, loved.*

"How do you feel?" he asks in my ear. My cries settle slightly allowing me to hear his words.

My face, still buried in his neck, my eyes still squeezed shut, I manage to choke out the only word I've been feeling since I've dotted the I in Pierce. "Relief," I squeeze him tighter. "Don't mistake my tears for anything else."

"I didn't. This is normal." I feel him move. I wonder where we are going but I don't care. *I'd go anywhere with this man.* I feel him lower us, and then the plush couch underneath my shins allowing me to straddle him. I finally pull away from him allowing myself the first look at this gorgeous man since he scooped me into his arms.

"I love you. Thank you…for everything," I whisper. "You… saved me."

He smiles at me and I feel my heart skip a beat at how genuine it is. "Charley," he whispers, rubbing a hand over my face as I wipe the tears from my eyes. "I am so proud of you. I might have thrown you the life raft, but *you* saved you. You got yourself out and you'll be stronger for it," he tells me.

I giggle through my tears. "You're shrinking me."

"Comes with being in love with a doctor," he shrugs. "You'll eventually get used to it." He winks and it reminds me and it ignites something within.

"Can't wait." I want him. *Need him. Now.*

"I love you so much and I can't wait to start our life together," he cups my face and then his lips are on mine.

I pull back, slightly, my lips still resting against his. "Do you want to go to your room and…start it?" I ask, knowing that Will and I both need to be as close as possible to each other. He picks me up and carries me to his bedroom, his lips never leaving mine once. His mouth is loving, worshipping. A kiss of a devoted man accepting me as I finally give my whole self to him. I thought I had given him everything already, but something about being completely free adds something to the kiss. Knowing I don't have to look over my shoulder, that there's no more lies, no more secrets, no more hiding. That we can have dinner tonight out in the open. It does something to me. And through that kiss I tell him.

I'm yours. Completely. Always.

Every part of me is officially yours. Even the ring finger on my left hand.

I'm pulled from my slumber, when I feel lips trailing down my face. A lazy smile pulls at my mouth as my body recognizes his smell, his touch, and his kiss. His lips move from my face and find my neck, the bristles from his beard tickling the skin. His tongue follows the same trail, licking and sucking at the skin on my neck and collarbone. He stops his ministrations and when my eyes flutter open I see the most gorgeous blue eyes staring back at me. "What a way to wake up."

"I would get used to it because you'll be waking up in my bed every day for the rest of your life." I feel a flutter in both my heart and somewhere between my legs thinking about being in bed with this man every day for the rest of my life.

I stretch my arms to the head of the bed, the sheet falling beneath my breasts and reminding me that the air is cool when my nipples pebble instantly. His eyes immediately dart to the exposed skin, his tongue darting out to wet his lips as he watches the effects of the temperature on my body.

I clench as I watch the pink muscle sweep back and forth across his mouth and despite the soreness between my legs, I want it again. I crave the delicious ache, and from the way he's looking at me, he wants me again too.

"I'll never have my fill of you," he murmurs as he flings the covers back and stares down at me, love, lust and admiration shooting out of his eyes. He lies between my legs wrapping his hands around my thighs and spreading them, exposing my bare sex to him. I expect for him to attack my pussy instantly, with the way he's all but drooling at the sight, but his lips find my stomach instead. He rains gentle kisses all over the space just above my belly button, dipping his tongue in the tiny divot and part of me yearns for this feeling when my stomach is round and swollen with the life we create. He nips at the skin, before moving down further, running his tongue over the top of my mound.

I whimper, as he spreads my lips. "Fuck me."

"I need a taste first." He sucks my clit between his lips immediately, forgoing any of the foreplay of licking. He sucks harder, rolling the tiny bundle of nerves between his lips and grazing his teeth over the slick flesh.

"Omigod!" I scream, my hands fly to his head, pushing him harder against me. "Holy fuck, I'm already close," I tell him, my favorite feelings in the world slowly creeping into my senses.

I see his tongue lapping at me, his eyes never leaving mine. I smell our arousals filling the room and I can almost taste the bittersweet flavors. I hear my moans, my whispers, my declarations of love, lust and passion. I hear his groans, as he feels my orgasm approaching.

The feels. Oh God, the feelings that Will gives me as he pushes me closer to that sweet release. The climax that rips through me while he fucks me or fingers me or eats me. The tingles that start at the base of my spine are starting to build as I begin to move my hips in rhythm with his face. "Will!"

"Fuck, you're already there," he groans. "Come on baby, come in my mouth so I can fuck you with my cock." His fingers tighten around my thighs, his nails digging into the skin and there's just enough pain, coinciding with a perfectly timed lick against my clit that pushes me over the edge.

"Fuck, Will!" I moan, as my body shakes. The sobs wrack my body as I fall back onto the pillows.

He climbs on top of me and slides his dick between the lips of my sex, my body still humming with the aftershocks of my orgasm. He wraps his arms around my back, tucking his face into my neck and sucking at the skin behind my ear. "Five months, and I'm still in awe watching you cum. It's the most erotic thing I've ever seen. You are so beautiful, Charlotte."

My hands fly to the back of his head, pulling at the hair at the nape of his neck as my eyes begin to roll back in my head while he pounds into me mercilessly. My toes curl forward, my body already preparing itself for a second climax. "You always make me feel beautiful," I reply, my eyes fluttering closed and letting the feelings of fullness take over my body as his thick cock thrusts in and out of me. The sounds of our lovemaking bounce off the walls of the quiet room, our bodies slick with sweat and arousals slapping together, and making the most sensual sounds. It doesn't take long for both of us to find our releases, screaming the entire way down, him one beat after me as he shoots his seed deep inside of me.

———

We make love for days, taking breaks to eat and a few moments of sleep before one of us would wake the other up desperate to feel the connection again. We live in our tiny bubble, completely ignoring the outside world except when we are forced to engage. It isn't until Thursday, three days after my divorce was finalized, that I prepare to spend time away from Will, much to my reluctance.

"Are you sure you can't come with me?" I'm sitting on his bed next to an empty suitcase, my clothes strewn around the room from my very disorganized packing process. I had been planning to take a 'Divorce-moon' as I've so tactfully named it for weeks but what I hadn't banked on was Will not joining me. He comes out of the closet, that he opened up to me and my overwhelming amount of clothes, as he ties a tie around his neck. Over the past month, I managed to get all of my clothes out of the house I shared with Matt. Most of them are still at Lauren's, but there's a good amount piling up in Will's closet waiting to be moved to the house across town.

"As much as I would love to, I do have some sessions today and tomorrow. And I don't think you're supposed to take your 'Divorce-moon' with your boyfriend."

"I mean, I guess not if I'm trying to find a nice rebound guy to mourn my marriage with while on my trip," I say shooting him a wicked glare, and he's on me instantly, pushing me onto my back.

"Watch it." I giggle, and he slides my hands above my head capturing them in his one hand and kisses me passionately. His tongue invades my mouth and I moan, relishing in the feeling of his tongue moving with mine.

"Don't leave," I whimper when he pulls back and I sit up.

"Baby I have to."

I pout, knowing that when he leaves I won't see him for five straight days as I'm preparing to set out for Key West for some much needed rest and relaxation with Lauren. "I'm going to miss you."

"Me too, Charley. But you'll have fun with Lauren…" He shoots me a look. "But not too much. You need this. You need a vacation and I have to get things prepared for our move." Truth is, I love how much Will wants to take care of me and look out for me. *And I don't mean financially. Will wants to be the sole person in charge of keeping me safe, something he promised he'd do for the rest of my life.*

"I can do that for us when I get back, Will. Just come with me."

"As much as I want to, you need this time by yourself for closure." I'm about to interject that I won't be alone when he must sense what I'm going to say. "Lauren going with you is different."

I roll my eyes knowing that this man will probably spend the better part of the rest of our lives together being the logical voice of reason and the thought warms me despite how much I push back on it. "We will talk every day?"

"Multiple times. Nothing will stop me from calling you," he says, and I nod in agreement. "Send pictures. Preferably of you in this," he grins, picking up one of the string suits I have out and he fingers the small fabric. He holds my yellow bikini in his fingers as he runs his finger along the crotch of my swimsuit devilishly. The gesture sends a surge through me and sparks a feeling in my core.

I snatch the bathing suit from him, knowing he's not going to try and fuck me before he leaves and I don't need him touching any of my panties or other bathing suit bottoms. "Stop touching. You're making me horny." He shoots me a cocky grin before he pushes me gently on my back and rips the panties I'm wearing from my body instantly. "Hey!" I squeal, reaching for them as he pockets them in his pants. I reach for them and he puts an arm up effectively stopping me. "Are you sure you can't have sex before you leave?"

"I'm already late," he chuckles and I wrap a leg around his body in response. I feel his hand making contact with my sex cupping me, possessively.

"If you grind this on me I'm going to have to change," he says stopping me from making contact with the crotch of his pants like I was attempting.

"That's not a bad idea. I love seeing you naked."

"Ditto," he says flashing me his most breathtaking smile before pulling his t-shirt that I was wearing up around my waist so he's greeted with a perfect glimpse of my glistening pussy. "I need a kiss to last me the next five days," he says and before I can present my lips to him, he's on his knees his mouth pressed against my sex. He takes one slow lick through my folds before he dives in.

Oh, that kind of kiss.

CHAPTER

FIVE

WILL

"**S**OMETHING'S ON YOUR MIND," I HEAR FROM BEHIND ME AS I send the golf ball soaring into the air and veering to the right. The air is warm and yet there's a slight breeze that comes with Novembers in Atlanta. With Charley being out of town, I felt it was time that I disclose what's been going on the last several months—with _my_ therapist and mentor for several years, Dr. Mitch Tucker.

My head leans back as my eyes follow the ball and I realize how this first shot is setting me up to be way over par for this hole. I curse myself. "You always shoot to the right when your mind is elsewhere," I hear from behind me. I grip my hand tightly around the club and look at Tuck, the nickname I'd given him years ago. I shadowed him while I was in graduate school and he'd taken me under his wing shortly after I'd gotten my doctorate.

And then, of course, there was everything he'd done for me after that...

Tuck had been more of a father to me than my own had ever been, which is why I'd been avoiding this subject like the plague. Disappointing Tuck was something I hated, and I knew he would be less than pleased about this situation I'd gotten myself into.

I've wanted to tell him about Charley for months but I wasn't sure how to broach the subject. _How do you tell the man that_

*instilled so many core values and taught you everything you know,
that you had tossed everything out the window?*

I slide my club back into my bag and take a seat in the cart.
"I'm in love."

He's raised his club to hit the ball but sets it down immediately
upon hearing my words. "Well, that was certainly unexpected.
You tell me this over golf? Who is she?" He smiles as he lines his
nine-iron club with the small white ball.

*Where to begin about who exactly Charlotte Pierce is. The love
of my life? The woman who changed everything? The woman I want
knocked up by spring? Take your pick.* "Tuck, maybe we should call
it a day and grab some lunch?"

"Oh?" he says, looking away from the ball. His curious eyes
find mine behind the glasses that are perched on his face, sliding
down slightly as he looks at me from over the top of the rims. He
adjusts them and runs a hand through his curly brown hair that
has started to gray slightly, something he was in denial about as
he entered his fiftieth year of life. "Alright let me just hit this one.
Tell me about her, what is she like?"

"I bought her a house," I blurt out and I groan at this case of
word vomit I have. *That's how we're going to start this?* I rub my
forehead, already feeling the headache coming on, and wishing
that I was with anyone except Tuck at the moment, because I
needed something to calm my nerves.

I see him stumble forward slightly hearing my words, the club
hitting the ball and knocking it from the tee. "You did that on purpose," he says glaring at me. "That doesn't count, dammit," he says
as he picks up the ball and places it back on the tee.

"That's one stroke," I nod at the ball.

"Kiss my ass, Montgomery."

Two holes later, we call it a day, as Tuck is already a dog with
a bone wanting information about this mysterious woman in
my life. We are back in the golf cart making our way up to the

clubhouse when he asks again. "So, you're not going to tell me anything about her?"

"It's a long story."

"Start from the beginning. How did you meet?"

I know I'm not ready to start there. Maybe if I work backwards, it will be easier.

"We've been together for five months, and I can safely say that I've never felt like this, Tuck. Ever. She's the best thing that's ever happened to me. I love her more than…anything. And it's scary."

And it's true. It's scary thinking about how far I'd go to be with her. With each passing day, I realize just how much I'd be willing to give up for her. How much I would sacrifice for her. It's why I finally decided to talk to Tucker. Is my love for her clouding my judgment and I can't see that my life is going up in flames? *And if it does, will Charley still be there after the wreckage? If I self-destruct will she be there when the smoke clears?*

"Does she reciprocate these feelings?"

I lean back in the golf cart seat and cross my arms. "Yes. She loves me too."

"Why am I sensing that there's more to the story?"

"Because that is merely the tip of the iceberg, Tuck." I run a hand through my hair and let it drag down my face. "I've made a lot of mistakes. I crossed so many lines…"

He rubs a hand over his mouth and regards me warily. "When you say you've crossed a line…"

"She's a patient," I blurt out.

"I was not expecting that," he says. "Will, you're a marriage counselor."

"That's what it says on the door to my office," I reply and he gives me a shrewd look.

"So, you're in love with a married woman, then?"

"She's divorced."

"Officially? As in, she filed?"

"Yes."

"Well that's something."

"There's more."

"Of course, there is. Go on…"

"Her husband caught us."

"And you still have a job?" He raises an eyebrow at me as he pulls the cart to a stop.

I give him a quick rundown of what happened with her husband and the tape, how Wells had hired a private investigator, and how we'd run into his best friend that night, effectively setting the chaos into motion. When I finally stop, I think for the first time ever Mitch Tucker is speechless.

"Say something. Tell me, how bad it will be if it comes out that we were together while she was married. That I was sleeping with my patient."

He lets out a breath and steadies himself to speak. "Bad. They'll take your license, Will…how did this happen? This isn't like you."

I shake my head. "I know. Things just got out of control. In the beginning, I thought that if I just slept with her once I'd get it out of my system and that would be the end of it. I knew I was crossing a line but I was drawn to her like no one else. I tried everything to forget about her. I even slept with a woman that looked like her to try and get the fantasy out of my system."

I wince, remembering that night and how sleeping with a woman that favored Charlotte, a woman I'd been lusting after for weeks didn't even begin to scratch the itch.

She's here.

Those two words surround me, making me instantly hard as if my body is already pre-dispositioned to react to her presence. My eyes rake over her once, twice, three times before I narrow them slightly.

Is it her? I lean forward, trying to ignore my brother Drew as he talks about his current woman troubles. The last thing I want to do is my job when I'm off the clock. And yet my brother always had some issue. I guess that comes with the territory of fucking every woman in Atlanta.

Her brown hair is covering her face, the familiar waves cascading down and around her shoulders, curling just under her breasts. Breasts that just this morning, I thought about running my cock between.

I lick my lips and shift slightly, trying to relieve the ache in my dick as I picture Charlotte Pierce across the room.

Is it her?

The bar's lighting is low creating an intimate ambiance for people unwinding after a long day.

A long week.

Hell, for me, a long month.

One month, thirty tortuous days of breaking my dick off thinking about my married patient. Thinking about her soft curves underneath my fingertips, her full pouty lips that she sinks her teeth into. Lips I want to kiss. I want to kiss her so thoroughly she wouldn't have a coherent thought in her brain.

Certainly not that she had a husband.

I wanted to run my tongue between her lips, and make love to her mouth, tasting every inch of her.

Her eyes find mine and only then do I realize how long I've been staring.

Shit.

Not her.

I groan, running a hand over my face as I realize that I really am losing it. I look at her again, prepared to shoot her an apologetic glance when a smirk plays at her lips and a smile crosses her face.

Shit.

It wasn't until I grunted out Charlotte's name as I shot ropes of cum onto the woman's back—whose name I can't remember for the life of me—did I realize how completely fucked I was.

"Nothing worked, Tuck. And then one day, she looked at me," I say, recalling the first time I knew she wanted me just as badly. The day I realized I was going to fuck Matthew Wells' wife all over my office in a private session. "She looked at me like she wanted me. *Needed me.*"

"Will, you took advantage of her trust in you as her counselor. She was in an extremely vulnerable position, and she confided in you. She trusted you to help her. And you helped yourself to *her*!"

"It's not like that."

"Oh? What's it like?"

"I didn't coerce her into sleeping with me" I snap.

"Did you do engage in intercourse in your office?"

"Yes." *Where the fuck else would we have done it?*

"Where was her husband?"

"He wasn't there," I say through gritted teeth.

"Oh? Why is that?" he says, narrowing his eyes at me.

"Private session," I grumble.

"And who's idea was that?"

I clear my throat knowing where his train of thought is going. "Mine."

"And you don't see the coercion? Come now Will, you graduated top of your class at Harvard. This was premeditated and you know it."

I sigh and pinch the bridge of my nose. "What do you want me to say, Mitch? I know I fucked up. I should have walked away from her…from all of it. I shouldn't have continued to see her. The second I started picturing her straddling me during her sessions."

"How long were you having these feelings before you acted on them?"

"Two months."

"And when you did?" he asks.

"When I did what?"

"Once you slept with her…how did you feel? Guilty?"

I stare at him for a second before I look out into the vast green lands remembering the guilt and shame I felt every time I masturbated thinking about her. Every time I pulled my dick out the second her and her husband left the room, my cock aching just from the mere scent of her. Every time I whispered her name into my dark bedroom, in the dead of night while my hand was wrapped around my cock.

I felt guilty then.

"I felt a little guilty. But really, I was having the internal conflict of whether I could do it again or if it would just be a one time thing. Mitch, it wasn't just that the sex was incredible. We have this connection that I've never had with anyone."

When our eyes locked, when I was inside of her it was as if something shifted inside of me sending me into the most intense orgasm I'd ever experienced. She came apart in my arms right after, and I swear in that moment, I saw God.

"And then our affair began," I finish telling Mitch as we climb out of the cart. "But somewhere along the line, it became more. We fell in love. She's the love of my life." He rubs his head and looks me over and I can see his mind racing with a million theories. "What?"

"Have you explored every possible reason for your infatuation?"

"Infatuation? That sounds like a crush…Mitch, she's the one."

"Because she's unavailable? It would be the perfect woman for you based on your commitment issues."

"Excuse me? She's very much available now."

"I'm talking about when you first pursued her. Hear me out, before you fly off the handle. You and I have both decided, through your own self-diagnosis as well as my own that you have commitment issues, and you meet this woman that's unavailable. Thereby she's perfect because you don't have to fully commit to her because—"

"But I am fully committed to her. And at the risk of sounding like a pussy, I now realize why I had those issues with other women. Because they weren't Charley. Tuck, I know how this sounds. And if I were on the other side, I'd be saying all the same things. Urging me not to do this, to walk away. But I can't now. I love her."

"I just worry this is going to blow up in your face."

"That's why I'm talking to you now."

"To prepare you for the fallout? You asked me how bad it would be if the board finds out? You'll have to go before them and plead your case about why they shouldn't take your license. They're going to dissect and scrutinize every little thing that transpired down to what you wore the day you seduced her." He sighs. "But can we put a pin in this for a moment? What are you doing about the fact that some of your patient's privacy was violated? What are you thinking about that?" I roll my eyes at the common therapist vernacular.

"I think you know what I'm thinking. I owe it to my patients to tell them the truth."

He leans back in his chair, and I'm irritated by the look he's giving me. "Why?"

"Because it's the right thing to do."

"Now we're concerned about doing the right thing?"

"What the hell does that mean?"

"You were sleeping with your married patient for seven months, Will. You more or less broke up her marriage. Where was this moral compass then?"

"I know that what I did was wrong, but don't judge me. And it certainly has nothing to do with the people who were betrayed on my watch."

"You want to go to the board and explain to them what happened and somehow leave out Charley and her ex-husband? It's not possible, Will. You cannot spin this story. There is no way."

"So, you're saying I don't have the obligation to tell the board that a dozen of my patient's had their privacy violated?"

"I say you have the obligation to keep yourself out of Charley's pants." He crosses his arms as he looks down at me over his glasses and I resist the urge to break them —while they're still on his face.

"Okay, well, that's no longer an option, so how about you give me some actual advice and stop with the judgmental bullshit. And for the record, you and I both know that her being a consenting, competent adult that has no plans to sue me for malpractice obviously, in addition to the fact that she will swear under oath that I didn't force her to do anything will all work in my favor.

"Will, I'm not judging you. I'm being honest. As your mentor, your friend, your shrink, whatever you want to call me…This is not going to be easy. You can't reveal this information and expect it to go away in a few weeks. If this gets out…this will follow you. I assume the board will want you to take some time away, but if and when you start practicing again, it will still be there. The skeleton in your closet that you'll never be able to get rid of. You'll probably be done for as a marriage counselor. What man would want to bring his wife around you?"

"I would be with Charley, and I would *never* cheat on her."

"They don't know that! They'll be thinking you collect wives like baseball cards and when the conquest is over you toss them aside to collect dust in the attic. Don't you dare tell me you're that naive. If at that point, you and Charley are married, they'll suspect you as being a man that sees this as a game. 'How many wives can I fuck, how many marriages can I end?' Hell, maybe Charley will even be in on it. You'll have a reputation. And given that no one will know the story of Charley and her ex-husband unless she writes some sort of tell-all book, the assumption will be that you, Dr. William Montgomery, used your power as their counselor to seduce a wife and break up a marriage."

His words wash over me, and at this point I'm seething. "So, I'm done for."

"Will, I just don't see…" He trails off before he lets out a breath and closes the book in front of him where I know he's taken a novel worth of notes, "how you can come out of this unscathed."

"I don't want this to touch Charley…I don't want her to be affected by my mistakes."

"I do believe she is half to blame."

"That's not fair."

"Oh? You better have your story straight, Will, because if the board thinks even for a second that she's not culpable in that you coerced her into this affair, then you have a completely different problem. You're right, if you present this to them with all of the factors that you shared with me, it does change things. According to the AMA, the board judges cases of sexual misconduct involving a consenting adult on a case by case basis. So, it's a very real possibility, that there will only be minor consequences in that regard. But they're going to want to talk to Charley and evaluate her level of consent for themselves. So, if you make it seem like you were a slave to your hormones and she was just this innocent woman going along with your advances it won't work out well for you. If you want to paint Charley as—what? the victim—in all of this? Be my guest, it's not my career."

His voice softens and I think he regrets his choice of words. "I get that you don't want it to come across that she's some bored housewife, or a gold digger or any of the things you think could be said, but you have to stop focusing on what the perception of you and her will be separately and focus on what the perception is of you *together* as a couple." He sighs rubbing a hand through his hair and scratching his beard. "Will, let me asking you something. Have you…had anything to drink recently?"

My heart rate spikes hearing his question, and I remember that twelve month chip tucked into my sock drawer at home.

"Mitch, nothing is going on."

"Not what I asked you, Will. I'm asking…if you've had anything to drink." His tone is even, but with a hint of scolding.

I slide my Ray-Bans onto my face, not knowing how to look my old sponsor in the face and lie to him about the scotch I'd had before bed —and the beer I'd had before I met him on the course.

"No, Tuck. I haven't."

CHAPTER
Six

WILL

"I DON'T SEE WHY YOU TOLD YOUR MENTOR ANYWAY. IT'S LIKE you were looking for a lecture." My brother says as he slams his drink down in front of him, the liquid sloshing over the sides of the glass. I'd met him for a beer at a bar near his house that turned into a two which soon turned into four.

I could hear Tuck's pesky voice in my ear, asking me if I'd had everything under control. If the stress caused by my relationship with Charley had led me down a familiar road of self-destruction. *If I'd had a drink recently.* I scratch my beard and pinch the bridge of my nose, feeling suddenly antsy and fidgety.

Everything is under control. Tuck is way too intense. I'm not falling into old patterns.

Everything is fine.

I'm fine.

I clear my throat, preparing to explain why I felt the need to disclose everything I had with Tuck. "There's a good chance her husband is coming after my practice…." I trail off. "Well, there was until Dad got ahold of him."

"Poor bastard, probably didn't even see the wrath of J.R. coming." He snorts.

I frown, wondering what he knew about the wrath. Andrew Montgomery was the golden child, perfect in my parent's eyes. Star of the football team, Prom King, lacrosse captain, all around sports

God. His grades were…decent. But everyone overlooks that when you're All-American. My parents were over the moon when he'd gotten a full ride to play at Ohio State. They were devastated that he'd be so far away, but they were thrilled at the bragging rights it gave them to everyone in Georgia. I, on the other hand, was classified as Drew's younger brother. *The Other Montgomery* was my claim to fame. The second child. I'd grown up with a middle child complex and I didn't even have younger siblings. I tried my best to be like him so that my parents would notice me. So they'd pay more attention. I was decent at sports, but nothing to the caliber of my star older brother. It used to confuse the shit out of everyone that I wasn't better. I was smart as shit, acing my way through high school and scoring almost a perfect score on my SATs. *But no one seemed to care about that in comparison to my brother's ability to throw sixty-yard touchdown passes.*

I let his comment slide, suppressing my feelings just as I had done my entire life. I look up from my drink to see my brother making eyes with a redhead at the end of the bar. I watch as she tips the beer bottle back, running her tongue over the neck as if it's well, you know. I shake my head at her brazenness, but mostly I'm confused because, although my brother may be a manwhore, he was usually monogamous. "What happened to Olivia?" I ask, referring to the woman my brother was seeing just last week, if my memory serves me correctly.

"Oh, we broke up." He doesn't even glance in my direction, his gaze still fixed on the redhead who is currently twirling her curls around her finger. *How original.* "I wonder if the carpet matches the drapes?" He finally pulls his gaze away from her—or her chest that is practically exposed—to look at me.

"Did you actually just say that?"

"You'd be surprised, little bro. A lot of girls out here are dying their hair red these days. Fucking a woman with red pubes is like meeting a real-life mermaid. Ariel in the flesh, if you will." He waves his hand as if to say, *obviously.*

"Haven't we talked about not sexualizing children's movies?" I groan, remembering a particular traumatic conversation he'd had with his fraternity brothers that I'd had the misfortune of witnessing regarding who was the most fuckable Disney Princess.

"Haven't we talked about not shrinking me, Dr. Asshole?"

"Fine, go. Fuck Ariel. Don't come crying to me when she gives you crabs though."

His head whips to mine and then back to hers. "She has crabs!?"

"I was making a joke, dumbass. The Little Mermaid, her best friend was a crab?"

"Oh. Right." She looks at the woman before turning back to me. "Now all I can see is crabs. Thanks for ruining it for me. I was obviously going to wrap it up."

I lift the beer bottle to my lips, taking a long swig of the liquid. "Sure, bro."

"Stop being a cock block! Just because you're not getting laid right now, stop ruining it for the rest of us." He rolls his eyes. "Speaking of which, when is Charley coming back?"

Just hearing her name, makes the ache in my balls feel that much heavier, knowing that she won't be back for three more days. "Monday."

"Don't break your dick off before then." He chuckles.

"Says the man who spent the better part of his teenage years in the fucking bathroom."

"Hey, I wasn't always in there alone."

I roll my eyes remembering how Drew often had girls over. My parents were rarely home as we got older, my father working around the clock and my mother usually at luncheons for *The Junior League.* I would lock myself in my room, doing homework or reading while my brother had more than his fair share of girls moving through his room as if it were an assembly line.

I'll admit I'd been jealous at the time, but now, I didn't envy him in the slightest. A series of faceless women over and over, night after night. I'd engaged in casual sex from time to time before I met Charley, and rarely did it leave me feeling satisfied. Rarely was I sated. "Oh, I know. I had to help sneak girls out of your room on more than one occasion."

"Look I know you were saving yourself for marriage and all, but don't judge me for getting laid in high school." He waves at the bartender before pointing at his bottle indicating he needed another.

"I wasn't saving myself for marriage asshole, it's called not wanting my dick to fall off for sticking it in the wrong woman." I raise an eyebrow at him and he punches my shoulder in response.

"Well for your information, my dick is perfectly attached. Shall we compare? We can ask red to be the judge," he jokes. My eyes chance a glance at her, and sure enough her eyes are still fixed on my brother.

Move on, hon. He already has.

Whenever I spent any amount of time longer than one hour with Drew, I remember why I could only take him in small doses. He'd yet to grow up, and more often than not our time spent together was rather tedious.

"What are you doing here anyway?"

"Like…here in this bar? Here in this life? Are you getting philosophical on me?" My mind immediately begins to construct a monologue about my stance on Nietzsche's theories when he interrupts me.

"No, Einstein, like here in Atlanta. Your girl is in Florida, why didn't you go with her? Or why don't you go now? It's Friday, you can have the weekend with her," he answers as if it were that easy. *Charley needs space.*

"She's there to decompress from her divorce, Drew. I don't need to be there crowding her thoughts. She needs space and time. Besides she's with her best friend."

He raises his brows. "Is she hot?"

"Lauren? I mean she's okay, I guess? I don't know."

"God, do you no longer have eyes since you fell head over dick?"

"I believe the saying is head over *heels*."

"I stand by my statement." He pulls his phone out.

"I don't see what it has to do with anything, but yes, Lauren is pretty." *I only have eyes for Charlotte, but Lauren is an attractive woman.*

"I assumed as much. Hot women travel in packs." I go to protest about his reference to Charlotte when he puts a hand up, silencing me. "And before you lose your shit, I'm not the first person to notice that your girl is hot, and I certainly won't be the last, so relax. Anyway," he says as he scrolls through his phone, "there's a flight to Destin in three hours. We could be on it, and you could be with Charley tonight. It's a quick hour flight."

"*We?* Sorry, how do *you* fit into the equation?"

"Hey, if you're keeping Charlotte occupied, her friend will need someone to hang out with, right?" I look at him and then down at his phone. "Come on, I've got the frequent flyer miles, it'll cost literally nothing. I'll even spring for your ticket too."

"How do you have frequent flyer miles, you don't go anywhere." Drew is a CPA, and he rarely travels for work. The most traveling he does is to and from Ohio during football season or the occasional debaucherous weekend trip to Vegas when one of his douchebag friends is having a bachelor party.

That was hardly enough to spring for two tickets from Atlanta to the small Destin airport.

"Oh, did I say they were mine? I meant Ma's," he jokes.

"You have access to mom's frequent flyer miles?" I ask, narrowing my eyes at him.

"Of course, don't you?" He turns back to his phone, and I can hear him rambling about refusing to take the middle seat. I chug the rest of my beer, suddenly ten times more tense than I was thirty seconds ago. My brother has a way of flaunting in my face the very different positions we have in our family in the most nonchalant way. To this day, I'm not sure if he even realizes how his comments came across.

I need Charley.

And I need her now.

"Let's go see my girl."

———

Five hours later, we are checking into the hotel, and it's as if my dick can sense that she's near because it's been hard ever since we touched down in Florida.

"You got a suite? Pulling out all the stops, huh?" Drew asks as his eyes scan the lobby as we approach the front desk.

"Well I wasn't sure if you were planning to crash with me, so I figured a second bedroom was needed just in case."

"And hear you and Charlotte going at it? Pass. Besides, I'm hoping to need my own space as well." He raises his eyebrows up and down as he cranes his neck around me to follow a woman in a tennis skirt pad through the lobby.

"I'm almost afraid to turn you loose in here."

"I'm on vacation!"

"Right. Okay, well…I'm going to head up to my room. Want to meet at the bar in like an hour?" I look at my watch, and based on Charlotte's texts, including one picture in particular of her in a black dress that made my dick hard, it seems that she is heading to the hotel restaurant for dinner shortly.

I want to be there when she arrives.

CHAPTER
Seven

Charlotte

A Few hours prior

It's the second day of our trip to Destin—*two days of sand and clear waters that you can only get from the best beaches in Florida.* I'm lying on the beach, a margarita in my hand, soaking up the glorious rays, and I'm pretty sure I'm at least a shade darker already much to my excitement. I lift my sunhat slightly and look at Lauren who's deep in some trashy magazine she got at the airport.

"Hey I'm going to get another drink, I don't see our guy," I say, looking around the beach for the young waiter that had been making sure our drinks never dropped below half full. "Want one?"

"Ya, I'll take the same," she says, pointing at the glass that had been filled with a fruity, red wine sangria. I nod before heading towards the beach bar. I grab my phone as the Wi-Fi is spotty on the beach and as I get closer to the hotel—and the bar—I notice the connection strengthening with each step. I haven't heard from Will in a few hours, and while I know he wants to give me space, it's honestly the last thing I want. I wasn't expecting to miss him this much, and I wonder if that's healthy.

Maybe you should ask your therapist.

I roll my eyes at my snarky subconscious as I grab my drinks and head back towards our chairs. I hand Lauren hers and sit back down next to her, stretching my feet out and wiggling my toes.

"Want to try that restaurant on the other side of the hotel tonight?" I ask her.

Her eyes light up, probably thrilled that I'm not suggesting another night of staying in.

I know Lauren is itching to paint the town like we used to do. Yesterday, we were both tired and stayed in our room, getting drunk off champagne and watching a marathon of chick flicks. I knew my best friend, and she subscribed to the notion that a vacation gave you complete carte blanche to take a walk on the wild side.

Well, Lauren actually lived on the wild side.

"I'm game. Do you want to go out later? Three guys have slid into my DMs ever since I posted that Instagram of us on the beach. Apparently, there's only like three bars in this family friendly town. But one is having a party!" She holds up her phone and I squint as I try to see the picture despite the glare of the sun. I vaguely make out a group of people taking shots with bracelet glow sticks around their wrists.

"Sounds good." I smile, knowing that if there is a party within a three-mile radius, Lauren would find it, even in a town where there are more antique shops than trendy bars.

The Palm restaurant is nestled into the side of the hotel facing the beach with open air seating, allowing you to feel the ocean breeze while you dine. Lauren and I are seated in the patio area, the winds cooling my heated skin every time a wave crashes onto the shore. My eyes pan the restaurant, eyeing all of the other patrons, and I can't help but smile at everyone's good spirits despite the ache I feel from being away from Will. We'd talked this morning, which eventually turned into phone sex while Lo had scoured the breakfast buffet for all of the carbs to try and combat our champagne hangovers.

But it only filled the void for half a second. I know this isn't healthy, and if I'm still feeling this clingy in two years I'll deal with it, but I've only officially been with him two days and then I had to leave him. I'm allowed to feel clingy, right? Honeymoon phase?

The waiter, who's been making eyes at Lauren all night much to her appreciation, approaches our table and sits down two very different drinks. A glass of Malbec that Lauren had been downing like it was water all night and a Manhattan for me. I look up at him. "I'm sorry I didn't order this?"

"From the gentleman at our bar." He gives me that knowing smile, as if he'd seen this scenario play out a hundred times. *Don't fight it lady, you're on vacation.* I can almost hear his thoughts.

A giggle leaves a drunken Lauren. "Ooh, a guy sent you a drink? He's totally trying to slide in there."

I shake my head and pick up the glass, holding it out for him to take. "Oh, that's sweet but can you tell him thank you and send it back?"

"No can do, ma'am. He said to tell you that Perfect Manhattans are ridiculous. Nothing in life is perfect…except for you. And if you're going to continue to drink these, which I know you will, you at least need to drink them correctly." He points to the drink in front of me. "That's an *Imperfect* Manhattan. The difference is in the vermouth."

My mouth drops open as I read between the lines, and I know it means Will is here poking fun at me and Matt's "Wells Manhattan." *Oh my God, Will is here!* I go through a range of emotions all while the waiter stands in front of me. Shocked, disbelief and finally excitement. I smile before taking a healthy sip. "It's great." I look around and don't see the bar in my direct line of sight. "Where's the bar?"

"You're actually going over there? For what? Hot Doc will

have a fit." She takes a long sip of her wine and gives me a confused look as to why I am potentially entertaining some other guy.

Little does she know.

"Around that corner and to your left," the waiter answers my question, pointing a finger to the other side of the restaurant, and I nod. Excitement courses through my veins over seeing the love of my life.

"Lauren, I'll be right back."

Then I'm out of my chair, not giving her a chance to ask a thousand questions and draw her conclusion that Will Montgomery is crashing our vacation. I turn the corner and his eyes find mine immediately. Despite my four-inch heels, I'm running towards the bar and he meets me halfway pulling me into his arms. "Missed me that much, huh?" I say. "What happened to needing some time alone?"

"I gave you two days! What do you want from me?"

"Oh, so many things," I say devilishly as my hand dances down his chest and brushes his cock. Just the mere graze against his semi erection causes my insides to sizzle and his lips find my neck. "I'm so glad you're here."

He pulls back, raking his eyes over me from head to toe. "You've gotten some sun. You're glowing," he says appreciatively. I don't think I'll ever get used to being with a man that always has something positive or complimentary to say about me.

"Thank you," I say unable to find any other words as I'm still somewhat shocked that he's standing before me.

"I have a suite upstairs," he says. "The honeymoon suite was already booked but this one will suffice."

"I'd be happy with you anywhere so long as there's a bed," I say wrapping my arms around his neck. Much like normal, I don't notice anything else the second I laid eyes on Will, so when Andrew appears I'm shocked. "Oh my God! Hi! Sorry," I say hugging him, and he chuckles.

"Good to see you, Charley. I'm not here to crash your trip. Will thought I could keep your friend company."

"Did he now?" I hear behind me and I have a feeling this isn't going to end well. "So, what he crashes our girls' trip and I'm just supposed to spend the rest of it hanging out with some guy I've never met while you two defile a suite upstairs?" She looks at me. "Did you know he was coming? Was I just some substitute until he got here?"

I wince at her words, feeling terrible that she's come to this conclusion. "No, of course not. I wanted you here. I *want* you here"

"I didn't tell her I was coming, Lauren. She didn't know. And I didn't mean to interrupt—"

"That's why you sent the drink over? Because you didn't want to interrupt?" She crosses her arms, and years of experience as her best friend tells me she's pissed.

"Hey, lay off. He missed his woman and the way she basically climbed him and all but tried to mount him here in the restaurant, it's obvious that she missed him too," Andrew interjects and I wince.

Not the best course of action if you were hoping to make a good impression with Lauren.

Lauren nods her head, her demeanor changing as I know she's feeling somewhat burned by Andrew's words. "All I'm saying is, he's here now, there's really no point in me being here. You'll just be tugged back and forth between us and that's not fair, especially when he's who you want to be with."

"That's not true," I say.

And it's not. Lauren was there for me when I needed her. She's always there when I need her. And I can't treat her like an afterthought now, even if I want to spend the next three days in bed with Will.

"We are still going out tonight, right?" I ask her, knowing

that the idea of partying would perk her up and put her back in better spirits.

"I'm not really in the mood now." She puts her hands on her hips and cocks her head to the side, her ponytail dusting the skin of her shoulder. Her perfectly shaped eyebrows furrow together as she shoots me her signature '*I'm annoyed I'm not getting my way*' look.

"Well get the fuck in the mood. We're doing shots," I say matter of factly as I wave the bartender over and order four shots of tequila.

Lauren pouts, but I can see the smile hiding behind it at the idea of knocking this party into high gear with back to back shots of tequila. The bartender places them in front of us and I smack Will's hand away when he reaches for one. "What are you doing?"

"You ordered four?" he asks raising an eyebrow.

"Yeah, two for her, two for me," I shoot him a smile and I hear Andrew's deep laugh. "You guys will come though, right?"

"Like I want you parading around a club in this tiny ass dress and not be there to beat everyone off with a stick," he whispers in my ear before nibbling gently. It all makes sense now. I'd sent Will a picture of me in the short black dress I'd donned for the evening, but then the text had gone unanswered much to my disappointment. *He'd been on the plane to surprise me.*

I lick my lips as I stare at him before I brush my lips over his. "I'm glad you're here," I smile, hoping he didn't take my conversation with Lauren to mean otherwise. He nods and gives me a knowing smile. *This whole being in love with the voice of reason thing might be the best thing that ever happened to me.*

I turn to look at Lauren and shoot her a pointed glare. "You okay with them coming? I mean, you were going to be scamming on guys all night anyway *Miss Three Guys Slid into my DMs today.* I can have my boyfriend with me."

"Fine, but don't scare the guys away," Lauren says before taking her second shot and heading back to our table.

I roll my eyes at her sassiness and look at the two men on the other side of me. Andrew is staring after her with a look of interest. He had watched her collect the salt from her hand with her tongue rather *closely*, and I would know that look anywhere. He looks at me with a smile. "Tonight's going to be fun. I'm going to run upstairs to my room to get changed. When are we leaving?"

"Maybe an hour?"

"Perfect." He motions after Lauren. "She single?"

"Today." I shrug as I think about my best friend's dating habits.

"Even better." Drew rolls the sleeves of his white button down up to his elbows and runs a hand through his hair as he continues to stare after her.

"Come down when you're ready. We are in 706, we have a fully stocked bar." I tell him, my mind already predicting with how the night is going to go between them.

"Alright then, I'll see you in a bit," he says before he disappears with a swagger in his step that leads me to believe he has similar predictions.

"Your brother is going to try and fuck my friend, isn't he?"

"Oh absolutely," Will answers.

I chuckle to myself because, if I know Lauren as well as I think I do, she won't be putting up much of a fight.

———

Will and I have been doing an erotic dance all night. My hand grazing his crotch, his lips brushing against my neck, his hand dancing over my thigh, me sitting in his lap, me rubbing his back. And those were just our hands. The second I held his gaze longer than five seconds I could feel him undressing me with his eyes. His eyes telling me everything I already knew.

I can't wait to fuck you so hard tonight.

"Do you want to dance?" I ask, from over my drink.

Lauren and Andrew have disappeared, leaving us alone at our table for us to shamelessly eye fuck each other. My tongue finds the rim of the glass, and his eyes follow it, as if he's temporarily in a trance, watching me.

"I have a better idea." He pulls me into his lap, wrapping his arms around me and he presses his lips to mine, just as he's done a million times in the past hour. The taste of whiskey on his tongue successfully turning me on even more than I already was.

My eyes flutter open, and I run my fingers over his lips, smearing the red stain that was coating them. "I love seeing my lipstick on you." I look down, a mischievous grin finding my lips, "I love seeing it *everywhere.*"

He glances towards the dance floor, assumedly looking for Andrew and Lauren before he turns back to me. "Let me touch you," he whispers as his lips find my neck, his tongue darting out to lick the skin that has a thin sheen of sweat.

"Now?" My pussy throbs with need in response to his words as my eyes look around at the glasses and shot glasses that litter the table.

Who cares? Let. him. touch. you.

"Right now." His hands move between my legs, pushing them open and stroking me through the satin fabric.

Our faces are so close, I can feel his breath on my face as he's becoming aroused, touching my most intimate space. *A space he knew better than I did.* "But what if someone sees? What if Lauren and Andrew come back? Where are they anyway?"

"They're fine." He tells me, his hand pressing harder on my clitoris and I dig my nails into his shoulder.

"That feels...fuck. That feels good," I moan as I begin to move my hips in time with his hand. "Put your hand inside my panties, Will. Touch me, *there.*" I suck my bottom lip between my teeth for good measure and suddenly, I feel his hand behind my neck, hauling me towards his lips. He attacks my mouth with an intensity that leaves me breathless but I couldn't care less. I need this kiss more than air.

"Fuck you are so wet." He pulls away, growling in my ear as he slides his fingers between the lips of my sex.

I don't even have a chance to respond when I feel him rip my underwear on both sides, effectively removing them from my body.

"Will! I'm in a dress!"

"Don't bend over too far then." He grins. "Unless I'm behind you." He presses my underwear to his face, inhaling my scent and he manages to smear some of the wetness across his lips. His mouth is glistening from the evidence of my arousal and I gasp at the kinkiness of it.

"Touch me again." My words are like a desperate plea, my body needy for him. *For the orgasm I know was only moments away.*

"Part your legs, sweet girl."

He turns his back slightly, shielding me from the dance floor as he slides his hand up my leg and presses it against my sex, rubbing it through my slit, up and back several times. "Fuck." I can feel my clit pulsing already as he slides two fingers inside of me, hooking his finger around my G spot. "Oh God, Will!" I moan as I grip his hand harder against my pussy.

"Let go, baby. I know you can feel it." A glass shatters somewhere in the distance and I flinch. "Don't pay attention to any of that. Focus on me. I've got you. Focus on where I'm touching you," he tells me, his voice calm and soothing but also incredibly seductive. My feet flex on their own accord as my body begins to embrace the sweet release of my orgasm. His thumb continues to swirl my clit, rubbing the slick bundle as he continues to pump his fingers in and out of me.

He slips his fingers out of me as I come down from my high

and I watch engrossed as he sucks my juices from his fingers, running his tongue over each one lasciviously.

"Ready for that dance now?"

I freeze, my hand halting from bringing my gin and tonic to my lips. "I'm not wearing underwear, Will."

He raises an eyebrow at me before turning to look at the mass of people in the center of the club. "Come," he says and it's as if the word has a direct line to the space between my legs. He stands and holds his hand out, pulling me to my feet.

The second we make it to the dance floor, my ass finds his groin immediately and he pulls me hard against him, my back flush against his chest. I haven't danced with a man like this in years but it was if it all came back to me instantly. And Will can *move*. We are barely through the first song when I feel his lips dragging along my bare shoulder and up my neck causing me to shiver in his arms despite how hot I am.

The last song ends and I hear the DJ say something about 'slowing it down for all the lovers out there.' The first few notes of a familiar song waft through the speakers. Instinctively, I slow my movements to move in time with the sensual beat. His hands grip my hips hard as I circle them, grinding my ass more into him before moving myself down to the ground, bending almost completely over before I move back up, completely forgetting that I didn't have underwear on at the moment.

My eyes fly open as the air of the club hits my wet sex. That coupled with the sensation of Will's stubble against my shoulder has me weak in the knees. I bite my bottom lip and squeeze my eyes shut, trying to quiet the roar between my legs. I am hyper-aware that he's dragged his lips from my shoulder to my neck and I lean my head back against his shoulder.

"You smell so good," I hear him say, and it takes everything in me not to melt into a puddle of need right here on the dance floor.

I feel his hand move from my hips downward, and his hand finds my thigh. He begins to stroke the skin softly and I clench instantly.

"Will," I whimper as I let my eyes flutter closed, the feeling of his fingertips stroking my skin causing my brain to completely shut off. The only thing I'm aware of is the sizzle moving through my body.

Please don't touch my pussy. My brain thinks.

Please touch my pussy. My body responds.

He spins me around to face him, and my eyes fly open, his hooded gaze finding mine, both of us breathing like we had just run a marathon. Our chests are heaving and my heart feels as if it could beat out of my chest. I bite down on my bottom lip, as I'm too overcome with lust to speak and his eyes flit to my mouth. His hand comes into view as he pulls my bottom lip from my teeth before running his thumb over it.

"We have to go. *Now.*"

———

I'm in a fit of giggles as Lauren and I walk hand in hand down the street, our two bodyguards behind us.

Or at very least that's what it's felt like all night. He was within arm's reach of me all night and anytime anyone hit on Lauren, Andrew was there successfully cockblocking him. At first, she was pissed, but then she figured out his game and she thought—two could play it.

"Are you going to sleep with Andrew?" I ask as I try and keep my voice down, but I think it ended coming out louder than I intended when I hear snickers behind me.

"Shhh, keep your voice down," she says at equal volume. She turns around to look at him and then back at me. "He is cute."

"Mmmhmm," I say. "So, you won't mind if I go to Will's room tonight?"

She shakes her head. "No. And I'm sorry I got so snappy with you earlier. I was just feeling sensitive and maybe a little jealous. Are you mad at me?" Her voice slurs, and I wonder if maybe we shouldn't have had those last fireball shots.

"No, of course not. I understand. I would be kind of annoyed too. I mean I dragged you on this trip and then you thought I was just ditching you."

"Which you thought about…" she says raising an eyebrow at me before shooting me a smile.

"I mean…Lauren," I drawl. "But I'm not going to ditch you, we still have our spa appointments in the morning and then we're going to go to brunch."

She hitches her thumb behind her to point at the two men following behind us. "Aren't they coming too?"

"Not if you don't want them to?" I shrug.

"We'll talk in the morning."

I purse my lips and do my best to whisper my question. "So, if the sex is bad, no brunch?"

A sly grin finds her lips. "Something like that," she giggles and I shake my head.

CHAPTER

Eight

Charlotte

THE ELEVATOR RIDE IS PERHAPS THE MOST EROTIC EXPERIENCE of my life, both of us too worried to touch each other out of fear that we'd give the camera nestled in the ceiling quite the show. It doesn't stop the air from crackling between us, from the arousal forming on the lips of my sex, threatening to trickle down my thighs as we ascend to the suite on the top floor. My fingers tingle with an itch to touch the man in the elevator and the sensation begins to overwhelm me with each passing second. I peek up at him through my eyelashes and my breath gets caught in my throat when I see his blue eyes have become dark sapphires staring straight at me.

I don't know how we make it down the hall and into the room. The heartbeat in my sex pounds with every step I take making me weak in the knees. The second we cross the threshold he pushes me hard against the wall. His hands make their way underneath my dress, squeezing my ass cheeks so hard I wonder if I'll have marks from his possessive touch tomorrow.

"Fuck I've missed you." His nostrils flare and his lips part slightly allowing me a tiny glimpse into his sexy mouth that I know will be between my legs within the minute.

Thank fuck.

"I've missed you too," I moan as he slides his hand between

us and rubs it through my pussy that has been practically dripping with arousal for him all night.

His other hand finds my breast, groping me through the chiffon fabric of my dress. It's thin, making me hyper-aware of every brush over my nipple. He rubs his thumb back and forth over them, making them pucker and poke through the material.

His thumb continues its torturous assault of stroking them back and forth. I curl my toes as I feel the orgasm brewing already. "I thought about you every second you were gone. I could barely focus at work." He whispers in my ear as I begin to rock against his hand.

My eyes flutter closed and I rest my head against the wall, "I'm always thinking about you."

His eyes dart up to mine, and a look crosses over his face that I can't quite understand before he turns his attention back to my chest. "You have the most perfect breasts." I look up to find him staring at my chest in fascination, watching as my nipples pebble. He traces the tops of my breasts, across the minor cleavage exposed and slowly lowers my dress and my bra below my breasts, forcing them upwards. He rolls one nipple between his fingers while he takes the other in his hot, wet mouth and I'm fairly certain for a brief moment I black out from pleasure overload.

"Will."

He lets me go with a pop, and his tongue darts out, making a long trail from one breast to the other. I watch in fascination as he licks his way along my flushed skin. My cheeks heat up watching this man make sure no inch of my skin has gone untouched.

Un-*licked.*

"Take my dress off."

His lips find my neck as he begins to nip and suck on the skin under my ear. *Fuck this feels incredible.* He pulls away and his hands reach behind me to unzip my dress and shove it to my feet. His eyes rake my naked body twice as if he's not sure that I'm really in front of him before he reaches out a hand to touch me.

"I'm always thinking about you too, baby," he says, when I feel him lift me off my feet and carry me through the suite and towards the bedroom. My sex is bumping his hard torso every few steps, as my legs have wrapped around him. He lays me on the bed and takes his time slowly pulling his clothes off.

I whimper, knowing he's doing this on purpose. I sit up on my knees and pull him to me by his belt. I undo the buckle slowly, letting my hands trace the leather before pulling the strap out of the loops. Slowly unzipping his pants, I let them fall to the floor, careful not to touch his penis. He kicks them off and I get off the bed and kneel before him. "Charley, I want to be inside of you."

"You will be," I say with a wicked grin as I place a kiss on his penis that's hardening by the second under my gaze. His gray briefs allow my saliva to show instantly as I begin to lick and suck him through his underwear. I wrap my lips completely around him and suck, tasting the cotton fabric but also the precum dripping out of him, and coating the insides of his briefs.

"Take them off," he says, his voice barely above a whisper.

I slide them slow down his body and he steps out of them leaving him completely naked. I take one slow lick up his shaft before I wrap my lips around him and suck, *hard*. I had only ever done this to one other man and although he was much smaller and thereby easier to do, he didn't taste half as good as the man in my mouth. Will was large, and I had to learn to really relax and open up my throat to get as much as I could in my mouth but he tasted like pure sex. And as kinky as it was, the times I loved sucking him best was when I could taste myself on him. The times that our arousals mixed and coated his dick. He runs a hand through my hair and pulls causing me to look up into his eyes.

"On the bed, Charlotte. *Now.*" I let him fall from my lips that are already swollen and red from his nibbling the skin. I lie back and before I have a chance to get comfortable I feel his dick, warm from being inside of my hot mouth, probing my sex, his thick member stretching me. Filling me.

"Oh God!" I moan as he hits the spot that only he's been able to find. "Right there," I tell him, my nails dragging down his back. My lips find his shoulder and I bite down hard. He grunts, pushing himself harder inside of me as he slams his hand down next to me. "Don't stop."

"I'll never stop. God dammit, Charley. When you squeeze me like that, I can't control myself. Do it again."

I do what he demands and his thrusts slowly become more rapid. "Don't…want to come… so soon," I manage to whimper between his aggressive thrusts when his hand finds my face and squeezes my jaw.

"I am going to fuck you so many times tonight that you'll lose track of how many orgasms I give you. But right now, I need you to fucking come. Don't make me tell you again," he says sternly. "Stop holding back on me. I need you to come like I need fucking air, Charlotte. Give it to me."

I was already close, but his words mixed with his lips on my nipple has my orgasm rocking through me. "Will," I almost scream as my insides shatter. I close my eyes, the feeling disallowing me from keeping them open as the tremors wrack my body. I hear him say my name and *yes* but I don't see or hear much else. Despite the room being illuminated by the lights that we never turned off, I see nothing. All I can feel is Will. I sense him everywhere around me. His touch, him pulsing inside of me, his lips pressed to mine. I flutter my eyes open and I see my favorite pair of eyes staring back at me. "It gets better and better every time."

"We're fucking explosive," he grins.

I let out a breath and reach up to brush the sweat from his brow. "I love you," I say, the exhaustion setting in. All of the alcohol

I've had tonight is starting to catch up with me. The alcohol mixed with the fatigue post-orgasm has my body feel like it's floating towards sleep.

"I love you too," he mumbles against my shoulder, as he peppers kisses onto my skin. "Are you going to sleep?" he asks.

I actually didn't realize my eyes had closed as my body is still recovering from the force of the orgasm. "Not asleep, just resting my eyes," I mumble.

I hear him laugh and then his lips are on my forehead, pressing gentle kisses to the skin. "Get some sleep, sweetheart." I'm on the precipice of sleep when I feel his mouth between my legs, cleaning up the mess we made and my eyes flutter open as no amount of exhaustion could stop me from paying attention to him when he does *this*.

"What are you doing down there?"

"You smelled so good, I could smell the sun on your skin. I just needed a taste."

"Mmmm, keep going," I say as I melt into the pillows. Sleep, completely forgotten about I perk my head up to watch this intimate display of affection. His eyes find mine and although I can't see his mouth, I can tell he's smiling. My mouth drops open and I let my head fall back allowing the pleasure to take over. It isn't long before I'm coming and coming *and coming,* his name leaving my lips in a chant. My hands find his hair and I pull him up to me immediately, locking my legs around his back and I kiss him, tasting my cum.

It doesn't take long for me to feel us move and me being pulled to lay across him. I snuggle my face into his chest and then I'm out like a light.

———

The next time I open my eyes the room is pitch black, making me wonder if it's still night time or if the suite has blackout curtains.

Will is no longer underneath me and I sit up completely alone in our bed, the thought chilling me more than the loss of his body heat. I frown, wondering where he is when I get up, still completely naked. Pulling the sheet from the bed, I wrap it around me and pad into the main room in search of him. My eyes find him instantly, sitting on the couch, on the phone, wearing nothing but his briefs. He smiles at me appreciatively although it doesn't reach his eyes. "Thank you for letting me know. Please call me if you hear anything else."

His aggravation unnerves me and I immediately move to be in his arms. He ends the call and I settle into his lap. "You know…I went to sleep in your arms, and I woke up alone…I don't think I like that." I press my face into his neck, running my lips along his collarbone. I tell myself that I'm trying to calm him, but really nothing made me more at ease than curling up against him.

"I'm sorry, I got a phone call…I needed to take it." His hand makes its way inside of the sheet and begins to rub circles on my naked back.

I pull away to look up at him. "You sound upset, is everything okay?"

He looks away and then back to me, giving me a sad smile. "There are times where I will want to keep things from you. Things that I will shield you from because I don't want you to get hurt." He tucks a lock of my messy bedhead behind my ear. "But leaving you in the dark about some things will do more harm than good."

"I don't want to be in the dark," I whisper. "Tell me what's going on. Let me help," I say.

"No," he says firmly. "I don't want you anywhere near this. But I will tell you what's going on."

I nod, knowing if he's trying to keep me out of something, it's for a reason that more than likely involves my safety. "Okay."

"I got a call about an hour ago." He leans back against the couch, bringing me closer to him, "from our security company."

"Ours?"

"For our house." My sex pulses in response. *Our house.*

My mind refocuses, remembering that Will isn't happy. "Okay?"

"Someone threw a brick through one of the first floor windows," he says with a sigh and I can almost hear the blaring thoughts in his head.

"Were there other houses vandalized on our street? Maybe it was a—"

"Just ours, Charley," he interrupts giving me a look. "The cameras on the outside aren't set up yet, so we have no way of knowing who it was but…I have an idea," he says looking at me.

Fuck. I bite my bottom lip to stop the tears from forming as my head lowers in shame. "I'm sorry," I whisper.

"Why are you sorry?" He lifts my chin up. "I thought I broke you of that bad habit."

"My past—"

"Is just that…the past," he tells me. "We deal with it but we don't let it affect *our* future."

"But what if it happens again…and we're there… or our… children are there." I don't miss the way my body reacts to the thought of me having his babies. I see him tense slightly thinking about it as well.

"I'll monitor the situation. Do you think I would let you move in if I thought it wasn't safe? Do you think I'd let our family be in harm's way, ever?"

I shake my head. "No. But—"

"I'll put the house back on the market, Charley." He shrugs. "We find a new place and, in the meantime, you move into my place with me. There is plenty of room for us both."

"Will, you just bought that house," I remind him.

"I'm aware, but I'm not going to gamble with your safety either.

I plan to have you knocked up by spring, I don't have time to deal with that bullshit."

"Spring?" My eyes are wide and unblinking. *He wants a baby that soon? I can actually feel my ovaries exploding at the idea.* "It's November."

"Your point?"

I smile as I think about how excited he is to have a family with me when the man before him wouldn't even discuss it. "Are you going to put a ring on it first?" I ask.

"Are you asking me to marry you?" he jokes, and I raise an eyebrow in response.

"Maybe I am? What's your answer, Montgomery? Or should I get down on one knee? There's something else I can do while I'm down there," I smile cheekily and he squeezes me tighter.

"I didn't think you would be ready so soon to get married."

"I want to be with you…forever," I whisper. "And I want to start forever…now."

"I want that too," he says brushing his lips across mine.

"So, will you?"

"Will I, what?"

"Marry me?"

"I think I'm supposed to ask you that," he says, narrowing his eyes at me, but I can see the twinkle there that means he's pleased with this course of action I've taken.

"My shrink taught me to go after what I want. He taught me to be brave and strong and be the person I want to be instead of the person someone else wants me to be. Well…I want you. I want to be Mrs. Charlotte Montgomery. I'm ready. I know it's soon but… I've known for months that you were the one. And you waited for me, and you were so patient and kind and yes, the way we fell in love was inconvenient, but it happened. You're the best thing that's ever happened to me and I want to be with you for the rest of my life." Tears are streaming down my cheeks as I put my entire heart on the line for the man I love more than anything in the world. I pull myself out of his grasp and lower myself to one knee in front of him. "William Montgomery…will you marry me?"

The man in front of me doesn't even try to stop the tears building in his eyes and although he swallows them down I know the emotion is there. He stands pulling me to my feet. "Yes. Of course, I'll marry you. Tomorrow if you'd let me," he says before his lips find mine in a passionate kiss. The sheets are ripped from me as he carries me back to our bedroom.

"I'm sorry I don't have a ring," I say with a cheeky smile.

"It's okay. *I* do."

My breath hitches in my throat hearing his confession. "You have it?"

"It's been picked out…I didn't know you were ready so I didn't have them rush it. If I wasn't so turned on, I'd take you over my knee for stealing my thunder."

I giggle. "Sorry. You'll get used to it," I wink.

"I can't wait."

We consummate our engagement over and over that night, enjoying the bubble of my *divorce moon* as much as we can, knowing that a storm was brewing back home.

CHAPTER
Nine

Will

A SIGH LEAVES CHARLEY'S LIPS THAT MAKES MY COCK TWITCH. My eyes trace over that perfect mouth just before her tongue darts out to wet her lips, successfully turning my dick to granite. Her eyes flutter open just as the wheels of the plane hit the ground in Atlanta and I watch as a smile finds her face when she sees we are home again. I'd learned that Charley was a bit of a nervous flyer; she clung to me upon takeoff, her nails all but digging into my skin every time we hit the slightest patch of turbulence. It was only about a seventy five minute flight, but Charley had forced herself to sleep after take-off. I was too tense to sleep, my mind floating back to the broken window in the house I'd just purchased.

The police came to my house in response to the tripped alarm and called me within minutes of the security company. I had already been in touch with them as well as the investigator *I* had used to get information regarding Charley's stepfather. *I was sure Matt was the guilty party but I needed proof.* Thank God, the entire window hadn't shattered, so until I got home, they had placed a board over it to prevent potential flooding or a bird from flying in. None of our belongings had been moved in so I wasn't too concerned; it was a good neighborhood and the officer assured me they'd pass by once a day to ensure no further damage had occurred.

That was until my father got wind of what happened.

Imagine my irritation, not to mention shock, when my father began to call me incessantly while a naked Charlotte hovered above me, her lips wrapped around my cock as I submerged my face in her pussy.

"For the love of God, J.R. WHAT?" I growl into the phone, wiping my face of the cum that was currently coating it.

"Oh, you're irritated with me? Excuse me, for wanting to help you." His tone matches mine, giving me the impression that he is even less thrilled with this conversation than I am.

"Help me with what, I'm a little busy at the moment." I pinch the bridge of my nose, the tension back in full force after Charley had spent the better part of the morning sucking it out of me. Literally.

He snorts. "Yeah, I'll bet. Were you honestly not going to fly home? You were just going to leave your investment exposed like that? Thank God, Drew called me."

My blood runs cold and I immediately look at the ceiling praying for divine intervention to save me from having to go through this conversation. And what the fuck Drew? Why the hell would you call J.R.? "I'm assuming you're talking about the window, then?"

"What the hell is this bullshit board going to do? Someone could easily break in, or what if an animal got in? Honestly, William, are you more concerned with being inside of Charlotte than with your home? Priorities, son. You can be so irresponsible." My nostrils flare and my fist forms a ball as I struggle to keep my rage intact. How fucking dare he? I'M irresponsible?

My mind is stopped from going down a road of anger and resentment when I feel Charlotte's lips on my fist. My eyes meet hers and she gives me a smile after she'd gotten my hand to open up, successfully releasing the tension. Relief floods me as she climbs back on top of me and lies down, her head resting directly over my heart. The smell of her shampoo floods my nostrils, coconut with a hint of vanilla. Her lips press against the skin just over my heart.

When she looks up at me she smiles, and just like that, I'm lost in her warm brown eyes.

"Can we do this later? I'll be home tomorrow afternoon."

"If you insist. I was only calling to tell you that I've had your window replaced."

"Wait —what?" I ask, breaking me out of the trance caused by Charlotte's gaze.

"Did you think I was just going to leave it like this? No, I had someone come out and replace it, obviously."

"Who asked you to do that?"

"I think the words you're looking for are 'thank you.' Clearly you weren't going to ask me."

"Because I was handling it."

"You're in Florida! And honestly, son, if I'm going to continue to clean up your messes, I'd at least appreciate some gratitude."

I grit my teeth knowing that nothing good will come from speaking my mind, so I opt for the high road. "You're right. Thank you for taking care of that."

"Was that so hard? It'll be fixed by the time you're home, and you won't have to deal with it."

"Right." To an onlooker that had no knowledge of the longstanding, tumultuous relationship between myself and my father, I probably sounded like an ungrateful asshole. And hell, I probably was. But I also knew J.R., and he didn't do anything for free. I didn't mean monetary compensation; no, my father had more money than he knew what to do with. I imagine he wasn't batting an eye over the cost but would somehow use this against me. His comment about my responsibility was already seeping into my subconscious.

"Well, we'll be in touch when you get home. Your mother is just beside herself."

Bingo.

I groan inwardly, knowing that on top of everything, Diana Montgomery was now involved.

Fuck.

"Did you sleep at all?" Charley asks me, breaking me from my thoughts as she unbuckles her seatbelt.

"No."

She frowns, her lips turning downward slightly. I reach forward rubbing my thumb along her lips. "Why the long face?"

"You've been tense and anxious ever since you talked to your Dad. You barely slept a wink last night…"

"Well to be fair, neither did you." I smile at her as I recall all of the various positions I'd taken my new fiancée in last night.

"You know what I mean." She gives me a pointed look and I have to admit this authoritative side of her is turning me the fuck on. "You need to get some sleep when we get home."

"I have to go into the office. I pushed my session to five since I knew we'd be back relatively early today. My Mondays are back to being pretty busy now that I don't block out my entire morning for your *private* sessions." I shoot her a lascivious grin and I'm rewarded with those teeth of hers sinking into her bottom lip as she fights the smile creeping onto her face. "I also want to go over to the house."

"I can go with you," she says immediately.

"No." Our house has just been vandalized, more than likely by her ex-husband, and who knows if he still has a PI on her or me or both of us. The last thing I want is to take her there, before I have a chance to speak with the police in person and evaluate the situation myself.

"Why?"

People are starting to stand and collect their belongings, and I follow suit, pulling Charley's carry-on luggage from the overhead compartment. "Because." *Way to use your words, Will.*

"Because why?"

"Charley, can we get off the plane and talk about this later?" I pinch the bridge of my nose as I begin to wish I'd asked for a second whiskey ginger when the flight attendant came around to collect my first.

"It's a simple question, Will."

"Charlotte," I look at her, "I said no. If that's not good enough, I'm sorry. But as I said we can talk about it later." My voice is low, and my face close to hers not wanting the people that are in close proximity to hear our conversation.

She lets out a breath of defiance before she narrows her eyes slightly. "You had a drink?"

I swallow, as if that somehow would mask the scent. "Just one."

She looks toward the line of people that are slowly inching their way to the front of the plane, as we wait for our turn to move into the aisle. "I just figured we'd both need a break after last night." She shrugs.

The night prior Charlotte, Drew, Lauren and I had gone to dinner, had far too many bottles of wine and then found ourselves at a club on the other side of town where we proceeded to take shots like we didn't have any morals. *Or a flight to board at eleven am.*

"I just…I needed something to calm my nerves; that's all." She seems to accept my explanation, but thankfully it's our turn to proceed towards the exit and at very least the conversation has to be put on hold. I let her move in front of me, and I find myself transfixed by her ass as she sashays up the aisle.

You're going to need to tell Charley, that tiny voice not enthralled with her body tells me.

Why? I ask myself. *I have a handle on it. This isn't like last time.* *Yet.*

———

I step through the door of my waiting area and I'm not surprised to see Vanessa typing away on her computer outside of my personal office. "Dr. Montgomery, welcome back." She stands immediately and makes her way towards me. "I've left coffee on your desk as well as your mail." She has a stack of notes in her hand, which I assume are my messages. "Your mother called, twice," she gives me a smile as if to say *don't kill the messenger*, "and Dr. Tucker called."

"Did you tell Dr. Tucker where I was?" *The last thing I need is him on my ass about my weekend in Destin with Charlotte, my brother, and far too much alcohol. I can already see that vein pulsing in his forehead.*

"No, sir."

"Great, if he calls again, just go ahead and put him through. If my mother calls, tell her I'm in a session. *Even if I'm not.*" My mother started calling me yesterday, presumably after she'd spoken with my father. I'd already dealt with one Montgomery parent yesterday, I certainly wasn't about to take on the other. So, I proceeded to send her to voicemail…*six times.*

I move towards my office door, closing it behind me immediately. I run a hand through my hair as I sit down at my desk preparing to go through the stack of mail sitting on top, in a neat pile. Vanessa is orderly and meticulous. Keeping my secrets aside, she is truly the best assistant I've ever had. I bring the piping hot cup of coffee to my lips, coffee that I know is from Starbucks, but Vanessa always insists on putting in a mug because *"it tastes better this way."* I scan through the mail, tossing some aside without opening it, when I find a plain white envelope with the words *Urgent* and *Confidential* marked across the front. There is no return address, and my information is printed as if done with a typewriter. If I hadn't spent the last three days in Charley's arms, and knew she wasn't home in my bed sleeping soundly, I'd half expect this to be some sort of ransom note.

I rip open the contents to find a USB flash drive and nothing else. *No note. Nothing.* I lean back in my chair, fiddling with it in my hands wondering what in the world this could be. A part of me wonders if this is the tape that my father had forced Matt to hand over that had been evidence of Charlotte's and my affair, but *what would be the point of that?*

What if it's someone who has footage of who threw the brick?

Or perhaps it has nothing to do with Charley at all?

Good one, Will. You know your life lacked any real excitement until Charlotte Pierce came strutting into it.

I shake my head, not prepared to deal with whatever is on this drive when I hear commotion in my office and then in the flesh, is my mother, walking through the door, yanking her signature white gloves from her hands angrily.

"WILLIAM PATRICK MONTGOMERY!"

Shit.

———

Diana Montgomery is known for her composure. She is calm, cool, and collected even in the most tense or hostile situations. She'd suffered through at least four of my father's affairs and yet a smile is planted firmly on her face whenever she's in public. In true WASP fashion, she'd hidden her pain and resentment under fake smiles and luncheons that are infamous amongst Atlanta's elite. Once when I was fifteen, I'd watched her find a pair of underwear in my father's coat pocket—underwear that had not belonged to her—launder them, put them back into his pocket, and then prepare a dinner for twelve of her closest friends.

My mother is stoic, almost cold, with a poker face that could bring down Vegas. The only emotion that my mother really can emit is judgment which is currently radiating off her as she slams the door behind her. *Chanel Number 5 and judgment:* the true essence of Diana Hamilton Montgomery.

"You can't call your mother back? Honestly, William, I raised you better than that. It's quite rude." She slams her gloves into her bag before setting it down on the table. She walks towards me, wearing a tailored, long sleeved pants suit despite the warm temperatures, and her auburn hair is pulled into her signature chignon. "Your father has told me everything that has been going on, and frankly I am shocked that you kept this from me for so long! A married woman, really, William? You're a marriage counselor!" The condescension drips from her voice as her hazel eyes bore into mine.

"Now is really not the time, mother. I have a session in twenty." *Try an hour.* But I certainly wasn't about to entertain her for the next sixty minutes.

"Darling, I'm on your side, but you have dug yourself into quite a hole, son. What are you going to do if that woman's husband goes to your board, or heaven forbid the press?! Your name will be dragged through the mud." She shudders, and I truly believe she's spooked. My mother believes that perception is reality and appearances are everything.

"He's not going to be talking to anyone. J.R. and I handled Charlotte's *ex*-husband."

"For *now*. Things like this don't go away. Not at least without…a hefty compensation."

"He does not want to risk going to jail."

My mother presses a hand to her chest, a gasp falling from her lips. "Jail, my goodness, Will, what have you gotten yourself mixed up with?"

I ignore her question, opting to speak the language she knows well. "And he's certainly not interested in causing a scandal and ruining his reputation. He does well at his job."

My mother nods in complete understanding, as if everyone treated life as if it were a chess match. As if she believed that people weren't slaves to their emotions and didn't respond accordingly. *As if everyone had it together all the time.* "Well…that makes sense. If only my son thought the same way. Do you have any water, dear?" I make my way over to the refrigerator when she stops me. "Sparkling, please."

I roll my eyes as I pull the *Perrier* from the fridge and begin to pour its contents into a glass, knowing that my mother would never drink from a bottle. I hand her the glass and she smiles just before she takes a tentative sip. "As I was saying, it seems *you* don't seem to care about your reputation as a marriage counselor or causing a scandal."

I shoot her a look, knowing that the truth probably won't move her as much as I hope, but I go for it. "I fell in love with her."

I expected a scoff, an eye roll, for her to fiddle with my grand-mother's string of pearls that were always perched proudly on her neck. What I hadn't expected was for tears to flood her eyes.

My mother is showing—emotion?

"I was afraid you'd say that." She clears her throat, probably remembering herself and effectively removing the emotion from her voice. "Will, you are my son and I love you. So, I feel it's my duty to tell you, all love will do is ruin your life."

The words hit me hard, hearing the pain so evident in her voice making me believe that perhaps my mother stayed with my father out of love...and not just appearances. My eyes dart to the opened envelope on my desk, and the USB sitting on top of it, as if the knee jerk reaction to hearing her words is to suspect that what's on that drive would test the love I have for Charlotte.

Is that why you don't want to open it?

"Mom…" She pulls her handkerchief from her jacket pocket and dabs at her eyes. "I love her. She's the one."

"She was married, son. Haven't you heard the phrase 'once a cheater, always a cheater?'" She raises an eyebrow, straightening her suit and running her hand down her arms as if to brush off any imaginary dust. "Will, I understand that you feel a bit respon-sible for breaking up her marriage, but this is not your issue to take on. She cheated on her husband. It's not *your* job to fix the mess she created of her life."

"It's not like that," I tell her. "She's the love of my life. You'll understand when you meet her." I'm not prepared to tell anyone that Charlotte and I are technically engaged. Even if her ring finger is still bare, she is still my future wife. When we tell our children and our grandchildren we'll say that she was naked at a hotel in Florida, covered only by a sheet, she asked me, and I said yes. *Well, something like that.*

"I can't say I'm thrilled at the idea of meeting your *adulteress.*"

I knew this situation would be a hard sell to my mother, who'd spent the better part of her marriage turning a blind eye to my father's indiscretions. "Don't call her that." I try to keep the snarl out of my voice, but what I've quickly come to learn is that I'd defend Charlotte to anyone. *My family included.*

"Well, it's what she is, no?"

"I'm not discussing this further with you—or anyone for that matter. Charlotte is a part of my life. That's not up for debate. I am sure your tune will change when she starts popping out your grandchildren."

Her eyes widen, her mouth drops open, her poker face slipping for just a moment before she corrects herself. "Is she—I mean—you're having—?"

"She is not pregnant—yet." There's a spark in my groin thinking about shooting my seed deep inside of her, fathering a child. *Fathering her child.* A small Montgomery running around, followed by several more Montgomery's.

She stares at me for a moment, before she looks down at the vintage Rolex that sits proudly on her wrist every day. "Well, I know you have a session soon, and I'm late for lunch at the club with Tish Reynolds, *but* this is not over young man."

CHAPTER
Ten

WILL

FOR THE ENTIRETY OF MY SESSION I'M DISTRACTED, MY EYES moving on their own accord to the envelope sitting on my desk. Even my patients can see I'm not entirely focused. The second that I close the door behind them, I'm in my seat pouring a glass of scotch, welcoming the burn of the liquid, but it doesn't come.

Normally, I would make note of that, but the thought escapes me as I hold the drive between my fingers. Before I can stop myself, I've pressed it firmly into the side of my computer. A sound I would know anywhere, one that has a direct line to my dick comes out of my speakers first. Before I can see anything, I hear the moan of a woman—my woman. I watch as a dick, that does not belong to me penetrates the pussy I pray doesn't belong to Charlotte.

No. It's not her. It's definitely not.

"Oh fuck! Matt, right there. That's it!" she whimpers and immediately I feel the bile rising in my throat. I swallow it down, with a swig of my drink. The camera slowly moves upwards from where they're conjoined between her legs and I take in her toned flat stomach and tits that I would know anywhere. Tits I've had in my hands, my mouth, tits I've pushed together and slid my dick between. My cock throbs at the idea of gliding between the valley of her breasts. Her nipples pucker and one hand reaches up and touches her, strokes her, rolls her nipple between fingers that don't belong to me.

Will stop watching this. Turn this shit off now.

Turn it off before—

Her face comes into view. Except, it's not *my* Charlotte. No, this woman is much younger, her eyes wild and innocent, yet shy and unsure. That bottom lip moves between her teeth, telling me that she's had that sexy as fuck habit for years. Her hands move up her body to rub her breasts, and I breathe a sigh of relief when I don't see any rings on her left finger alerting me that this was before they were married. *Still makes me want to throw my computer out the window.* My heart feels like it could beat out of my chest at any moment as I watch an old sex tape between my fiancée and her ex-husband.

You know they fucked, Will. They were married.

But seeing it fucking sucks.

I feel as if someone has taken a knife to my inside and is slowly carving me out. My body, which was full of love and passion and devotion to the woman on the screen suddenly feels hollow, empty and broken the second the words *I love you* fall from her plump lips.

"You are so beautiful, Charlotte. God, you make me so fucking hard. Come for me, baby."

Don't make her come. Don't make her come. My mind is almost screaming at me at this point. *Stop fucking watching!*

"Fuck, Matt. I'm so close." She cries out, her eyes scrunched together, her lips parted, as her tongue darts out to lick her lips. She begins to bounce on top of his dick faster, her breasts swaying more aggressively with every bounce. "Oh my God, I'm coming!" Her eyes pop open and she looks down at that moment, into the camera, and the look in her eyes shatters me.

I would know that look anywhere.

Charlotte Pierce was in love.

And she came.

———

The video stops sometime after that, just as Charlotte was gearing up to put his cock in her mouth, the screen fades to black. The words that proceed after make my blood run cold.

I had to listen to you fuck my wife, how does it feel to watch me fuck your girlfriend?

The rational part, the stronger part of me knows that it was years ago. That Charlotte isn't the same woman as the one on that video, but the weaker part, the part that is currently fueled by one too many glasses of Macallan 18 and a blind, jealous rage, felt ready to attack.

Matt.

Charlotte.

Anyone.

———

Charlotte

I have been staring at my screen for what feels like hours trying to make sense of the five-year gap in my resume and how I was going to somehow *bridge* that gap with no actual experience. I'm sitting in Will's office, when the sound of slamming cabinets breaks me out of my concentration. I'm out of my seat before my brain can communicate to the rest of my body that I needed to approach the kitchen with caution.

My feet propel me towards the kitchen as Will rips his tie from his neck and throws it aggressively towards the floor just as he slams a bottle of alcohol onto the counter so hard I'm shocked it didn't shatter under the force. I jump, a tiny squeak coming out of me, and his attention turns slowly to me. His eyes soften slightly but I can still see the hurt and anger lurking there. His hands are balled into fists and I notice a tremor move through him, making me believe that he's so tense that he's actually shaking. I bite my lip, mostly out of nervousness, but also in the attempt to try and appeal to another side of him. "Will," I whisper. I take a tentative step towards him and his arm immediately shoots up towards me.

"No, Charley."

"No?" I ask, my eyes widen in shock. I don't remember Will ever not wanting me near him. *If we are in a room alone together, we are touching.*

That's part of what got us into trouble in the first place.

"I'm too angry with you."

"With…me? What did I do?" My heart begins to race, never having witnessed this level of anger and wondering what I possibly could have done to provoke him. This morning, Will and I couldn't even get out of bed, our bodies clinging to each other like magnets as we went through waves of passion we'd never experienced together. I don't think I'd ever come that many times in a short period. *What happened between then and now?*

He doesn't answer; he simply drains the contents of the glass in front of him and I move towards him, not letting his half-hearted *no* stop me.

He needs me.

"Hey," I move so that I'm in front of him and I can stare at him straight on. "What's wrong?"

"Just a long day," he says, his eyes finding mine but his gaze doesn't penetrate me like it usually does with blazing fire and passion.

No, his eyes are vacant.

Expressionless.

He tries to move out of my grasp and I stop him. "Stop that," I tell him as I wrap my arms around him tightly. "Don't walk away from me. Tell me what's wrong."

He's tense in my arms, and my heart begins to accelerate even faster as I notice that he's not putting his arms around me. Instead, I feel him pulling himself out of my grasp. "Charley, just…give me some space." Against my better judgment, I let him go, allowing him to move out of the room without so much as a glance back at me.

Dr. Montgomery's words ring in my head. *"A lack of communication is poisonous to your marriage. It seeps into those tiny cracks that you think aren't problems and rips them open creating monumental rifts in your marriage. It breaks down all of your strength until you're left with nothing."*

No. No fucking way.

My feet are moving quick as lighting as I dart into his office, to find him seated at his desk with his head in his hands. I push myself through the room and move into his lap. I don't think he even realizes I'm there until I put my hands on his cheeks to make him look at me. He gives me a small smile and I can see the glaze washing over his eyes.

Is he…he's drunk?

"You're so beautiful, Charlotte," he says softly as he reaches out to touch my cheek. His hands move into my hair and begin to play with the strands. "I've never met anyone like you. And I just…had to have you. But you weren't mine to have. I took you from someone else. You weren't mine to look at—to touch—to fuck."

Where is this coming from? I silence him, putting a hand over his mouth. "Stop it. Will, I am yours. I've always been yours to have."

He shrugs and leans back in his chair. "He's never going to give you up, Charley."

"Who?" He gives me a look as he reaches for a glass sitting behind me. I stop his hand and bring it to my mouth letting his fingertips graze my bottom lip. "Tell me what's going on."

"Your husband—"

"Ex-husband," I interrupt.

"Whatever he is. He's not going to quit until he has you back. Or I leave you," he says sadly. The thought makes my blood run cold. *He's thought about leaving me?* "He did make that promise, remember," he continues. "When he was 'finished with us' all you'd have left would be the money from the settlement. He may not turn me in, he may not tell anyone about our affair, but he's going to do everything in his power to break us up. He wants us to be as miserable as he is, which means we don't get to be together. Which means…I can't have you."

"You have me. I'm yours! You promised we were on the same side. We agreed we wouldn't let anything turn us against each other." The tears are already pouring from my eyes, hearing the love of my life express what sounds like defeat.

He's giving up on us.

"The whole time you were still married, it used to drive me crazy wondering if you were sleeping with him. If you were letting him touch you, kiss you, see you the way that you said you only let *me* see you." *Is that what this is about? He thinks I was sleeping with Matt once we were together?*

"I didn't!" My eyes are wide as I shake my head vigorously back and forth. "What makes you think that?"

"But you did at some point," he says sadly.

My face morphs into a look of confusion. "Well yes, we were married, Will. But…once *we* started, he never touched me. I've belonged to you since the moment you kissed me." I shiver at the mere memory of him sliding through my folds for the first time. "Even before then." An involuntary blush finds my cheeks, as I think about how my infatuation with my marriage counselor made it so I didn't even want Matt to touch me.

"Seeing you fuck him didn't destroy me, Charlotte."

"Wha—what?" *Seeing me? He's drunk. What in the world is he talking about?*

"I shouldn't have watched it. I should have burned it when I got it. But…I don't know, call it morbid curiosity." He shrugs as he lets his head fall, his chin connecting with his chest.

"I don't understand." I sniffle as I try to get a control on the tears that are still rapidly falling, hearing him profess his wariness about everything.

Me. Us. Our love.

He pulls a USB drive from behind me that I didn't realize was sitting on his desk and plays with it in his fingers. I look down at what he's holding and look up at him. I see pure defeat in Will's eyes and it shakes me to my very core.

"What is this?" I ask.

"Wells sent me this. Of course, before I watched it, I didn't know. I should break it." He balls it into his fist, and I wonder if he's trying to break the object that seems to have broken *him*.

"What is it?" I ask, though a part of me, somewhere deep inside knows what's on this drive and how it might destroy the one thing—the one person I love the most.

"I had to listen to you fuck my wife, how does it feel to watch me fuck your girlfriend?" He looks up at me and I feel the blood draining from my face upon hearing his words. I feel like I'm going to be sick.

My stomach churns as waves of nausea flow through me. "Tell me you didn't watch it," I choke out.

"I thought seeing another man fuck the woman I love would be the hardest part. But it wasn't. It was surprisingly easy. I mean it pissed me off, but you were married. I knew you had sex with him." He grimaces. "But no, it was the way you looked at him. The way you came apart in his arms…the way you told him you *loved* him. *That* destroyed me."

The tears are sliding down my cheeks as I push myself

further into his arms, wrapping my arms around his neck. "Why did you watch it!? How!? You're never going to look at me the same!" I shriek. I don't hear him reply and that only spurs me on further, my sobs becoming louder and more hysterical. "How could you do this!?"

"What do you mean how?"

"You knew watching this would change you…change us. Why would you do this!? Why didn't you stop, when you saw what was on it?" I push hard against his chest, needing him to feel my pain. I grip his shirt and my head finds his shoulder.

"I know, Charley. I know. I should have stopped."

"How long did you watch it?" I say lifting my head, my vision blurry from all of the tears that are constantly brimming under my lids.

"About two minutes. Enough to watch you come." His hands find his hair and then he looks up at me with sad eyes. "I had to watch him make you come. I'd convinced myself he could never give you that. That only I gave you that mind-numbing pleasure. And then I had to hear you tell him you love him. I watched as the words fell from your lips. I saw the look in your eyes…You meant it."

"I did love him, Will, once upon a time. Or at least I thought I did. You can't punish me over the man that came before you. You more than anyone know that I have a past."

"What does that mean?" he barks, and his aggression coupled with the stench of alcohol surrounding us, makes me wonder if now is the best time to continue this conversation.

"It just means that you know I have a past. You know I was in a relationship with someone else before you." I shake my head. "Will…don't do this."

"Do what?"

"Push me away. I need…" I wonder what it is I need right now, when the words leave my lips on their own. "I need Dr.

Montgomery right now," I say, knowing that appealing to his reasonable side is the only way to get through this.

"He's unavailable. You've got the insanely jealous boyfriend who watched his fiancé's sex tape with her ex-husband. Don't you see how fucked up this is?"

This is the first time he's called me his fiancé and I can't even enjoy the feeling that washes over me hearing the term.

"Don't you see that this is what he wants? To create a divide between us? He's manipulative and calculating…we can't let him do this to us. We are stronger than that."

"I don't know, Charley…the brick, and then this…what's next? Is he ever going to stop?"

Goosebumps rise on my skin instantly, the frost from his words chilling me to my bone. My teeth find my bottom lip as I look down sadly. *Is he ending it? Is he saying I'm not worth the trouble?* My lip trembles and his hand finds my face. He draws his finger along my cheek and my heart skips a beat at the minor contact. "Are you breaking up with me?" I ask quietly, and I hate that I have no conviction in my voice. I feel weak, something I swore I'd never feel again after I left Matt.

I'm stronger than this.

"I don't know," he whispers.

I let out a breath, doing my best not to fly off the handle. Trying my best to be the rational one as I understand that he's not thinking clearly. "You don't want this."

"No shit," he chuckles as he shuts his eyes. "You think I want to deal with Matthew Wells for the rest of my life?"

"I mean…" I start, wanting to make sure we are on the same page about what Will does and does not want, "I mean you don't want to break up."

"I don't know what I want," he says simply, and those six words feel like they're enough to slide into those cracks Will warned us about.

I chuckle sarcastically. "So that's it? Shit gets hard and you walk?" Despite my chuckle, the words that come out of my mouth are anything but funny. *He promised he was in this with me.*

"Gets hard? Charley, where have you been? Shit has *been* hard. Or did you forget that he threw a brick through our window? That he recorded our sessions? That he has a private investigator following us. That he sent me a Goddamn sex tape!"

I feel myself starting to spiral, my blood pressure is rising, my heart is pounding so fast it might beat out of my chest, and I'm resisting the urge to scream. My breaths are coming out in short spurts and I feel as if someone is standing on my chest, making it hard to breathe. In short, I'm about to fucking lose it. I move out of his lap.

"You said we were in this together. If you do this…there's no going back, Will. If you don't want to fight for me…with me…for us…then let me go. Because I'm not going to go through this with you every time my ex retaliates. It's been one week and he's hurt and angry and he's lashing out. This won't go on forever. But I'm not going to be in a relationship where I feel like you could leave me the second things get tough. That's not what I signed up for." I'm out of his office door before he has a chance to respond.

Do I believe that his "I don't know what I want" talk is just fueled by alcohol? Yes. But that isn't the point. Somewhere deep inside of him he thinks those things. It had been a week, and he is already giving up. We are finally free to be together, and he alluded to wanting out. Why did he watch that fucking tape? My fists flex angrily as I think about what I'll do to Matt if and when I ever see him again. *Fucking dick.*

I manage to get myself into bed, and as soon as I'm horizontal, the tears begin to fall more rapidly. I wonder how long before he comes to find me and argue with myself on whether

I want him to stay away or come to me, wrap his arms around me, and rock me to sleep. I don't have to wait long for my answer when I feel the bed dip behind me and his arms wrap around me tightly. The smell of alcohol is all around me but the faint smell of Will is what I cling to. I can't make out what he's saying over my cries but he seems to grip me even tighter every time he says something. I'm not sure how long we lie there, him holding onto me like a life raft as he desperately tries not to drown in all of this.

I'm asleep before I figure it out.

CHAPTER
Eleven

WILL

F UCK, THIS IS MISERABLE.

I already know what's in store for me the second I open my eyes, so I keep them closed for a while longer, mentally preparing myself for the hangover I know awaits me. Those kinds of hangovers where you really can *hear* light. The ones that cause a pounding in your head so loud it can't be quieted even by an entire bottle of Advil. The kind where just the smell of food makes you sick. The type of nausea that is so overwhelming all you can do is lie still while you wallow in your self-destruction and the pity. And this was all while being under the age of twenty-five. It's been years since I've been hungover, and I'm waiting for my body to tell me *you're too old for this shit.*

Prepared for the nausea, headache, and feelings of self-loathing, I open my eyes just as I feel Charley prying herself out of my arms. *Fuck.* Nothing could have prepared me for watching her climb out of bed, the tension radiating off of her in waves. My hangover is temporarily forgotten as a new feeling unfurls in my chest. *Anxiety.* "Baby, come back to bed."

"I have to pee," she tells me without another word or glance towards me.

I climbed into bed shortly after she'd stormed out of my office and held her in my arms while she slept, a sense of irrational panic washing over me that she may flee in the middle of the night. I manage to sit up, and I stare at the bathroom door, willing it to open. Charley finally appears, her face freshly washed and her chestnut locks piled in a bun at the top of her head. "Hey."

"How are you feeling?" she crosses her arms defensively as her brown eyes bore into me.

"Like I got hit by a truck," I tell her honestly.

She looks at me as if to say *serves you right.* "How much of that bottle did you put away?"

I can feel my jaw tick, a sense of shame running through me as I think about the fact that she has no idea how hard her words hit me. *You have to fucking tell her. Especially if you're going to be drinking this aggressively.*

No, Will. Never again. You swore to a lot of people you weren't going down this road again.

I'm not.

My mind argues, and a pesky little voice inside of me whispers, *"Denial."*

"I'm not sure," I tell her. Now was not the time to tell her there was a *second* bottle involved as well.

Having an alcohol problem was like riding a bike. *Your body never forgot.*

It's as if my body is suddenly on high alert hearing that word roaring in my brain.

Alcohol. Problem. Alcohol problem.

How do I tell Charley that her stepfather and I have something in common?

Had.

Everything is fine. It's under control.

I push the beginnings of the breakthrough back down and stand up, my body screaming in pain at every step towards her. "Charley, baby, I'm so sorry. I—I fucked up."

Her arms which were crossed in front of her chest lower to her sides upon hearing my words and she looks up at me once

I'm close enough to touch her as if she's slowly letting her guard back down. I run my hands up her bare arms, her skin breaking out into goosebumps instantly as she takes a step back out of my reach, her walls going back up.

"No, that doesn't make it all better," she says. I open my mouth to tell her that I'm not trying to use sex to beg for the forgiveness I know I need to ask for when she puts a hand up silencing me. "I'm not taking your shit," she tells me, and my eyes widen hearing her words. "I spent years taking shit from Matt, and I didn't get myself out of that relationship just to become another man's punching bag. No. You told me you were different—you told me *this* was different. And then last night, you tell me you're not sure what you want? Well, you need to figure it out. Like now, because I'm not going to be in this relationship by myself. You said we were in this together, that we'd face the man that came before you *together*. And yet the second he attacks, you turn on me? What Matt did was childish, and I'm angry too, but taking your anger out on me was completely unwarranted! That video was from *years* ago. Before we were even married! Are you really telling me you're *that* irrationally jealous?" Her eyes are wide and angry, her hands shaking with how worked up she is. Her nostrils have flared a few times and then she shakes her head. "You said you loved me. Last night, was not love, it was fear. And there's no room for it here. We are stronger than that." Her words are sobering, both emotionally and mentally as I feel myself trying to quiet the roaring headache I have.

"I didn't mean what I said." I'm not sure if she's finished speaking but I want her to be aware I want her. *That I will always want her.*

"I thought it was just the hurt and the alcohol talking, but that doesn't make your words hurt less. You made me wonder if things were over between us."

"Never." I sit on the bed, my head falling into my hands as I wonder how I let things escalate to that. *Why do I keep drinking?* "I hate being that drunk. I should've talked to you. I knew getting drunk would just add fuel to the flames that were burning. I knew I would end up taking it out on you. The moment I said those words, even in my drunk mind I knew, I fucked up." The words are on the tip of my tongue.

I have something to tell you.

I had a problem.

I have a problem.

I shake the thoughts from my head knowing I am nowhere near the rock bottom I'd hit years back. This was a minor setback, but this was also the realization I needed.

A lack of control triggered my thirst for alcohol. I could usually get it under control without *losing* control but watching Charlotte with her husband broke my resolve. *Hell, it almost broke me completely in that moment.*

"How could you watch that?" she whispers as she makes her way to the bed. My body immediately notices she doesn't sit in my lap like she usually does when we're seated in the same room.

I'm immediately on edge as I prepare to answer her question. The feelings of dread flood my body as my mind flashes to her tits in his mouth, her cunt full of another man's cock. Just like that, the thirst was back. I clear my throat, swallowing the saliva that has pooled in my mouth thinking about the bottle of whiskey in my office which still has enough for at least two drinks.

"At first, I think I was in shock," I tell her, grabbing her hand, desperate for a connection to anything other than the substance that always seems to be there when I needed it. *Unlike everyone else that claimed to love me, alcohol never left my side. It never made me feel weak or less than what I was. As a matter of fact, I usually felt powerful, sexy, masculine. It's a heady feeling alcoholics try to forget.*

There's that word again.

Alcoholic.

"You're not visible until a few seconds in," I continue, stroking the soft skin of her hand back and forth. "He was holding the camera and the first few seconds are just—him going in and out of you and then he raises the camera and the first thing I see are your breasts. Ones I'd know anywhere. All I could think was *keep them out of his mouth.*"

I chance a glance, and her eyes are soft with hints of sadness behind their brown warmth. There's a hint of pink in her cheeks as if she's just as uncomfortable as I am. "I'm sorry you had to see that," she whispers. "I'm angry at how you handled it, but, no one was ever supposed to see it in the first place. You're certainly the last person I ever would have ever wanted to see that."

"Your eyes." I start. "I see your eyes and you're so…happy. I see the lust in your eyes. I recognized the look because you've given it to me on so many occasions. Watching you in the throes of passion with someone else, hearing those words…it was a bitter pill to swallow. I know I should have stopped, but I just couldn't pull away," I tell her honestly. Call it morbid curiosity, like when you can't pull your eyes away from the car accident as you pass it, even though you know you need to keep your eyes on your own lane.

"That was almost nine years ago." There's a hint of placation in her tone I wish I couldn't detect. "I don't even know who that girl is anymore, Will. I was happy once upon a time, when I married him. But I changed, *we* changed." Her eyes trace my face. Eyes full of love and devotion—*for me.* "I love *you.*"

"I know you do, baby." I stroke her face gently, rubbing my thumb over the apples of her cheeks and down her face, dipping it slowly into her mouth. "I love you. I'm sorry about how I behaved." She moves closer, letting her legs slide over my lap and I relish the closeness.

"Are you going to let this go?"

"Yes. I don't want anything between us. It just might take me some time to stop picturing another man giving you an orgasm." I roll my eyes and she scoffs.

"I was probably faking it."

My eyes flash to hers. "I know what it looks like when you come, baby. Unless you've been faking it with me."

Her brows furrow and within a second, she's in my arms and I'm on my back. A sense of calm comes over me as I feel her luscious body on top of mine. The apex of her thighs, which is covered with only a scrap of fabric is pressed up against my groin and she grinds down slightly on me making me groan. "I resent that." She presses her hands to my chest and leans down holding her face just above mine. "I've never faked it with you. You've known how to make my body come alive with just a look for so long. The second you touched me I was ready to combust. The first swipe of your tongue over my clit I almost lost it. The first thrust inside of me sealed our fate, Will. I'm yours. I don't care what's come before you, there's only *you* now. And forever."

"Charley." My eyes close, the ramifications of last night finally setting in, making my lids heavy with sleep. I open them again, my eyes weaker as sleep looms over my head. "I don't want to fuck this up."

"You won't."

You don't even know what I'm referring to, baby.

"I'll love you forever, Charlotte," I whisper, as the rest of the energy leaves my body letting me fall into a deep and troubled sleep before I can hear her reply.

—

Charlotte

Will has been asleep for the better part of the day making me wonder just how much of that bottle he did put away. I've checked in on him a few times, but he's out cold. I sit on his deck at the rear of his townhome, feeling as the warm wind whips around me. I look up and notice the trees are starting to turn from the green to yellow and red and brown as the last of the Indian summer fades away. The wind rustles through the leaves giving me a sense of calm that I haven't felt in twenty-four hours. My mind makes a mental note of all the things that have occurred in the past day.

Things I know:

Matt is petty. I mean really, sending Will our sex tape was beyond childish. What was he even thinking?

He's hurt and he wanted to hurt Will, and by extension—you, I argue with myself.

I cross my arms as I pull the cup of chamomile tea to my lips, hoping that the herbs are strong enough to keep my nerves at bay. Last night was the first time Will had expressed any apprehension with proceeding with our relationship, and it did nothing for the nagging thought in the back of my brain that when it was all said and done, Will would leave.

I would be alone.

Was this the first step of Matt making good on his promise? Making Will doubt me and us?

Will apologized, Charlotte.

Yeah, apologized for being an irrational drunk. Who knows how long it'll take for him to get over the images of me having an orgasm at the hands—and cock—of my ex-husband.

I wrack my brain, trying to remember just what he could have seen on that tape, but it escapes me, like most of the good times that took place early on in my relationship. Good times that sadly got overwhelmed and eventually erased by the bad that came in the later years.

My thoughts are interrupted by Will's voice. "There you are."

I look up and I'm amazed at what just his presence does to me. My heart races. It seems he's showered and changed and now looks like a human again. *My human.* I give him a shy smile, trying not to give away how much he turns me into a puddle of need, especially when things are still a bit tense between us. His hair is freshly washed; the tips of his hair are wetting his gray t-shirt with water droplets. His shirt isn't tight anywhere except around his biceps, which are usually hidden under well-tailored suits and sweaters. My eyes scan down his body to a pair of sweatpants and I resist the urge to stare too long in search of his dick. If that wasn't enough, I try to ignore the fact that he has his glasses on, which do nothing but amplify the intensity of the gaze he's giving me. I swallow, doing my best to wet my dry mouth.

"Are you trying to seduce me?" I say as he sits in the chair next to me. He lets out a laugh, and as if he knows just what to do to make my clit pulse, he adjusts his glasses.

Bastard.

Before he's even fully seated I'm on my feet ready to take my place in his lap. He welcomes me instantly, wrapping his arms around me and leaning his head back against the chair. I'm straddling him at this point, our pelvises perfectly aligned and I begin to move back and forth on the appendage I feel growing with each passing second underneath me.

"Are you trying to seduce *me?*" He throws my words back at me and I giggle.

"You started it, what do you need these for?" I tap his glasses and raise an eyebrow at him as I wait for his explanation that he came out here to read something. He gives me a guilty smile and I lift my chin. "Exactly."

He narrows his eyes slightly. "You're mad at me, and I was hoping you'd let me give you an orgasm or two to fix it. And yeah—I know you like the glasses."

"I'm not mad at you," I reassure him, and I watch as the relief spreads across his face. It's in that moment I suddenly realize, all this time I haven't been dealing with my level-headed marriage counselor, but my possessive boyfriend. Usually there's a balance between the two, but for the past day and a half, Dr. Montgomery has been nowhere in sight.

"Oh, well, my need to give you an orgasm still stands." His words have a direct line to my sex, my body fiending for the release that is imminent.

"Well, who am I to deny you?" I smile and as if I weigh nothing more than a feather, he stands with me in his arms and carries me back inside, pressing me against the wall immediately, his cock pressing up and into my sex as I'm still just in a t-shirt and a pair of panties. I groan and dig my nails into his shoulders. "Fuck, Will." My clit feels as if it's on fire, desperate for any friction to lessen the ache between my thighs. My heartbeat thumps in my sex, almost pounding against the inside of my panties and I would do anything for him to drop to his knees and quiet the noise with his mouth.

His mouth is on mine, his tongue snaking between my lips and making love to my mouth as he grinds his hips upwards, grinding his cock against me harder in perfect rhythm with the strokes of his tongue. "You are mine," he growls when he pulls away, staring straight into my eyes. His tongue darts out and I watch fascinated as he runs it across his bottom lip. "You'll never know just how much I need you, Charley."

"I think I do know because I need you just as desperately." I close my eyes, the orgasm that I felt building merely by the ridges of his cock rubbing against me still sends tingles through every part of my body.

He carries me through his house, his hands firmly under my butt, cupping the cheeks hard, as his teeth nip at the flesh of my neck.

Within seconds, I'm flat on my back reaching for the hem of my shirt, yanking it over my head as I watch him do the same. He's on me instantly, his shirt gone, allowing me to rub my hands along his broad chest, my fingers moving through the smattering of chest hair. "I am going to fuck you so hard you won't know your own name." He tells me as he rips my panties from me in one quick motion.

I let out a breath as he moves up my body, skimming his lips up my heated skin and finding my mouth again. He still has his underwear on, and every time I feel the cotton of his briefs between the lips of my sex I groan, feeling the fabric graze my clit. "Will…ooo-ff," I stammer, as all coherent thoughts leave my brain. I can't focus on anything except getting some part of his body inside of me.

Cock. Fingers. Mouth. SOMETHING.

He obliges my request, and lines himself up at my opening. "So, fucking beautiful." His lips are on my nipple, suckling the skin, dragging the peak between his teeth and biting gently. His hand palms the other one, rolling the nipple between his fingertips as the blunt tip of his cock continues to rub through my folds. It feels as if we're moving in slow motion, to the lyrics of a song that can't be heard, it's a melody our bodies only know. His cock slides inside, pushing harder, deeper, slower than he has ever gone. He pulls back slowly, his hands finding my hips as he holds me down—as if he needs to keep me still. His gaze is transfixed on where we're connected, his attention captivated at him burying himself to the hilt over and over.

"Will," I whimper.

"I need you so much," he chokes out as his pace picks up slightly, his cock going deeper with each thrust. "Fuck, baby." The tips of his fingers dig into the flesh of my ass and I find myself straddling the line between pleasure and pain.

"Will!" I moan as my eyes squeeze shut.

"Look at me, baby," he tells me, and my eyes pop open feeling my climax building inside of me.

"I'm never letting you go."

"Never let me go," I tell him just as I feel my orgasm begin to rip through me. "Will! Fuuuuck!" I groan as the orgasm shoots through me, flexing my feet forward and making me claw at the sheets underneath me. I'm vaguely aware of him telling me how beautiful I am when I come and then I feel him moving faster and a warm feeling in my sex—an expanding and releasing that spreads straight to my heart.

He's on me instantly, his lips attacking mine as he rolls us so I'm on top, refusing to break the powerful connection I've never had with anyone else. His hands wind in my hair, pulling at the root and I clench around him in response.

"Oh God," I moan as I pull off of his dick, letting his cock—that's not completely flaccid—fall out of me. I sit on his pelvis, just above his cock as our orgasms begin to flow out of me and I catch his gaze watching the stream.

"I want you off the pill," he says as he watches his cum coat his torso. His face is serious yet I can sense his nervousness of dropping this bomb on me.

"Now?" I ask. He's made comments about having me knocked up by spring, about dying to see my stomach round with his child, but they were always in the heat of the moment while he was trying to assert his dominance and lay his claim over me.

"Can we talk about this while we aren't in this sex haze?" I moan, desperate not to have this heavy conversation now when I'm dying to get his cock back inside of me.

"No," he growls. "I've never had this primal urge to *mate*. But I need this Charlotte, I need you off the pill so I can fuck you and breed you. I need every part of you to belong to *me*."

Fuck, that's hot.

And probably a direct response to Matt's little stunt. Think about this, Charlotte!

Think about what? I want a baby, he wants a baby. What am I thinking about?

Um, how about his motives? He wants to knock you up because he's afraid of losing you.

Or because he wants a baby...

I squeeze my eyes shut, trying to quiet the voices and I nod, knowing that nothing has to be decided now when I'm just trying to get his dick into my pussy for round two. "Really?"

I resign myself to the fact that round two may not be happening as soon as I'd hoped. "I think we should talk about this when we're both thinking rationally and not when I'm naked, sitting on top of you, feeling your cock harden underneath me."

"My feelings won't change...will yours?"

"No. God, when did you become such a buzzkill?" I move off him and close my legs as I attempt to calm my heated body and racing heart.

"I'm not. I just don't want you to agree to something you don't want."

"No, that's really more your speed, right? Saying things you don't mean?" I rub a hand over my eyes. "I already told you I wanted a family with you. I'm sorry I'm not ready to make a decision right this second just because you're feeling insecure."

"I'm not insecure, Charlotte." His voice is low and cold and I know without a doubt I struck a nerve.

"I just wanted to talk about this when we'd cooled down and not when we're..." I point to our naked bodies. "Since when did I become the rational one? I did not sign up for that role," I snap, sarcasm evident in my tone.

"Don't be a smartass, Charlotte." He sits up and gets off the bed. My eyes find the appendage between his legs that is still pointing directly at me. "Stop looking at it."

"Where else would you like me to look? It's staring at *me!*"

"Look. You want a baby. That was what brought you to me—wanting a baby, and being with someone who couldn't give you one."

"I'm not with you because you said *you* would. You're not my sperm donor or my personal baby maker. I want a baby, but I also want time alone with you without stolen moments or racing against the clock. Without an ex-husband who's trying to break us up. I think we need time alone to be a couple. Just you and me." I move towards him on my knees and look up at him. "You can't knock me up to ensure I won't go back to him or leave you. My word that I love you and I want to be with you for the rest of my life should be enough. Don't you trust me?" I voice my concerns and his eyes, which have been following his hand as he draws circles into my clavicle, move to mine in a flash.

"Of course, I do."

"Do you trust I'm not going to leave you?" His eyes trace my face but they are almost vacant, as if he's gone somewhere else, and I narrow my gaze wondering why it feels as if he's looking *through* me and not *at* me. He nods once and I frown. *What is that about?* "Say the words, Will."

"I believe you *don't want* to leave." He backs up from me, rubbing a hand over his jaw as I hear the qualifier in his statement.

"What—" I go to ask him what that even means when he shakes his head and pulls his briefs up his legs. "Will?"

"I have to tell you something."

My heart beats wildly in my chest hearing his ominous words. My mind, filled with the most ridiculous things I can muster, is not prepared for the words that fall from those perfect lips.

CHAPTER
Twelve

WILL

BABY, *I HAVE A PROBLEM. AND I THINK IT'S ABOUT TO GET worse.*

The words stall, not wanting to leave my lips.

I'm fine.

Everything is fine.

I clear my throat wondering what I'm going to tell her instead.

They say the first step is admitting that you have a problem. Reaching into your soul and allowing yourself to force the words out, purging yourself of the guilt and shame associated with the problem. I was powerless in defeating the problem and thus my life has become unmanageable.

The next step is realizing that a greater power could restore your sanity.

The love I have for Charlotte is that higher power. She is the incentive I needed to stop things from escalating any further.

She'll leave you if she knows. She'll be terrified that you share any common characteristics with her stepfather.

She'll run.

Suddenly, it hits me—and that's the thing about this *problem*: it hits you in waves and at the worst times. Sometimes, it's easier to manage, easier to avoid the voice in the back of your head that tells you you're dying to have a drink. But other times, times like now when I'm thinking of a life without Charlotte it is... *unmanageable.*

Suddenly, the need to have a drink overwhelms me.

Just one to take the edge off. Just to get back in control. To clear your mind.

Knowing I need to tell her something, I blurt out, "I need to tell my patients their privacy has been violated. I'm going to email my supervisor to set up a meeting with our ethics board."

I know she wasn't expecting me to say that because I watch as her eyebrows shoot to her hairline. "I get that you feel you need to do that, but…now?"

"The longer I let this go on, the worse it will be. My patient's trust me and their privacy was violated. They deserve to know. But the board needs to know first, I'm not sure how they'll want to handle it. I'm sure our lawyers will need to get involved."

"But you'll get in trouble, right? They'll wonder why he planted the device, they'll start asking questions and it will lead them back to me. To *you and me.*" The look in her eyes guts me, hearing her speak about us that way.

"I don't regret it for a second. Any of it. We are meant to be together, Charley. Maybe in another life things would have been easier, but there's only this life. Here. Now. And we're together and that's the only thing that matters."

"Them disbarring you or taking you to jail or…"

"I won't go to jail."

"It's possible. A doctor having sex with a patient isn't just a slap on the wrist."

"It can be. These things are handled on a case by case basis."

"And you want to risk it?"

"What other choice do I have?"

"Not to say anything?"

"I took an oath, Charlotte." I can feel myself getting irritated that she's not understanding my need to do the right thing.

Because you've been so concerned with that lately?

"I know, and I get it, but maybe you should talk to your dad?"

she asks weakly. I can't even contain the fire burning inside of me which shoots out of my eyes towards her. I need to calm the roaring fires before I explode, and I know just the extinguisher I need.

My thumb and index finger rub together as I think about turning that familiar lid.

I put the amber liquid out of my mind for the time being. "Oh, you think *that's* the answer?" I shake my head. "J.R. cannot fix this."

"I wasn't saying that," she whispers, and I wonder if it's time I tell her a little bit more about my childhood and the man that for all intents and purposes is my father. "But he's your lawyer, perhaps he can advise you—."

"My father can't advise me on anything except how to take what you want. How to lie and deceive and still come out on top. How to cheat on you and get away with it," I snap at her. "He can teach me *that*." I step back from her, my eyes leaving her as I know there's pain behind them hearing my words. When I finally look at her, she has her gaze cast downward and I feel like shit for speaking those words aloud. I'm on my knees in front of her in an instant. "I would never cheat on you," I tell her as I lift her chin. "I love you more than anything."

"I didn't think I would cheat on Matt either." Her lips tremble and I can see she's trying to keep the emotion out of her voice, but failing miserably.

"We've been over this."

"I know. I just… you don't get along with your dad?"

I chuckle, contemplating how complex that statement really is and how I couldn't even begin to unpack it. I'd spent years going back and forth with Tuck about it and I still feel like I haven't had the breakthrough. I still hold onto too much anger and resentment. It makes it impossible to have any true realizations about myself or my parents. I have enough self-awareness, and experience as a therapist to understand that. "My father is just…not the man I want to be."

"He…he's cheated on your mom?" She furrows her brows together and I can see the wheels turning.

"I would never do that, I'm sorry I said that." I sigh, wishing I hadn't put the thoughts in her head. "But yes, often. I don't know if he still does in his older years; my guess is yes, because he hires women that absolutely reek of daddy issues but I don't know for sure."

"When you were a kid?" She winces.

"Childhood, teenage years, adolescence…he was actually late to my college graduation. Showed up forty minutes late in the same clothes he was in the night before, when we'd all gone to dinner to celebrate my degree." I'm still kneeling in front of Charlotte and before I can think, I've placed my head in her lap, seeking the comfort I know alcohol could give me, but wanting to grasp for the higher power I was hoping could pull me out of the darkness that is hovering over me. Her hands find my head instantly and begin to stroke my hair and massage my scalp. Her fingertips quiet the roaring thoughts swirling in my brain as I remember the fact that he didn't even attend my master's graduation. *Though that fact had more to do with Diana Montgomery.* "They missed my grad school graduation."

She gasps. "They? As in…?"

"Both my parents. Drew came with whatever flavor of the week at the time."

"How—?"

"They had tickets for a cruise around the Mediterranean." I hear a sharp intake of air. "And before you empathize with them at all, they weren't non-refundable tickets."

"I wasn't…I was just going to say that's pretty shitty."

"The sad part is I was used to it by then." I sit up, as I look her in the eye, wondering if the breakthrough is on its way. "I've never had what felt like any real connection to anyone in my immediate family. My mom was…is the stereotypical Stepford wife, but lacks any real emotion. I couldn't tell you the last time I felt any real affection from her. My father…" I swallow, wishing this conversation was over so I could go hide out in my office for the rest of the day. "I'm sorry they'll be your in-laws." I grimace and she frowns, finding my face.

"I'm sorry they hurt you. I'm sorry they *continue* to hurt you." She blinks away her tears. "What about your brother? It seems you two are quite close?"

I roll my eyes. *Honestly, that's more on Drew's part. I tried to put distance between us; hiding the resentment I have for him is exhausting.* "Drew had a different upbringing than I did. It's almost as if we were born to different parents. He had parents that worshipped him, supported his dreams, encouraged his passions. He was a sports God, perfect at anything that required athleticism—something I lacked. He bonded with my father over that, whereas J.R. couldn't understand why I lacked the physical ability to keep up. Drew was my mother's firstborn, her pride and joy. A baby made out of love. J.R. was there for everything in the beginning for Drew—first steps, first words, everything. I came five years later, as my mother struggled to keep my father interested. I came in response to my father's first affair. The band-aid my mother hoped would fix everything. Instead, it just pushed him into the arms of another woman and my mother was left essentially raising me on her own." I shake my head as I remember coming to that first realization. "My mother resented me for it. Or maybe she resented her actions of getting pregnant to keep my father. Either way, I'm far from the favorite child."

I watch as the tears trickle down her cheek, her eyes red and glassy. "Oh Will." She shakes her head and puts her hands over her eyes, then drops them, and moves to the floor to press her knees against mine, placing her hands on my thighs. "I love you so much. Thank you for sharing that with me. I hate that you felt so alone growing up, but I hope you know you never have to feel that way again."

I never have to feel alone again. My heart reacts to her words and I have her in my lap kissing her like our lives depend on it before she can say anything else. I don't speak, I let my mouth do the talking for me as my tongue winds with hers. I wrap my arms around her, holding her tight against me as the pain of talking about my past bubbles inside of me. My mouth waters again thinking about what I planned to do after I left this room, but Charley's tongue wipes away the feeling just as quickly. I pull away from her when I feel like we both need a breath and rest my forehead against hers. "God, where have you been all my life?"

She doesn't say anything, because I don't think she really has the answer. Finally, she speaks, her voice just above a whisper. "I would have wanted you if we met in high school. Or college. I would have made you feel wanted. Special. I would have protected you from them. I'll protect you from them now. You're not alone, Will. Not anymore." My nose rubs against hers, my eyes fixed on hers as they penetrate me.

Seeing me.

Feeling me.

Knowing me.

That's the thing about meeting your soulmate. They know what you need to hear sometimes before *you* do. I'd never used the word alone. *Or lonely* and it's like she could feel it just by looking in my eyes.

"I love you," I tell her as my heart pounds so hard I wonder if it'll fly out of my chest. A part of me wishes it would so she could see my heart only beat for her.

Even if I was keeping a secret from her.

"I love you too. I wish you'd open up to me. Stop hiding from me. Whatever it is you're holding onto, let it go. You don't have to carry it all on your own."

I'd said that so many times, I wonder if she's just merely telling me to practice what I preach. *Share things with your partner. You're in this together and you need to share the weight of the baggage you bring into your relationship. One person can't do it alone.*

But what happens when the baggage is too much? So heavy it overpowers the relationship and forces it to break creating irreparable damage?

This is why people have secrets.

This is why people feel they have to carry things alone.

It's why marriages end.

It's why I have a job.

CHAPTER
Thirteen

WILL

THE SMELL OF BAD COFFEE OVERWHELMS MY SENSES AS I STEP foot into the diner across town. The *Peachgrove Diner* is known for two things—pancakes and sponsor meetings. Alcoholics flocked from all over to the seedy establishment with their sponsors in hopes that a stack of the sweet cakes could make them forget their troubles for just a second.

For a second, they traded one vice for another because, make no mistake, the pancakes were addictive.

A man with an unlit cigarette tucked between his lips stares at me with a snide grin.

"You can't cover it up with a fancy suit, rich boy."

My eyes narrow into slits. "Excuse me?"

"You think your fancy threads make you better than anyone? You think it hides your problem? I can spot an addict a mile away." His eyes sweep me from top to bottom and I do the same making note of his Falcons hat that seems to cover up quite a bit of white hair. A worn brown leather jacket covers his torso followed by dark jeans with more than a few holes.

"Then you know better than to call them out on it," I snap, wondering who the hell allowed this man loose on any alcoholic. Putting an addict down in any way rarely worked. Especially a re-covering one like myself, who'd used alcohol as a way of escaping all the people in life who *did* put me down.

"I only call out the ones that are so obviously in denial."

"You're a seriously shitty sponsor, you know that?" I growl as I scan the restaurant looking for Tuck. I frown, not seeing him in our usual booth, but knowing that in the ten years I'd known him, he was never late.

"I ain't a sponsor, which means I can say that you wear your addiction all over your face. You're not hiding it from anyone." He pulls his cigarette from his mouth and points it at me, waving it in a circle.

Rage blooms in my chest hearing this man speak so casually about the demons threatening to break out of me.

I knew I shouldn't have had that drink this morning.

"Joe, don't you have someone else to harass?" I feel a familiar hand on my shoulder and relief floods me as I sense Tuck has come to my rescue—*for the millionth time.* They share a look and I watch as the smile tugs at Tuck's lips; I wonder if it's at my expense. My nostrils flare, feeling as if I'm left out of some inside joke.

"He one of yours? You always did have a soft spot for the uppity drunks," Joe chuckles as if this is all one big joke.

I shoot a look at Tuck daring him to laugh. "I am not uppity..." It's not lost on me that *uppity* was the word that stuck out to me first. "I'm not a drunk," I add for good measure. "So, you can fuck off."

I feel a hand on my chest keeping me from taking a step forward. "Send Cass our way, will ya?" Tuck says as he leads me towards a different table in the opposite corner.

"Who the fuck is that guy?"

"He's harmless, Will. Calm down," he says as we take our seats in the booth.

"He's rude as hell."

"What, can't handle the truth?"

I ignore his comment. "Is he drunk?"

"He better not be. He works here as a condition of his charge."

"Charge?"

"DUI. Like four of them," he says not looking up from his menu.

"You're not supposed to tell me that."

Tuck's eyes meet mine. "You can't keep a secret now?" He gives me a pointed look and sets his menu down just as who I assume to be Cass approaches our table.

"Hi, Mitch! It's so good to see you!" She's young, very young. Probably younger than Charley. Her jet black hair is pulled into a messy bun on the top of her head and her face is completely void of makeup with the exception of a pink balm on her lips. Her white tee shirt has the name of the diner scrawled across her chest and an apron is wrapped around her waist covering what I assume to be very short shorts. She was young enough to be his daughter. I shoot him a look instantly, raising an eyebrow at him. He pretends not to notice it.

"Always good to see you, Cassie, how's school?"

Her powder blue eyes roll in a circle. "A pain in the ass. I'm taking twenty-six credits this semester."

"If anyone can do it, it's you." A pink blush coats her cheeks hiding the freckles that dot her face.

"And what about you? How is everything." Her eyes dart to mine as if she hadn't realized there was another person at the table. "How are you today, sir?"

"No need for sirs. I'm younger than him." I point, taking note at her formality with me versus my older mentor.

"I was raised to say sir and ma'am unless instructed otherwise. And you're older than *me*."

I shoot another look at Tuck wondering just how close he's gotten with this girl before turning back to her. "You can call me Will."

"Will." She turns to look at Tuck again. "The usual?"

"Please. And a side of scrambled eggs."

She raises an eyebrow at him. "Is that really good for your cholesterol?"

"You been talking to my doctor now?"

"I'm just sayin'." She shrugs as she gives him a toothy grin and sashays away.

"She knows about your cholesterol, huh?" I say, taking a look at the menu despite the fact that he'd already put in his usual which happened to be my usual as well.

"Don't deflect."

"What's going on with you and that girl who's young enough to be your granddaughter?"

He scoffs. "Don't be an asshole. She's twenty-three. Daughter at best."

"Sure, Tuck."

"And nothing. She sees me as a father figure."

I snort. "Yeah, I'll bet she does."

"Nothing even mildly inappropriate has happened between us. So just get your mind out of the gutter."

I raise my hands in defeat, knowing that now isn't the time to interrogate him about his *friend* even though there is so clearly a story there. "Fine."

"So, tell me why we're here."

"You know why we're here."

"You didn't say explicitly."

"I've been thinking about drinking."

"Just thinking?"

My brain blanks for a moment. I had a monologue prepared about how I'd been thinking about having a drink. How I'd gone to the store and bought a bottle of Macallan 18 but I hadn't drunk it.

I clear my throat. "It's consuming my thoughts."

"But you haven't drunk anything. This is good. It's smart that you're getting in front of this." His voice is even, not giving anything away and a part of me deep in the crevices of my mind believes that Tuck knows the truth.

Cassie returns with our mugs and the putrid liquid they call coffee. I watch as she pours both of our cups before retreating without another glance at me. My eyes follow her away from the table and then back to Tuck still not convinced about his story. "I have to come clean about what I did."

"And that is why you're thinking about alcohol?"

I nod. There was some truth to it. The idea of throwing myself at the mercy of our ethics board has me wanting to drain the contents of every bottle in a two-mile radius. *He just didn't know that I'd already started.* "Charlotte doesn't know."

"Doesn't know…"

"About my past with alcohol."

"You mean that you let things get so out of control?"

"Yes."

"Almost ruined your future?"

"Yes."

"Almost killed yourself?"

I grit my teeth. "You're not helping."

"Frankly, neither are you." He leans forward, taking a sip of his coffee and not even making a face as it slides down his throat.

His words are like an electric shock to my insides. "I'm afraid to tell her."

"Because of her stepfather?"

"How do you—"

He cocks his head at me. "Come on now, you weren't giving me any information. I wanted to see who had my boy so smitten." My heart thuds in my chest as I think about how differently he phrases things in comparison to my own father. Tuck truly was the father I wanted. *The one I needed.*

"I don't know how she'll take it."

"What are you afraid of?"

"That she'll leave me."

"For being honest with her?"

"For lying to her."

"What have you lied about? You have a past with alcohol. Why would she leave you over that?" He steeples his hands under his chin and gives me a look that says *unless there's something you're not telling me.*

"I just…"

"Unless you're drinking now and not being honest with her about how serious it is."

I shake my head, not having the words to say aloud. I lift the coffee just as a tremor moves through me. Tuck's eyes find my hands instantly as I try and still their shaking before his eyes dart back to mine. "Will."

"What, Tuck?" I can't face him. My eyes are staring out the window watching as a man and his sponsor embrace and the sponsor hands his sponsee a chip. *The chip that sat in my drawer but didn't mean all that much now.*

"Look at me."

I finally do, and when I meet his eyes they're not laced with judgment or scolding like I expected, but with understanding, acceptance, and perhaps a hint of something else. *Love maybe?*

"Are you drinking again?"

"No. I'm good, Tuck. I swear."

He purses his lips and I know he wants to say something further but, in that moment, Cassie returns with a tray full of pancakes effectively ending the conversation.

No one discussed their problems over *Peachgrove Diner* pancakes.

It's why everyone got the bottomless.

CHAPTER

Fourteen

WILL

F EELINGS OF GUILT WRACK MY BRAIN AS I PULL INTO MY townhouse later that evening. I'd had a session that afternoon that I had basically coasted through. I nodded in the right places, asked the cliché questions, and at the stroke of one hour, I told them I would see them next week without another glance towards them as they walked out of my office.

I was distracted, unfocused, and stressed beyond belief.

Harboring a secret is exhausting.

I scrub a hand down my face as I walk into my townhouse wondering where I'd find Charlotte—her car is parked out front. *I wish she'd just park in the garage.* For so long it was just me, and a one car garage was all I needed. *But now I need something to accommodate a black Audi Q3 as well.*

I make my way through my house, climbing the stairs to my bedroom, pulling my jacket off. I make my way into the bedroom and I'm instantly calmed knowing where she is as I hear the water running.

She's naked and wet.

I toe off my shoes and begin to loosen the tie from around my neck as I make my way into the ensuite bathroom. I watch in fascination through the glass as the soap trickles down her body, turning my cock to granite. Her eyes are shut, her lips slightly parted as she works the suds from her hair. I grab at my cock, desperate to relieve the ache when she must feel my predatory gaze because her eyes fly open. She doesn't say anything, she just summons me towards her with one finger.

Before I've even closed the shower door behind me, I feel hands on my stomach moving up towards my chest and then back down, grazing my dick with her hand. I lean my head back, the water beating down on me as I feel her luscious breasts pressed into my back. Her tongue darts out and she licks the skin at my neck and it's as if all of the stress from the day just melts away. Her hand moves down my body and strokes my cock gently causing it to harden further in her hand. I feel her lips again, this time on my back and she hums, sending vibrations through my body. "You are perfect." Her words are breathy and more than likely fueled by her raging libido, although I wouldn't be surprised if Charley actually thought I was perfect.

Because she doesn't know everything about you.

You need to tell her the truth.

I turn in her arms wanting to see her perfect face, and as usual she takes my breath away. *God, she is so fucking beautiful.* I scan down her body and I almost come at the sight of her slick body waiting for me to kiss, to lick, to fuck. Her nipples harden completely under my gaze and I can practically see her sex glistening—and not from the water. *Fuck I need her.* My mouth finds her neck instantly and I feel her knees buckle so I wrap an arm around her keeping her upright.

"Welcome home," she purrs as her tits rub against me and her hand begins to work me over between us. "How was your day?"

"Long," I tell her honestly, recalling my lunch with Tuck followed by a tedious session. "I missed you."

She sighs and her eyes float down my body, landing on my cock watching as she strokes my dick from root to tip. "I missed you too."

"I want to be inside you, *now,*" I tell her as I the familiar tingle in my balls begins to spread throughout my body.

I lift her into my arms before she can reply and press her against the wall of my shower, sliding my cock through her folds one time. I try to do it again, teasing her a second time but her pussy sucks me deep inside, burying me to the hilt. "Shit." I moan as the feeling of her tight cunt wrapped around my dick has me ready to blow before I even thrust once. I let out a breath and drop my forehead to her shoulder, trying to calm myself from climaxing this soon when she begins to wiggle in my arms.

"Baby, move."

"Wait a second," I growl.

"No." She squeezes my dick hard, and my eyes shoot open as a crack of lightning shoots through my body.

"Fuck," I oblige her request, as I begin to glide in and out of her. She leans her head back against the wall of the shower, her bottom lip between her teeth and her eyes squeezed shut as I begin to pump into her harder and harder as the water continues to cleanse us.

I'd do anything if this shower could just wash away the sins and the secrets that I've been keeping from Charlotte. I look down for a second, watching as the water slides down the drain, and I shut my eyes wishing that all the wrong that I'd done was being washed away as well.

A gasp leaving Charlotte's lips draws my attention back to her. "Something's wrong?" she whispers.

"No."

"You're distracted."

Tell her.

"No, I'm not." I put one hand in her hair, pulling at the strands gently as I press my lips to hers. "You're my only focus, Charlotte. You're the only thing I see."

She shudders in my arms and pushes herself harder against

me. "I need you to come, Will. Come inside of me, please," she begs, and the way she's talking makes me wonder if she's stopped taking her pill.

Come inside of me. Get me pregnant. I can almost hear her begging me.

Visions of Charley pregnant with my baby move through my brain and it sends me over the edge. I freeze as cum shoots out of me and inside of her, stretching her, filling her. "Fuck! God dammit, Charley. You're a goddess." I slap my hand on the tile next to her head as I continue to pump the remainder of my orgasm into her. "I need you to come now," I order her.

She looks up at me through her wet lashes, making me hard inside of her all over again. "Touch me." Her voice is so shaky, for a brief second, I wonder if she's nervous about asking, but then I realize that the lust coursing through her has taken her voice.

"Touch you where, Charlotte? Tell me." *I know what she wants. But I want to hear the words fall from those pouty lips.*

I can see the shyness in her eyes and it's because she hasn't started to build yet. When she is in the moments leading up to her climax, she is unashamed at asking for what she wants. Just yesterday, she'd been completely clear in asking for me to touch her there but only because my mouth was on her pussy at the time. I press my thumb to her clit, my cock still inside of her and I push down slightly and she gasps. "Tell me what you want, Charlotte." I smile at her and she begins to rock slowly against my hand.

"I want you to fuck me with your mouth from behind. And then fuck my ass with your mouth."

"You have quite the mouth on you."

Her eyes are so penetrating it takes me a second to find my voice as I pull out of her. "What is it?" I ask her. I frame her face with my hands desperate to know what she's thinking.

"I just can't believe that we're here now. That we're together. I am so happy with you, Will," My heart soars at her words. "It almost makes all of the shit I've been through worth it." And just as quickly my heart sinks.

I don't answer before I push my lips to hers. I continue to hold her up with one hand and weave my other in her wet wavy locks as I make love to her mouth with my tongue, stroking slowly against hers. We kiss for I don't know how long, only stopping when I feel the water starting to cool. I pull away from her, her lips red and raw from my beard and I'm sure my lips look similar given how many times her teeth nipped at the skin.

Her chest heaves up and down quickly and the look in her eyes tells me that she feels the intensity of that kiss *everywhere,* just like I did. I feel a twinge of guilt hearing her talk about how happy she is, knowing I've been keeping something from her.

"I've never been as happy as I have been with you, Charlotte." She gives me a smile as I shut the water off and I lead her out of the shower. I'm still naked and dripping wet as I pull her towel off the back of my door and begin to towel dry her body and her hair. Only when she's somewhat dry do I do the same for myself. She props herself up on the sink after her hair is tied up in a towel and watches as I dry off.

"Enjoying the show?"

"Very much." She smiles. Her eyes dart to my cock as I run my towel over it, and she watches as it bobs up and down, still slightly hard from our shower activities. Her tongue darts out and runs over her bottom lip, and I don't miss the fact that she's still staring at my cock.

"You seem tense. Let me make it better." She gnaws on her bottom lip, a seductive grin spreading across her lips and then she hops off the counter falling to her knees in front of me sheathing her mouth around my dick.

Fuck. I can already feel the familiar tingle starting at the base of my spine as she moves up and back on my cock. One hand wraps around my ass as the other makes its way between my legs to stroke my perineum. I fist her hair as I begin to move my hips against her face. "Oh God, Charley."

She looks up at me, her mouth full of my cock with those eyes and cheeks slightly pink and I almost lose it right then and there. She lets me fall from her lips and tilts her head back.

"Fuck my mouth." I can see the wicked gleam in her eye.

"Charlotte…"

"I want your cock down my throat. Trust me. I can handle it."

I know she can. She sucks my dick like a champ. I move so that I'm almost straddling her face, thankful for how short she is. On her knees, she fits perfectly between my legs without me having to do any legwork. Her mouth opens excitedly, and I don't waste a second before pushing my cock literally down her throat.

"Breathe through your nose." She nods, and her teeth graze my shaft in the process. "Fuck." I rest my hand on her head, pulling the towel from her hair as I begin to push slowly in and out of her, our eyes never breaking contact once. "Your mouth is so incredible, Charley. You're so fucking beautiful. I want to take a picture and remember this moment forever." Her eyes widen and I wonder if she's worried that I would make good on my comment, so I shake my head. *I'm not sure if this is in reaction to my recent viewing of a certain sex tape, and I hate myself for still feeling slightly insecure.* "I won't."

She shakes her head and based on the way she's looking at me, I wonder if I misread her eyes. "You want me to do that?" I ask. "You want me to take a picture of you like this? With my cock in your pretty little mouth?" She bobs her head yes. "How about with my cum coating your beautiful tits."

She nods again.

I smell her arousal floating through the air and I can't see exactly what she's doing but I have to ask. "Charlotte, are you touching yourself, at the thought of me taking your picture?"

Another nod.

"You're fingering your perfect pussy? Tell me does it feel good, baby?"

I can see the smile in her eyes and I know the answer without feeling her head move. *Fuck, I'm about to come again, and she hasn't come once yet. We will be fixing that immediately.*

I put my other hand on her head, careful not to move her too much, but just to keep her in place as I fuck her mouth. "Fuck," I manage to choke out. I feel her hand, undoubtedly the hand that was just between her legs, cupping my balls and then floating slowly upward towards the space between my balls and my ass, and the feeling of her arousal being rubbed into my skin is enough to send me over the edge. I come with a roar, the ropes of the salty liquid shooting out of my dick and into her waiting mouth. Her mouth is full in no time, despite just having come not too long ago. Her cheeks puff out slightly before she begins to suck it down. I slide out of her mouth, dragging my cock over her lips leaving them wet and slightly white with my leftover cum.

I don't even think before I'm hauling her over my shoulder and carrying her back to my room, tossing her onto my bed like she's weightless. She giggles a few times but they're immediately halted when I place a long lingering kiss on her pussy. "Tell me, Charley. Do you want me to do what I did last night?"

She nods and I waste no time flipping her over and pulling her to her knees in front of me. She drops her head and I can see her clenching in anticipation. I spread her cheeks slowly, allowing for a better look at the pink flesh between her legs. Her folds are still swollen from both my dick and her own assault, and I can faintly make out her clit from this angle. I press my face against her ass, allowing me to eat her from behind, lapping at her entrance, knowing that she's desperate for stimulation at both holes. I drag my tongue upwards, finding what she wants and running my tongue over it. I feel her clench and my cock bobs in response. "Rub your clit for me, baby," I order her.

"But…" She trails off, knowing that yesterday I did it for her. "Trust me."

She whimpers, and I feel her fingers touching herself, rubbing that swollen bundle of nerves that has become one of the wonders of my world. I hold her cheeks open with both hands, my chin rubbing against her with each lick. My facial hair is just short enough that she probably feels a bit of pain from the bristles, but if she does, you wouldn't know it by the way she's crying out in pleasure. I continue to rim her, as she fingers herself and it's not long before I can feel her quivering.

"Will, I'm going to…" Her whole body trembles with the force of her impending orgasm and before the word can leave her lips, she screams out my name instead and falls to the bed, completely removing herself from my mouth. She lands on her stomach, her hand still wedged between her legs as she rides the rest of her high. "Holy fuck," she moans. "You are incredible." She moves to her back.

I place a final kiss to her pussy and she shivers. "No, no. Stay away," I chuckle as I make my way into the bathroom to brush my teeth and grab a warm cloth to clean her off.

I'm not surprised that she's asleep by the time I'm back. I stare at her, hearing her words playing on repeat in my head.

You told her you love her but you aren't being honest with her.

I squeeze my eyes together as I climb into bed, trying to quiet the roaring thoughts in my brain and most importantly the fact that I'm dying for a drink. I wrap my arms around her, praying for sleep to claim me as easily as it had claimed Charlotte.

It doesn't.

CHAPTER
Fifteen

Charlotte

ARM LIPS ROUSE ME FROM SLEEP THE NEXT MORNING, pulling me out of my final moments of slumber. I open one eye to find Will completely dressed, hovering over me looking at me as if he wishes he *wasn't* dressed. "Good morning, beautiful," he murmurs against my cheek as he drags his lips across them again. He smells of mint and his cologne and it's a heady scent that makes me wet instantly. I rub my thighs together and I can already feel the slick arousal forming between my legs.

"Why didn't you wake me?" I pout, and I don't even miss the breathiness in my voice caused by the final moments of sleep. "I would have joined you in the shower."

"And then I would have been late for my session." He looks at his watch and then back to me. "I used to be that guy that loved to get out of bed in the morning, and now it's a struggle leaving because I hate leaving *you*. I hate prying myself off of you when you're like this." His eyes trail down my body as he slowly pulls the covers back revealing inches of unclothed skin. "Fuck, you're sexy."

I smile at his words, recalling the night of sweet and gentle lovemaking that came after the crazed and primal fucking. It was as if Will and I couldn't get enough of each other. There was only us in these moments. No ex-husband, no lies, no deceit, only me and the man I love. Our bodies doing the dance they know by heart. He looks at me as if I am the only woman in the world. *As if I am his world.* Will's feelings for me run deep and have the intensity that perhaps others would call unhealthy.

Co-dependency.

It's a word that has sat in the back of my mind for the past few weeks. I love Will with all my heart, but even I can see that we are using our love to shield us from things that we don't want to face. *My past for instance.* I'm sure what Will is hiding, but every time I looked in his eyes, I sense there is something he isn't telling me. That there is a secret he's hiding.

I just hoped that it isn't a secret that will end everything.

I sit up in bed, wrapping the sheets around me so as to not have my naked breasts on display when I have to talk to Will about something important. "I'm meeting with a recruiter." I sigh. I had resigned myself to the fact that after a five-year gap in my resume, I would need a bit of help securing a job.

He grabs my hand, rubbing his thumb back and forth over them as if he can feel the tension building regarding my unemployment. I'd received a hefty sum of money in my settlement, but I wouldn't see the money until next year and, anyway, I wanted to learn to stand on my own two feet. Will had come around to support it, after a few arguments where he'd told me I didn't ever need to work.

Coming from a marriage to a man that told me just that, it was the last thing I wanted. "Do you want me to go with you?"

My scalp prickles at his question. *God, he was sweet.* "No, I'll be fine."

"Of course you will, it's not like going on an interview. I just wasn't sure if you were nervous." He brings my knuckles to his lips, his beard tickling my skin as he kisses it.

"I am, but...I can do this."

"You can do anything, baby."

"You make me feel like I can do anything—be anything. You are my biggest supporter." I swallow, trying to keep the words down but they move out of me quickly anyway. "You know I'm your biggest supporter too, right? I am always on your side, Will. No matter what."

He cocks his head to the side as if he's unsure why I'm saying any of this, but then nods. "I shouldn't be too late." He kisses me gently, his hands stroking my cheek with each lick of his tongue against mine before he pulls away just as I was planning to climb on top of him to keep him from getting up. "I love you."

"I love you too."

He shoots me a wink effectively making me even wetter, before he leaves the room. His scent still lingers in the sheets and all over me.

Time to go make use of that retractable shower head.

———

"You alright, Char?" The voice of my vivacious best friend, Lauren Michaels, interrupts my thoughts just as two salads are set in front of us in the small bistro by her office. I'd come to meet her after she rang our figurative *best friend bat signal,* but as soon as she sat down she just started firing off questions about Will and me. I didn't have the courage to tell her I sensed that Will was keeping something from me. I don't have the strength to endure a lecture or whatever Lauren would potentially say after I voiced my thoughts. I could hear her now:

"Have you asked him straight up?"

"I mean this is what happens when you rush into relationships."

Lauren wouldn't say that, my mind argues.

She would be thinking it.

Well, so are you…right?

"I'm fine, but you summoned me, and now you're just asking me a bunch of questions about my relationship." I rub my forehead. "You could have at least done me the courtesy of doing this over drinks at happy hour."

"Sorry, right." She pokes at the chicken in her salad before setting the fork down. "I just want to know that you'll be okay. That…you'll always be okay. Even if…I'm not here. You're my best friend, Charley, but I want to make sure someone has your back…when I'm not around to watch it."

"Oh God." Tears flood my eyes. "Are you okay? What's wrong? Are you sick?" The words come out like word vomit.

"No, no! I'm fine, I swear." She shakes her head; loose curls sweep back and forth across her shoulders and rain down her back. She tucks a hair behind her ear and gives me a weak smile. "I got promoted."

"Oh my God, Lo! That's fantastic! Why aren't we celebrating! Champagne later tonight?" My eyes narrow wondering why she's not more excited. Why she's so morose. I cock my head to the side when she still hasn't joined in my celebrating. My heart sinks as her mood begins to set in. "You have to move, don't you?"

"Chicago."

I let out a breath, picturing what my life would be like if I hadn't spent the last ten years of it calling Lauren Michaels my person. A person that was never further than a phone call or a few miles away. Now she would be several hundred miles away.

"Lo."

"I know, this fucking sucks. I'll miss you so much. And the best sex of my life. I barely even got to enjoy it." She pouts and my brows furrow.

"You mean…"

"Big dicks must run in the Montgomery family." She snickers and I blanch thinking about Will's older brother.

"Can you not?"

"His dick is fantastic, Char. Like sets the bar." She stands up and raises her hand toward the ceiling as high as she can go. "And his mouth game." Her thumb and index finger form the okay symbol as she sits back down.

"Thanks for sharing." I roll my eyes, not wanting to think about my future brother in law's appendage. The thought sends a spark to my heart. *In law.*

Will and I are getting married.

"Seriously, saying goodbye to that third leg of Drew Montgomery's is going to be tough." She pouts and her words snap me out of a particularly dirty wedding night fantasy involving Will and me in that sexy number position.

"But you'll be close to your sister, and your niece. So, that's good?"

"Yes, that's the biggest reason I'm taking the job. Besides the money of course. But Emma is three now and I want to see her grow up. Face Timing is getting hard."

"You could just have a baby of your own," I tease, and I can't even stop the stars from forming in my eyes as I picture Lauren's child. Gorgeous amber colored irises and tanned skin. Lauren's babies would hit the genetic lottery.

She scoffs. "With who? Drew? Although that would be cute. Our kids would be cousins!" She giggles. "But in all seriousness, Drew and I are just having fun."

"I don't know. I see the way he looks at you."

"Like I have magic in my vagina and he's trying to see my next trick."

I ignore her joke. "I see the way you look at him."

She purses her lips, the joke failing her. "He's sweet. And he's fun. And…it doesn't matter Char, I'm moving. And Drew is barely the monogamous type when the girl is in the same state!"

I huff and my brows thread together. "Is he fucking other girls?"

"No…I don't think so. Calm down. I'm just saying—Drew Montgomery has a lot of fun."

"Well, maybe you're the kind of girl to get him to settle down?"

"Sure, Char. He can come live with me in the Windy City. Me, him, Emma, and her parents: one big happy family."

"Never know." I shrug. "Have you told him?"

"We were supposed to get drinks tonight but something came up. He said something about dinner with his parents."

Without Will? I hadn't heard anything about a family gathering; it made me wonder if the three of them were having dinner alone. Will's words regarding his upbringing and his relationships with everyone in his immediate family come to mind making my heart sink slightly.

"Well, when do you move?" I ask her, not wanting to disclose private information about Will and his family.

"End of the month. It's bittersweet, but I think I'm ready for the change."

―――

Me: Lauren just told me she's moving :(

The frown is still on my face long after lunch with Lauren as I drop my keys on the counter of Will's townhouse. I don't have to wait long for a response, making me glad I know his schedule as well as I do.

Will: I'm sorry, baby. Why?

Me: Work. and wants to be closer to family.

Will: Well that's good for her. I'm sure she'll miss you though. Where is she moving?

Me: Chicago. We will go visit?

Will: Absolutely. How is your day?

Me: Besides that bomb? Not bad.

I neglect to tell him what Lo had said about Drew having dinner with their parents.

Will: Well unfortunately it's about to get worse.

I sit up straight on his couch, my body on high alert, waiting for his follow up when I see the familiar three dots indicating that he's typing.

> **Will: My parents are coming over.**
>
> **Me: PARENTS? As in PLURAL? As in J.R. who's not my biggest fan AND your mother who is even less of a fan?**

He doesn't answer my text, and I begin texting furiously as jump from the couch and break into a run towards the kitchen, realizing dinner is going to be *here*.

FUCK.

My phone starts ringing and I answer on the first ring.

"UH HUH?!?" My voice is panicked to the point of shrill and his voice comes over the receiver even, calm, and feels like warm honey all over me.

"Baby," he says softly, "please breathe. Everything is going to be fine."

"What—when—who?"

"Unfortunately, it's my fault how this happened. When you call J.R. for anything it's always a goddamn production," he groans.

"What do you mean?"

"I called him to see what he thought about me coming clean."

"Based on what you've told me, I assume he didn't agree with the idea?"

"You're learning." I can hear the chuckle, but it's dark. "When and if I do, he needs to be there so this conversation is inevitable. It escalated into him and my mother coming over." I open the refrigerator wondering what I have time to prepare and if I need to go to the store.

"And Drew?" I ask, wondering where he fits into these dinner plans.

"Drew? I don't—"

"Lauren mentioned that they had plans but that he canceled for dinner with your parents… maybe I'm mistaken." I backtrack not wanting to draw his attention to the fact that they probably had plans without him. *Like I thought.*

"News to me. But sounds about right." He snorts, and I twist my mouth to prevent the tears that are building. He is just as nervous about this as I am, and here I am panicking that my in-laws won't like me—when *Will* feels like they didn't even like *him*.

"We'll get through this together, baby."

CHAPTER
Sixteen

WILL

I COME HOME TO A WHIRLWIND MOVING AROUND THE KITCHEN and the smell of marinara in the air. My mouth waters both from the smell and the vision of Charlotte's ass in a tight pair of spandex leggings bending over the oven.

I move behind her as she stands up. My hand grips her ass hard before sliding around her waist and cupping her sex. I can feel the heat radiating through the material just from that one touch and it taps into the possessive caveman in me as I think about the power I have to turn her on.

"Are you barefoot in my kitchen, Miss Pierce?" My fingers stroking the space between her legs. Her leggings are so tight I can almost make out that tiny swollen bundle that was no doubt slightly peeking out between the lips of her sex.

"Will," she whines, "can you not?" She turns in my arms, presenting her lips to me, and I happily lean down to capture her lips. I'm desperate to feel her tongue moving against mine when she pulls away. "I don't have time for that."

"We have plenty of time. Why are you even cooking? You don't have to make anything for them. I don't think they are planning to stay for dinner."

"You invited your parents over at dinner time! Of course, I am expected to make something," she shrieks. "They already hate me. At least let me feed them." I don't tell her my mother has been off carbs since 1997 and there is a zero percent chance she'd have even a bite of the lasagna that she'd just slid into the oven. I run a hand through my hair as I can already hear the comments my mother will undoubtedly make.

"Thank you, baby, it's very sweet. But… it's going to be late, my parents eat at like…five." I want to prepare her for my mother not touching her food. *My father, on the other hand, will be thrilled. I don't think there's been red sauce anywhere near the white carpets of my parents' house in years. My mother rarely even allows red wine in the house.*

"Well," she furrows her brows, "at least they'll know I'm feeding you." She shrugs before she heads out of the kitchen. I grab her by her waist as she attempts to pass me and pull her towards me, wrapping my arms around her.

"Everything is going to be okay."

"Will it though?" she asks. "Your parents aren't exactly my biggest fans." I can see the tears forming in her eyes, and I pull her closer, brushing my lips across hers gently.

"Don't cry." My heart lurches in my chest as I watch one lone tear slide down her cheek. I reach my hand out to wipe her face.

"I just wish we could have talked about this more extensively first, without them."

"Baby, he *is* my lawyer, and I just don't want this hanging over my head anymore. It's constantly on my mind and I'm losing sleep over it. I just want us to move on."

"I understand that, and I get you want to know where you stand legally but I'm…" she trails off and sighs. "I just thought we'd be making decisions together about our future, that's all," she says before she disappears from the kitchen.

I follow behind her after a few minutes and lean against the doorframe as I watch her shed her clothes to prepare for a shower. My eyes follow her around the room lustfully before I press off the frame and pull her naked body into my arms. I pick her up and her arms and legs immediately go around me, clinging to me like a life raft and my body automatically reacts to her soft, womanly curves pressed up against me. "We are making these decisions together, baby." I rest my forehead against hers. "It's just you and me, okay? We'll hear what he thinks and decide together what's best."

She eyes me as if she doesn't totally believe my words before she nods once. She's silent for a moment before she shoots me a devilish grin and locks her ankles tighter behind me. "Do you want to shower with me? Maybe an orgasm will help take the edge off." I feel my dick respond to her words, answering for me as I walk us into the bathroom.

After our shower, that served to sate us both, I realize I left my phone in the kitchen. I step out of my bedroom and I'm immediately hit with a familiar scent that is almost overpowering the smell of the lasagna. *Chanel No. 5.*

Fuck. What are they doing here?

I pull the door to my bedroom shut behind me and jog down the stairs, my heart racing as I think about the fact that my family just showed up—two hours early. "What the hell are you doing here?"

"Well, hello to you too, son," my father says. His laptop rests in his lap, with his feet propped up on my custom made coffee table, and I resist the urge to knock them down. "I do believe you summoned us here to help fix this mess you're in."

"Yeah, two hours from now. I do believe we agreed for you to arrive around seven. What happened to calling, if you're going to be early? Or I don't know, knocking?" I cross my arms, irritated with their intrusion.

"We did knock, dear," my mother interjects as she brings a cup of tea to her lips. *If she's had time to prepare tea that means they've been here at least fifteen minutes.* I sigh, knowing they probably know what Charley and I were just doing, especially since the last orgasm I gave Charley had her screaming. "When you didn't answer after some time, we used our key."

Note to self: Take their keys.

"It sounded like you were busy," she continues, her teacup still raised, as she narrows her gaze at me over the rim. "I made myself some tea, I hope that's okay." Her lips form a straight line as she gives me a look, letting me know she knew just what was keeping me *busy*. It's one of those rare times I've seen my mother with her hair down, both sides are tucked behind her ear and curled almost perfectly. She looks exhausted, as if she hasn't been sleeping, and I begin to ask if she's getting enough rest in an attempt to deflect.

"Honey, did you check on the—" Charley's voice floods the room and I kick myself for not telling her they were here the second I smelled my mother's perfume. I breathe a sigh of relief when I see she's completely dressed, although her hair is still wet and she's pulled it into a bun high on her head. Her face is completely void of makeup and, despite my parents' presence, I want to take her back into my room and make love to her for the rest of the day. I reach for her hand and rub my thumb over the back of it trying to calm her racing thoughts—and heart.

"My parents decided to come early," I say, so she knows that this is just as much of a surprise to me.

She swallows and gives me a look, showing the worry all over her beautiful features. "That's not a problem, is it?" my mother asks, and I shoot her a look.

Charley immediately changes her expression and gives my mother a smile. "Of course not, dinner is just not quite ready." She moves towards my mother and holds her hand out towards her. "I'm Charlotte, it's very nice to meet you." I can sense her warm smile although I'm standing behind her, and I watch as my mother stares at her hand for a beat longer than is appropriate before reluctantly setting her tea down. *Where are those manners you instilled, Mother?*

I expect her usual curt greeting. I can already hear "The pleasure is all mine, darling." *Cue air kiss.* But what I did not expect was for her eyes to narrow slightly as she stands to her feet, dusting the imaginary dust from her lap and staring Charlotte square in the eye. I can see a slight tremor move through Charley as if she's bracing for impact. "So, you're the woman who has my son beside himself and risking his entire practice."

"Mother," I grit out, as I move to stand next to Charlotte, pulling her back slightly.

"I—I…" Charlotte stammers.

My mother raises her hands in exasperation. "You have nothing to say? Can you imagine how this will make you look if this gets out, Will? Honestly, dear, it'll completely tarnish your good name."

"That I fell in love?" I ask her.

"That you slept with your *married* patient!" I hear a sniffle and I can sense that Charley is seconds from losing it. "Oh, for Heaven's sake, now is *not* the time to cry. What are you going to do if my son loses his career over you?"

I go to interject when Charlotte's confident voice rings through the air. "I think about it every day. How I would be able to look at myself in the mirror knowing I cost the man I love…everything. How he would view me and us—how our relationship would change. If we could even have one at all. I wonder if he would eventually resent me."

Never, baby. I don't interrupt, I just slide my hand into hers and squeeze, praying that the gesture will translate. She looks at me and if I ever needed any confirmation that she and I were on the same wavelength, she nods her head.

"Frankly, Mrs. Montgomery, I don't know what I would do. Love him? Try and be there for him as best I can? Try to live with myself. I'm not going to walk away from him, if that's what you're asking. I love him. More than anything. I know you don't believe that. Maybe you never will. But I just hope you'll give me a chance to show you that I'm not a bad person. I'm not a—"

"Liar? Cheater? Manipulator?" my mother interrupts and I feel the fury flash across my face. "I hate to break it to you, honey, but you are those things," she snaps.

"That is *enough*," I snarl. "Baby, can you go check on the food?" I wanting her away from my mother as soon as possible. I chance a glance at J.R. who's still seated, mindlessly going through his phone as if he's oblivious to the scene unfolding in front of him.

"Yes, I…see you're preparing lasagna," she grits her teeth. "I haven't had carbs in years." She sticks her nose in the air and shudders as if the thought abhors her.

Charlotte's back straightens slightly and I can see a small glimpse of the confident Charley shining through. "I've done bad things, it doesn't make me a bad person. I'm just asking for a chance to—" She ignores the petty comment about her choice of meal preparation. *Good girl, don't feed into that bullshit.*

"What? Break my son's heart? Ruin his life? Take half his money? J.R. told me you're coming out of your previous marriage with some pretty significant wealth."

"Frankly, that's not any of your business." Her voice is even, not combative or angry. "Will is not my ex-husband and you don't know anything about my prior marriage."

"Marriage is hard work. You don't get to throw a temper tantrum and end your marriage just because you aren't getting enough attention. Get a hobby, dear. Once upon a time you would have thrived in the junior league." She crosses her arms and backs away slightly, moving toward the bar cart in the corner of my room. "Of course, not now. No, now, your *lifestyle choices* would make it very difficult for you to be accepted."

"I'm not interested," Charley says immediately.

"Hmmm." My mom opens a bottle of *Tanqueray* gin and shoots me a look. "Olives, dear?"

I don't answer her, and with my hand wrapped around Charlotte's forearm, I haul her into the kitchen. Once we are safely out of earshot, I reach for her. "Baby." It's as if that simple word causes her to break down because the tears are streaming down her cheeks.

"She hates me. Which I somewhat expected but…that?" She points at the doorway. I wrap her in my arms and push her face into my chest.

"Shhh, she doesn't hate you. She doesn't know you and my mother is just…" *How do I even put her into words?* "She hates any sign of scandal."

"She thinks I'm all wrong for you." She pulls back, her eyes teary and red, her skin slightly blotchy but she's still as radiant as ever.

"Good thing she doesn't get a say in the matter then." I kiss her lips gently, sliding my tongue between them in an effort to calm her.

"Is she always…" she starts. "Has she always been like that?" I can hear the question she's really trying to ask. *Does she treat you like that?*

"As long as I can remember." *Yes,* I answer her unspoken question.

Empathy flashes in her eyes, and then she's back in my arms, wrapping hers around me and pressing a kiss just over my heart. "I'm sorry."

I lift her chin upwards towards me and allow my lips to hover over hers. "I love you," I tell her just before I press my lips to hers. "And I'm sorry for what she said to you." I press my forehead to hers.

Her eyes flutter closed and I take a minute to just enjoy the stillness between us, ignoring the fact that my parents are one room over, probably preparing for round two with my fiancée.

A throat being cleared penetrates our bubble and I turn around to see my mother holding her gin martini at the stem of her glass. "Olives? Also, Tanqueray over Hendrick's?" She wrinkles her nose. "Not my first choice for entertaining. Did you not read the book I gave you for the drinks that should always be on hand?" She moves towards my cabinet and opens it, in search of the olives I know are not in there.

"Mother I don't have any olives. And I'm sure you have Hendrick's at *home*."

"A gin martini without olives?" She puts a hand across her chest in the most dramatic fashion, and had it been anyone else on the face of the Earth, I would think they're kidding. *But no, my mother is definitely serious.* "I might as well drink this out of one of those red plastic cups." She moves out of the kitchen without another word. Charlotte is staring after her, mouth slightly open in shock. She looks at me and then back to the door and then back to me again.

"I have no words," she whispers. "Literally not even one."

"I've been trying to come up with the words for years." I follow her gaze. "They fail me every time."

—

I walk out of the kitchen, leaving Charley alone and shoot my mother a look. "Can you not?"

"What?" she asks as if she's clueless to her calculated comments.

"Watch your tone with her, *Diana,* I mean it," I growl, knowing she hates it when I call her by her first name. "*I am not J.R., you will address me as the woman that spent fourteen hours in labor bringing you into this world,*" she would say.

And then the next eighteen years making me wish you hadn't.

"William, what do you even know about this girl, really? I am just trying to understand—"

I snort. "No, you're not. You're using the fact that you're my mother to stomp all over her, when you know Charlotte does ultimately want your approval. And I won't have it. *Ever.* But you are damn sure not going to insult the woman I love under my roof."

She huffs. "She shouldn't be so sensitive."

"I am warning you, *Mother.* Don't make me do it again." I walk by her, daring her to walk into the kitchen to bother the woman who is probably still shaking like a leaf.

I move into the living room and my father immediately drops his phone from his ear, a hushed "I'll call you later," falls from his lips and I resist the urge to chuckle.

"Really? Your *wife* is in the other room." I don't even try to hide my disgust and disapproval.

"Keep your voice down," he says half-heartedly, as if my mother finding out that he was talking to *whoever* didn't concern him. "I have plans for dinner, so let's get started, shall we?" I frown, not because I think he's having dinner with a woman, but because I remember what Charlotte said about them having dinner plans with Drew.

It's probably for the best anyway, my mind attempts to rationalize in an attempt to hide the hurt.

"Why did you even bring her here?"

"She is your mother, and she's concerned."

"Maybe she should be more concerned with *her* relationship and less concerned with mine."

"What goes on between your mother and me is not your business and it works for us."

My eyebrows almost shoot off my face. "Works for who? You? Your infidelity works for Mom? How?"

"Trust me, your mother is fine." I watch as he drowns the contents of his highball glass, and I feel the itch to join him. *No Will, no drinks while they're here.* Having a drink around my parents is a slippery slope. Once I open that door, it wouldn't take me long to be completely obliterated as I would be taking a sip every time either one of them pissed me off. I'd once gone through four drinks in the span of an hour.

"Fine, whatever. I can't have this conversation with you for the millionth time. Can we talk about why I called you over here?"

"Yes, that would be lovely." My mother comes back into the

room, and I wonder if she waited until after she knew we were no longer discussing my father's latest indiscretion.

It is much easier to ignore it that way.

She sits in the chair that she handpicked for me, telling the decorator she hired that it was the perfect addition to the room. It was beige and hard and *I fucking hate it.* She is literally the only person who ever sits there.

I believe my father is about to start talking when Charley reappears in the room. "It's ready if you want to eat first or…" she trails off, and I can hear the nerves in her voice. "Mrs. Montgomery, I can make you something else?"

My mother doesn't move and my father's eyes are glued to his laptop he'd just opened. I watch in disbelief as neither one of them acknowledge her.

After a moment, my mother remembers her manners and smiles. "It's really much too late for me to eat anything."

Charley frowns and looks down at her watch, visibly confused at my mother's inability to eat past five. My mother must mistake Charley's confusion for judgment because she continues. "Once your metabolism slows, you'll understand. Usually around a woman's late twenties early thirties, one has to watch what they eat and when they eat it," she nods.

I roll my eyes. "Baby, come sit with me," I tell her as I wave her over, ignoring my mother's jab at my fiancée. I sit down and pull her as close as she can get to me without being in my lap and wrap an arm around her waist before giving her a gentle squeeze.

"Let's forget about food for now, we ate before we came anyway," my father says and I want to kick them both out for the insensitivity towards Charley's feelings. "So, let's weigh the options, shall we?" He sets his computer to the side. "You go to the board, explain everything, they suspend your license." He opens his arms as if to say 'what's next?' "What happens?"

"I don't know. There's a lot of factors. I wasn't *just* messing around with a patient. I fell in love with her. She wanted to leave her husband. She's of a consenting age—"

"Well, I would certainly hope so!" my mother exclaims.

"I just mean she's of an age to make her own decisions without suspicion of being coerced," I say before turning back to my father. "I don't know what the future holds if I tell them everything. The AMA condemns any kind of sexual relationship between a doctor and a patient, but our situation is a little different. It's against the code of conduct, but—"

"But what, Will?" J.R. interjects, and I'm getting so irritated with them for prohibiting me from getting my thoughts out with their constant interruptions. "I was just reading an article that there are some members of the AMA that believe under no circumstances can a patient give consent at all. Let's put the violation of patient privacy aside, which is a completely different bear, what will they do when they learn about you and Charley?"

"Worst case scenario, I lose my license."

"And then what exactly comes next?"

"I do something else. I can do other things. I can counsel other people. Some help centers don't require a license, and a variety of degrees which I have will suffice. In my situation, I could file for a reissue in which case I could be reinstated. It just might be hard to stay in Atlanta and practice again with my reputation. But I could very well start somewhere new."

My mother gasps. "And now you're leaving?!" She shakes her head. "There has to be some other way."

"Not if he's hell-bent on telling them."

"You make it seem like doing the right thing is so terrible. God J.R., your lawyer is showing," I groan as I rub my head. "It's the right thing to do, I took an oath for fuck's sake. Try to understand that!"

"In relation to those patients whose privacy was violated, those people are none the wiser. Charley's ex-husband agreed he wasn't going to say anything. We are the only people that know! What is the point of turning your life upside down? I understand the principle, but…you don't have to cut off your nose to spite your face," J.R. bites back.

"I can't have this over me anymore. The guilt will eventually eat away at me," I tell him honestly. *And that's if I don't drink myself to death first.*

"Why?! They're not going to know. If you're feeling guilty, stop counseling them. Recommend them to someone else and move on," my mother adds.

"Will, we got the tape from Matt when we met with him. There's no chance of it getting back to them," my father says.

"And what happens if he made a copy?" I ask.

"I made it clear what would happen if he made trouble in that regard. He gets it."

I sigh. "So, you're saying I just say nothing, pretend it didn't happen?"

"That's my vote," J.R. says, as he leans back in his chair, crossing one leg over the other.

"And if it comes out later that I knew about it, I'm fucked."

Both of my parents are silent, and I turn to my side, and study Charley for a moment. Her head is bowed slightly, her hands fidgeting nervously in her lap, and I swear I can hear her heart pounding from where I sit. "What do you think, baby?"

She looks up at me and then at my parents who've now turned their attention to her as well. "I think…" she starts. "Only you have to live with yourself and the choices you make. If you don't say anything, and you get to keep everything intact, but you're miserable and unhappy…is it worth it? I don't want to watch this eat you alive. That's when people turn to other vices instead of the people that love them. I don't want to watch you spiral."

Does she know? Can she sense the inner turmoil that is building within me? Does she know I have another vice—besides her?

"He's stronger than that. And as his mother I resent the insinuation that he's not," I hear my mother say, and I don't think for one second that Charley was calling me weak. *She's right. One hundred percent. It doesn't matter what any of us say. It's about whether I'll be able to look at myself in the mirror every morning.*

"He's the strongest man I know." Charley smiles before she turns her gaze to me and rubs her hand over my jaw. "But guilt..." she trails off before she turns back to my parents. "I've had quite a lot of experience with guilt lately and...it will consume you." She looks back at me and her eyes penetrate me. "I want you to do what's best for you, and I will support whatever you need to do so long as it's...nothing crazy. I love you. I will always support you. If we have to leave Atlanta, then we leave Atlanta. I would follow you anywhere." She smiles and I resist the urge to pull her into my lap and kiss her with everything in me.

I settle for cupping her face and placing a gentle kiss on her lips that I hope conveys how much I love her. I let my forehead rest against hers just letting myself be calmed by her gentle breathing.

"I love you too," I tell her.

I hear my father clear his throat and I see the pink in her cheeks as I think she may have forgotten we weren't alone.

"It seems like you've got your mind made up. So, I guess the only question is—when is this going down?"

CHAPTER
Seventeen

Will

T HE MEETING IS SET FOR MONDAY, ALLOWING ME ONE FINAL weekend of normalcy before I turn my life completely upside down. I hate the unknown; it makes me feel out of control, something that triggers me to drink more than usual, but I am trying my best to ignore the little voice that urges me to have *just one glass*. I haven't had a drink in two days, after I'd soaked my liver in scotch the night that J.R. and my mother stopped by and voiced their opinions while Charlotte tried to relieve her tension through a two-hour bubble bath. Once she was out, I buried myself inside of her over and over again, wringing every ounce of pleasure from her delicious little body.

It's Saturday, and Charlotte and I have decided to spend the weekend not worrying about the future and just enjoying each other. It's the first time we are out in the open in Atlanta as a couple, and we want to enjoy the newfound freedom. I haven't been able to keep my eyes off Charlotte all night, her black dress that exposes tanned skin and sexy curves gives me a hard-on that I can't shake. Lips coated in red, smile up at me over her menu. "You're staring again."

"It's just because you're the most beautiful woman I've ever laid eyes on." I look around the restaurant and catch more than a few people looking at us. "Every man is jealous that you're here with me and not them."

A pink tint finds her cheeks as she bites down on her lip. "You always make me feel beautiful."

"And I will continue to do so for the rest of our lives, future Mrs. Montgomery." Desire flashes in her eyes and I notice she squirms in her seat. I raise an eyebrow at her. "Are you wet?"

She swallows and nods her head several times as she sets her menu down. "I want you to fuck me."

"And here I thought my tongue in your pussy right before we left would be enough to get you through the night." My voice is low, not wanting to alert any of the patrons of our sexual banter, but equally seductive.

Her hand reaches across the table and grips my forearm. "Well, you've been looking at me like you want to devour me all night. You know I react to your looks. All of them. I always have."

"Always, huh?"

She nods. "When…he would be late, and I arrived on time, you always complimented what I was wearing, particularly when I wore dresses. You told me I looked lovely, nice, I think once you told me I looked beautiful. I almost dropped to the ground and spread my legs for you right then and there. It's why I started wearing them every time. Because I thought you liked them."

"I love you in everything. *And nothing,*" I add and she giggles. "I had no idea, you noticed."

"I noticed everything. Because…you noticed everything about *me.*"

And it was true, I had noticed everything about her, from the beginning, all I could see was her.

The waiter comes over with the bottle of champagne we ordered. I hadn't planned to drink, but Charlotte absentmindedly said something about celebrating our first official date and asked what champagne I thought was best.

See what happens when you aren't honest with your partner? I'd seen it time and time again in counseling. If one partner has an addiction problem—alcohol specifically—it can be the spouse without the problem that can accidentally drag them back in with something as harmless as a champagne toast.

Case in point. I look at the champagne as he pours our glasses, and I watch as the bubbles make it almost to the surface but begin to dissolve just before they begin to spill over the edge. *Veuve Clicquot* champagne had become my favorite by default, having been raised that *Moet* and *Dom Perignon* were simply *too flashy*. Besides, *that's what Ingrid and Humphrey drink in Casablanca,* my mother would giggle as she downed the bubbly liquid amongst her friends.

"Cheers, baby." She lifts her glass and holds it out for me to tap mine against and I do so without hesitation.

"Cheers to you." I nod at her, before letting my eyes close as I take a long sip. There's an explosion in my mouth and throughout my body as it recognizes the taste instantly.

I knew you couldn't stay away.

I swallow past the lump forming in my throat as I set the glass down, not wanting to drain the entire thing in one gulp.

"Are you nervous for Monday?" *Ah fuck it.* I pick up the glass and down it before sitting it back down. "I guess that's a yes." She reaches across the table and grabs my hand. "Don't be nervous, I'll be right there with you the whole time."

I nod, knowing that it was never an argument I could have won. When I planned the meeting, I started to tell her that she didn't need to be there. The words weren't even out of my mouth before she was shooting me a glare and telling me to "not fucking go there."

"I know, it's just a big risk."

"But you'll feel much better afterwards, getting it out in the open. Secrets always find a way of coming out. And like you said, you want to be able to live with yourself."

I repeat her words in my head. *Secrets always find a way of coming out.*

Secrets.

I have a secret.

I let out a breath and sit back against my chair, my eyes raking over the vision in front of me and trying to forget the fact that there's something I need to tell her.

Not tonight.

Do it tomorrow. Just enjoy tonight.

"When did you want to get married?" I ask changing the subject.

Her eyes light up so bright, it almost stops my heart. "When you're ready."

"Are *you* ready?"

"Yes," she tells me without hesitation. "I love you and I want to be with you…forever."

You better not marry this woman without being honest with her about everything. Would she be this willing to dive into marriage with you when she learns that she's not your first love like she believes?

That title belongs to alcohol. And she is a jealous fucking bitch.

"Sometime early next year?"

"I don't need a big wedding. I've done that and…I just need you and Lauren and my mom and whoever else you want."

"I don't want anything big."

"I'm sure your mother will want to invite everyone in Atlanta." She rolls her eyes in a circle as she takes another sip and the itch in my fingers to pour myself another glass overtakes me. "Do you want more?" Charlotte asks as she points at my empty glass. She lifts the bottle to pour it for me as I nod.

Then no more.

Two hours and two bottles of champagne later, Charlotte and I have switched to harder drinks and I've moved my chair to allow myself to touch every inch of her skin. We are tucked into a corner of the restaurant where there aren't as many eyes witnessing our slightly drunken public displays of affection.

"You mean the world to me, Charlotte. You know that?" I mindlessly play with her hair as her hand strokes my thigh, her hand moving up higher each time. I strain against my pants, my cock rising to the fact that her hand is wandering dangerously close to it.

"Of course. You tell me all the time!" She giggles, her voice a little louder than usual and I wonder if the whiskey in her Manhattan is getting to her.

"Because it's the truth."

"Do you know that you mean the world to *me*? I didn't even know it was possible to love someone this much. I read all those romance novels where women were like bursting with love for a guy, and I always wondered what that was like? But I am just consumed by you. Is that unhealthy? That's unhealthy, right? What is your official Doctor opinion?" she rambles and I chuckle at her ability to go off on tangents so easily. *God, I love her.*

"I think…" I start. "That our love has been extremely healthy for both of us. We needed this. We deserve this after trusting our hearts with people that didn't deserve it. *We* deserve to be happy."

"See and that, you always know just what to say." She sighs and puts her hand under her head and stares up at me dreamily. "You're perfect."

"I am far from perfect, Charley." I laugh.

Really far.

"Well, you're perfect for me."

I hope you still think so after tomorrow.

"You would never lie to me," she says with a smile. I think she's still talking, but my brain has shut down hearing those six words.

You would never lie to me.

You would never lie to me.

You would never lie to me.

"I'm sorry, what did you say, baby?" I ask.

"You're honest and compassionate and you are such a good man, Will. I feel so lucky to know you."

Charlotte has been unabashed about her feelings from the beginning but hearing her voice them so emphatically has me wanting to fuck her on this table.

Maybe, just maybe I had a shot at keeping her when this was all over. When she had all the facts, she'd look up at me with tears in her eyes and tell me she loved me and that we would get through this together.

It's all I could hope for.

—

We'd long since decided that we would leave my car here and come back for it in the morning, and had opted to walk a bit down Main Street before calling it a night. This is how we came to be at a lounge that has a speakeasy feel. Exposed brick and dim lights that flicker line the walls, and amber hues reflect off the shiny mahogany bar.

A bar where Matthew Wells is sitting, his hand moving up the skirt of a blonde woman with breasts up to her ears. I freeze, hesitating to take another step. I turn to Charlotte, trying to block her vision of what's behind me. "Let's go, the place next door seems better."

"What! Oh, come on, this place is so cool." She steps around me and takes in the atmosphere with almost a childlike expression. She moves towards the bar before immediately stopping in her tracks. The bar is somewhat dark but lit enough for me to follow her gaze to see that she'd located her ex-husband. I watch as the color leaves her face.

"You are much more beautiful," I murmur in her ear, unsure of what is going through that mind of hers. She scoffs and shakes her head.

"I'm not jealous. But you're right, we should go. Nothing good can come from the three of us being here."

I nod in agreement, just as his eyes find us. "Fuck," I whisper and Charlotte's sharp intake of breath is enough for me to make the call for us. "We're out of here." I grab her hand and begin moving back through the door when I feel something pulling me back followed by a squeal. I turn my head to see that Matt has wrapped his arm around Charlotte's forearm staring at her with a murderous expression.

"If you don't let her the fuck go, I will break your arm off," I growl at him as I put myself between them and force his hand off of her.

He still hasn't said anything when Charley starts to pull on my arm. "Baby, let's go."

"BABY?" he roars, and the thing about speakeasies is they're quiet, unlike raging clubs and bars; the vibe is relaxed, the volume just above a dull roar. So, when Matt bellows, everyone turns to look at us.

"There a problem here, folks?" the host asks, his eyes scanning the circle and landing on Charlotte as if he's quickly putting together what *exactly* that problem is.

"He," Matt sticks his finger in my face, and I resist the urge to break it, "is fucking my *wife*."

"Oh my God," Charlotte groans and a look of dread crosses her face as I imagine she's picturing the worst.

"She's his *ex*-wife," I snarl, as I look at the man who's probably regretting even asking.

"This sounds like a domestic problem. And you can handle that outside. I won't have you disrupting our establishment."

"That's fine. We were just leaving when he manhandled her." I shoot him a glare, as I stand protectively in front of Charlotte.

"I have some fucking things I want to say to you. So yeah, let's go." He points his finger in my face and then towards the door.

"Matt, now is really not the time." Charley's voice wavers alerting me of the panic she feels. *I wish she wasn't here because this could get ugly.*

"I have some things to say to you as well, like how you sent me a sex tape, you spineless prick." I put my hands on my hips, daring him to fuck with me. My heart rapidly pounds in my chest as I have flashes of them together.

Thrusting.

Panting.

Fucking.

FUCK.

"Okay that's it, all of you, OUT," the host barks as he begins to all but shove Matt and me out the door, and I'm grateful for the few seconds that we aren't staring each other down. Charley scurries in front of me and when we make it into the cool night air, I immediately pull her back behind me.

"You're really whining about that? How do you think I felt *hearing* you have sex with my wife? All the things you said…" Matt stops talking and shuts his eyes for a second, more than likely remembering that we confessed our love to each other on the very same tape. I don't even try to wipe the smug look off my face. When his eyes pop back open, they're filled with rage and directed at Charley who'd moved next to me. "I wanted you to feel how I felt after I had to hear your little tape."

"That was a fucking visual, Matt!" Charley yells. She's so angry she's shaking, and under any other circumstances I would be turned on. *Hell, I think I am anyway, watching her protect me and us so fiercely to the man she'd essentially left to be with me.* "You unlawfully planted an audio recording device, that is *not* the fucking same."

"You're right, you cheating on me after five years of marriage is *not* the fucking same."

She lets out a breath, her cheeks puffing out as I know she's not really sure what to say to that. "You were never supposed to hear that, and I'm sorry you did. But you maliciously sent a tape to the man I love. You intentionally sent the tape out of retaliation. To hurt him. To hurt *me*."

"What about me? You think I didn't love you? Do you just not give a fuck about my feelings at all? It doesn't matter that you hurt me? That you destroyed our marriage?"

"I didn't—Matt, can we not do this now? We've had a bit to drink and—"

"Everything has to be done on your terms, right? Never mind that you cheated on me and broke us. Never mind that it was with our fucking therapist!" He pauses. "I always thought that laundry list of reasons you gave was bullshit."

"They weren't bullshit! I didn't destroy this marriage all on my own, Matt."

"You certainly played a larger part," he snarls. "I wasn't around enough, I worked too much, I didn't give you a baby…but you neglected to tell me the biggest reason. You needed to be fucked constantly like the whore you are and our fucking marriage counselor was taking care of that for you." He gets in her face, yelling at her, and I press my hand to his chest, pushing him backwards. My fist flexes, preparing myself for his retaliation.

"Back off, Wells, and watch your fucking mouth."

"Tell me does she suck your dick? Because that's a luxury I had in the beginning but that goes away. She turned into a frigid bitch in the third year of our marriage. The sex was like going through the motions. I barely enjoyed it half the time. I hate to break it to you, Charlotte, but you're kind of a boring lay. In case you were wondering why I stopped fucking you."

"Enough," I growl, my hands flex before balling into a fist and my brain is screaming at me to calm down, to not engage in this psychological warfare. *If you swing at him, it will be bad.*

If you swing at him, you will lose everything.

You'll lose Charlotte.

I'm not sure if that is true, but I need to keep my rage in check, and allowing her asshole ex-husband to get under my skin is the quickest way to lose my temper.

"Everything is all sunshine and blow jobs in the beginning and then it just stops."

"You're being disgusting," Charlotte interjects. "I forgot you can get like this when you're drunk." Her words are like a punch to the gut. *Is this how she felt about me when I found the sex tape?* I feel her hands lacing with mine and then pulling me down the street away from potential disaster.

"Don't fucking walk away from me. I'm not finished."

"Well, we are," I tell him. "I'll be damned if I'm going to sit back and let you insult her."

I hear his heavy breathing and I know he's only a few steps behind us. "And fuck you and your so-called therapy. I ought to kick your ass. God, I was paying you three hundred dollars an hour to fuck my wife? You know prostitution is illegal in Georgia. I don't like that I unknowingly became your pimp, Charlotte," he growls.

I spin around to face him. My nostrils flare, and my heart pounds in my chest. Sweat beads on the back of my neck and trickles down as the anger boils inside. I let out a deep breath, trying to extinguish the fire blazing within.

Call her a name, one more fucking time.

Charley's voice cuts through the tension calming me slightly. "Don't be disgusting."

"You spread your legs for the first man that gave you a second glance, Charlotte. Don't call *me* disgusting. Look in the fucking mirror."

She gasps and I prepare myself to tear him a new one for speaking to her in such a hateful manner when she explodes. "Are you fucking kidding me? Are you really that self-involved? First of all, I didn't *spread* my legs for anyone. I gave myself fully to a man that loves and cherishes me. To a man that I love more than anything." She purses her lips, and I know she feels good having gotten that small dig in. "But circling back to 'the first man that gave me a second glance.' PLEASE!" She puts her hand up. "Men gave me second glances all the time. Sometimes third and fourth glances too. Do you know how many of *your* associates, clients, and partners have hit on me? Sometimes in front of you! I always thought it didn't bother you, because you never reacted to it. But you're telling me you just didn't notice? I don't know why I'm surprised, you never noticed anything when it came to me." I hear the sadness in her voice, and I want to pull her away and kiss the pain out of her. I want her to know that I notice everything about her. That I will always notice her. That she will always be the center of my universe.

Matt is silent, and I think he's taking a moment to recall the instances in question. "What did he do that I didn't? How did this motherfucker," he points at me *again*, "weasel in and steal my wife right out from under my nose?"

I'm struggling with whether to step away and let her handle this on her own and wanting to stay, to keep Matt in check and his hands off of my fiancée. "So many things," Charlotte whispers. "You fell out of love with me, Matt. I could feel it and so could you. When you looked at me it was as if you were looking through me. You stopped seeing me. Will saw me. He didn't steal me either. I was drowning in my own misery, depressed with a low self-image due to a husband that didn't pay me the time of day. You took me for granted. You made me feel that I wasn't important. Like I was your property to do with what you wanted and when you didn't need me I was irrelevant." She lowers her head in shame and I wrap my arm around her waist pulling her closer to me.

"Why didn't you ever tell me that?" he yells, his eyes darting to where we are connected and she flinches.

See? She wants me to protect her now.

She wants me.

She's mine.

"I did. Before we even went to therapy. And *in* therapy! You walked out on me so many times when I was trying to have this conversation with you. Matt, I tried to leave you once. This isn't the first time you've heard this."

"You never said it like that."

"Yes, I did. You just weren't listening. I was screaming for your attention, your affection. But you couldn't hear me. Or maybe you just didn't *want* to."

He puts his hands on his hips as he takes a step back. He turns around and I wonder if he's going to walk away, but he turns back to us, his body shaking with anger, his eyes glazing over and I wonder if it's fueled by too much alcohol or if his emotions are just running high. Either way, I'm on high alert ready to put myself between them.

"We can try again." *Oh, fuck that.* "You and me, we can put this behind us. I can forgive you for what you did. *For this.*" His eyes are clearer as they glare at me, but still cold and angry leading me to believe that despite his words, he would never be able to truly forgive her for what she did. *He damn sure wouldn't be able to forget.*

"No, Matt. This isn't a fling. This is real." She looks up at me, a look in her eyes telling me she's sorry, and I squeeze her tighter against me.

"What the fuck do you mean *real?* YOU WERE MY WIFE! THERE IS NOTHING MORE REAL!" he screams as he takes another step closer to us. I move in between them again and push him harder against his chest.

I've been trying my best to keep my voice even but the anger seeps out of me as he screams at her. "Get the fuck away from her!" I push him back out of her personal space. "You act like she's the only one that had a hand in destroying your marriage. But this is your MO, right? Placing blame everywhere except for where it belongs. Blaming others for your fucking mistakes." My voice gets louder, and I note a couple in the corner of my eye scurrying past me.

"You were a shitty fucking husband," I continue and I watch as his face falls slightly. *Good. You deserve to know the truth.* "Charley was done taking your shit! She moved on to someone who cares about her. Who gave a shit. Because it was obvious you *did not.*" I'm so angry at this point that I'm actually shaking. I ball my hands into a fist to try and stop the tremors moving through me.

I know my words are harsh. Ones said out of anger. The doctor in me is silently condemning my behavior. *This is not the answer, Will.* But the other part of me, the much larger part, the one that promised to protect the woman shaking like a leaf beside me is gearing up for battle.

This is the end of a yearlong war.

Against my feelings, my conscious, my morals and now the ex-husband of the woman I love.

This is the man that sent a brick through my window, that sent me a fucking sex tape, that tried to break Charley.

Fuck him.

He's back in my face, the whiskey from his breath swirling around me and making me wish I had a glass at that moment. "You have a lot of fucking nerve, you prick. Is this how you *counsel?*" he spits out.

Hit him. The alcohol tells me.

I'm shaking with rage, my hand curling into a fist, ready to hit his arrogant face.

I'm toe to toe with him, he's about my height, putting us nose to nose and I stare at him square in the eye. "Listen to me," my voice is low, cold, hard, "if you don't watch your fucking tone, I will put my fist through your face. Your insults and petulant comments are only proof of just what a pathetic man you are. Charlotte was always too good for you and she's better off without you."

He stares at me with equally angry eyes, and within a split second, his hands are wrapped around the collar of my jacket. "Fuck you, asshole." He turns to Charlotte. "*This* is who you chose over me? This pretentious prick?" He lets me go, shoving me backwards and all of the alcohol in my system makes me stumble slightly.

Charlotte wraps her arms around me, holding me upright. "Matt, I'm sorry that I've turned you into this hateful man. But I—" she starts.

I'm so focused on Charlotte, hearing her gear up to speak that I don't see it coming or I don't see his fist flying through the air. I hear him grunt out *asshole* and then Charlotte's eyes widen. But it all happens so fast.

I turn back towards him and she screams just as his fist connects with my jaw.

Hard.

———

The car ride is silent, only the sounds of late night talk radio blare through the speakers as we move towards my house. Charlotte is pressed up against me, her lips having found my cheek every few seconds soothing the searing pain shooting through my face. I hadn't looked at the damage yet but I could feel my cheek swelling up and the fire bubbling under the surface.

Fuck, that was one hell of a hit. I hope that felt good, Wells. Because that was your one.

Charlotte hailed a cab that was driving by and all but forced me into it before I could make the snap decision to punch Matt back.

"I am so sorry," she whispers against my cheek as she strokes the other, rubbing her nose along the inflamed skin.

"It's okay, baby. Not your fault."

I look over to find tears brimming under her lids, a direct reflection of the sorrow lurking. "How can you say that? This whole thing is my fault." She sniffles and pushes herself harder against me.

I turn my face towards her and rub my nose against her. "Not. Your. Fault. I provoked him, Charley."

Her eyes aren't looking at me, but at my cheek, and she winces as she begins to run her fingertips over it. "We should ice that when we get home."

"How bad is it?"

"You're still perfect." She smiles and I have to resist the urge to roll my eyes. "Does it hurt?"

"It's fine. But you see why I was always so worried about you around him? I thought you said he wasn't the violent type?"

"I said he'd never hit *me*."

"I'm still not convinced."

She shivers and I wonder if the thought had crossed her mind as well. "Do you still feel the same?" she whispers, and even in the darkness of the cab I can see that her eyelids are drooping.

"What do you mean?"

"The same as you said you felt at the restaurant? Do you still love me? Despite…this?" She hiccups and buries her face in my chest.

"Charley." I pull her so that she's almost in my lap and kiss her forehead. "We can talk about this tomorrow when we're both sober, but of course I still love you. I will always love you. I don't give a damn about what your ex-husband says or does. It's you and me, *forever*."

CHAPTER
Eighteen

Charlotte

I WAKE UP THE NEXT MORNING, MY BODY ON HIGH ALERT THAT I'm alone in bed. I sit up, rubbing a hand over my head as I try to quiet the pounding against my temple. I'm not sure which is more aggressive at the moment: the physical or emotional hangover. I hadn't given much thought to what it would be like to run into Matt again, especially with Will in tow. But if last night was any indication, hell, maybe leaving Atlanta would be for the best. My eyes sweep the length of the room before falling on the empty space next to me. I run my hand over the cool sheets making me wonder just how long Will has been awake.

When we got home last night, I half expected Will to throw me against the wall and fuck me like he was a jealous man on a mission. But he merely tucked me into bed before climbing in next to me as he rested the ice pack on his face. Matt's words come back to me in an instant.

It was like going through the motions. I barely enjoyed the sex half the time. I scoff. *At least you got off.*

We were in therapy for seven months and he never thought to mention that he'd grown bored with our sex life? The very minimal sex life we *did* have? *Is that why he avoided me like the plague?* My mind drifts to Will, wondering if he'll eventually feel the same once the honeymoon phase is over. No more forbidden, exciting trysts, no more sneaking around, and no more Matt. *What if in a few years he grows bored as well? What if it's me?*

"What a dick," I grumble to myself, hearing my insecurities rear their ugly heads. I climb out of bed in search of Will knowing that just a simple kiss from him is all the reassurance I need. I move through his townhouse in nothing more than his t-shirt in hopes he'll rip it off me so I can show him just how much *I* enjoy the sex between us. I push open the door to his office slowly to find him sitting on his couch reading a newspaper and my body comes alive instantly watching his arm flex as he lifts the coffee to his lips and then back to the table in front of him. He's sporting quite a bruise on his cheek just below his eye and my heart constricts remembering how he got it.

"Hey."

His eyes look up to find mine after a very long and lascivious look from my toes up. They linger on my legs for a beat longer than everywhere else and a smile tugs at his lips.

"Come here, baby."

My feet move before it even registers that he's told me to come, as if my body understood the words first. I'm in his lap in an instant kissing him, *hard.* My hands cup his face and I stroke his spiky beard. "I love you," I say in between kisses. My tongue finds his and I stroke it feverishly as I grind myself down onto his growing member. I still taste a hint of alcohol, and I assume it's still in his system. *We did drink a lot last night.* I stroke his cheek gently, before pulling off his lips and giving the inflamed skin some attention. "I can't believe he punched you."

He snorts. "I can. Kinda comes with the territory of sleeping with another man's wife. Given that you ended up divorcing him and you're now with me, I'm going to say I probably deserved it."

"No, you didn't."

"Okay, I expected it."

"Not the point, Will."

"Well, what is the point?" His lips are on my jaw, kissing his way along the line and nibbling gently on my ear.

"That I'm sorry."

"For…sleeping with me or getting a divorce?" He raises an eyebrow at me and I roll my eyes. "Because those things are what led to last night."

"I'm sorry for…everything bad that's happened to you since you met me," I whisper.

He cocks his head to the side. "I'm not. I made certain decisions. Those decisions had consequences, but I don't regret the choices I made. I don't regret *you*. Anything "bad" that has happened is far outweighed by all of the good. *You* are the good, Charley."

"You say that now…but what happens if they revoke your license? What happens if you can no longer practice?"

"Then we go from there. Like I told my father, there are other things I can do."

"What if you realize this was all a mistake?"

"What if you realize it?"

"I won't."

"Neither will I. We're in this together, Charlotte."

I'm silent for a second, letting his words wash over me. "Am I boring?" He narrows his eyes in question. "Like in bed. Am I boring in bed?"

"I knew you were going to fixate on that. Baby, don't listen to Matt. He's an asshole. And the only thing worse than an asshole is an egotistical asshole. You left him, seemingly for another man. He's hurt, he's angry, his ego is bruised. He's trying to get in your head. He knew what to say to play on your emotions to hurt you, to destroy you. And most importantly to make you question everything about yourself, especially your relationship with me." He shakes his head and pinches the bridge of his nose as he squeezes his eyes shut. "Charley, you've said on numerous occasions that you weren't happy with your sex life. Sex can be one-sided, obviously. But for good sex, amazing sex, soul-shattering sex like we have, it has to be good for both parties. So, if you felt the disconnect, you don't think he could?" He lifts my chin to look at him. "I know it stings, but I figured you'd take anything he said with a grain of salt."

I can sense the irritation in his voice, and his pulse flickers in his neck. I frown. "I just…wonder what happens when all of this is just a distant memory? I just want to keep you happy. I don't want you to get bored and start feeling like you can't even come to bed until after I'm asleep so you don't have the arduous task of having sex with me." At this point, the tears have started to fall down my cheeks and I don't have the energy to wipe them. My gaze is cast downward so I don't have to see the pity in Will's eyes.

"Charlotte, look at me," he commands, and my watery eyes find his angry ones. I'm shocked at his response. He shakes his head and runs his tongue over his teeth and I wonder what he's going to say. He puts a hand on either side of my head. "I thought we got rid of this low self-esteem you have. I thought I worked that out of you."

No. This is different. I don't have low self-esteem. Matt made a generalization about our sex life and it stung. What woman wants to hear that their husband of five years was unhappy with your sex life for half of your marriage?

"No, it's not—"

"Fuck what *he* said, Charlotte. How many times has he lied to you over the course of eight years?" My mind drifts back over the past and when I don't say anything Will answers his own question. "Countless! Matt is a liar. And what do liars do? They lie. What do they do when they feel like they're backed into a corner? They lash out. And the liar you were with for almost a decade still knows where to hit you to make you feel like you're two inches tall. He spent the majority of your marriage doing it to you," he barks. His jaw immediately clenches and I can feel the tension in his shoulders. He lets out a breath, trying to calm himself down before looking up at me. "Do you think I don't enjoy our sex life? Do you think I'd be potentially sending my life up in flames if I didn't love you? If I didn't have insane chemistry with you? I didn't think that I had to say this, but since you seem to be a bit on the needy side right now, I'll give it to you. You are the best sex of my life and that's not going to change."

I scoff. "I am not needy. Excuse me for being a little hurt by what Matt said." I go to move off his lap when he grips my thighs keeping me in place.

"Don't move."

"I don't want to talk to you right now. You're trying to be a shrink and my fiancé and you're doing a shitty job at both to be honest," I snap as I effectively move off his lap and start moving towards the door.

I'm almost out of his office before I'm being hauled backwards and pushed up against the wall, his arms boxing me in. "Maybe I should *show* you how much I enjoy our sex life."

"I'm not having sex with you."

"Oh?" he asks as he cocks one eyebrow while staring me down. "You don't want to fuck me?" *Shut up, Will. Shut up, shut up, shut up!* I scream, trying to prevent my body from responding to his question. "You don't want to suck my cock into that perfect little mouth of yours so far down your throat that you gag? The tears form in your eyes, like they always do when you go too far? But you don't care, do you?" He groans into my ear as his lips trace the skin on my neck. I whimper in response as he continues.

"You love deep throating me. I've spent the last seven months with a hard-on thinking about those lips and that tongue wrapped around my cock, Charlotte. Did you know that?" He grips my jaw as his tongue finds my pulse point and he moves it back and forth devastatingly slow. My thighs press together and my toes curl. "Sometimes when you're on your knees, you look up at me with those beautiful brown eyes and I have to talk myself down from coming right then and there." He pulls back and my eyes flutter open just in time to see him staring at me with a cocky smile. I want nothing more than to wipe it from his face but it would require me to have control over my body. *And right now, I don't.* William Montgomery has complete control over it, and he knows it. *And what's worse, is so do I.* "Do you want to suck my cock, Charlotte?"

Yes. Say yes, Charley. SAY. YES. I roll my eyes at my horny subconscious and before I can stop myself I nod once.

"Good girl," he says and the two words set my body on fire. "Do you know why I'm doing this?"

Do I? "I'm...I'm not sure. Maybe?"

"Yes, you do."

"Does everything have to feel like a session? Can't you just tell me what you're thinking? Stop making me feel like I have to figure everything out on my own."

I think I've finally gotten through to him as I see his face go through a wide range of emotions. He looks away from me and then back at me. He nods once and then I hear the unmistakable sound of him unbuckling his pants and them hitting the floor. "Get on your knees, Charlotte."

"Are you kidding me?" I ask him, as I try and move away from him. He puts an arm up effectively keeping me in place. He takes a step closer to me and he's so close that our lips are almost touching but not quite.

"Anything I say is going to go in one ear and out the other. You let your ex-husband get in your head and make you question everything about the sexual woman that you are. Sure, I could tell you that no one has ever made me feel the way you do. No one has ever made me come like you do. No woman but you has ever done things to my asshole that would make most people blush.

That until you, I was never one for going down on a woman, and now my mouth sets up shop between your legs at least four times a day. I could tell you that I love you, that I worship the ground you fucking walk on, and you'd still have that nagging thought in the back of your mind that you weren't good enough, weren't sexy enough. That you weren't pleasing me. So, no, Charlotte I'm not going to tell you anything. And you are going to prove to *yourself* that you are the sexiest woman that walked this Earth and there isn't a boring bone in your body. Because I already fucking know that. I'm *making* you figure it out on your own because it's the only way to get it through your head. So, get. the. fuck. on. your. knees. now."

His words wash over me; I blink the tears out of my eyes and before I can think, I feel the hard ground beneath my knees. I reach for his briefs and slide them slowly down his legs. His erection juts out immediately, and my mouth waters in response to being within arm's reach of one of my favorite parts of him. I feel his hands in my hair and then he pulls slightly, to get me to look up at him. "I love you," he tells me simply.

I nod before looking back at the impressive appendage at my eye level. *Well more like mouth level.* I rest my hands on his thighs gently and it's not lost on me that the minor touch makes him clench his fists which I know he does when he's turned on. I grip his penis with one hand and run my tongue from root to tip. I hear his hum of approval. I use my other hand to run my fingers up his inner thigh before I make him separate his legs slightly so that I can cup his balls gently. I wrap my lips around the head of his penis, swirling my tongue around it, collecting the beads of pre-cum leaking out of him and letting them slide down my throat before I push myself further down his shaft, inch by delicious inch.

I drop my hand from fondling his balls and reach around with both hands and grip his ass tightly as I begin to fuck him with my mouth, the saliva forming around the corners of my mouth as I let him glide in and out forcefully. I push him to the back of my throat and tilt my head back so he can push himself in a little further when I hear him groan out my name.

"Fuck baby, only you know how to suck my cock." His hand finds my hair and when he fists it hard I wince slightly, but it quickly turns to pleasure as I think about how quickly I can bring this man to his knees.

I am hot. I am sexy. I am a goddess. I am not boring.

I chance a glance at the man above me and a surge of pride moves through me as I see his head tilted back and his chest rising and falling at a rapid pace. That coupled with his hand still wound tightly in my hair only tells me one thing.

He's going to come. Hard.

"Charley," he groans as I feel his penis start to pulse, and he begins to thrust into my mouth as I slide up and back on him. My hand drops from his ass and rubs the spot between the bottom of his shaft and his balls and I hear a loud bang which I assume is his hand hitting the wall above him. "FUCK!" he roars as his breathing becomes more erratic and his thrusts into my mouth become more aggressive. "Right there, baby. I'm going to come. Look at me, Charley," I look up at him and see him staring down at me, a mix of emotions all over his face.

Love. Lust. Adoration. Devotion.

Our eyes meet as he pushes one final time into my mouth, his seed spilling down my throat. I continue to suck as I swallow down every drop he has to offer. I continue to suck even after he's finished coming, until he stops me, sliding my lips off of his cock. He lifts my chin and rubs his thumb over my bruised lips that are coated with my saliva and any leftover cum. He helps me to my feet and stares down at me for what feels like forever before I'm off my feet being carried through his townhouse.

We make it to his bedroom and I'm barely through the door before he has my shirt over my head. "You have fantastic breasts,

Charlotte." He unclasps my bra and lets it fall to the floor. I expect his mouth to find one of my nipples but I look up to see him staring at them hungrily. He pushes me onto the bed to lay on my back. "Your breasts are perfect." His hands touch them and I immediately shiver when he makes contact. "They're the perfect size and they're perky and the right fit for my mouth. Your tits were made for my mouth," he says as his lips enclose around one of my nipples. He sucks on one and then the other before turning me over so that I'm lying on my stomach.

"Have *you* seen your ass? It is undoubtedly the best thing that ever happened to a pair of jeans. He squeezes my ass, one cheek in each hand, and I feel his nails digging into my flesh. I whimper at the painful pleasure coursing through me. His hands leave my ass and I feel his teeth nibbling the sensitive skin. "Your ass is one of the wonders of *my* world, Charlotte. I feel him spread me slightly and tug gently at the string between my crack. I clench in response causing him to chuckle. "I'm not going to fuck you there now. I need a lot of time with your pussy, first. Turn over." I do as he says and I'm greeted with a dangerous look that leaves me short of breath. He slides my panties down my legs and drops to his knees in front of me. "And this," he murmurs as he runs one finger through my folds that are soaking wet with my arousal. "This is everything." He stares at me as if I'm the most fascinating thing he's ever seen. "You have the prettiest pussy, Charlotte." He opens me up gently with his fingers and I can feel my clit throb under his gaze. His tongue slides through my sex once and I shudder.

"Oh, fuck."

He pulls back as one hand begins to work me over, and the other keeps me open for him. He rolls my clit between his thumb and index finger and pinches slightly. "You can't really believe that I'd ever get bored with you," he asks, looking up at me, my clit still between his fingers.

God, what kind of psychological foreplay is this? Where if I answer correctly I get the orgasm?

I yelp when I feel another pinch. "Answer me."

"I... I don't know."

His hands leave my pussy and I get my answer. "Manipulative bastard," I murmur.

"What was that?"

I sit up slightly, resting on my elbows. "You heard me. I know what you're doing. I took Psychology in college."

He chuckles and moves up my body to straddle my waist. "Is that so?"

"Yes," I say as confident as I can in this vulnerable position.

"So, tell me, what am I doing"

"You want me to give you a specific answer. You want me to associate me thinking that I'm not good in bed with not coming. If I were to say that I didn't believe it, I'd be having an orgasm right now."

He gives me a wicked smirk. "And does your answer stand?"

"You can't use your fancy doctor degree to fuck me, Montgomery"

"Who says?"

"You're a pain in the ass," I bark.

"I would love to be a pain in your ass."

"Fuck me first and then we can talk about it," I say thrusting my hips upward as best as I can with this man on top of me.

"Tell me what I want to hear."

"*You* want to hear it?"

"*You* need to say it"

"Say what?"

"Don't be cute, Charlotte."

I close my eyes slowly and take a deep breath. *If this man is willing to do all this for me just to show me that Matt was wrong, get the fuck out of your own head and listen. He risked everything for you. Do you think he'd do it for someone he felt was boring? He was sleeping with you long before he was in love with you, Charley.* "I'm not boring," I whisper.

He leans down slightly and ghosts his lips across mine. "What was that?"

"I'm…not…boring," I say slowly as I let the words seep into my brain.

"Don't say it if you don't mean it. I'm more than happy to continue with this exercise."

"I mean it."

"Are you sure because I don't want to have this conversation again." I nod, and my words, his words, mixed with the fact that I'm naked underneath him, unable to move, has my vision blurry with tears. I close my eyes as they leak out of the corners and slide into my hair. I feel him move from sitting on top of me and feel his breath on my face. I open my eyes to see him a mere inch from my face and he wipes the tears from my eyes. "You're not boring, Charley. You are extraordinary." He smiles as he lowers his face to nuzzle my neck.

"What did I do to deserve you?" I choke out, the tears prohibiting my ability to speak clearly. "I love you," I say as I wrap my arms around his neck and pull him closer to me. "I love you so much."

"You exist," he whispers in my ear. "That's all you did to be deserving of me, Charlotte." His words do nothing to stop the tears from falling from my eyes. "I'm going to make love to you now, are you okay with that?"

I nod as I try and get myself together and stop the flow of tears that have been flowing for what seems like forever. He slides inside of me and just like that, I'm home.

CHAPTER
Nineteen

WILL

HAD PLANNED TO TELL CHARLOTTE EVERYTHING YESTERDAY. I woke up early, leaving her in bed so I could be alone with my thoughts, without her soft body pressed up against me. I had written out a list of things we needed to discuss. I may have made myself an Irish coffee that morning, but it was just one cup and it was only to take the edge off. I was completely prepared to tell her everything yesterday, but then she entered my office in nothing more than a t-shirt and a sad smile, feeling somewhat dejected over what Matt had said the night before.

Suddenly, the idea of revealing a secret that I kept from her sounded like the worst idea.

She needed comfort, not the realization that yet another man who professed to love her hadn't been honest with her.

So, I didn't tell her.

Again.

God, I was a pussy.

I can't seem to quiet the racing thoughts as we sit outside the conference room even as Charlotte sits next to me stroking my hand. I watch as J.R., dressed in a smart power suit, paces in front of us, his ear glued to his cell phone as he's yelling at what I assume to be some poor intern at his firm. He'd commented on the fact that I wasn't wearing a tie and how unprofessional it was. *Amazing.* Two minutes with my father, and I already needed a drink. *I think that is some sort of record.* I feel hands on my face turning me towards familiar lips. Charley's mouth is on mine in an instant, moving against my lips slowly, her tongue parting my lips and rubbing against mine. I moan quietly into her mouth as her hand cups my cheek and she winds her fingers through my hair.

"Don't worry," she whispers. "I'll be right there." Relief floods my body, hearing her words, and just as I'm about to respond, I hear J.R.'s voice piercing the air.

"Must you do that, *here? Now?*" he asks, and we pull apart slowly, our eyes not leaving each other's for the first few seconds. *To be honest, I forgot where we were.*

"So beautiful," I tell her as I bring her hand to my mouth and brush my lips across them.

"J.R. don't you have someone else to bother?" I don't take my eyes off the woman in front of me, who is currently blushing over being scolded by my father. "We need a moment alone."

"So, you can continue what you're doing? No, Will. Someone needs to be here and keep an eye on you two and possibly turn a hose on you. Besides, you need to focus on what you're going to say."

"I already know what I'm going to say. I'm nervous enough. She's keeping me calm." I turn my attention back to her. "Don't let go of my hand."

"Never," she whispers.

"Dr. Montgomery," I hear a voice booming into the lobby and the three of us are ushered into a room with a long conference table and seven people sitting on one side of the brown polished wood.

Well, this is intense. I squeeze Charley's hand, seeking her comfort and she squeezes it back.

The three of us sit, myself in the middle, with J.R. and Charley on either side of me.

"You called this meeting, Dr. Montgomery. What can we help

you with?" the man seated in the middle says. Dr. Preston Marks, the head of the board of Directors of the AMA in Georgia. He's bald, with a handlebar mustache, one I'd only seen in movies and I can't help but feel like I am in a movie. *How did this become my life?*

"Yes," I clear my throat and shift in my chair nervously. "There are some things I believe you need to be made aware of. Everything is under control but—in case things come to light in the future, I think it would be best that you know now."

A few of the members lean back in their chairs, judgment evident on their faces. "Go on, Dr. Montgomery."

"Dr. Marks," I address the Director before looking at the rest of the members, "members of the Board of Doctors for the State of Georgia, I'm asking that you keep an open mind in what I'm about to divulge." I try to hide my feelings of unease as I do my best to sound confident and strong. "There's been a…situation in which I've become involved with…a patient." There's some whispering amongst a few of the members. Although I can't make out what's being said, I can only imagine.

"Is that so? Is this the patient in question?" Dr. Marks says as he looks at Charlotte over thick rimmed glasses.

"Yes sir, this is Charlotte Pierce." I shoot her a small smile, trying to calm her nerves. "My fiancée."

J.R. had suggested it may play in our favor if we mention how serious we are already. Although she doesn't have a ring, we are technically still engaged and plan to be married sometime before the end of next year.

"You're engaged?" Someone chimes in.

"How long ago did you stop counseling her? You know the wait period after you're finished counseling a patient is two years, although a lot of boards are doing away with that in certain situations…so if you haven't been counseling her for some time now…" one interjects, as he strokes his chin.

"Two months ago," I say before they can go on a tangent that would end with stating that this may not be a huge indiscretion. I let out a breath, preparing to drop the bomb that may seal my fate. "We were involved while I was counseling her."

"I see. Well, that changes things," Dr. Marks says. "And based on your field I take it to mean you were a counselor for both her and her husband?"

"Yes, sir," I nod.

"So, you were sleeping with your *married* patient."

"Yes."

"Is she still married?" I hate that they're talking about her like she's not in the room. I look at her, and I can tell she's fighting the tears in her eyes. *It's going to be okay, baby.* I squeeze her hand hoping she hears my thoughts.

"She's recently divorced."

"So, then she left her husband…for you."

"There's more to the story—" I start, because there is. But something tells me there's no room for gray here. They are only going to see it in black and white.

She was married.

We started having an affair.

She got divorced.

"Simple question, Dr. Montgomery. Yes or no?"

"It's complicated."

"Yes. Or. No?" Dr. Marks spits out. I hadn't had too many interactions with him, but enough to know that he didn't take any bullshit.

"I think what my client is trying to—" J.R. starts when Dr. Marks interrupts him.

"I asked a question. Your *client* needs to answer it."

He even put J.R. in his place. Well, I'm fucked. A bottle of Macallan 18 flashes through my head.

No.

You really think you're not going to need a drink after this?

No. I need to tell Charlotte the truth.

But then she'll probably purge the house of alcohol.

I blink my eyes a few times, trying to quiet my thoughts as Dr. Marks continues. "I understand it's complicated. What I want to know is if the patient in question who was married when she started seeing Dr. Montgomery, decided to terminate her marriage *after* she started sleeping with him."

"Yes," I answer. I'd made my bed...*one I had fucked Charlotte in,* and now I had to lie in it.

Dr. Marks rubs a hand over his eyes. "I want your patient's file, and I assume, since they are now divorced you are no longer seeing them?"

"That is correct."

"When did you stop counseling them?"

"When she filed, about two and a half months ago."

"How long were you involved before then?"

"Five months," I answer as I slide Charlotte and Matt's file across the table.

"Five?" Dr. Marks looks at me and then at Charlotte. "You know better than this. You're one of the finest doctors in the field."

"Does the husband know?" another member asks.

"When did you become engaged?" another asks.

"Are you living together?" the questions are coming at me rapid fire when Dr. Marks silences the group.

"Does the husband know and is he going to make trouble? What is the likelihood that he will sue for malpractice?"

"Charlotte's ex-husband knows, and there is no chance he's going to make trouble."

"Legally?" he looks at J.R. who's currently leaned back in his chair arrogantly. I resist the urge to roll my eyes. He nods once.

"Well, that's one less thing to worry about." Dr. Marks opens their file. There are seven month's worth of notes in there ranging from Matt's narcissism, Charlotte's need to apologize for everything, and the fact that they weren't having sex. I'd painted the picture of two people that had no business being married. *But it wasn't enough to excuse me for fucking her all over my office for months.*

"Sort of," I hold my breath, preparing to divulge the other half of the situation.

"What the hell do you mean sort of, Dr. Montgomery? Either her husband is an issue or he's not."

"We don't have to worry about him suing," J.R. interjects.

"Okay?" Dr. Marks says as if to say, *get on with it.*

"He suspected that we were…having a relationship. He then planted a bug in my office to gain proof."

"Tell me it just recorded your time with Ms. Pierce here," Dr. Marks says as his thumb and index finger pinch the bridge of his nose.

"Not exactly."

Dr. Marks' hand slams on the table. "What do you mean, not exactly!? How long was the device there, Dr. Montgomery? How many people are on that tape?"

"Four couples," I admit, shakily.

"EIGHT PEOPLE?!" he bellows.

"I know, this is bad." The hand not clasped with Charlotte's runs through my hair. She squeezes the hand I'm holding hard in an attempt to ground me.

"I hope you are taking care of this? Taking legal action?" Dr. Marks says as his eyes find my father.

"We are handling it."

"Have you met with any of your patients since then?"

"I've met with each of them once, but I haven't told them anything. I wanted to discuss this with you to figure out the best course of action."

"Great. Your contact ends with them effective immediately.

We will take it from here." All I can do is nod my head once. "Do you have the tape in question?"

"Yes."

"You'll be needing to hand that over. Are we sure there isn't a copy?"

"I can't imagine he would have one."

"I don't want you imagining anything. Is there a copy, yes or no?"

"No." *I hope not.*

"He's signed an NDA, so if he's got a copy there's nothing he can do with it," J.R. chimes in.

"We'll be needing to meet with you, as well Ms. Pierce."

She nods. I prepared her for this, so I know she's ready. "Yes, whenever you'd like to meet. I'm very flexible."

"How is tomorrow, Ms. Pierce? The sooner we get this taken care of the sooner we can come to a conclusion about the fate of Dr. Montgomery here. Until further notice, Dr. Montgomery you are suspended. You cannot practice or meet with any of your patients until this investigation is complete, do you understand?

"Yes."

"You'll need to give us the keys to your office, and we will be doing a thorough sweep. Is there anything in there we will find? It's better if you tell us now."

"No, sir."

"Pornographic photos…videos…?"

"No."

"I imagine if you're engaged to be married that she was the only one, but I have to ask—" he starts.

"Charlotte is the only one," I pause. "I fell in love with her." I look from one end of the table to the other. "I know how this looks. It looks like a sordid affair with a married woman—"

"That's exactly what it is. Except, when men have sordid affairs they are legal and not breaking a hundred different rules. When a

Doctor has a sordid affair it's DIFFERENT!" one of the men bellows so loud I wouldn't be surprised if it was heard throughout the building. "You know better, Dr. Montgomery!"

I try to swallow his words and simultaneously the bile rising in my throat. "I know. I…should have left her alone. But I couldn't. She's the love of my life."

"You've known her five minutes, William." I wince, hearing Dr. Marks use my first name in such a condescending manner. I feel like I'm being scolded like a child.

I feel like I'm being scolded by J.R. My eyes flit to him for a second. "Was it worth your entire practice?" another member asks, drawing my attention back to them.

"Yes," I feel like a hand is being wrapped around my throat as I hear the potential ramifications of my actions spelled out for me. It's as if I'm watching years of my hard work go up in flames. My gaze looks to my other side, finding Charlotte, who stares up at me, and a sad smile crosses her face. "I'd do it again in a heartbeat," I say more to her than to the seven people on the other side of the table.

"Dr. Montgomery, security will follow you to your office to take any personal belongings you may need."

"I took everything home with me yesterday."

Dr. Marks nods, before he shuts Charlotte's file and crosses his hands over it. "I am very disappointed in you, Dr. Montgomery."

"I know."

"We'll be needing an official testimony of your time with Ms. Pierce and the time leading up to it as well. Which will be done in private. You may keep your lawyer," Dr. Marks says, looking at Charlotte as if to say *she has to go.*

I feel Charlotte tense next to me and I imagine she hears the implication as well. "I can go." She moves to her feet as all of the gentlemen in the room stand up with me. I grip her hand, alerting her that I would be walking out with her.

"I'll be just a moment," I tell them as I follow her out.

Once we are out of the room, I feel like I can breathe now that the tension is no longer swirling around me. Charlotte is in my arms instantly.

"You're doing so well," she tells me, pulling back to look up at me. "I love you."

"Will you stay?" I whisper as she squeezes me tighter and peppers kisses on my neck.

"Of course, I'll be right over there." She points at the loveseat we were sitting on earlier. I nod, thankful she won't be too far away from me. "How about a kiss?"

I nod and she wraps her arms around my neck and presses herself flush against me. "I love you so much, Will Montgomery. And when you leave, we're going to go home and make love all of over your house because *nothing* will be held over our heads any longer. Everything is out in the open. We. are. *free.*"

"Free," I whisper.

Except I'm not.

CHAPTER
Twenty

Charlotte

"**D**O YOU KNOW WHAT THEY'RE GOING TO ASK ME?" I ASK Will. My head rests on his chest, allowing me to listen to every beat of his heart. We'd already made love once, but the way he's rubbing his hand down my back and grazing my ass gently, it's safe to assume we'll be doing so again very shortly.

I feel his hand move up my back and begin to play with my hair, twisting it around his index finger. "I can imagine that it's something along the lines of whether or not you felt that I pressured you into the affair."

"Affair?" I ask, lifting my head to look at him. "Is that what you would call us?"

"No, but that's what *they'll* call us."

I lay my head back down and rest my leg over his legs, rubbing my core against his thigh in the process. I feel myself begin to tingle as my folds make direct contact with his body. "Is there anything I shouldn't say?"

"No, baby." He moves so that he's hovering over me. "Just tell the truth." He rubs his nose against mine. "Everything is going to be okay. I'll be right outside waiting for you."

I nod as I run my hand across his cheek and rub his growing beard. "I am so proud of you," I tell him again. His eyes narrow slightly at what I assume to be confusion over my comment. "You stood by your morals and you did the right thing. The world would be better with more people like you, Will Montgomery." He frowns slightly and I'm not sure why.

His face eventually finds my neck and I wonder if it's because he knows I can read him like a book. "I'm sorry that I brought you into this. That you're involved…" His voice breaks.

"I've been involved for a while now, Montgomery," I giggle as my mouth finds his shoulder and I sink my teeth into the taut flesh. He groans and moves, allowing his cock to rest against the apex of my thighs but not quite where I need him most. I part my legs, wrapping them around his body and he takes it as the invitation to slide inside of me. His lips find mine and he licks into my mouth, his tongue massaging mine as he thrusts slowly into my aching core.

Every time we make love it's better than the last, and I let out a sigh of contentedness as his left hand finds my nipple. "I love you," he murmurs against my mouth. "I can't wait to make you mine."

"I am yours," I moan, even though I know what he means. *Officially his. Husband. Wife. Marriage.*

I squeeze my eyes together tight, as I feel the orgasm brewing just over those three words flashing through my mind. He moves to his back in response to my words, bringing me to be on top, not breaking our connection for a second. I sit up and begin to ride him as both hands find my breasts.

"You are so beautiful, Charlotte." He sits up, holding me in place as I continue to move up and down on his cock. "You're the most beautiful woman I've ever laid eyes on." His eyes close and his fingertips find my hips as he guides me up and down on his shaft. "Fuck." He opens his eyes and fixes his gaze on where we are connected between us, his shaft glistening with the arousal from my wet core. "You're so incredible. How was I supposed to see you three times a week and *not* fall in love with you? How was I supposed to leave you alone?"

"I didn't want you to leave me alone, Will."

"I thought if I just…tasted you once, it would get you out of my system." He growls as he quickens his pace. "But you're my addiction, Charlotte Pierce. One taste wasn't enough. One taste of you could never be enough. I want all of you. *Need all of you.* Everyday. For the rest of my life."

"Yes!" I throw my head back as I feel the beginnings of my orgasm.

"Tell me you feel the same," he says, his voice hoarse and my head shoots up to find his eyes boring into mine.

"You know that I do," I say softly, as my hand finds his face. I cup his jaw and for the first time since my divorce was finalized I see something in his eyes that unnerves me.

Uneasiness.

"Will, you know I feel the same." I clench my muscles around him and I feel him twitch inside of me. "Should we talk about this first? Or finish?" I cock my head to the side knowing that we need to discuss where these doubts are coming from, but I also know we need this connection as well.

"You need to come," he says as his hands find my ass. He palms them tightly, letting his fingers graze the area between my cheeks. An involuntary shiver moves through me as I feel his fingers in such an intimate place.

"What do *you* need?" I ask him knowing that his complete possession of me might be just what he needs to calm his fears.

He sits up, so that we are nose to nose but he's still inside of me when his mouth finds the space behind my ear. He nibbles gently on the space. "I want a baby. I want to get you pregnant. *Now.*"

"Now?" I ask him as I pull his head away from my neck. This was the second time he'd mentioned it in a month and something tells me he isn't going to let this go until he'd successfully knocked me up.

He nods. "You asked what I needed. That's it. To get you pregnant. To see your belly swollen with my baby. I need to know that

no one can take you from me. That you won't leave me… even…"
He trails off.

*Even what? No one could take me from you, Will. How could
you even think that?*

"I could lose everything, Charlotte. What then?"

"We've talked about this, Will…I'm never going anywhere,"
I tell him as my hands find his jaw. I press a kiss to his lips and
I move to attempt to break our connection as I realize that this
conversation can't happen while he's balls deep inside of me. He
grips my hips again keeping me in place, my folds pressed firmly
against him, as he's completely submerged inside of me.

"It's easy to talk about it when it's hypotheticals. It's a very real
thing now. And I just…I don't know how the rest of these proceedings are going to go. If they begin to be too much…you can
walk away from all of this."

My eyes widen in horror as he lays his fears all out on the table
for me. He's avoiding my gaze, his vulnerability making it difficult
to look me in the eye. I grab his face and make him look at me.

"I am *never* going anywhere, Will. You and me. Forever. No
matter what. I know what I'm signing up for. I'm in this with you."
I press my lips to his and push him gently onto his back as we pick
up where we left off.

———

The first thing I notice are the walls. They're stark white; four stark
white walls. Not eggshell, not ecru, not any of the many colors
on the white spectrum I agonized over when I was redecorating
the townhouse I shared with Matt. They are white and blank. No
artwork, no windows, nothing, a huge contrast to Will's office
that was so warm and inviting. This feels clinical, and I'm having
the startling realization that I may not be able to get through this
without having a breakdown fueled by claustrophobia.

The slamming of the office door breaks me out of my thoughts as two people who I assume must be from the board enter the room. A middle aged man, and a woman that's probably only a few years older than me sit across from me at the table. *This feels like an interrogation in the making.*

"Ms. Pierce, how are you today?" the man asks. "I'm Dr. Lenox and this is Dr. Norwood," he says, gesturing to the woman on his left that is staring at me with cold, judgmental eyes. *Great.* "We just have a couple of questions and then you'll be on your way." He gives me a smile that I've seen before.

The infamous Doctor smile. That fake smile they give that doesn't quite reach the eyes before they deliver that news that you just don't want to hear. I wonder if it's a requirement for all doctors.

"So, you do understand why you are here today?" Dr. Norwood asks, although it sounds more like an accusation. My eyes dart to hers and I see them narrow slightly.

My teeth find my bottom lip and I bite down gently not wanting to give away how nervous I am. "Yes."

"Okay, so we'll just jump right in then," Dr. Lenox says as he opens up the file. "Why don't you tell me in your own words, a little bit about your relationship with Dr. Montgomery."

My heart flutters in my chest hearing his name, and I can feel the blood rushing to my cheeks as the words leave my mouth. "I'm in love with him," I say simply. "I am unbelievably in love with him," I state more confidently, without hesitation. "I never meant to hurt anyone. *We* never meant to hurt anyone."

"Not even your ex-husband?" Dr. Norwood asks.

"My relationship with my ex-husband was…complicated. And to be honest it's not really your business."

"It's our business in part because you essentially left your husband for Dr. Montgomery."

"That's not true." I shake my head. "There were monumentally huge problems in our marriage before we started counseling."

"But you have to admit, you go to counseling to try and better your marriage. To *fix* those problems. And yet, I don't think that's what Dr. Montgomery did, wouldn't you agree?"

I shrug, not knowing what to say to that. "Some problems are unfixable. Some marriages are irreparable. My ex-husband and I didn't realize that going in. Dr. Montgomery tried, it…didn't work."

"So, he tried a different type of therapy?" Dr. Norwood asks, and I resist the urge to tell her to shut up with her snarky comments.

"Dr. Norwood, we are getting off track," Dr. Lenox says. "I would like to know a little bit more about your relationship with Dr. Montgomery while you were in therapy."

"It was very professional."

"You were sleeping with him," Dr. Norwood says, and I wince.

"Yes, but…that was later. That was after months of…Dr. Montgomery trying to fix the problems in my marriage. That was after my ex-husband and I had spent months arguing, screaming…"

"Do you think that he used that to his advantage?"

"No. No, of course not! Why…are you trying to make this into something that it's not! We fell in love. And I understand that it went against the rules, but…in love there are no rules."

"There are in the medical world, Miss Pierce. Dr. Montgomery knew the rules and he knowingly broke them."

"Because he loves me. This isn't some sick game or whatever it is you're trying to turn this into. Dr. Montgomery and I love each other. We want to get married and have a family. Start a life together," I say, hoping that it's okay that I'm divulging all of this.

"Why is it that you keep calling him Dr. Montgomery?"

"I don't understand…"

"You're calling him, Dr. Montgomery. Not Will? Is that what you call him in a more… intimate setting as well?"

"No! Of course not. God is that what this is about? You think I have some weird fantasy about sleeping with my doctor? Stop fetishizing him! I didn't leave my husband for my marriage counselor. I left my husband for another man," I blurt out, and my eyes widen at the words that have just left my mouth. I shake my head as I let my words wash over me and my gaze finds a spot on the floor. "I left my husband…for another…man," I whisper slowly. "A man that loves me and cherishes me. A man that put me before his job." My heart lurches as I say the words aloud. The words that have been tucked away neatly in my brain inside of a box that says *do not open.* "He's the complete opposite of Matthew. Oh my God," I whisper as my hands find my face. "But he didn't…" I hiccup. "He was so professional…He never pressured me into anything. If anything, I made the first move, I made the first hundred moves. The brushes against him, the looks I'd give him when I knew my husband wasn't looking. Hell, the first day I met him, before I even set foot into his office, I wanted him—" I start when Dr. Lenox interrupts me.

"Pardon the interruption, but…you found yourself attracted to him physically that early on?"

"Absolutely. I was struggling with my attraction to him for months. The first time I saw him…" My teeth find my bottom lip as I remember the first time I ever laid eyes on him. "I thought he was the most gorgeous man I'd ever seen. And he was always so kind and caring…I know he was paid to do that, but I felt like it was different with me."

"Different how?"

"It's hard to describe. We just…clicked. And not in a sexual way…"

"Charlotte, in leaving your husband for Dr. Montgomery—" Dr. Lennox starts, and I shake my head.

"Will," I interrupt, "he tried to tell me we should stop…that it wasn't right. It wasn't ethical. We were both in tough spots as our minds battled our hearts." I shake my head as I lean back in my chair.

"So, you say that he tried to stop, I take that to mean that was after you had already started the affair?"

There's that word Will warned me about—affair. It was like a bright, blinding, neon light I couldn't avoid.

"Yes. He suggested on more than one occasion that it wasn't right and that we should stop."

"And why didn't you?"

I bite my bottom lip. "I didn't want to. Maybe he didn't want to either...I don't know. The chemistry we have, the attraction between us is...explosive. We couldn't deny what was happening between us."

"And the whole time your husband was oblivious to what was happening underneath his nose?"

My lips form a straight line as I nod my head slowly. "That's correct."

I see them both scribble something frantically in their notebook and I can already imagine what the words say. '*Bored housewife. Neglectful husband. Crying out for attention.*

"Miss Pierce are you familiar with the *Knight and Shining Armor Complex*?"

Here we go. "I can draw my own conclusions," I say simply. "I assume you're going to say that I fell for a man because I believe he saved me from something." I roll my eyes. "That's not why I fell for him. If he wasn't my counselor, I would just be a woman that fell for a man."

"But he *was* your counselor. And that makes things complicated," Dr. Norwood says.

"I don't know what you want me to say," I whisper. "I never meant for this to happen...but if I could do it all over again...I would."

CHAPTER
Twenty-One

WILL

M Y EYES SNAP UP FROM THE SPOT ON THE FLOOR I'D BEEN staring at for the past hour as I hear the door open. I smile, seeing Charley walk through the door but as quick as it finds my face it fades when I see the person behind her.

Dr. Audrey Norwood.

My eyes close slowly, a clear sign of my irritation; Charley picks up on it immediately and her brows furrow together in question.

Audrey Norwood has been a colleague of mine for years. She's also a woman that I was sleeping with for a few months when I first started practicing five years ago. I had assumed we were just having fun, but then she mentioned meeting her parents and in true commitment-phobe fashion, I panicked. I told her I wasn't ready for that step and fed her a story about how it was unethical for us to be sleeping and working together. I don't know if it's in violation of our code of conduct not to screw your coworkers… but I went with it. Needless to say, she was pissed.

And now here we are years later, and she's investigating me over a relationship with a patient.

Where are these so-called ethics now, Montgomery? I can almost hear her thoughts as she shoots daggers at me, and now Charley who has found her way into my arms.

"Hi," Charley breathes, and her face finds my neck, her arms wrapping around my back. She looks up at me, her eyes full of question. "Everything okay?"

I don't have a chance to answer her when Norwood's voice rings through the air. "Dr. Montgomery, a word please?" she asks, and I shoot her a look.

"Is that really necessary?"

She looks taken aback by my response and crosses her arms across her chest successfully pushing her breasts upwards which doesn't have the same effect that it used to. "It really is. Or did you forget the mess that you've gotten yourself into due to this violation of *ethics?*" she spits out.

I resist the urge to roll my eyes. *And there it is.*

"It's okay, I'll wait here," I hear next to me. *Charley probably has a million questions running through her mind.* I cup her cheeks lightly and brush my lips over hers.

"Five minutes," I tell her, and wonder if she's feeling uncomfortable with this public display of affection in front of the person that was interviewing her just minutes earlier, because a hint of pink colors her cheeks.

"Unbelievable," I hear murmured and Charley turns her gaze away from me to Audrey, breaking my grasp on her face.

"Excuse me?" she asks, and I wonder if she's getting a vibe from her causing her to get territorial.

I can see Dr. Norwood struggling with a nasty case of word vomit, and before I can suggest moving to another room so that she doesn't blow all over my fiancé, she speaks. "So, you break up with me because it's 'not right' and yet you can sleep with a patient?" Audrey asks and my shoulders sag instantly as I feel Charley tense next to me.

"I'm not *sleeping* with a patient." I snarl. "And you're out of line."

"*I'm* out of line? You are literally the biggest hypocrite, you know that?"

"Call me what you want, Audrey. But I'm not going to stand here and let you disrespect my relationship with my fiancée."

"Your fiancée, huh? That's a mighty small ring," she says eyeing Charley's left hand. "Tell me, was this all a scheme? You got caught with your pants down with a married woman so you came up with this whole scheme so that the board will go easier on you? I will say, you are doing an excellent job of selling this *love* affair," she snorts.

"A scheme? One that involved me getting an expensive divorce? You think I got divorced just to keep up appearances and we are just pretending? Are you stupid as well as jealous?" Charley perks up. "You're not even making sense."

"Excuse me, you can't talk to me like that."

"Actually, I can, and I'm pretty sure your board wouldn't appreciate the conflict of interest that comes with you being on this investigation," Charley says.

I can't help the smile creeping onto my face.

"What…are you going to tell them that your precious fiancé couldn't keep it in his pants with *another* woman?" Charley is seething, and I decide to derail this conversation, but before I can speak, Audrey continues. "Well, if you're going to tell them, be sure you have all the facts," she spits out. "Your therapist sought *me* out."

"Audrey, enough," I growl.

"Told me that I was the most beautiful woman he'd ever seen."

"Stop it," I bark as I begin to pull Charley from the room.

"That he'd thought about fucking me for weeks. It was so hot when we finally did. We fucked *everywhere*."

Charley pulls herself from my grip and I'm resisting the urge to haul her over my shoulder so she doesn't have to listen to any more of this shit. *But if I know my girl like I think I do, she has some words for this bitch.*

The beginnings of what looks like Audrey's psychotic break continues. "You did it in his office, right? I hope he didn't tell you that you were the first to christen his desk, the coffee table… Vanessa's desk?" She snickers and I notice Charley clench her fist.

"Baby, let's go," I tell her.

"Baby? God Montgomery, you're so cliché." She shakes her head before tucking a blonde hair behind her ear. "And then after months of sleeping together, and basically living at each other's places, when I suggested he come to dinner to meet my family, he turned into a colossal asshole. Told me he didn't think it was 'ethical'. I assume the thrill wore off. Fucking his co-worker was no longer exciting. I didn't give him the adrenaline rush any-more. I guess he had to step up his game." She puts up a finger. "Married." She puts up another finger. "Patient." She puts up a third finger. "Neglectful husband whose wife he could fuck right under his nose. Montgomery you really hit the trifecta with this one." She rolls her eyes.

"You can kiss your job goodbye, Audrey," I growl.

She snorts. "That's rich coming from you. You honestly think they'd get rid of *me* before *you*? I know you went to Harvard, but don't tell me you're that clueless." I roll my eyes thinking about how she'd gone to Stanford, and we had a long-standing compe-tition over which school was better.

My focus turns back to Charley where it's been for the ma-jority of her monologue. "Are you done?" she asks with the most indifferent, monotone expression, as if she's bored and not af-fected in the slightest. *Not sure I buy that.* "What did you think you'd succeed in doing with this whole "woman scorned" act? Are you kidding me right now? Is this supposed to make me feel… threatened? I'm coming out of a five-year marriage to a man that didn't pay me the time of day and you're complaining about a man that you were screwing for a few months that lost interest? Please! And maybe he used you guys working together as an ex-cuse because, GUESS WHAT?" She raises her voice slightly. "He just wasn't that into you. And he didn't want to hurt your feelings."

She shrugs. "Couldn't imagine why though, you seem like a heart-less bitch to me."

Audrey smirks, possibly guessing that despite Charley's words, she was affected. "Look all I'm saying, is be careful."

"Is that all you're saying?" Charley interrupts. "It sounds a little bit like you're trying to come between me and my fiancé. Which hate to break it to you." she leans forward and whispers, "you're failing."

"So, you completely trust him then?"

"Not that it's any of your business, but yes."

She shouldn't. My mind quips.

"So, you know about the women that came before me...came after me...the woman that was... hmmm..." She looks down at the file in her hands and then back at us. "What would appear to be right before you? Who knows maybe there was even some overlap. I'm a little hazy on the timeline details of when exactly you two started breaking all the rules."

At this point, I feel like I could break her neck, but I settle for aggressively pulling Charley out of there, not wanting her around that woman for another second.

———

"I want her off the case," I growl the second we are in the eleva-tor. I pull out my phone to call J.R. when I realize that Charley is looking straight forward and not at me. I slide the phone back into my pocket and slam my hand against the stop button not wanting to move another floor until I can assure that Charley and I are okay. "Look at me," I tell her, as I push her up against the wall of the elevator.

Her eyes find mine, and though they aren't watery, they're hurt. "You know everything about me." She shakes her head. "Everything about the only relationship I've ever been in. I never thought..." She winces, scrunching her nose slightly and I notice the goosebumps popping up all over her skin. "We spent so much time talking about my relationship I never thought to ask you about any of yours." She rubs her forehead and reaches around me to start the elevator. "I just need to think."

"Think about what, Charlotte?"

"Was there an overlap?" she asks. "Were you—"

"After we first slept together, I never slept with anyone else."

"Just when we *started* sleeping together?"

"What do you mean?"

"It means according to you, you were thinking about me for months before we were first intimate…were you sleeping with other women to… fill the void of not having me?"

"We should talk about this at home," I tell her, and her eyes widen.

"Oh my God! You know at one point, I thought that it was kind of hot thinking about you using other women…maybe even calling them my name in bed but now…" she crosses her arms, "I'm pissed."

"What do you want from me, Charley!? I couldn't have you. I couldn't touch you. I had no idea…I had no idea that we were going to get here. That we'd eventually fall in love. At the time, I didn't even know we'd ever sleep together! Was I supposed to break my dick off jacking it thinking about you for the rest of my life?"

She scoffs as the elevator dings and walks out without so much as a backwards glance. "Whatever."

"You're being irrational, Charley."

"Excuse me?"

"I understand you being pissed about Audrey and the way she talked to you. Believe me, there was so much more I wanted to say, but being in the position I'm in, I was trying to keep my cool. Fuck her. You were spot on. She's jealous. But are you really going to be upset about women I slept with years ago?"

"Uh, you slept with them less than one year ago."

"Charley it was two faceless women. I slept with two women when I first started seeing you and Wells."

"How many times?"

"What?"

"How many times did you sleep with each of them?"

"Just one time each. I was trying to forget you, Charlotte. They didn't mean anything."

"Just twice?" she grits out as we make our way to my car. "Why?"

"Charley, I don't want to do this."

"Why? You know why Matt and I stopped having sex. Why weren't you?"

"Trust me, not by choice," I snort.

"Uhhhh," she says sarcastically. "No one made you do anything. You took our case, you agreed to counsel us. You could have gotten out at any time. So, I'm asking, why did you stop?" she asks as she leans against my car.

I place my arms on either side of her, pinning her to my Beamer. "Charlotte Pierce."

"What, Will?" She crosses her arms and looks away from me.

I grip her jaw hard and pull her face to look at me. "You're sexy when you're jealous."

"This isn't funny, and you can't fuck your way out of this."

"I know that. But there's no need to talk about any of the women before you."

"Why? Are you hiding something?"

"No, Charley. Because they didn't mean anything. You were in a relationship for eight years and married for five. You'd need to discuss that with any new relationship. I dated women casually for a few months here and there. You're my first, real relationship, Charlotte. So, no, it's not necessary to talk about."

"How many were there?" she whispers, and it's the million-dollar question I was hoping she wouldn't ask. "Audrey made it seem like there were quite a few." I sigh sending a hand through my hair and wondering how much I should downplay this number. "Don't lie to me, Montgomery."

"Ever in my life?"

She shrugs and I can see the insecurities of me being the second man that she's been with written all over her beautiful face. "I guess it's a lot, huh?" She looks up at me sadly, and I feel my heart constrict. "I don't mean to act so crazy. I just…never really thought about you and other women."

"It's not a lot, baby," I whisper. "Comparative to you, yes. But… not a lot."

"More than ten?" she asks, and I press my lips to hers hoping that will suffice as an answer for now.

"I've only ever made love to you, Charley. I didn't have *earth moving, soul shattering, hot, passionate, amazing sex* until you."

"We should go," she whispers and although she's letting this go from now, I have a feeling this conversation is far from over.

CHAPTER
Twenty-Two

Will

S HE KICKS HER SHOES OFF AS SOON AS WE CROSS THE THRESHOLD to my townhouse and her hands find the back of her pencil skirt, unzipping it and sending it down her legs. She walks to the kitchen, leaving her shoes and skirt scattered across the floor before beelining for the refrigerator. She pulls out a bottle of wine that she'd opened last night at dinner. *It was the first time probably ever that I didn't join her, but I was preparing to tell her the truth and I needed to start weaning myself off of alcohol.*

I'm not sure if she's trying to seduce me or torture me with her lack of clothes but she leans over the bar as she sips her wine before handing me a glass. "Sit," she demands.

Fuck.

She sighs. "How much time was there between you having sex with them and with me?" She freezes momentarily. "If you say something like two days, I will throw this wine in your face. So, if it's that close, I suggest you *lie.*"

I sigh and move around the counter so I can be within arm's reach of what seems to be my very wary fiancée. She takes a step back and raises her eyebrows as if to say, *answer first.*

"I started seeing you in January. We slept together in May. I realized in late February, early March that I was attracted to you and it was growing by the day. I'd gone out one night with my brother, had far too many drinks. I slept with a woman that night.

That was in March." I rub the back of my neck. "I did use her to try and fill the void of not being able to have you. I fantasized that it was you, when I fucked her. *I said your name* when I fucked her. It was the beginning of April when I cut it off. My feelings for you were so strong at this point and getting more intense. Every time I came when I was alone, I said your name. I tried it again a few weeks later, still the same. I couldn't get you out of my head. So, in short, a month," I tell her, and hope she's pleased enough with my answer to let it go.

She swallows before she nods once and takes another healthy sip. "Was there anyone else besides Audrey and me? I mean…is that your thing? Sleeping with women you can't have?"

"Audrey is a bitch for putting that in your head. And she's a fucking counselor." I shake my head as I wrap my arms around her, grateful that she's letting me touch her. "It was just you. There's nothing that said I couldn't be with Audrey. I just didn't want to be."

"Well, you really shouldn't sleep with your co-workers."

"There's nothing in our code of conduct on it. It might be frowned upon but it's not forbidden."

"You had sex with her in your office?" she asks, and I don't miss her lip slightly trembling.

"Charley…" I trail off, my finger finding her soft cheek. "Baby, please don't be upset."

"I'm not," she says as she looks away from me, her hand finding the space under her left eye and wiping gently. She clears her throat and sniffles and I've officially had enough. I pull her to the couch and bring her into my lap, cupping her face.

"I love *you* so much, do you know that?" I rub my nose against hers.

"Do you think I'm prettier than her?"

"Do you even have to ask?"

She nods. "You said…I mean she said you said that she was the most beautiful."

"You know I think you're the most insanely beautiful woman I've ever seen. When I met you…I think I was speechless for a few seconds. You are stunning."

She sighs. "I'm officially over this conversation. I'm exhausted after meeting your ex-girlfriend. She's a gem, by the way."

"I was perfectly content not having this conversation. We could be fucking right now." *Or you could use this time to talk to her about what she needs to know.*

She snorts and I don't like her reaction to the idea of making love when it's obvious we both need it. "Tell me about Audrey."

"No, Charley."

"Why?"

"Because she's fucking irrelevant, and I'm not arguing with you about her."

"I don't need a blow by blow of your sex life, I mean what happened in the relationship?" She rolls her eyes as she stands and pours another glass of wine. *Time to slow this train down.*

I let her keep the glass but I pull the bottle of wine off the counter and hold it in my hands resisting the urge to put it to my lips and take a long drink. "Stop saying shit like that, Charlotte, or I'm taking you the fuck over my knee until you can remember just who *I* belong to."

"Apparently the woman that's the juiciest forbidden fruit." She shrugs. My nostrils flare, my eyes widen, and I resist the urge to snatch her wine and throw it at the wall. "How do you think it made me feel to hear that?" she yells. "That you'll lose interest in me once the chase and the initial excitement is over?"

"Fuck you, Charley," I growl pulling her glass from her hand and setting it on the counter. The rational thing to do would be to go to my office to put some space between myself and this infuriating woman. But instead, I push her hard against the wall, ripping her blouse off of her. The buttons fly everywhere, and before I even take her bra—one of the ones I had bought her all those months ago—off, I'm sucking her thin lace covered nipple into my mouth and biting down *hard.*

She yelps, which quickly turns into a moan as I lightly tickle her nipple with my tongue. "I've only *ever* belonged to you. And you know that. You're just trying to get under my skin," I say as my hands fist the lace material. "And it's fucking working. Stop putting yourself on the same level as anyone that came before you. Stop comparing yourself to anyone else because there is no comparison." I rip the bra at the point between her breasts and slide it off her before trailing my tongue through the valley of her breasts.

"You are so sweet," I murmur into her skin. "No woman has ever tasted like you. I've always liked the way your skin tasted. Even after your runs…" My lips find her left nipple and I enclose my lips around it. My eyes finding hers, and I look up at her as I suckle her perky breast.

"You think I wanted to fuck my patient? Fuck a married woman? No. That's not why I wanted to fuck you or why my thoughts were consumed with you every waking moment. Why I couldn't get you out of my head when I masturbated. I wanted to fuck *you,* Charlotte. Kiss you. Lick you. Worship you. And right before we finally got together, I realized I didn't want to only fuck you, but I wanted to make love to you. I've told you this before. My feelings for you started off pretty strong and then got to be unbreakable."

She moans as her leg finds its way around my waist, in an attempt to bring me closer to her. "I'm sorry," she whimpers, "for being so crazy."

"You should be sorry," I growl, hating that I've spent the last hour or so convincing my fiancée no one mattered before her. "I love you. And you acting like you doubt that pisses me the fuck off."

"I don't doubt it." She whimpers and her eyes look up at me nervously.

"Oh? It certainly sounded like you weren't sure. That you don't trust me."

"I trust you." She assures me as her grip tightens around my biceps. Her fingernails digging into the skin as if my skepticism scares her.

"Do you?" *She shouldn't*

"Yes!" she cries out. My fingers have found their way into her panties and have thrusted upwards. "Yes, of course I trust you," she says as her jaw goes slack and her head rests up against the wall behind her.

"Look at me, Charlotte."

She obeys my order immediately. "Yes?"

I begin to rub my fingers against her vaginal wall and she clenches. "*No one* mattered before you." I begin to slow my ministrations, pulling my fingers from inside of her and ghosting them slowly over her slippery clit. "My therapist thinks I had commitment issues…well, until you. I ran from relationships. Never let myself get too close to women," I whisper in her ear, pressing a kiss to the side of her neck. "And then I met you, and you brought me to my knees so easily. I thought about you constantly, from the first day I met you. I want to marry you, father your children, grow old with you. *You* broke me of my fear of commitments. I've been committed to you from the moment you asked if I saw myself getting married or if I was too jaded from my profession."

She gasps, and I don't know if it's because I'm still fingering her or if she's recalling that conversation and realizing that it was before we ever slept together.

"I've been yours long before I ever touched you, Charlotte."

—

Seven months prior

"*So why aren't you married, Dr. Montgomery?*" Charley asks as she leans back in her usual seat. This has become a bit of a routine for us. Matt is always late, so we usually spend the first twenty minutes of their scheduled session talking about—anything. Everything. "Has this job made you jaded? You've seen too much?" Her legs are crossed, her nude pump, moving up and down slowly and the way it contrasts with her slender, tanned ankle is mesmerizing.

Realizing I need to answer, I shake my head at her invasion of privacy. Anyone else I'd sidestep the question or accuse them of being inappropriate. But not Charlotte. Not the woman that is starring in every single one of my dirty fantasies. Not the woman I'd jacked off thinking about not thirty minutes ago. No, she could know the truth.

"I just haven't met the right one, I guess," I say.

How can I when I spend most of my day trying to get you out of my mind, Charlotte?

"Are you sure you haven't met her?" she asks, her eyes slightly narrowed. "I mean how does anyone know who the one is?"

I'm slightly taken aback by the first part of her question. What does that mean? "You just… know," I tell her.

"That's not very…specific. Your fancy degrees teach you that?" she chirps as she nods at my framed diplomas hanging on the wall behind me.

I smile at her cheekiness. Another thing I love about Charley. My eyes blink several times having caught the word blaring in my head like a bright neon light.

Fuck. Fuck. Fuck.

Every feeling that I've ever felt about Charlotte Pierce is coming at me all at once. The first time we met, the first time I got a whiff of her hair, the first time I touched her soft skin, the first time she wrapped her arms around me and hugged me after a particularly rough session; her soft breasts, pressed up against me. The first time I masturbated thinking about her.

And the second…
and third…
and fourth…

And now, the first time I've had a startling realization. I am in love with Charlotte Pierce.

A smile crosses my lips as I face this epiphany, before everything comes crashing down when reality sets in.

"Sorry I'm late," Matt says as he enters the room and pulls the woman I love to her feet and presses a kiss to her cheek.

"I thought you were looking at me weird that entire session," she giggles as I kneel before her, pulling her panties down her legs. She looks down at me as they reach her feet and she steps out of them. I move up her body, sliding my hands up her silky smooth legs and over the curve of her ass to cup her cheeks. Her hands find my shoulders as she looks me square in the eye wondering what I'm going to do next.

I brush my lips once against hers. "I knew then. I just…didn't know what to do. I didn't know how I was going to handle counseling you…watching you with your husband. I actively tried to push the feelings to the side, ignore them. But they wouldn't go away and then one day… I caught a look." I smile as I recall the lustful gaze I saw in her eyes. "You say you always looked at me with stars in your eyes, but you must have hidden it well because I never got any indication that you might want me. And then one day…you did. I was calling you in for your solo session the next day. I didn't even know what I was going to do then," I tell her, as I begin to unbuckle my pants.

"Tell me what you were thinking," she whispers.

"That I wasn't sure if I could fuck you. What if you were interested but weren't interested in going that far. What if I completely misread the signals? I could've been in a ton of trouble if I had read the situation wrong."

"Like we are now?" She opens her eyes and winces slightly.

"Worth it. But no, it's different. You could have sued for sexual harassment."

"I wouldn't have," she whispers. "Even if I didn't want to go as far as we did. I wouldn't have told anyone if you made a pass at me. I liked you too much." She brushes her hand softly against my jaw and I push my head further into it letting her fingers stroke the bristles on my skin.

I nod, pressing a kiss to her palm. "Not that it matters now. It all worked out in the end."

She nods, and in a moment, I see her wall moving back up slightly. "Is Dr. Norwood going to be a problem?"

"I'll take care of it."

"How?"

"I'll talk to my father, see what he can do."

"But won't you have to tell them you slept with her?"

"Do you have a better idea? They vote on my fate, Charley. And if she has a vote…or she's in anyone's ear…" I trail off. "I have a feeling this is going to be a pretty split case. One vote could tip the scales."

"Why didn't you tell me?" she sighs as she pushes against my chest lightly, the sexy intimate moment we just had long forgotten. "I could have been better prepared. She wasn't exactly neutral in there. I thought it was all in my head, but I knew she sounded like a jealous ex-girlfriend." She shakes her head as she picks up her blouse and pulls it back on, the vulnerability she feels at being naked for this conversation evident by her body language.

"Tell you what? I had no idea she'd be on this investigation. She's not even on the board, but sometimes they bring in other doctors for this part. But hold on a second, what did she say to you?"

"Nothing completely out of line, just some things that raised a flag, and now that I know that you fucked her, it all makes sense."

"Okay…Charley? Can you let this go? I have a fucking past, I'm sorry!"

"Don't be sorry." She shrugs. "It just sucks that this person actually directly affects our relationship now."

"How?" I ask narrowing my eyes. "This investigation has nothing to do with you and me being together. We are together whether I get fried or I walk." *I know she's jealous and upset but I'm getting tired of this little attitude of hers.*

Not everyone marries the first person they have sex with.

"Oh? You don't think that her telling me that maybe there was some overlap between me and another woman doesn't directly affect me? You don't think that her asking if I can totally trust you isn't blaring in my head right now?" She puts a hand up. "I do trust you. I don't think you'd ever cheat on me or..." She shakes her head. "No, I don't. It doesn't mean I wanted to hear it. Then to hear that you broke up with her because the excitement wore off? It's like she knew exactly what to say to me."

"You know it's more than that with us. We've been over this."

"I know, Will," she snaps. "I'm fully aware. I'm just...struggling with my feelings a little bit, okay? Give me a fucking break." She moves towards our bedroom, I think as a way to end the conversation but I'm not having it. I'm behind her instantly and stand in my doorframe as she moves around the room. Within moments, she's in a pair of sweatpants and my Harvard t-shirt that she wears more than I do now. She brings it to her nose before a pout finds her face and she pulls it off immediately. "I need a different one. That smells too much like me."

I smile as I watch her rummage through one of my drawers and find another t-shirt. "I don't know why you're getting dressed, I'm just about to rip the clothes off of you," I say moving towards her.

She puts a hand up, stopping me from moving any closer. "No. We haven't solved anything."

"What's there to solve?"

"These feelings are so fucking foreign," she says sadly as she sits on the bed, her head in her hands. "I didn't even care that Matt slept with Bree. I'd met his ex-girlfriend—granted he was only twenty-two when we met but..." She winces. "He was kind of a ho before he met me." She chuckles. "And nothing ever bothered me." She looks at me and the first thing that catches my attention is how bright her eyes are as the tears intensify the color. "I didn't know that I was the jealous type." She looks down and fidgets with her hands.

"Hey," I whisper against her skin, as I bring her face closer to mine. "It's okay."

"You're pissed at me."

I shake my head. "No, I'm not. I just don't want you fixating on that."

"Did you have any serious relationships before me?"

I let out a deep breath wondering why we can't just drop this. "No, not really? I dated someone on and off all through college, but…it was college. She's married now, I think. I don't know." I shrug and really, I don't. We didn't have some awful breakup, we just grew apart when we graduated. Truth was, I never felt as intense about anyone as Charlotte Pierce.

The one woman I really should have left alone.

"Charley, baby. I understand jealousy. I've always had a bit of a jealous streak. Of course, it got worse when I met you. But you know all about the issues in my family—with my brother. You know I've always been jealous of him. And that's something I've dealt with all my life… even now. Although it's not nearly as bad." I narrow my eyes at her. "But with *you*. Do you have any idea how hard it is to be in love with a woman you can't touch? To be in love with a woman who has to sit in front of you three times a week with the man she actually does belong to? I was out of my mind with jealousy, Charley."

My mind floats back to one of the few times I saw him kiss her, one of the few times I saw them at least mildly affectionate. He tucked a hair behind her ear, she giggled, playfully smacked his arm and he kissed her. I watched this display for thirty seconds before I realized I was awkwardly standing in the entrance to my office staring at them. I faked a phone call and told them I needed a few minutes before proceeding to angrily pace the length of my office, trying to calm down.

I hadn't even touched her then.

"Charley, he sent me a tape of you having sex," I say, the anger coursing through my veins like it was just yesterday.

Her hands find my face, breaking my thoughts. "I know," she whispers. "I'm not blaming you...I'm just trying to process everything." She licks her lips once and I wonder if she'll let me touch her. I need her. She needs me.

We need each other.

"Charley," I say as I run my hand up her arm and gently push her hair behind her back. Her skin is covered with goosebumps within seconds and I smirk, thinking about the effect I have on her.

"Yes?" she asks, her resolve weakening by the second.

I rest my chin on her shoulder and wrap my arms around her. "I'm sorry about Audrey," I whisper.

She nods and I take that to mean that she's not so angry with me anymore. I move to trail kisses down her face, starting from her temple to her chin. She turns her head towards me, our faces an inch apart, our lips so close that I can taste her breath. She looks down at my mouth and before I can attach our lips she raises her arms slowly straight up over her head, indicating she wants me to undress her.

I stand up in front of her and slide my shirt over her head. She leans back and stretches her legs towards me, wiggling her toes, and I smile. I reach for the waistband of her sweatpants and slide them slowly down her legs and toss them somewhere behind me.

"Your body is perfect, Charlotte. You turn the heads of men everywhere and you think that doesn't piss me off?"

"But you're the only man who can touch me," she says, her teeth sinking into those pouty lips of hers.

"Fucking right," I say more aggressively than I intended and her eyes widen at my tone. I wonder if she thinks I'm mad at her when she speaks.

"What do you want to do to me? What do you need me to do to show you that I'm yours?"

A million things flash through my head all at once. Some sexual some not so sexual but all of them have my eyes zoning in on one appendage in particular.

Her left ring finger.

Her eyes follow mine and she looks up at me when she puts it together. "When?" she whispers as she lets her left hand trail down her body towards the place between her legs that is already showing signs of her arousal. Her left ring finger slides between her folds once and she moans. My dick reacts immediately.

I'm completely dressed in the suit I wore earlier and I don't think I have the brainpower to take my clothes off as I'm too pre-occupied watching Charley touch herself with the finger that will soon house the ring I buy her. I don't even realize what's happening before I'm on my knees in front of her, my face an inch from her entrance watching her perfect fingers move in and out of her.

I pull her hand from her and bring her fingers to my nose briefly, taking in her sweet scent before I slide her three fingers into my mouth, sucking her juices from them. I let my tongue linger over her ring finger much longer than the other two before I bite down gently. "Soon," I tell her as I pull her from my mouth. My eyes trail up her body to her eyes and I raise an eyebrow at her before letting my eyes fall to her core, letting her know what I am going to do next. I open her folds, exposing her completely to me and I see her clench when the cool air hits her slick opening. Her clit is enlarged with arousal and I'm dying to take it into my mouth and suck, but I don't want her coming so soon.

"Will," she whines, and when I look up she's staring down at me through hooded eyes. "I need you."

"I know, baby. I need you too."

"Kiss me," she whispers. "Please." She throws her head back and sighs before looking down at me again. "You know you want to."

My gaze goes back to her opening. "Touch yourself."

"What?" she breathes out. *I know you're at the edge and you're about to snap, but just play along, baby.*

"Touch yourself, I want an up close and personal show," I say looking up at her from between her legs.

"I want *you* to make me come."

"I will. Just start it. So, I can watch. I'll take over soon."

I still have my fingers holding her open so when her hand slides down her body and joins my hands between her legs I almost lose it. I can feel the cum dripping out of me and into my shorts, some of it streaming down my shaft towards my balls. My dick is throbbing with how much it needs her pussy, and I wonder if I can come just by her throaty moans and the taste of her cum once my mouth hits her sex.

"Fuck," she moans as she begins to rub herself. Her fingers haven't entered her wet channel, as they are focused strictly on her clit. *I know it's only a matter of time before she shatters.* I push her hands away and replace them with my mouth. I swipe my tongue across that sensitive bundle and her hands find my head immediately, pushing me harder against her. My hands find her thighs, gripping them so hard, I wonder if I will leave bruises on her porcelain skin, but at the moment I'm too turned on to care. I lift them and slide them over my shoulders.

"You're my favorite taste. Nothing tastes like your cum, Charley."

"I'm going to…" she manages to get out before she cries out and the heels of her bare feet press hard into my back. "Oh God!" she screams as she shatters at the torturous assault of my lips wrapped around her clit, sucking her into my mouth. She sits up, her right hand winding in my hair and her left hand holding her up as she rides out the rest of her orgasm on my face. I can still feel her reeling underneath my tongue, as I swallow down everything her body has to offer.

I groan when I feel her move her legs and pull me up her body, connecting her lips with mine. "Fuck me," she moans as her hands unzip my pants and they fall down my legs.

"Turn over," I grit out, knowing that I'm seconds from exploding and I'm not taking the time to get undressed. I slide my underwear down slightly, leaving me still clothed with the exception of my dick which doesn't want to wait another second.

She does as I ask, getting on her hands and knees, sticking her ass out towards me, and giving me a cheeky grin. I press my face to her ass, sinking my teeth into her left cheek before running my tongue along my teeth marks. I move onto the bed behind her, and slam into her. She jolts forward, the frame of my bed hitting the wall with the force I've used to enter her.

"Will!" she cries out and I wonder if she's gearing up for another orgasm already.

"Hold it," I tell her. "Wait for me."

She nods as I begin to pound forcefully into her, my balls slapping against her pussy with each thrust. "Tell me you'll never let anyone come between us," She moans in response and I smack her behind to get her to focus. "Say it!" I demand as I tighten my grip on her hips.

"Never! No one."

"It's just you and me, Charley. Tell me you know that."

"I know!" she cries as her head drops to the mattress. "Will, I'm going to come again."

I smile knowing that I know how to make her come so easily. "Not yet."

She groans. "God dammit, Will. Get there! I know you need to cum."

"I've been ready to come since we got home, I'm trying to make it last," I grit out.

"Well, stop," she growls and I feel her hands on my balls. I groan feeling her petite hand stroke them and when she squeezes, I hiss.

"Charley!" I'm pounding into her at a relentless speed when I feel her clenching around me multiple times which only means one thing.

"I'm coming, I can't…." she whimpers and then she explodes around my cock. Her hands grip the sheets below her and she screams so loud I wonder if my neighbors heard her. "Oh God." My orgasm follows a beat behind her, thankfully. I know she's about to collapse after these two intense orgasms. "Come deep inside of me, Will. Give us what we both want." The words send a shock through me hearing her voice her need for me to get her pregnant.

"FUCK!" I cum with a roar, as the last thrust presses against her cervix and sends my seed deep inside of her.

I'm leaning over her, my chest pressed against her back, my arms holding myself up so I don't put all my weight on the small woman underneath me. We are both breathing like we've run a marathon, when I place a kiss on her back and roll off of her, immediately bringing her to lie on top of me. My hands find her face and I kiss her mouth, her cheeks, her nose, her eyelids. Anywhere that my mouth can find.

"I love you," she tells me in between kisses. She kisses me one final time before her head finds my chest after the force of her orgasms having taken the last of her strength. I had never been one for cuddling after sex, but I find myself longing for these moments just as much. The period where there are no words exchanged.

Just peace.

Quiet.

The only things I can hear are the sounds of her breathing and the beat of her heart. I wrap my arms around her and kiss the top of her head before I move slightly. She grips me tightly not wanting to move.

"Just let me grab the blanket. You're sweating and I don't want you to get cold," I whisper against her skin. I've barely had the blanket halfway up her back before I can feel her breathing even out indicating she's asleep.

⸻

I wake up to a dark room and I'm immediately on alert that I don't feel Charley's body on top of mine. I'm not wrapped around her like I usually am, so it's safe to assume she's not in bed with me. I sit up slightly and see that my bathroom light is on. I get up and make my way into the bathroom to find my fiancée, in my tub, submerged up to her neck with bubbles. Her hair is tied up in a messy bun, but a few errant curls have escaped, the tips grazing the bubbles.

Her head turns to meet mine and she smiles.

"I was hoping you'd join me soon."

I move towards her and sit on the edge of the tub. I lean forward and press a kiss to her forehead and put my hand on her cheek. "How are you feeling?" I ask her, wondering if the bath and the candles were to help calm her nerves.

She shrugs. "I'm fine. The orgasms helped," she says weakly.

I narrow my eyes at her knowing that she's still feeling something even if she doesn't want to admit it or know what it is for that matter. "Can I join you?"

She nods and I expect her to move forward so I can slide in behind her but she shakes her head and points to the other end of the tub. "I want to see your pretty face," she giggles.

I remove my clothes and sink into the water across from her, sliding my legs around her petite ones. My tub is long, so her feet only come up to about mid thigh and I feel her running her toes over the tops of them under the water. "Full disclosure?" she asks.

I nod once, hoping we can bury this once and for all.

"Did you love her? Audrey? Maybe looking back, you don't think you did. But at the time? Did you?"

I shake my head. "No. I knew what our relationship was. Even if she didn't."

"But you said you were a commitment-phobe. That doesn't necessarily mean you didn't love her. Just that you were too afraid to admit it."

I lean back, impressed by her statement. "You'd make an excellent shrink."

"I learned from the best." She smiles and my heart skips a beat hearing her talk about me that way.

"I don't think I loved her," I say finally. "I think I cared for her, and I hurt her. But I didn't love her."

"Have you ever been in love?" She pauses. "Besides me?"

I sigh, wracking my brain for any of the similar signs that I exhibit with Charlotte every day. I try to remember having any of the symptoms I was experiencing as I fell hard for her. Nothing even comes close.

"No. I never felt for anyone a fraction of what I feel for you."

She nods and I pause, wondering if I want to open this can of worms, but I figure while we are on the subject we might as well get everything out in the open. "When do you think you fell out of love with Wells?"

"Shouldn't you know that?" she giggles.

"Charley…" I trail off.

Truth is, I'm not sure. I wonder if she had already fallen out of love with him before they started coming to me.

"I don't know," she shrugs. "Probably sometime before the first time I asked for a divorce. Somewhere in our third year of marriage."

"And you stayed with him another two years, Charley?"

She shrugs sadly. "I didn't know what else to do, Will. I thought…I felt so alone." The tears well up in her eyes and before I know it water is sloshing out of the tub as I pull her swiftly through it and into my lap. I pull her to me, her hands resting on my chest as she straddles my thighs.

"We don't have to talk about it. Just know that you're not alone now. I never want you to feel that way again."

"I know. You were so good to me...even before...I should have known that I was different. That you didn't treat all of your wife patients like me."

"None like you," I whisper as my lips find hers.

"You were the first man to ask me about my day in years." She sighs. "I think I fell in love with you then." I look into her eyes where I can still see a few traces of hurt behind them, and I decide to end this for good.

"Charley...I know today was difficult for you, but you know me," I tell her as I press her hand to my heart. "You know me better than anyone. You know that what we have is real. What I feel for you is real. I hate to say it like this, but if I wasn't invested, if I wasn't all in...I wouldn't have pushed you to leave Wells. I'm never going to get bored of you or of this. The spark will never die between us. It will always be exciting. I love you, Charley." I guide her onto my cock, feeling her slide down on me. "I love you so much."

CHAPTER
Twenty-Three

Charlotte

WATCH THE LOVE OF MY LIFE STAND TO HIS FEET AS A PANEL of seven decide his fate as a doctor. I frown as I watch as his father, his lawyer, stands beside him. I'm seated behind him in the crowd and I wonder if he can feel the vibes I'm sending him. I look nervously to the right to see his mother tapping her fingertips against the armrest a few seats down. I was seated first, having arrived with Will hours ago. Diana arrived later and immediately chose her seat, making a point that she'd rather not sit next to me. I offer her a weak smile, but her cold eyes give away nothing.

I turn my gaze forward again, ignoring the tension radiating between me and my future mother-in-law.

"Dr. Montgomery, in all of my years as a psychologist, and the years I've served on this board, never have I ever been on a case this—circumstantial. This…objective. A case with such an exorbitant amount of gray area. I understand that you fell in love and I do wish you well, but the fact of the matter is you broke a number of rules that led you to where we are now. And after both of your testimonies, it appears that you have very little regard for the rules that you broke. You made your choice, Dr. Montgomery. It was *not* your career. The cards were always in your hand regarding your future."

My blood runs cold hearing Dr. Marks' words and I hear a gasp from a few seats down. *She knows it too. We all know it.*

This is it.

I can't escape the tears that spring to my eyes as I know that this isn't going to end the way we hoped. We knew this was a possibility. J.R. prepared us, Will prepared *me*. It's funny, this is directly affecting Will the most, and yet he was talking me off the ledge last night. I didn't mean to break down…it just happened. The thought of Will losing everything made me sick to my stomach.

My stomach turns again, and I wince, praying that the nausea can be kept at bay until we either recess or the proceedings are over. I take a deep breath and let it out slowly before reaching for the cup of water sitting on the floor under my feet with shaky hands.

"Dr. Montgomery, do you understand what it would mean if we were to revoke your license completely?"

My eyes widen and my teeth find my bottom lip nervously. *Revoke? As in…permanently? We were holding onto hope that it would merely be a suspension and he could apply for an appeal after a certain amount of time but revocation is… He can't be reinstated.*

"Yes, Dr. Marks," I hear him say.

Dr. Marks leans back in his chair slightly and narrows his eyes at him. "Do you think that you deserve a punishment to that extent?"

Will looks up and although I can't see his face, I know there's confusion written all over it as if to say, *you're asking me?*

"No, sir, I don't."

"And why is that?"

"With all due respect, haven't we been over that?"

"Humor me," he challenges.

"Miss Pierce and I had a relationship, yes…"

"A relationship that violates everything in the code of ethics. Revocation, Dr. Montgomery is well within the scope of punishments we could administer." He opens a folder, laying it flat in front of him and looks at him over his glasses. "Revocation is justified when the license holder is guilty of unlawful or improper conduct." He puts his glasses down. "Would you call your relationship with Miss Pierce unlawful?"

"No sir."

"Improper?"

God, this man is a dick. I roll my eyes. *What a condescending asshole.*

"Oh please," I hear murmured and I catch a glimpse of Will's mother who is shooting daggers at Dr. Marks.

"Yes, my behavior with Miss Pierce was improper. I should not have engaged with her while she was my patient—"

"And married," Dr. Marks interrupts.

"And married," Will repeats, and I can hear the defeat in his voice.

"Dr. Montgomery you've been listed as one of the top, world-renowned doctor's year after year. You've received award after award, and accolades for your service. Graduated top of your class at Harvard, Dr. Montgomery. Your resume is impressive, and yet you knowingly entered into a sexual relationship with a patient, being fully aware of the risks that you were taking. Knowing that it was against everything being a doctor stands for. You were *not* acting in the best interest of your patients, but in your own best interest. How does that make you a good doctor?"

How could they say those things? I'm ready to jump out of my seat to come to his rescue when I feel a hand slipping through mine and squeezing. I look over to the person in question and I see the last person I would have expected: *Diana Montgomery.* She shakes her head slowly as if to say, *don't do what you're thinking.*

"I can't let them do this to him," I whisper. "I have to say something."

"You've said enough. They're taking your testimony into account. If you cause a scene or have an outburst, you could be removed and Will needs to keep his head in the game. My son needs you here, Charlotte." My eyebrows furrow hearing her say those words.

Now you see that he needs me? That I need him?

"There is also the matter of the violation of your patients' privacy. We've been conducting our own investigation on the matter. We summoned Matthew Wells for his testimony."

My head snaps back to the panel upon hearing my ex-husband's name and my heart rate quickens immediately. *What happened with that? Fuck!*

"He admitted to everything, but he's also been very cooperative and signed a number of documents stating he wouldn't say anything. He was more than willing to avoid the possibility of incarceration."

I fiddle with my fingers in my lap, having pulled away from the Ice Queen's grasp.

"Despite all of this we," he looks at the table of Doctors, "are Doctors first, and members of this board, second. Our job is to detect basic human emotions and interactions. Based on the testimony of Dr. Lenox, when he interviewed one Miss Charlotte Pierce, his recommendation was that she, in fact, was in love with you, and was competent enough to understand the gravity of what your love meant. Of what your love meant for her, for you, for all parties involved. She sacrificed a marriage, security, possible protection from what appears to be an abusive stepfather?" He looks at what I assume to be my file. "And yet, she stated on record that she'd do it all again if she had the choice."

I notice Will visibly relax hearing a recount of my testimony and a brief smile crosses my face knowing that it's brought him a moment of peace.

"Miss Pierce also mentioned, and I don't think she really understands the pertinence of her statement that she was attracted to you from the moment she saw you, before she set foot in your office. Thereby, her attraction for you technically started before you were her doctor. If we were going to proceed further with re-vocation, we would need to prove to a jury in a court of law that you seduced her as her doctor. Her testimony throws that out, and heaven forbid we put her on the stand."

My eyes widen as I hear what seems to be a *loophole.*

He steeples his fingers under his chin. "Dr. Montgomery, I don't think I'll ever sit on a case of this *nature.* So, we as a board, vote for the motion to suspend you for twenty-four months. Reinstatement will be allowed in December 2019. We will start from left to right, starting with Dr. Lenox; please state whether you agree or disagree. If the majority disagrees we will proceed with trying this case in a court of law for complete revocation of your license."

"Agree," Dr. Lenox states.

"Agree."

"Agree."

"Disagree." My eyes narrow at the man staring cold eyes at Will.

"Asshole," I hear Diana mumble under her breath, and under any other circumstances I would giggle.

"Disagree." My heart plummets as it's now 3-2.

"Disagree."

No. No. No.

Dr. Marks is the final person to vote and he narrows his eyes at Will. "Dr. Montgomery, I urge you to take the next two years and make something of them. Do not waste them thinking of the past. Write a book, write three books. Start an organization. Counsel troubled youths. You are still a doctor whether you can legally practice or not." He nods and shoots him a small smile. "Agree. Dr. Montgomery, we'll see you in two years." He slams his gavel against the table and I feel the air leave my lungs almost immediately.

CHAPTER
Twenty-Four

Charlotte

I**T'S BEEN TWO DAYS SINCE THE VERDICT, AND WILL HASN'T LEFT** his townhouse once. Not only has he not left the house, but he hasn't left his office which means I've barely seen him. I've gone to bed alone and woken up alone, and I wonder if he's even come to bed at all which feels all too familiar. I'm trying to give him space, but I'm wondering if he needs me more than this space.

Will hasn't eaten much over the past few days. He's been surviving off bourbon and the toast I've been shoving down his throat in the morning, but tonight I'm making him dinner. As I do I feel my phone vibrate.

"Hello?"

"Hey, Charley, it's Drew."

I pull my phone away from my ear and frown slightly as I'm not really in the mood to talk to anyone. "Oh… hey."

"I hope you don't mind, Lauren gave me your number."

Oh right. "Not a problem, what's up?"

"Well, my brother isn't answering his phone and J.R. told me what happened. I was just checking in on him."

"Oh." I put a hand over my eyes, knowing that there was no way Will would want to talk to Drew when he was barely speaking to *me.* "He's just taking it one day at a time. I think he's in a bit of shock still. The whole situation kind of sucks."

"But he got you in the end, and that's what he wanted, right? So, he can't be too upset?"

Tears spring to my eyes hearing what I hoped to be Will's reaction. Instead, he'd been pushing me away and asking for space. "Right of course, but I understand…it was his livelihood."

"Can I talk to him?" he asks.

"He's…sleeping, I think? I can have him call you back?"

There's silence on the other end followed by, "Don't let him push you away, Charley. He pushed all of us away years ago. I should have pushed back. He needed someone to do that and now it's too late. But you…he's crazy about you. He needs you, Charley."

"I need him too," I whisper into the phone, the emotions taking all of the conviction out of my voice.

"Well, be there for him…even when he says not to."

I hang up the phone and move towards his office. I open the door to find him asleep on the couch, a drink sitting on his glass coffee table the color of amber, collecting condensation from the ice. *I wonder what he's drinking today.* I turn on the light, illuminating the once dark room. "Will," I say softly.

"Hmmm," he says before he turns away from me.

"Will, we need to talk," I tell him as I sit on the couch next to him. I put a hand on his shoulder and rub it gently. "Please."

He turns to look at me, his eyes squinting as the light of the room meets them. "What is it, Charlotte?"

I shake my head, never having heard him take that tone with me. "Your brother called."

He groans, "I don't want to talk to Drew."

"I figured, given that you don't even want to talk to me. I told him you were sleeping."

"Don't start."

"Start what? You've barely talked to me in two days. I was trying to give you space, but are you trying to tell me something? We talked about this; you said you wouldn't push me away. That you wouldn't hate or resent me if things didn't go the way you wanted."

"Don't make this about you, Charlotte," he snaps as he sits up. "I don't resent you. I'm not saying I want out, if that's what you're thinking. I'm not mad at you, I'm mad at myself." He takes a long sip of his drink.

It feels like a slap in the face hearing his words. "You being angry with yourself just means you're having regrets…and that hurts just as much as you resenting me."

"I just should have stopped seeing you and Wells once I started having feelings. I should have stopped counseling you and pursued you then. I knew better."

"Dr. Marks said you shouldn't dwell on the past," I whisper.

"Fuck that asshole. He could have given me a lesser sentence." My lips form a straight line. "You don't agree?" he accuses, and I can tell that I need to get out of this now before he explodes and I'm a casualty of the explosion.

"I don't know enough about the rules and precedent…I thought two years was standard."

"You heard him, this was a special case."

"I don't want to argue with you, Will. I'm on your side. I'm always on your side," I tell him. "You heard him, my testimony was probably what got you out of the line of fire of complete revocation."

He looks up at me, the sadness lurking behind his blue eyes. "Thank you for that, by the way. You didn't tell me you said that."

I shrug. "I told you. I told the truth about everything. If I could have taken the blame for this I would have," I tell him sadly. "I hate that this cost you so much." His head finds my chest and I hear him breathe in deeply. I stroke the back of his head, letting my hand ghost down his back. "But I'm here. I'm here for you, Will. You can't shut me out. Let me make this better. Or… try."

I kiss his forehead and his arms move around me and tighten

as he buries his head further into my chest. "I just want to be the best man I can for you," he mumbles into my shirt.

"Who says that you aren't? You are the best man I know, Will. I know you're feeling defeated and upset and you feel like the world is against you but…I'm here. And I know this isn't what you pictured, but two years is better than forever. Two years is nothing. There's so much we can do in that time. Or you can do…"

"Like what?" he asks sadly.

"Marks suggested a few things…what if you wrote a book?"

"Who would want to read what I have to say?"

I've never known Will to be someone that would have feelings of self-loathing, but hearing his words expressing his shattered confidence hurts me deeply. "Will, there are so many things you could write. A self-help book for instance. You could give people advice…"

"On breaking up a marriage?" He snorts as he pulls his face away from my chest and looks at the ceiling.

"Hey," I grip his jaw, pulling his gaze to mine, "you didn't break up a marriage." I kiss his lips gently. "You did nothing wrong," I whisper.

He snorts again. "Okay, Charley. I did about a hundred things wrong."

"But it led to us being together…it can't be so wrong." I want to convey just how much I feel that us being together is the right thing.

He cocks his head to the side and narrows his eyes. "Nice try."

"Baby, I just want you to feel better. I hate seeing you like this."

"I know, Charley. I hate being like this. I'm sorry that I'm taking it out on you."

"You're not, it's okay. I just don't want you being so hard on yourself." I climb into his lap and stroke both of his cheeks, my thumbs stroking the skin under his eyes. "I love you and I just want you to be happy. That's all I've ever wanted for you."

His eyes study mine for a moment before he leans forward and presses his lips to mine. "You make me happy," he whispers against my lips. "You're all I've ever wanted."

———

Two weeks later

My foot hasn't stopped bouncing since I sat down, the seconds ticking by at a snail's pace as I wait for the two minutes to be up. My eyes go back and forth between my watch and the bathroom counter. I will myself not to look at the pregnancy test until the time is up, but I'm on pins and needles wondering what it will say.

I am two days late for my period; that wasn't completely out of the norm, but something told me to pick up the tests when I was at the pharmacy earlier. I'm not exhibiting any telltale signs but it's a feeling. A feeling that I'm hoping will be correct.

Will and I both want children, and while Will isn't exactly himself, maybe a baby on the way would be the perfect thing to snap him out of it.

Charley, babies don't fix everything. Actually they rarely fix anything.

The words run through my mind on a loop and I wrap my arms around myself, suddenly cold. Maybe I should have asked Will to wait with me.

It's been two weeks since Will was suspended, and while he's left the four corners of his office, and the townhouse, he hasn't gone far. Drew dragged him out of the house a few nights ago to get a drink, and Will came home on the precipice of blackout drunk. I could count on one hand the number of times I'd seen Will lose control with his drinking, but in the past two weeks it had almost tripled.

I'd been worried that if Will had to live with the guilt of our actions he could have turned to other vices. I hadn't taken into account that he still could have turned to other things for turning himself in.

I stand slowly to look at the test and my heart flutters in my chest as I see the two pink lines staring at me in the face.

Pregnant.

I'm pregnant.

We are having a baby.

Oh. My. God.

A smile crosses my face as the tears find my eyes and before I can wipe them, they're flying down my cheeks. I look at the second test and see the word *Pregnant* staring at me straight in the face.

I hear movement in his bedroom, and when I walk out I'm startled to see Will with a full glass of bourbon in his hand.

"Will, it's not even noon," I tell him, my eyes narrowing slightly. I can hear the judgment in my voice, but to be honest I don't give a fuck.

This shit ends now.

"What are you? My mother? Relax, baby."

"Relax? Are you fucking kidding me?" I move towards him. "You reek of liquor, ALL. THE. TIME. You're so distant and cold to me. You barely talk to me. Look at me. You're a fucking ghost, Will. I understand you're upset. I do…but you have got to snap out of this. If not for me then…" I wrap my arms around myself again feeling the chill once again. *Now isn't the time to tell him.* "Then for yourself."

"I would do anything for you," he says. "I think I've proven that, haven't I?" He takes another long sip.

"Wow," I tell him. "Really?"

"I didn't mean it like that," he says.

"How did you mean it?"

"Charley, can we not do this right now?" He sits on the bed, his head in his hands.

"Yes, we need to do this *right* now." He shakes his head and raises the glass to his lips but before he can drink the poisonous liquid I snatch it from his hands, the drink sloshing along the side of the glass and onto my hand. "Stop this shit, right now, Will."

He tries to reach for it, and instead of letting him have it, I throw it. Hard. Against the wall. The glass shatters, and the brown liquid streaking down the white walls.

"God, Charley. WHAT THE FUCK?" he roars, and I'm so angry in this moment, I could scream.

"What the fuck is right! You are a mess, Will. A MESS!" I scream at him. I take a few calming breaths, trying to slow my accelerated heartbeat and move towards the bathroom slamming the door behind me. I grab the tests holding them in my hands before I grip them hard. I'm surprised that he wasn't hot on my heels right behind me. I wait a few minutes to calm down, knowing that despite our anger this will be the happiest moment of our lives.

I move back into the bedroom to find him lying flat on his back on our bed, and I wonder if he's asleep, making me wonder just how drunk he already was to be able to pass out that quickly.

"Will," I say sadly, the tears moving down my face.

No answer.

"Will." My eyes find the tests in my hands before they shoot up to find the passed out father snoring on the bed.

—

Will

The roar of the pounding in my head wakes me up as I move my head to the side. The sun blares against my face as it streams through the blinds of our bedroom. I wonder if Charlotte opened them to give me a rude awakening. Her angry words come flooding back to me.

You're a mess.

You're a ghost.

You reek of alcohol.

I groan, thinking about this bender I've been on. I've gone through almost two bottles a day since the hearing, and I can see the fear in Charley's eyes every time I look at her.

She knows your secret.

You have a problem.

And she's denying it like you are.

I sit up, resting my elbows on my knees. I try to quiet the splitting headache as the hangover I've been avoiding for the better part of two weeks comes at me full force.

I trudge to the bathroom and take a few Advil before swishing the taste of alcohol out of my mouth. I glance at my watch and I see that it's not even three pm.

Three pm and you've already passed out from drinking.

I run a hand through my hair and frown as I look at myself in the mirror hating the person staring back at me. My eyes are tired and red, dark bags circle my eyes and it looks as if I've aged five years. I look exhausted, having barely slept last night. I tossed and turned on the couch in my den not wanting to disturb Charley with my insomnia. I haven't shaved in at least a week, and my beard has grown in, slightly unkempt. My hair is sticking up all over the place, and for a brief second, I have to recall when the last time it was I'd showered. I'm sure Charlotte would be all over this mountain man look, if I didn't look more like a *homeless* mountain man.

My heart constricts as I think about Charley's face when she threw my drink against the wall, the anger shooting out of her eyes at me.

It's official, I'm at rock bottom.

I run a hand over my face, scratching the skin before I turn on the tap. I collect the cool water in my hands and submerge my face in it. I brush my teeth, and I cringe thinking about the last time I'd even done this.

At least before, I was a functioning alcoholic.

What are you doing to yourself, Will?

My stomach flips in response, the anxiety of facing Charlotte coursing through me.

"Charley!" I call out, but there's no answer. "Charlotte," I call a second time, as I make my way downstairs.

I find her on the deck, staring out into the fall day. You can feel the chill in the air that indicates fall is coming, but it's still warm enough to only need a sweater. She's pulled her knees up to her chin, with a blanket wrapped around her. A box of tissues sits next to her, and what appears to be a cup of tea. "Hey." I'm wary about approaching her, wondering what kind of mood she's in after what happened earlier. Her eyes flash to mine, anger running rampant in her eyes, but I can tell she's been crying. "I'm —"

"Sorry?" she asks. I'd yet to witness this level of anger towards me, and I feel out of my depth.

Not to mention hungover.

"Charlotte…" I try my best to tell her with my eyes how sorry I am. How much I love her. How much she means to me. But the look that she's giving me tells me she's not hearing it.

"Is there something you want to tell me?"

That I've relapsed? Yes, but not at the moment.

I drop to the seat next to her, and stare at her willing her to answer her own question. "What do you mean?" She moves her gaze around me and focuses on something on the other side of her.

I crane my neck slightly and only now do I see that there's a box on the floor next to her. She pulls out an empty bottle of Macallan and sets it on the table. "Found your little stash." Her eyes flit to the box on the ground and I swallow knowing exactly what else is in there. A lot of empty bottles. I was too nervous to throw them out; I knew Charlotte would see just how much I was putting away if they were in the trash. I knew I had to get rid of the evidence, but I hadn't yet. I was hoarding them until trash day, when I could sneak out in the middle of the night and put them in the bins that sit outside of my house. If I have to guess there's close to fifteen bottles in there, showing her just how much I've drunk in the last week.

"Charlotte."

"Will, you have a problem," she whispers. Her lip trembles and her eyes well up with tears as if she's realizing that not only do I have a problem, but a dangerous one.

I swallow, not knowing how I'm going to explain this.

You should have told her weeks ago. Hell, months ago. You should have been honest about your past. So she could help you avoid it. So she could help you fight the demons.

"I'm just stressed out, Charlotte. I did lose my job." *Not an excuse.*

But maybe she'll see it as one. She'll tell me to stop, I'll go to some AA classes, and this will be over. This is just what I needed, Charlotte's kick in the ass to get me back on track.

She leans forward and puts her hand on my knee, squeezing it gently. Her features have softened dramatically, and I breathe a sigh of relief as she touches me. *So, she's not too angry.* "I know. And you have no idea how terrible I feel. I wish I could take all of the pain away. I wish I could fix it, but—"

I interrupt her, knowing where she's going with this. "I know things have gotten a little out of control. But I'm done. No more drinking, I swear."

"See, Will, that's the thing. I don't think it's that simple." Her eyes well up with tears, and in my gut, I know that somehow, she knows. She opens up her hand revealing the twelve-month chip that was in my sock drawer.

No.

Nausea bubbles to the surface making my body convulse with the need to be sick. I swallow it down, not wanting to be sick in front of Charlotte, even though if she tells me she's leaving me she won't be able to avoid it.

"Charley…" my voice is quiet and timid, fearing what she's going to say next. "I love you so much."

"You've been lying to me." She pulls another tissue from the box and wipes at her eyes. My chest aches with the need to comfort her.

"I didn't…"

"You surely haven't been honest. I had no idea you struggled with…this. You having this chip means…" She bites her bottom lip, and her shoulders droop slightly. "When?"

"Charlotte, I was young and—"

"WHEN!?" She shoots to her feet and stares down at me. "God dammit, Will. You should have told me this. I let…" She sniffles and pulls the blanket tighter around her. "I let you spiral. I didn't know, I didn't see the signs until now. And now it's too late!"

"Baby…" I stand up, trying to be closer to her and she backs up shaking her head profusely.

"No. If you touch me, I'll crumble and I can't afford to crumble. I have to be strong for—" She pauses and blinks the tears out of her eyes before scanning the land behind my house. "I want the truth, Will, and I want it *now.*"

This is it. You have to put it all out on the line for her.

I just pray she'll still want me after she hears it all.

CHAPTER
Twenty-Five

WILL

"I'M SORRY I DIDN'T TELL YOU," I TELL HER HONESTLY. "THERE were so many times I planned to, but there was so much going on between Matt and your divorce and then learning he'd planted the device and then the hearing and Audrey and..." I stand up. "I just wanted a minute alone with you with no bullshit. I wanted to be a normal couple with no problems for a little while. Is that so wrong?" I shoot her a look but she's still staring at the chip in her hands. *My chip.* "Give me that."

"Why? It doesn't make much difference now, does it?"

Her words are like a slap in the face. I shake my head at her as I lean over the railing of my deck, not wanting to hold her gaze. "You would have been afraid of me if you knew," I tell her quietly.

"Afraid? Why?" I can hear her moving towards me, but she's wary as if she is slightly afraid to get near me.

"Because of your stepfather."

She doesn't say anything. She just stands next to me, not touching me, as she follows my gaze. She stares at the trees rustling in the wind and finally after a few moments of silence her eyes find mine. "Were you violent? I mean can you get..."

"I've never hit anyone, Charlotte. I would never hit you. See this is what I mean. You're afraid of me. *Me.*"

"I'm not afraid but...all..." she takes a breath, "*drunks* say they would never hit you when they're sober." Her voice is somber and it's a punch in the gut as I think about the fact that perhaps her stepfather made those same promises in the beginning. "Things escalate. They get worse. At first, it's a slap, or grabbing you so hard they leave a mark. It's not always being pushed down a flight of stairs or breaking your bones." She swallows hard. "But it's comforting to know that you don't have much experience with that the first time around."

"I am not a violent person, Charley."

"You're not *you* when you've been drinking. People with alcoholism are rarely the same person when they're sober. *The few times they are sober.* Will, I just want to understand, how— you're a counselor. You stress the importance of honesty and trusting your partner. You talk about the dangers of addiction. I just don't understand how things spiraled. Why you kept me in the dark. I would have helped. I surely wouldn't have been drinking around you—or at all. I certainly would never sacrifice your mental or physical health."

"I know."

"You knew if you told me, I would keep you accountable. You didn't think you had a problem. Or you thought you had it under control. You were in denial."

"Charlotte…"

"You should have told me, Will. God, what else are you keeping from me?"

"Nothing!" I exclaim. "Charlotte, this was before you came into my life. Before I was a therapist. This was years ago!"

"And yet it still affects you!"

"Of course, it does, that's what alcoholism is, Charlotte!" Her lip trembles and I take a deep breath trying to calm my agitation. "The things I've told you about my family, my childhood…my relationship with Drew. It went a little deeper than that. I used alcohol to cope with feeling like an outsider in my own family. I used it because alcohol never made me feel like an outsider. It made me feel like I belonged. Or maybe it just numbed the pain." I rest my elbows over the railing.

"How long?"

I let out a breath. "I started in high school, nothing aggressive, but I did my fair share of partying. I told myself once I got away I would stop. And I did, I went to college and grad school back to back, foregoing summer vacations and winter breaks because I couldn't bear being around them. I threw myself into work, taking four years to do what it took most people six. It wasn't until I graduated from grad school, that I picked it up again. I was relying heavily on alcohol to temper the pain. I was lonely, in crippling debt from grad school having come from a family with *too* much money for scholarships. I hadn't wanted to use a dime of my trust fund, and I was making next to nothing as an intern. I was barely speaking to my parents, the resentment for them and my brother after a childhood of hell still coursing through my veins. In short, I was miserable. Tuck took me under his wing. Helped me get clean. I guess you could call him my sponsor. My family never knew."

"How...? How could they not know?" she asks. "I know you didn't want much to do with them, but they didn't take an interest...*in you*?"

"No," I say without another word. She clears her throat slightly and I can see she's struggling with telling me something. "What is it, baby?" I know she's angry with me, and in the deep, dark places of my mind, I fear that this is the end of us—but that doesn't stop me from pushing.

"Drew said—I mean—earlier when he called, he said not to let you push me away." She purses her lips. "That he should have fought harder for you when you pushed *him* away."

Of course, that mother fucker would act like the victim. Like I hurt him. Like he wasn't the problem.

But was he?

Was it his fault that your parents favored him?

No, but he certainly ate it up.

"Don't buy that bullshit Drew is selling, Charley."

"He sounded—"

"You bought that 'he pushed me away crap' because you don't know him like I do."

"And how is that? Because he's somewhat involved with my best friend, and I don't want her to get hurt."

"Then she should probably end her involvement," I snort, thinking about how he's slept with half of Atlanta.

"We're getting off topic." *Good, off topic means maybe I have a chance at keeping her. Making her stay.* "How did you get clean, back then? Did you go to rehab?"

"No...I didn't go. I was worried about how that would look being brand new in the field and a first-year intern. I went to Alcoholics Anonymous meetings and Tuck basically followed me around like a bodyguard making sure I didn't slip up. I didn't touch alcohol again until..." I pause, giving her a solemn stare.

"Until...me?"

I hesitate, before resting my hands on her shoulders. "This is not your fault, Charlotte. None of this is your fault. I use alcohol to cope with things that are out of my control. And falling in love with you—with a patient—was completely out of control. At first, I was drinking in a way to combat the feelings that I was having for you. *Because* I couldn't have you. But then we slept together and the itch that I thought I scratched wasn't going away. I thought I may have been falling in love with you, but I prayed it was just lust. *It wasn't.* It was painful not being able to have you whenever I wanted you. Not being able to touch you when I wanted...Having to sit in therapy and watch you *married* to someone else. To someone that wasn't *me.* It drove me crazy and I had no control over the situation. So, the drinking got worse. It was enough just to take the edge off at first. And then to numb...whatever I was feeling."

She narrows her eyes slightly. "I had no idea…I mean…were you ever drinking or drunk during our sessions?"

Lord knows I wanted to. Having to watch the woman I was sleeping with argue with another man about all the sex they weren't having made me irate. That went double the times he attempted to touch her. "No. I kept it to after hours. And it wasn't as bad as my first time around. I wasn't getting drunk necessarily. It was a drink here or there. But as the people of AA so eloquently put it, there is no drink here or there." I sit back down in the chair, the exhaustion of this conversation and the remainder of my slight hangover taking over. "I'm so sorry," I tell her as I put my head in my hands. "I'm sorry I didn't tell you."

"I'm worried about you, Will. What happens when you start feeling out of control again? How do I know you're not going to go back to drinking to calm your nerves or give you some sense of control? You'll keep it from me. Or at least you'll try to."

That doesn't sound like she's leaving you.

Or she's weighing the options.

"Baby, no. I won't, I swear, this is it. You have to believe me. I've never lied to you before."

"You didn't tell me about any of this. This is a big deal. You used to say that lying by omission is just as bad."

I chuckle, hearing my words thrown back at me. She lets her arms fall and moves back towards me, sitting on the table in front of me and putting my hands in hers. She brings them to her lips and then puts them over her heart.

I don't like where this is going.

"I love you. So incredibly much," she starts. "You came into my life like a tornado…stirring up things inside of me that I had never felt. You challenge me and push me and love me harder than anyone ever has. *I love you* harder than anyone I ever have. But we just jumped feet first into this without really getting to know each other. Without really building a connection outside of our affair."

"Charlotte…"

"I think I should stay with Lauren for now."

Panic blooms in my chest. "What? You're leaving me?"

"No! I just…"

No. She can't go. She swore we were in this together.

You didn't act like you were, why should she?

I ignore the thoughts. "You're leaving me, when I need you?"

"That's not fair." Her eyes are full of tears as they slide down her cheeks. "I will always be there for you." Her hand reaches out to stroke my cheek. "I love you."

"Then why are you leaving? How can you leave?"

"Because I can't set myself on fire…just to keep you warm."

The words are a bitter pill. I know the sentiment; I'd spoken them to some couples. But hearing her think she has to do that for me… "That's bullshit."

"Will, there are almost twenty bottles of liquor—*hard* liquor—in that box. This is something you struggle with, and I just want you to get a handle on it before I further complicate your life."

"You're not a complication." *Baby, you're everything.*

"You just got suspended over my involvement in your life."

"Yes, and your response to that is to run?" My heart hammers in my chest, as I speak the words. *I can't lose her.*

"I'm not running! I want to give you space."

You're the last person I want space from.

Don't let her leave. If she walks out of that door, you'll lose her forever. "I don't want space."

"Fine. Maybe *I* need the space."

Well, that certainly changes things… "Wh—what? Space from… me?"

She swallows and fidgets in her lap. "I took a test."

My eyes furrow together for a moment, not knowing what she means when realization dawns on me. *A test…* Her eyes look

up to meet mine and they're watery and full of worry. "Like a...
pregnancy test?"

"Like a pregnancy test."

"And?" *Well, she's not telling you she's leaving because the test
is negative.*

"I'm pregnant..." she says. "We are pregnant."

I don't say anything at first, unsure of how she feels. *How I
should feel...*

"A...baby?" I choke out.

"Yes." The tears flood her eyes, and before I can think I've
dropped to my knees in front of her, wrapping my arms around
her stomach.

"A baby," I whisper as I press my face to her stomach. "Oh my
God." I lift her shirt and press a kiss to the skin before standing up
and wrapping her in my arms. My heart sinks as I don't feel her
hugging me back. I pull back and she doesn't seem as happy as I am.

"This should be the happiest moment of my life. I'm finally
getting what I always wanted. A baby with a man that loves me."

"Then what's the problem? I'm here, I love you, I want a family with you." *I've been coming inside of you for the past month just
praying to get you pregnant.*

"The problem is the novelty wears off, Will! And when that
happens you seem to turn to other vices instead of me. I can't risk
raising this baby with someone who passes out on me mid-sentence,
or who goes on benders from time to time, soaking their liver in
scotch! I've seen what alcoholics can do to children. I've seen what
alcohol can do to families, Will. I'm not saying you'll be Michael.
I'm not. In my heart of hearts, I don't think you'd ever lay a hand on
me. But there are so many other factors. What if you hurt yourself
or someone else? What happens if you relapse and I'm not around?
What happens if you pass out when you're watching our children?
What about when they're older and you miss birthdays or recitals
or soccer games because you're off somewhere getting drunk?"

My hands begin to shake as she lists off some of her biggest fears. *Hell, some of mine too.* "Charlotte, that won't happen. I'll stop. I'll get help."

"AA meetings aren't enough. You've been through this once. Maybe you'll stop for a while, but what happens when something else happens and you feel out of control. What if in two years you can't get your license reinstated for whatever reason? What if something else happens that throws a wrench in your life? And maybe you won't turn to alcohol next time. Maybe it'll be something harder or more dangerous. Words aren't enough, Will. Maybe if it was just me…but I'm not risking anything when it comes to our baby."

"I would never hurt you or our baby."

"I know that. But you'd say anything to keep me here right now. You kept this from me for so long, because you were afraid I'd leave if I knew."

"AND YOU'RE LEAVING!" I bellow as I stand up.

"I just don't want you to use me as a crutch, Will. I can't be your entire incentive. I want you to get better for *you*."

The words are bubbling to the surface and they're flying from my mouth before I can catch them. "You can't fucking do this," I growl. I don't think I've ever taken this tone with her, but I'm angry. *Livid.* "You do this…you leave and it's over. It'll break us."

You don't mean that.

If she leaves me now when I need her most, how the hell am I supposed to trust her?

That's not fair. She's afraid of you.

No, she's not. She's afraid of what your relationship with her could do to you if you don't get help.

Her eyes widen and she looks down, the tears trickling down her cheeks again. "I'm sorry you feel that way."

"You told me you loved me."

"I do. Which is why I'm doing this. I love you too much to watch you self-destruct."

I'm not self-destructing, I had a slip up. I made a mistake. Like you've never made a mistake, Charlotte?

Don't say that. "But I need you."

"And I'll be there for you if you need me to go with you to meetings or—"

"Fuck that, Charlotte. I need YOU. Here. In my house with me. In *our* house, I bought for us across town." *You asked me to fucking marry you. We're having a baby! I'll be damned if we aren't living in the same house.*

"I want to be there too."

"Then why are you leaving?"

"I just suggested that maybe I should stay at Lauren's while you get yourself together. I went from a house I shared with Matt to a house I share with you and…I never even had a second to decompress."

"But you knew that," I argue. *That's kind of what happens when you leave your husband for another man, Charlotte.*

"I know."

"What's changed?"

"You." My palms begin to sweat, as I come to the startling realization that I don't think I'll be able to talk her into staying.

She's leaving me.

"I'm not, though. I'm the same man you fell for," I plead.

"Are you?" She looks up at me and it's like a punch to the gut.

"You are breaking my heart!" I yell, as I avoid her rhetorical question

"I know. I'm breaking mine too."

I kneel in front of her, taking her face in my hands. The tears are forming in my eyes, and I'm not even ashamed that I'm crying in front of her. *Something I was told never to do. Real men don't cry.* "Please, Charley. I'll do anything."

She puts her hands over mine, that are still cupping her cheeks, the tears in her eyes a direct reflection of my own. "I just want you to get help."

"I will. Tomorrow. *Now*. I'll go. Please. Just stay here. I need to know that you're here waiting for me. That you'll be here when I get out."

"I'll wait for you forever," she tells me softly, but it doesn't soothe my shattered heart like I hoped.

"Here?"

"Will…"

"Please. I've lost everything…I can't lose you too," I beg.

"Will, you've taught me so much in the past seven months. But most importantly, you've taught me how to be strong. How to be everything I need for myself. I can't be your only source of happiness, Will. I can't be the only thing in your life that you love. You don't speak to your family, I don't know that you have many friends, and you need other people in your life that support you. You taught me how to love myself after I'd spent so long doing just the opposite. But…do you love the person you see when you look in the mirror? Do you love him as much as I do? If you don't love yourself—how can you love me?"

"Charlotte…" I choke out, not wanting to go down this road with her.

"Your family hurt you—"

This was not the time to talk about them. "Not worse than what you're doing."

"Can't you see why I'm doing this?"

"No." *Forgive me for not thinking like a counselor as you stomp all over my heart.*

"Well…maybe one day, we'll look back on this together and you'll understand."

"I'm going to fight for you, Charlotte."

"I need you to fight for yourself, first."

CHAPTER
Twenty-Six

Charlotte

4:00 pm

I somehow manage to get myself out of Will's house before completely breaking down. I'm barely out of sight of his townhouse before I pull the car over, the tears clouding my vision.

Oh God, what did I do?!

I look in the rearview mirror, wondering if I should turn back.

No, Charlotte. This is for the best.

But he needs me.

As much as he thinks he needs alcohol?

Space is good. Space doesn't always translate to a breakup.

But he doesn't have anyone else but me.

That's the problem.

I shut my eyes and let out a scream so loud I wouldn't be surprised if Will could hear me. Once all of the air has left my lungs I stop, letting my head rest on the steering wheel before I make my way to the one person who'd always been there for me.

Hi, you've reached Lauren, I'm not here, but my phone is! Leave me some love!

I sigh, wondering where she is that she wouldn't be answering her phone. "Lo, it's Charley, I'll be at your place in approximately..." I look at the clock in my car, "thirty minutes. Please be home. Please have wine. Actually *fuck*. I can't have wine because I'm pregnant. FUCK! I didn't mean that. I mean, it's true but I didn't mean to blurt it out on the answering machine, I'm sure you'll never check. Please don't check this because I know you'll be pissed that this is how you found out that I'm pregnant. Pregnant with Will's baby and he's got a drinking problem. Like full fledged, and I just left his house, he thinks I've left him…and, oh my God, why am I still talking!? I'm coming over. I pray to God you're home, because I have a problem."

—

WILL

5:00 pm

It's been an hour since Charlotte left. An hour of me staring at the door that she walked out of. An hour of feeling a monumental hole in my chest where my heart used to be. A heart that a teary-eyed Charley left with. She didn't take all of her things with her, leaving me some shred of hope that maybe she was just scared and that this wasn't really over.

You think she could have hauled everything out of here in one trip? You know the girl's got a lot of shit.

I finally manage to pull myself off the floor, wiping the tears that had slid down my face for the millionth time and pick up the phone to call the one person who'd never forsaken me. I could sit here in the dark forever, feeling sorry for myself, or I could make a change. A change that would get me my girl back. And once I had her, I was *never* letting her go again.

"Tuck," I speak into the phone, "I have a problem."

—

Charlotte

5:30 pm

I had to pull over two more times, my body wracked with sobs as I drove to Lauren's. I was shocked that she had yet to call me back or even text me, making me wonder if she had to go into work and she wasn't near her phone. *Hopefully nothing is wrong.*

I pull into the parking lot of her apartment complex and make my way into the building, avoiding eye contact with everyone in the lobby including the guy at the front desk who's eyeing me as I sign in.

"Are you alright, miss?" he asks.

Not in the slightest. "Yes, I'm fine, thank you." I tell him with the most confidence I can muster. I'm practically flying down the hall the second I make it to her floor and pushing my key into her door. My lip trembles as I see boxes littering the floor, dishes out of her cabinets, and her bookshelf is almost completely empty.

She's already packing? She's leaving…this soon? My lip trembles thinking about how I am going to get through life with no Will *and* no Lauren.

Matt was right, I am going to be alone.

No! Will is going to make it right and we are going to be together.

"Lo?" I notice her cell phone lighting up on her table. *So, she's here. Maybe she's napping. Perfect, I can crawl into bed with her and sleep for the next week.* I spy her bedroom door slightly ajar at the end of the hallway and I move towards it, noting that she'd already taken a few pictures off the walls. I spy one of us from college and I stroke the frame. *Best Friends Forever* in script is inscribed along the metal frame and the tears flood my eyes again.

I miss you already, Lo.

I push open her bedroom door and my heart plummets. My eyes find what I assume to be a very naked Drew Montgomery spooning her as they sleep. They are both wrapped up in a sheet, his arms around her, and his face submerged in her hair. It's amazing how much he really does look like Will, and my heart skips a beat thinking about the man I wish was holding me while I slept. I look at Lauren, and she looks so peaceful, a serene smile on her face even in slumber.

It must be nice.

I close the door behind me, not wanting to disturb them and move into the living room. I would try and lie down but I'm worried that my mind isn't ready to be alone in the quiet with my thoughts. *I need background noise.*

I turn on the television and pull out my phone. I'm not surprised that I have a missed call from Will. *Well, several missed calls.*

The little red number next to the text message icon haunts me and before I can tell myself that it isn't a good idea, I've clicked on it.

———

Will: Please let me know you make it to Lauren's safely. I love you.
Me:Made it. I love you too.

I squeeze my eyes shut, knowing I shouldn't have done that as soon as I see the bubbles responding.

Will: I'm going to fix this. Take care of our little one.

I've known I was pregnant for literally six hours, and I've spent half of that time sobbing my eyes out over the father. *We never even celebrated.* I let out a breath just as a very naked Drew comes trudging out of their bedroom and into the kitchen. He's yet to notice me and I turn my eyes away from the kitchen so as to not get a glimpse of *all* of him. "Ummm, Drew?"

"Holy fuck, Charlotte!" He drops the bottle of water that he had pulled to his lips and opens the fridge so that I don't have a view of his dick. "What—what are you? Why are you here in the dark? Yo, Lauren!" he calls for her, and I pull my legs up to my chin and put my head on my knees as I try and stop the tears that are falling yet again. *God, I didn't even cry this much when I left Matt.*

"Drew, I—"

"Oh my God, Char!" Lauren bolts for me, her body wrapped in one of her cashmere robes and engulfs me in her arms. "What are you doing here? Not that I'm not thrilled to see you, but how long have you been here?"

"About ten minutes. I saw you…had a visitor." I nod to where Drew is standing, but he's gone, making me believe he had slipped out to hopefully put on clothes.

"Babe, why are you crying? What's going on?" She clasps her hand with mine and squeezes. "Did you and Will have a fight?"

"Sort of…" I whisper. "Lauren, everything is so…*hard!*"

"Okay, why don't we start from the beginning."

"Well, I'm pregnant."

"No shit!" I hear from the entryway, and I look up to see Drew staring at me with the largest smile on his face, completely dressed. "Congratulations, future sis! Why aren't we celebrating? Popping some bubbly…though none for you." He points at me. "Where's that asshole brother of mine? I—"

"Drew!" Lauren starts. "Can't you see that she is *clearly* not in the celebrating mood? Now either hush or leave." She turns to me. "Do you want him to leave?"

"Well…"

"Go!" she orders Drew immediately and he crosses his arms across his chest as he shoots her a look.

"I think it would be best if maybe you checked on your brother?" I tell him. *I'm not sure if he has anyone to turn to, and I don't want him wallowing in self-pity. I want someone who loves him. Even if Will doesn't think they do.*

"What…what exactly am I walking in to? Did you…did you leave him?"

"He thinks I did." I bite my bottom lip. "But I love him. I did it for us. I swear I just…"

"Okay," Lauren says wrapping her arms around me. "Drew, go and call me once you know what's going on."

"On it, boss." He salutes her and if that didn't make me smile, then him being two steps from the door, turning around and walking back towards us to plant a kiss on her lips followed by one on her nose, brings a smile to my face despite the tears leaking from my eyes. He looks at me. "I don't know what happened but…my brother loves you so much. You make him happier than…I've ever seen him." He smiles at me. "Congratulations."

"Thanks, Drew."

—

Will

6:00 pm

I ignore Drew's call for the fourth time in the span of five minutes. He is the last person I want to talk to. He is probably calling to see if I want to go to some bullshit nightclub. I'm lying on my bed flat on my back when the phone rings again. I'm hoping for either Charley or Tuck to call me back but this time it's my mother.

Fuck that.

I turn over, groaning, as I can already hear the passive aggressive voicemail she's about to leave me. *Well, since you can't be bothered to answer the phone…*

"How did I let my fucked up relationship with my parents ruin the one thing I love the most?" I say to myself as I sit up hearing my front door open. "Charlotte?" I call out, praying for her to manifest in my doorway. "Baby?"

I'm so sorry I left, Will. I love you so much, we'll work this out. I'm here, I'll never leave your side.

I can almost hear her voice saying the words. I stand up, my brain having convinced my body that Charlotte is on the premises when my brother appears in my doorway. I drop like a log to my bed.

"What are you doing here? I'm really not in the mood to go out or whatever it is you're hearing bugging me for."

I look up and he looks as if he's been punched and the wind knocked out of him. He looks forlorn, almost sad. "I just came to check on you, bro." He makes his way through my room slowly before standing up against the wall, his hands in his pockets. "You and Charlotte have a fight?"

How the hell does he know that? Do I look that bad?

I don't even have to look in the mirror to know the answer to that question.

"I don't want to talk about it."

"Well, get over it, because she's in hysterics at Lauren's house right now. What the hell happened? You're pregnant, shouldn't you be like over the moon right now? You don't think it's that asshole ex-husbands of hers, do you?"

The thought makes me enraged. "It's mine," I grit out.

He puts his hands up in defeat. "Then what happened? What's going on?"

"How the fuck do you even know?" *Did Lauren call Drew when Charley showed up? Did Charley call Drew?*

"I was at Lauren's when she showed up. I overheard them talking."

I nod in understanding. To be honest, I wasn't aware that they were still seeing each other that frequently. *Not that you ever know much about your brother and his sexcapades.*

"What else did she say?" *Does he know everything?*

"That's all. She didn't say what happened. She just asked if I could come check on you."

I breathe a sigh of relief. Not that I thought Charlotte would unleash all of my issues on him, but I'm grateful that at least he doesn't know much. "I'm good, Drew. I don't need anything."

He rubs the area behind his neck and gives me a worried look. "She said you think she left you."

What's there to think about? I begged you not to go, and you did anyway. "You don't see her here, do you? She *did* leave me."

"It didn't sound like she agreed with that."

"Fine, if you're determined to talk, you may want to sit."

"Sounds like there's a story, should I grab us some beers?"

I blanche, my blood feeling like ice in my veins. "You have no idea how bad I want to say yes."

———

Charlotte

6:00 pm

I'm lying flat on my back on Lauren's bed as she lies next to me, both of us silent. I imagine she's trying to let everything sink in. She has a glass of vodka next to her that she's been nursing since I started explaining. She'd said she *needed something stronger than wine for this* before she promptly poured it down the sink. She looks over at me and gives me a small smile. "How are you feeling?"

"Like shit."

"You did the right thing, Charley."

I turn my head towards her. "Did I?"

"Yes. Will needs help, and you're right he was so dependent on you to make him happy."

"Is that so wrong?" *I made him happy and he wanted to be with me, maybe I was overreacting.*

"No, but it could get exhausting. It's a lot to be everything for someone."

"He was everything for me."

She scoffs. "Um false. You have me."

"Not for much longer."

She rolls her eyes. "And you have hobbies. What does Will do besides work and worship the ground you walk on?"

"He plays golf and umm…" I sit up, trying to think about what he's done in the past few months besides dote over me.

"Drink, evidently," she says before she takes a sip of her drink.

"That's not funny," I warn her.

"I wasn't joking."

"Lo…" I shake my head. "How did everything get so screwed up? A year ago, today I was…"

"Way more miserable. Don't start."

"I just mean my life was less complicated."

"A loveless marriage probably does that. You were also bored out of your mind. At least now your life is interesting."

"Cute." I nod.

"Should we start thinking of names? Obviously, Lauren if it's a girl…" she jokes, and I smile at her attempt to make me feel better.

"He said if I left it was over." The tears spring to my eyes remembering his threat. *What if he makes good on it?*

"You know he didn't mean that."

"What if he did?"

"Will is angry and upset and he thinks you abandoned him, but eventually he will see that you did this for him. For *you*. For your family."

WILL

"What the fuck!?" Drew screams as he paces my bedroom. I lay on the bed with an icepack on my head as I try to numb the headache. "I should have known something was off when we went out last weekend. You *never* go that hard. What the fuck, man?"

"I know. I *know*." I pull off the icepack and stare at my angry brother who hasn't stopped yelling since I told him everything that has been happening the last two weeks.

"Fuck." He drops like a log next to me on my bed. "But she's a wreck, man. You know she loves you."

"The rational part of me knows that."

"And the irrational?" he asks.

"The irrational wants me to go over to Lauren's and drag her out of there and bring her back here where she belongs."

"It sounds like she just wants you to get yourself together."

"Thank you, Dr. Obvious. It's not that simple. And you need a support system. One she up and bailed from."

"She's not bailing, Will."

"And how would you know?"

"Because I know what it looks like when someone bails, and that's not it. She knew if she stayed you wouldn't change, or it would be a temporary fix, and then you'd fall back into old patterns. She had to show you she was serious. You're hurting yourself, Will, and she doesn't want to sit around and watch you do that. That's not bailing. That's love."

"You would know what it looks like when someone bails," I snort as I get up and make my way out of my bedroom.

I can hear him right on my heels. "What the fuck does that mean?"

"Forget it, you hungry? I haven't eaten today, and I'm fucking starving."

"No Will, what does that even mean?"

"Pizza okay?"

"WILL!" he screams, and I turn to look at him.

"What?"

He's silent, and it's as if I don't need to answer, because his face falls. "I didn't bail on you."

"Oh? What would you call it?"

"Fed up with your bullshit to be honest."

"Excuse me?"

"I never did understand your issue with me. It was like you hated me so much, and I never understood why. So finally, I just stopped trying." He shrugs. "You didn't try either, so I figured that was that. Only in the last year or so have you started coming around, and my guess is that has to do with Charlotte. I saw a change in you. She made you happy. You should have seen your face that first time we went to that bar all those months ago. I knew *then*. I knew there was someone."

"I didn't hate you, Drew," I murmur as I lean on the counter, putting my head in my hands. "I envied you."

"Envied me?" I look up and he's equal parts confused and horrified. "Why would you envy me? You have a badass house, and a job that you love, helping people. You have a woman that loves you."

"I don't have those things anymore."

"You have them, they're just on hiatus. But what could you have to be jealous of?"

"All those years ago, I mean. I envied you because you had the one thing I didn't have. The one thing I'll never have."

"What is that? A big dick?" He smiles.

I raise an eyebrow at him and shake my head. "No. Mom and Dad's approval."

"Mom and Dad? Like...*our* mom and dad?"

What the fuck? God, he really is clueless. "Yes, who the fuck do you think?"

He drops onto one of my stools that line my marble bar. He doesn't say anything for a second and his face is one of pure realization as if all it took was my words for him to see things in a new light. "Will..."

"You are Mom and Dad's favorite. The favorite Montgomery child." I rest my arms on the counter, as I stare into similar eyes. "You were right, I did push you away. I hated you when we were kids. You always got your way, they always took *your* side. You were the model child, the first born, I was the second born that never lived up to you. I lived in your shadows for...my whole life."

"That's not true. Mom and Dad were thrilled when you became a doctor."

"What parent wouldn't? It took years and three degrees, one of which they didn't even see me receive, for them to recognize me. Do you know what that does to a person? Do you know what that kind of rejection did to *me*? It's why I can't handle Charlotte walking out right now. It feels like everyone else that's left me, because I wasn't perfect."

"Charlotte didn't leave you because you aren't perfect, Will. She left you because you need help. She left you because she chose your child over you...and herself. And I wouldn't necessarily call it *leaving* you."

"What would you call it?" I clench my fists. *She left me, stop fucking sugar coating it.*

"Space."

"Well, that's not what I want!" My voice booms through my kitchen, reverberating off the walls.

"What about what you *need*?"

I'm about to speak when I hear my front door opening again and my ears perk up immediately. "Charley?"

Charlotte

8:00 pm

"I should call him." I set down the sausage pizza I suddenly craved and look up at Lauren.

"And say what?" Lauren grabs my phone before I can pick it up and sets it in her lap, out of reach.

"That I love him. That this isn't over. He thinks I left him!"

"Drew says he's handling it, and that he's trying to talk some sense into him. He says his therapist showed up?"

"Tucker?" I groan, letting my head fall into my hands. "God, he probably hates me."

"Why would he hate you?"

"I don't know, breaking his protégé? How the hell should I know? Will is so loyal to him, I can't imagine the feeling isn't mutual."

"He's a *therapist*. I'm sure he understands."

"I want him to know that I'm still here, even though it may not feel like it."

"You're supposed to be giving him space." She raises an eyebrow at me.

"It doesn't mean I don't want to be supportive."

She grabs my hand and squeezes, "Char, one day he will see that you did this for him."

I frown, knowing she's right, but hating that he doesn't realize that *now*. Now, he thinks I've abandoned him like everyone else in his life. "And until then?"

"Until then, you focus on keeping that little one healthy." She cocks her head to the side. "I swear did you get pregnant just to try and keep me here?"

I smile, letting my hands find my flat stomach that I can't wait to get bigger. *I'm having a baby!* A warm sensation spreads throughout my body and I realize I haven't really allowed myself to think about how much my life is about to change. I shut my eyes picturing a baby that is equal parts myself and Will. A little boy or girl with Will's piercing blue eyes. His eyes, his nose, his... heart. The man with the kindest heart I'd ever met. The man that loves me with every inch of it.

He understands, Charley.

CHAPTER

Twenty-Seven

WILL

It had been two days since I'd seen Charley. Two days without seeing her smile or holding her in my arms—or making love to her. It had been almost *two weeks* since I'd done that, and my body had definitely taken notice. I rub my dick through my pants, as a vision of her underneath me floods my brain.

Fuck.

We'd spoken on the phone a few times, and I'd let her know that I would be spending the week in a rehabilitation center of sorts. I wasn't thrilled at the idea, knowing just how those facilities can be, having worked at the very one I was attending, but I needed to turn my life around, and not just for Charlotte.

But not just for me either.

There's a baby now.

A baby that will need their father, *sober.*

"*When do you leave?*" she speaks softly and slowly, as if she *can't get the words out.*

"*Monday.*"

"*Can…can I see you before you go?*" she stutters slightly.

"*I would like that.*" *A feeling of hope runs through me and I can't help the small smile. I miss her so fucking much.*

"*How are you getting there?*"

"*Drew offered to drive.*"

"*Oh?*"

"*Yes, I've been forced into a bit of a breakthrough,*" I chuckle.

Drew and I had sat on my kitchen floor, a large pizza between us, and talked about everything. And nothing. It had been unreal just how much I'd missed in my brother's life.

Who knew that he'd recently started doing yoga—with Lauren.

That he was training to run a half marathon—with Lauren.

That he thought he might be in love—with Lauren.

I felt like an asshole for not being more involved in his life. For not caring enough to try and have a relationship with him because of what had happened when we were kids.

We're adults now, and I always urged people to try and repair their broken childhood relationships once they were in adolescence.

It's Monday and I haven't heard from Charley. *Did she decide not to come?*

No, she wouldn't just not show up. She would at least call.

I glance at my watch. I asked her to come earlier than Drew, so we could have a few moments alone before I have to leave.

Where is she?

Charley is always on time. It's one of the things I always admired about her, and not for the same reasons I was punctual as well. She wasn't brought up on waspy cotillions and "proper etiquette classes." No that was me, and the thing about being someone that grew up with that chain around your neck disguised as an eighteenth century social construct was you always recognized when someone else had the same past.

No, Charlotte was on time because she genuinely cared about people's time and not because she had some deep instilled fear of bringing shame to the family name.

God, no wonder I drink.

The sound of a key in my front door snaps me from my thoughts and I stand up as I prepare to see the love of my life for the first time in two days.

Please God, don't be Drew.

She appears in the doorway like a vision and my heart stops. Her brown hair is wild, like when she showers and lets it air dry, giving her a beachy look. Her skin is completely clear, and free from makeup and I wonder if it's because she's worried that she'll cry. Her eyes are red and already a bit glassy. My eyes trail down her body, fixating on her stomach as if in the last two days there would have been a change to show her pregnancy. *Our* pregnancy.

"Charley," I whisper and it's as if it sparks something inside of her because she runs towards me. I meet her halfway, scooping her into my arms as she breaks down. Her legs immediately wrap around my waist as her face presses into my neck. I wrap my arms around her tight, feeling her sobs against my chest. "Shhh, baby. Please don't cry. I'm sorry. I fucked up," I whisper in her ear as I lift her into my arms and carry her to the couch.

She doesn't say anything just continues to cry against my chest, the sobs wracking her body. I pull her head away and cup her face gently, wiping the tears away despite the constant flow of fresh ones and her continuous hiccups. She's straddling my lap, and despite this position, there's nothing sexual about it. I rub her back gently as her sobs subside, before pulling her back to look at her.

I see the love she has for me underneath all of the pain in her eyes. "Thank you," I whisper at the same time she whispers, "I'm sorry."

"No. Charlotte, don't be sorry." I stroke her face gently. "You did what you had to do," I tell her. "It knocked some sense into me. I needed a wake-up call. I was spiraling." I shake my head. "I know the signs. I could see the signs but I ignored them."

The tears are sliding down her cheeks as she sniffles every few seconds. "I am so proud of you."

"You are?" I don't even attempt to hide my shock. Her feelings and opinion of me mean the world to me and hearing her words makes my heart soar.

"Yes. So proud. You're the best man I've ever known, and loving you has been the best thing that's ever happened to me. I don't regret one second of our story."

I narrow my eyes slightly as I recall everything that's happened in our relationship. "Not even one?" A low chuckle escapes me and she rolls her eyes at my dark humor.

A frown finds her perfect face and I regret being the one who put it there, making her think about the past. "I regret anything I've done that's hurt you."

"You did what you had to do for all of us. I understand, Charley. I'm sorry about keeping this from you for so long. For my behavior the last two weeks…all of it. I let you down."

"Don't say that." Her words waver, the emotions running through her, affecting her voice. She looks down at her stomach. "We both love you so much."

I touch her stomach gently, the first time I've done so since she told me we were having a baby. "I can't believe we're having a baby." She shivers as I reach under her shirt and stroke her bare skin and the feeling of her trembling in my arms sends a spark to my cock.

She must feel it too because she gives me a shy smile. "I'm assuming we don't have time for…"

"Maybe if you were on time," I tease. God knows I want to take her upstairs and have my way with her, but Drew will be here any minute, and I'm due at the facility at nine am. My heart begins to race as I think about being away from Charlotte for another seven days. Not making love to her for yet another week. *I can't wait until this is all over.* I feel like the hurdles that Charlotte and I have had to jump over have been endless in our quest to be together.

But it's worth it.

It is worth it.

"Sorry, I was late. I was…a mess this morning."

I bring her head back to my chest as her lip begins to tremble.

"It's going to be fine, baby," I whisper in her ear. "I see you brought your stuff?" I look at the small bag she took with her that first day when she left.

"Yes." She follows my gaze and clears her throat. "I thought I could...stay here while—."

"Yes," I interrupt her. "Stay here."

She nods before resting her head against my chest again. I don't know how long we stay like this, with her in my arms, me stroking her head, and her gripping my biceps like she never wants to let go. But soon, I hear a key in the door, and just like that, our time is over.

Charlotte

The ride to the rehab facility is quiet. Too quiet. I think even Drew feels uncomfortable at some point because he turns the radio on for at least some white noise. Will is seated in the back of Drew's Mercedes next to me in order to give us our last few moments of closeness. I lift my head from his shoulder when I feel his finger drawing circles on the inside of my palm.

"I'll call you when I can. And you can come on Thursday...if you want. Apparently, that's their family day."

"I'll be there." The idea of needing space went out the window the second he told me he was getting help. I smile at him, and he places a kiss on my forehead. He holds his lips there a beat longer than usual and I wonder if he's putting up a brave front for me.

The rest of the ride is silent, my head on his shoulder and our hands clasped. When the car slows to a stop I feel a full panic attack coming on, but through some deep breathing I manage to stop it. He helps me out of the car and presses a kiss to my lips when I hear a throat being cleared. Will's lips move from mine, much to my disappointment, when I see a man in a dark brown sports coat and jeans walking towards us. I furrow my brow into a scowl at this man's intrusion of our privacy while we're trying to say goodbye. *Can you give us a minute? He's not even on the premises yet, good God.*

"Tuck," he nods at the older man and my eyes widen. *His therapist?* His eyes seem to be fixed on me and I give him a small smile. "This is Charlotte Pierce, my beautiful fiancée. Charley, this is my mentor, Mitch Tucker."

He smiles a warm smile at me. "It's very nice to meet you. Will speaks very highly of you. I am sure you will be the main focus of his time here."

I don't know if that's a good thing or a bad thing given that the main point of this stint in rehab is for him to work through the issues lurking below the surface. *Which brings me to a nagging question, am I an issue?*

"Being a better man for her is the number one priority," Will says and I look up at him.

"You're already the best," I whisper.

"Well, we want it to stay that way," Tucker interjects.

At this point, Drew gets out of the car and makes his way to where we are, probably wondering if someone needed to tell Tuck to give us some space.

Which I would not mind in the slightest. I know he means well, but can he give us a minute?

"Drew, just...check in on my girl every once in a while?" Will looks at his brother, and I'm happy to see the start of their relationship being repaired after so long.

"You got it. Everything is going to be fine. You go and get yourself better. I'll watch out for these two while you're gone."

Tuck's eyes snap to me immediately in question and then back to Will. Drew puts a hand over his mouth and then looks at me and then at Tucker. "Shit, you hadn't told him? Were you not planning to?"

Will shakes his head at him and rolls his eyes. "I was planning to."

"Well, we have even more to talk about than I thought." Tucker looks at me. "Congratulations," he nods, "on the baby…and the divorce, of course."

Will looks as if he could ring his neck. My face falls even more hearing the judgment laced through his words, and Will tightens his hold on my hand.

"Watch it," he growls, and I can sense the tension working through his back and shoulders instantly. "Give us a second, Tuck."

"Will, the sooner—" he starts, when I feel Will tense next to me.

"ONE SECOND," he raises his voice. His posture is rigid as he stares Tucker down.

Tucker puts his arms up in defense and takes a few steps back. Drew gets back in the car leaving me alone with Will. "I'm sorry about that," he whispers as he cups my face, and his lips find my right cheek, then my nose, then my left cheek before he rubs his nose against mine. "I have to go."

"I know." My eyes find the ground sadly.

He lifts my chin gently. "I love you."

A smile plays on my lips hearing his words. "I love you, too."

He leans in to kiss me and what I expect to be a short, sweet kiss, turns into a kiss that I feel in every bone in my body. His hand finds the car behind me, effectively boxing me in as his other hand weaves through my hair, and his tongue strokes against mine. I know this kiss, I love these kisses. These are the kisses that come just before we make love. The kisses we have *while* we make love. As much as I love this kiss now, I'm disappointed that this one in particular is leading to nothing. *Space actually*. It's leading to a week of space.

When I pull apart, his pupils are dilated, and his mouth a bit swollen from my nibbling on his lip. I stroke his jaw, and he kisses my open palm. "Get in the car, Charley. If you don't, I won't be able to walk away from you."

"But…"

"Please," he pleads.

I want to tell him that it's just as hard for me to walk away, but I know between the two of us I have to be the stronger one right now.

I give him one final peck before I slide into Drew's car. He waves at me once and I wave back, the feeling of devastation and an overall sense of dread creeping through my body by the second. I stare out the window as we pull away from him and Tucker. I keep staring as we pull out of the parking lot. Finally, when the facility is completely out of sight, I pry my gaze away from the window and face forward. We are barely back on the highway before the tears that I had been holding in since we got in the car start moving slowly down my cheeks.

CHAPTER

Charlotte

Tuesday: Day Two

I T TOOK EVERYTHING OUT OF ME NOT TO CALL HIM LAST NIGHT. I wanted to talk to him, reassure him that everything would be okay. I wanted him to reassure *me* that everything would be okay. So then, I wrote him a letter. A really long letter. A letter that pushed me to tears as I wrote the words of how much I loved him, how happy I was that I had found him despite the circumstances.

The sun had barely risen on Tuesday before I had the phone to my ear dialing the facility. I wasn't sure when the hours were, but I figured at very least someone could tell me when I could call back.

"Yes, I do see that you are at the top of Dr. Montgomery's emergency contacts. We will call you if anything happens. Don't worry," she'd said, her voice chirpy and perky.

"Wait wait wait, that's not why I'm calling. I'm calling to talk to him."

"Oh, I'm sorry Ms. Pierce, he is not permitted to use the phone at this time."

"He's voluntarily admitted!"

"Yes, but he still has to adhere to the rules whilst he's here."

"Fine. When can I speak to him?"

"The times that they are permitted to use the phone are between four and six pm."

"Great."

"But I suggest that you wait for him to call you, Ms. Pierce. They aren't always available to talk during that time if they're in a session."

"I'll call at four," I'd said, not bothering to wait for her reply before I angrily hit the end call button.

It's now, finally, four in the afternoon and I'm calling again in hopes that I can talk to him.

"Yes, I see you called earlier as well," a new woman says, her voice riddled with condescension. "Dr. Montgomery is not taking any phone calls right now."

"What? That's impossible. He will want to talk to me." *What if something is wrong...? Will would never just not take my calls.* The thought makes me panic. *What if they're doing something to him like some batshit crazy, insane asylum, scary movie nonsense?*

"Ms. Pierce, there's a note in his file that explicitly says he's not taking any calls today."

"Today?"

"Yes, ma'am."

I sigh. "Fine, when should I call back."

"Phone calls are allowed between four—"

"Bullshit!" I exclaim.

"Ma'am..."

I pinch the bridge of my nose, feeling my pressure rise slow and steadily. "Stop ma'aming me! Tuck...is Dr. Tucker there?"

"I'm not authorized—"

"THEN LET ME SPEAK TO SOMEONE WHO IS AUTHORIZED!"

"Please don't yell at me, ma'am. I really can't help you."

"Then what are you there for!? Listen, I'm pregnant," I bark into the phone. I hate that I have to pull this card, but I need answers and I need them yesterday. "I am pregnant and I know Will would very much like to speak to the mother of his child. Can you please..." I sigh feeling utterly defeated. "I just want to make sure he's okay."

There's silence on the other end before she begins to speak. "I can page one of the on-call doctors and have them call you. My eyes widen as I feel like I'm finally getting somewhere. "Tonight?"

"Yes, ma'am, tonight."

"Thank you...and...I'm sorry I yelled at you."

"Not a problem, ma'am. You aren't the first and I'm sure you won't be the last."

I hang up the phone and let out a breath. The feeling that I'll finally get to talk to Will has me the most relaxed since before I dropped him off and before I know it I'm asleep.

———

Sometime that same night, I shoot up in bed, the feeling of anxiety coursing through me at lightning speed.

What time is it? What day is it!?

I look at my phone that has a text from Drew and Lauren both, but no missed calls. *I've been out for five hours?* It was now nearing ten pm and I still haven't heard from anyone.

Should I call again?

I shake my head, knowing that I'm clearly not getting anywhere so I call probably the only other person he'd willingly take a phone call from.

"Drew," I say into the phone before he even says *hello*.

"Hey lady. I was just about to call you. How are you doing?"

"Terrible. Listen, have you talked to Will?"

"No...I haven't. But I figured he was using up all his free time talking to you."

"No! He's not calling me. I can't get him on the phone. Drew, what if something's wrong?" The panic is evident in my voice, bordering on shrill.

"Okay okay, breathe. Stress isn't good when you're pregnant, right?" My hands instinctively go to my stomach and I stroke the skin. *It's going to be okay, little one. Daddy is fine.*

"Not being able to get in touch with the father isn't good when you're pregnant, Drew."

"Touché, okay let's just call."

"I keep getting the Goddamn runaround."

"God Charley, how many times have you called?"

"Just…twice."

"Alright, do you have the number? We can three way call. Just don't fly off the handle."

I breathe a sigh of relief. "I won't!"

"Right. I can hear the anxiety in your voice."

I make a face at the phone as I hear him click off of our call to dial the facility. The next thing I know I hear the phone ringing.

"Atlanta Rehabilitation Facility, this is April."

"Hi, April, my name is Andrew Montgomery, my brother was admitted there yesterday, and I'm just checking on him. Is there any way I can speak to him?"

"Unfortunately, sir, it's after hours." I clench my hand around my phone, squeezing it harder. *I am going to fucking lose it.*

"I know, I know the hours are from four to six, but I was hoping you could help me out? His pregnant fiancée is here with me and she's about losing her mind that no one is letting her talk to him. Five minutes that's all I'm asking."

"Well…" April trails off.

"Come on, April…you sound like a nice lady. Help us out."

I can almost see Drew's flirty grin through the phone and I roll my eyes. *Do what you gotta do, just let me talk to my man.*

"Okay let me see what I can do. Can I place you on hold?"

"Yes, ma'am. I do appreciate you. William Montgomery is his name."

I definitely hear a giggle before hold music comes over the

phone. "Okay, well I can't do that," I say into the phone referring to his ways of getting what he wants through flirting with women.

"You probably sounded like a crazy person when you called too, didn't you?"

"Did not!"

"Did you yell?"

"Once. But she deserved it. And I apologized."

I'm sure Drew is about to say something smart back when April returns to the line. "Hi, Mr. Montgomery, it appears that Dr. Montgomery has gone to bed."

"Okay…April, is there any way we can wake him up? His fiancée is very worried…she might go into labor soon."

Smart! Way to go, Drew!

"Umm…Mr. Montgomery, his file says that his fiancée is newly pregnant and emergency calls outside of the permitted times can only be as a direct result of the hospitalization of Ms. Pierce, or any members of the immediate Montgomery family. Is…Ms. Pierce in the hospital?"

I hear him sigh in defeat. "No, she's not."

"Then…I'm afraid I can't help you, Mr. Montgomery."

"Someone told me that they were going to call me….I think her name was Betty?" I interject, completely fed up with this bullshit.

"Umm, who is this?"

"Ms. Pierce, obviously," I growl.

"Okay, Ms. Pierce. I don't know anything about that, it's possible that they haven't gotten around to returning your call? The on-call doctors are very busy with on-site patients. They don't have time to return every phone call the same day."

I put my head in my hand. *This is a nightmare.*

"Okay, so when would you suggest we call back?" Drew asks.

"Tomorrow between four and six is the best time to get your brother on the phone."

I fall backwards on the bed letting out a loud groan. "Oh, for the love of God."

"I'm sorry, but it's really all I can suggest."

"Fine. Wait!" I say. "Family Day…that's Thursday right?"

"Yes ma'am."

"What time? I haven't been able to talk to him, so I don't know."

"Noon until three."

"Great, thanks."

They better hope they let me talk to him before then, or else I am going to cause the biggest scene of my life.

———

Wednesday: Day Three

I am a nervous wreck. It's been three days since I talked to Will. Three goddamn days. Two nights I've gone to bed without hearing his voice. Last night, I stared at the ceiling for the majority of the night after Drew and I called, until I finally got up out of bed and started reading the fourth book I've downloaded since he left.

I've stress baked, cleaned, started researching ideas of where we could travel to, ordered almost two hundred dollars' worth of baby books on Amazon and Barnes and Noble. I've done everything to keep my mind off of the fact that I haven't talked to Will in over forty-eight hours.

Maybe if I could just get Tucker on the phone. He could tell me what is going on. But how do I even find him? I pull up my phone and Google his name and I'm pleased to see there's only one Doctor in Atlanta with that name. I dial his office and I'm met with someone I assume to be his secretary. *Great. More runaround.*

"Dr. Tucker is actually out of office for the week, is there something that another Doctor can help you with?"

This is a complete nightmare. Why can't I just wake up? "No, I really need Dr. Tucker. If he does return to his office at any point, please have him call Charlotte Pierce. Please do not pass along my message to any other doctor. Only Dr. Tucker."

"Yes, Ms. Pierce. We take confidentiality requests very seriously."

"Thank you. My phone number is 404-354-0981."

"I will pass along the message."

"Great, thank you." I fall back onto the pillows and hang up the phone, only to stare at it. *I should call again...*

"God dammit. It's not four pm," I say in a high-pitched voice as I mimic all three of the women who refuse to put me through to Will.

What if I just went...No, tomorrow is family day. You can go tomorrow.

Lauren has been calling me for two days so I'm not totally surprised when she shows up at Will's door with her hands on her hips and her head cocked to the side. "What the fuck?" she growls as she walks by me. "Why aren't you answering my calls?" She moves past me.

"Sorry, I'm just...a wreck." I put my head in my hands as I collapse on the couch in a heap. "I am literally one second from going off the deep end. I can't get him on the phone. I've been calling since yesterday. If I knew I wasn't going to be allowed to talk to him I could have prepared myself for it. But Will said we would be able to communicate at certain times. And now he's not talking to anyone."

"It's only been what—three days? Maybe they told him the first few days no phone access?"

"Well, he should have told them that someone should reach out to his pregnant fiancée that would worry about him, if that's the case." I'm silent for a moment as I prepare myself to voice my fears aloud for the first time. "Lauren, what if something is wrong? What if they're hurting him or...brainwashing him that this is all my fault? God, what if this is all my fault." I put my hands over my eyes as I feel the tears forming.

"Charley, this is absolutely not your fault." She pulls my hands from my eyes. "I don't know what made Will start drinking like that, but you know it's not because of you. He worships the ground you walk on, Char. And he just wants to get better, for you and the baby. Even if you convinced him not to turn himself in, and he was still practicing, the guilt could have eaten away at him."

I let out a sigh. "I'm calling again at four."

———

Despite Lauren's visit, I am still on edge most of the day. *Maybe I'm overreacting. Lauren is probably right. They told him that they didn't want him making any calls and just hadn't gotten around to calling me to let me know.* I purse my lips together. *Assholes. I'm not asking for a long phone call.* It's four pm as I settle in to call again.

"It's Ms. Pierce, *again*," I say, recognizing Betty's voice from the two days before.

"Hi, Ms. Pierce. You still haven't spoken with Dr. Montgomery?"

"Nope," I say. "Can I please speak with him, now?"

"Hold on for just a moment."

Lauren gives me two thumbs up and walks out of the living room towards the kitchen in an effort to give me some privacy.

"Ms. Pierce," I hear a familiar voice, but not the *right* familiar voice.

"Dr. Tucker?"

"Yes, hi, how are you?"

"I've been better, Doctor. I've been trying to talk to Will. I even called your office to see if you could help."

"Yes, I got the message. My secretary thought it might be important. You sounded…anxious."

"I am. I want to speak to Will, please."

"Ms. Pierce," he sighs and I immediately feel my palms begin to sweat. "A few of the other doctors here, and myself, have advised based on our evaluation that perhaps communication between you two isn't best."

"Wait…what?"

"Charlotte, it's obvious that Will loves you very much. We aren't in any way, shape, or form suggesting that you aren't good for him, please don't misread what I'm saying. But collectively we all want him to get better, to not want to use alcohol as a crutch."

"Okay…"

"And we've noticed some…triggers in him. Ones I hadn't caught onto because I wasn't seeing him as much when you began your relationship."

"I—you're saying *I'm* a trigger?"

"When someone is in rehab, we try to prevent any excess, aggressive stimulation."

"I'm aggressive?"

"His feelings for you are quite…strong."

"I'm aware. The feeling is pretty mutual. So, let me get this straight—you're hypothesizing that our love…his love for me caused him to drink?"

"We aren't saying one is a direct correlation to the other."

"What are you saying?"

"Charley, he wasn't drinking like this until just after he started seeing you and your husband. It was exacerbated after his license was suspended."

"So, it's my fault?"

"Not at all."

"But I'm a direct cause of it. So, what's going to happen when he's out?"

"The good news is we are early in the process. While he's been drinking more over the past several months, it does appear it was mostly in social settings. The last two to three weeks is where we see the problems."

I'm silent, stunned, speechless. *So, I was right.* "I can't even speak to him for just a moment, to tell him I love him?"

"Charley…he knows you love him."

"But I want to hear his voice."

"Do you want to hear his voice more than you want him home?"

"Of course, not but…"

"He's progressing really well already. He's just not…he's not in a place to handle talking to you right now. We have also noticed some signs of codependency, and we are thinking a week will do you both some good."

Codependency? We're in love and yes, it's intense, but who are you to fucking judge? "He said that?"

"Of course not, he's climbing the walls in here to talk to you."

"Is…he's okay, right?"

"Yes, he's fine, Ms. Pierce. Maybe a little homesick. But he knows that this is necessary."

I wipe at the constant flow of tears. "So, I can't come tomorrow?"

"We won't be allowing visitors tomorrow."

"None? Not even Drew?"

"Ms. Pierce, Drew is another one of his triggers so no, he wouldn't be allowed either."

"What kind of bullshit are you telling him? We're his family! You can't tell me we're triggers because we love him too much. What kind of quack are you?! And how can you even be telling me this, aren't you breaking doctor patient confidentiality?"

"I have in writing a signed form from Will authorizing me to speak with you on any and all matters."

"How is Drew a trigger?"

"There are…issues from their childhood that Will hasn't completely worked through."

I guess what he was telling me affects him more than he let on.

"Can he still come home Monday?" I whisper, fearing that they're about to tell me they want to keep him for the month, which I read online was a real thing.

"That is the plan we have in place. We are on track for that."

"If I send him something, can he have it?"

"Like what?"

"A letter?"

"How is that any different from talking to him?"

"So, he's just supposed to think that I've forgotten about him? That I don't care at all? That I haven't been trying to talk to him?"

"He knows, Ms. Pierce. He knows you've been calling."

At this point, Lauren finds her seat on the couch next to me, and gives me a sad smile, no doubt having heard my half of this conversation. She grabs my free hand and squeezes it. "Will you tell him…that I love him?"

"That I can do."

"And that I'll be there on Monday."

"Yes."

"Okay and—"

"Miss Pierce, I suggest you get some rest. Everything is going to be okay."

"Fine."

"Have a good night, Charlotte."

"Same, Doc," I say before I hang up and Lauren's arms are around me instantly as the tears stream down my face.

CHAPTER
Twenty-Nine

WILL

Thursday: Day Four

"**A**RE YOU OUT OF YOUR MIND!?" I SCREAM. "YOU CAN'T TELL her she can't come here. It is literally the ENTIRE point of having a Family Day. It's not just for the people in here, but for the people OUT THERE too!" I shout as I point out the window.

Tuck and Patterson have just sat me down to let me know that they'd informed Charley that I wasn't permitted to have any visitors. *This is on top of the rule that I can't even speak to her on the phone.*

"Will, I know that this is difficult to process, but as we've told you when we discussed the phone calls. We need to avoid any aggressive triggers until we get to the root of the issue and why you've returned to alcohol for a second time," Tuck says.

"Charley is not the problem," I grit out, my hand flexing angrily. *Don't come within swinging range of me Tuck, I mean it.*

"Problem is not the appropriate word. But she is the catalyst."

"This is bullshit. You can't keep me from her."

"Actually Montgomery, we can," Patterson interjects. "And we are. You entered voluntarily, but you know how it works even with voluntary admission."

"It's one week, Will," Tuck tells me, and I resist the urge to punch him square in the face, completely fed up with his *I'm on your side* rouse.

"What are you even telling her, *Mitch*?" Patients aren't technically supposed to refer to the doctors by their first names, but I'm sick of them acting like they don't know who the fuck I am in the medical community.

"I…told her what she needed to know."

"Which was?" *Don't beat around the fucking bush.*

"That the focus is to make sure that you don't return to alcohol. That once you leave you don't return to old habits. We need you focused and we don't need any distractions."

"She's not a distraction."

"You've certainly been very focused on her and when you could talk to her since you've arrived," Patterson says.

"Because she's my fiancée and I worry about her."

"Kip, I have it from here," Tuck says effectively dismissing Patterson. He nods before finding the exit.

As soon as the door closes behind him, he unleashes his thoughts on me in a very unprofessional manner. "You are obsessed with this woman, Will. She is absolutely the reason why you've started drinking again! How the hell can't you see that?!" I can literally feel the daggers coming out of my eyes in response to Tuck's outburst but he continues despite my deadly look. "You broke up a fucking marriage. AS. A. MARRIAGE COUNSELOR. You mentioned in your first evaluation that you started drinking earlier this year, around the time you started seeing Charley."

I feel my palms begin to sweat hearing him say her name.

"Do you really not see the correlation? You couldn't have her so you drank, then you had her but not on your terms. We both know lack of control is one of your triggers, so again, you drank. Are you REALLY telling me that you haven't put it all together yet? You haven't connected point A to point B? You wanted to be with her, you couldn't be with her—SO. YOU. DRANK. The question I want to know is HOW DO WE AVOID THIS IN THE FUTURE?!" he yells. "I'm not doing this with you every time you throw a temper tantrum for not getting your way, Will!"

I stare at him hard, my cold eyes angry and unforgiving. "How fucking dare you!"

"Will—" he sighs. "You and I both know, I'm not just your counselor in here. I won't sugarcoat it for you." I don't bother to listen to anything he has to say before I'm out the door slamming it behind me.

———

I'm hitting the pavement hard, one foot after the other as I run my eighth lap around the track indicating that I've hit two miles. If only I could hop over the fence in the distance and run home. I slow my feet to a stop and check the stopwatch on my wrist missing the Rolex that usually sits there instead. *Leave all valuables at home* is one of the rules that they stress the most before entering any rehabilitation facility. I shake my head as I think about the most precious of my valuables sitting at home probably thinking that I'm just avoiding her calls.

How could Tuck say all of that? He doesn't even know her!

But he does know you, My subconscious bites back.

"You ready to sit down and talk? Or are you just going to avoid me and spend the morning running laps around his track?"

I look over to see Tuck leaning against the rail separating the track from the stands and I feel a fiery rage building underneath my skin.

"Fuck you, Tuck," I growl, the last four days have been nothing short of what feels like a hostile takeover of my life; something I'd only witnessed in extreme situations. I've been drinking heavily again for the past two weeks and they're treating me as if I've had a bottle a day for the last forty years. Despite the issues that I've had with alcohol before, this is extreme. I look down at my watch.

Twelve minutes, not bad. How fast I can run a mile feels like the only thing that's gotten better since I've been here.

"I'm sorry for losing it like that," Tuck says and he shakes his head. "I just want what's best for you. I'm disappointed that you're in this situation…not just the alcohol, but getting suspended, getting involved with a patient…I thought you knew better."

"Save me the lecture, Tuck. I'm not in the mood." *Especially after you unleashed all that bullshit on me this morning.*

"I shouldn't have said what I said, but…you know, deep down, you're drinking again because of some deep-rooted issue that stems from her."

I scoff. "No. I was drinking because I lost my job."

He interrupts. "Because you were sleeping with her."

"It doesn't make it her fault."

"I know that, and I know you believe that, but somewhere inside of you…you may be fearing the resentment that may come later. The resentment towards her for losing your job even though it's not her fault—entirely. You did take a lot of risks in being with her—continuing your relationship. Maybe that's what's led you back to alcohol. Whatever it is, we need to exorcise it."

My hands are on my hips as I pace back and forth, trying to calm my racing heart.

"And you think keeping me away from Charley is helping? Not letting me talk to her? Not letting her come and visit me here?" I rub my head thinking about the screaming match from this morning. "You've never been like this. You've always had my back—"

"You think I don't have it now?"

"Why can't I talk to her? What if she needs me or something's wrong?"

"Will, she's fine. I relayed everything she said last night on the phone. She's okay. She misses you and she loves you. We've talked about why we advised severing communication."

"Because of this bullshit you're trying to pass off as your evaluation? Thinking that she's a trigger?"

"Will—" he starts.

I raise my hand, effectively cutting him off. *I can't listen to this shit anymore.* "No. Okay? I'm done. I'm fed up with this. It's like you're all in cahoots to punish me a step further than the suspension. I don't want to hear anything else from you or anyone here. Just leave me be for the next three days."

I begin running again, and hear him call after me. I let my mind drift back to the session on the second day where they informed me that they hadn't been letting Charley's calls through and that there would be no communication between us for the next five days. My blood begins to boil as I pick up the pace.

Two days prior:

"How did you sleep, Will?" Tuck asks as he sits across from me, sliding his frames over his eyes.

"As expected," I sigh as I run a hand over my face. It's been a little under twenty-four hours since I've seen or spoke to Charley and I already miss her. "Before we start today, can I have my phone back? I want to call Charley."

"Will, you know that's not how this works; phone calls are between four and six."

"Yeah, I know. On the main lines. Give me my cell, Tuck," I say holding my hand out.

"Will, I don't have it."

"What do you mean you don't have it?"

"I mean it's in Patterson's office just like everyone else's phones, away from patients so they don't get themselves into trouble."

"What?" I narrow my gaze into slits. "I'm a doctor, I certainly don't expect the same treatment as everyone else here. Once upon a time I was the on-call doctor here." I shake my head. "Go get it!"

"Will, you're not a doctor right now, you're a patient. And you're in rehab. It's the time to separate from your life and recover. You need...space, to get better."

"Are you fucking with me right now? This is a joke, right?"

"Will, do you want to get better?"

"I want to talk to my fiancée." He blinks his eyes a few times before I see him jot something down on his notepad. "For Christ sakes, Tuck, she's pregnant...and I'm not there."

"I'm aware of that. Tell me was this pregnancy planned?"

"Tuck, I swear to God, I'm not kidding around, give me my phone."

"Will, I'll see what I can do. But for now, can we just talk?"

My knee begins to bounce nervously that he's so adamant about me not talking to Charley. And now he's changing the subject. I know these signs. "About?"

"You know what about. Will I thought we had a handle on this?"

"We do...I do!" I cross my arms over my chest. "It's been a rough few weeks."

"I know."

"I can't practice for two years," I say, the burn in my throat returning both from the words and as a reminder that I haven't had any alcohol in a few days.

"Do you think that was fair?"

"Ummm," I rub my forehead. "I don't know, I think two years is a bit harsh."

"Is it? It's pretty standard. And...correct me if I'm wrong...but I do remember a certain conversation on a golf course when I told you that this was the potential outcome. Did you think I was making it up?"

"I knew it was a potential outcome."

"So, you just thought—what? The board would just eat up your love story like a bunch of women reading romance novels? Come on."

"There's no need for your fucking sarcasm."

"There's no need for your fucking language," he retorts.

"Screw you, Tuck. I'm in here so that I can break myself of this habit before it truly begins to form, but I don't need you questioning everything I've done over the past several months. I've already answered to someone, taken my punishment. I've been asked a thousand and one of these questions...I'm not doing it again." I am so over talking about my choice to have a relationship with a patient.

"Will, I didn't know...I didn't know that you had started drinking again at all. Your entry forms and in yesterday's session you stated that you'd been drinking socially for months. You knew that was a slippery slope. And I asked you, more than once. You lied to me."

I was lying to everyone, including myself. What makes you so special? "I wasn't out of control."

"That's not the point. After we got you through it the first time, I thought you were done."

"I wasn't drinking nearly as aggressively as I was then."

"You said you started earlier this year..."

"Yep."

"Right around the time you started seeing Charley and her husband."

"**Ex**-Husband," I growl.

"Fine, Will. Ex-husband. You had to know that was going to get out of hand. You were starting to have feelings for a woman while you were counseling her and the man she was married to. That could cause anyone to have a breakdown. I'm not blaming you. I just don't know why you didn't come to me. We could have worked through it."

"It was just here and there."

"Once you've established a history of problems with alcohol you know there is no 'just here and there'."

I'm quiet, letting the words I already know wash over me. "You want to know why I didn't come see you in the beginning? Because you'd know! And I couldn't face you." I rub my hand over my head *as I feel the headache forming more aggressively by the minute. "I didn't know things were going to escalate between us..." I say re-calling the first time I reached for alcohol all those months ago. "I thought it was hard not being able to have Charley at all." I shake my head. "But I was wrong. It was worse, having her but not when-ever I wanted."*

"It sounds like Charley—and I don't blame her—but it sounds like she was your catalyst for beginning to drink again."

My eyes shoot to his, knowing where he's going with this conclu-sion and I shake my head. "I want to speak to her...today."

"And it's my strong recommendation, that you don't."

———

He'd gone on to tell me that she'd already called once that morn-ing and that they would be letting her know that I wouldn't be allowed to accept any of her calls. I close my eyes hoping that she can hear my thoughts apologizing to her for this situation. I slow my feet as I finish another lap to find Tuck still in the same spot.

"I would never tell a patient that they couldn't have their sup-port system."

"Even if that support system is what caused them to drink in the first place?"

"Oh my God!" I yell out. "What the hell is your problem when it comes to Charley anyway? What do you have against her?"

"Why don't we go inside and—"

"No, I'm not going anywhere with you until you tell me why you're hellbent on keeping me from Charley."

He sighs and pulls his coat tighter around him as he comes through the gate to stand with me on the track. "Will, I'm not the enemy here. But talking to Charley right now is not particularly good for you."

My eyes widen having heard the person that used to know

me better than anyone speak such a ludicrous statement. "You're crazy."

"Let's walk." He nods to the track and I reluctantly begin to walk in time with him somewhat curious how he came to this bullshit conclusion. "Tell me about the first time you had a drink. What happened?"

I narrow my eyes as I shake my head. "I don't really remember."

"Yes, you do."

True. I do know.

"That night I slept with the girl that looked like her. I told you about it when we played golf? I'd gone out with Drew…met some girl at a bar. God, she looked just like Charley." I rub my forehead trying to remember her exact features but it's no use as the only brunette woman ingrained in my memory currently has my child growing inside of her. "I can't even remember what she actually looked like, but I remember almost doing a double take when I saw her. I couldn't even stop myself from getting hard thinking it was really Charley. She must have felt me staring at her because she looked at me. I realized it wasn't Charley and looked away, but it didn't stop her from coming over."

"I'd been drinking iced tea all night but for some reason, I ordered a scotch next. Maybe because she was drinking and I offered to buy her one, I don't know. But the more I drank, the more she began to look like Charley. At the end of the night, we were both drunk and…I took her home. I didn't realize how fucked I was until Charley's name left my lips when I came. I'd been masturbating like a crazy person thinking about her, but this was different. I was crushed. I wanted her so much and I couldn't have her."

"Had you slept with her at this point?"

"No." I shake my head. "But after that night, I knew that I had taken about a hundred steps back getting intoxicated and fucking a woman that reminded me of a patient. So, I just swept that night under the rug. Pretended it didn't happen. I tried to get my mind off Charley."

"Did it work?"

"It worked...until I saw her again," I admit. "I went out again with my brother and met another woman. Same thing. I used her to fill the void of not having Charley."

"I see. Were you drinking during this time too?"

"Yes, more socially though. I wasn't getting drunk, and it wasn't every day. Just to take the edge off and to...feel numb I guess. In the early stages of Charley and I sleeping together it was fine, I'd stopped altogether. I thought that I had everything under control. But then things began to get more real on both ends. I couldn't see her when I wanted, talk to her when I wanted. I had no control over the situation, and I started to spiral."

"Did Charley know about any of that?"

"No. I hid it from her until recently."

"Why did it take you so long to tell her? You would have thought that was something you should have disclosed when you were getting closer. When she was planning to leave her husband. When she actually *left* her husband," he says, as we begin walking back towards the main facility.

"Why do you think?" I ask him as we head through the glass doors towards one of the rooms for sessions. "I didn't want her to think less of me."

"Well, now do you understand why we're advising that you don't speak to her while you're here? There is a correlation between her, your feelings for her...this whole situation, and you drinking again. You were drinking because you wanted something that you couldn't have...which is always your trigger. With your family. And now with Charley."

"No. I was..." The words fail me. "I just..."

We make our way through the halls and back into the office

we'd been using, and I immediately drop to the couch, not caring that the sweat is still fresh on my skin from my run. I stare off into space, letting Tuck's words run through my mind on a loop.

"I can't lose her." I rub my jaw, feeling the tears form in my eyes. "It's not the same as with my parents. I don't question Charley's love for me. I'm not competing with anyone for Charley's attention or affection."

"But, *you were* competing for her. With her *husband.*"

"There was never a competition between myself and Wells once we started."

"Be that as it may, she wasn't yours. You didn't have her. She belonged to another man. You couldn't see her, touch her, or hold her when you wanted. And it made you crazy."

I rub my palms together trying to calm my nerves as I feel myself begin to get worked up. "Tuck…"

"So, you drank to numb the pain of not being able to be with her. And again, when you couldn't have her whenever she couldn't see you. When she couldn't take your calls…"

"Stop," I tell him not wanting to hear any more.

"And then when you finally got her, you lose the ability to practice. Will, you've been fighting for stability and balance… your entire adult life. When you were a child, you couldn't figure out why your brother got the attention you craved, which stayed with you for years, and then you meet this woman, and although you understand why she can't give you the attention and affection you yearn for, it doesn't stop you from craving it. From wanting Charley…" he trails off.

I pull at my hair wishing that it were enough to wake me up from this nightmare, when I feel as if everything is clear for the first time ever. I look up from the floor, my eyes brimming with unshed tears. "I'm not giving her up…for anything."

"Then be honest with her. Be fair to her. It's good that

you've talked to her about your past now so that you can be stronger for your future. For her and for the family that you're building with her."

"A part of me is afraid she'll leave me," I say finally, feeling all of my insecurities coming to a head.

"What makes you fear that?"

"I don't know...I know she loves me. But she had everything, and she walked away from it all. She risked everything just as I did. What if she wakes up one day and regrets it?"

"What if you do?"

"I won't."

"Okay, if you are sure you will never feel that way, why won't you take her word for it that she feels the same? I am sure that she's been equally transparent about her feelings in this whole ordeal."

I'm silent for what feels like an eternity, my thoughts and his words weighing on my brain. "Can we wrap this up for the day?" I ask him, wanting to be alone with my thoughts.

"Of course." He nods. "I've given you a lot to reflect on."

—

I walk through the facility and I'm not surprised that the majority of the occupants aren't in their rooms; they're with their families in one of the many common areas. I make it back to my room and drop to my bed, the events of the day having me barreling towards sleep despite the fact that it is only noon. I'm staring at the ceiling for what feels like an hour before I sit up, accepting defeat that sleep is evading me. I reach for my bag and pull out a book that I brought. When I open it, a picture falls out.

And not just any picture.

My favorite picture of Charley—one that I stare at often; it's the background to my cell phone.

She's lying on our bed giving the camera one of her signature shy smiles, her eyes teasing me as they always do. I notice an envelope that fell out of the bag when I grab the book, and I frown, wondering what it is.

I turn it over and it reads:

Read me when you're lonely.

I recognize the handwriting instantly and a smile finds my face as I open the envelope.

Will,

Thank you for loving me even when I didn't love myself. Thank you for being the support I needed, the shoulder to cry on, the hand to hold. My favorite hello, my hardest goodbye, all of the things that love songs are made of. Thank you for breathing life into me, metaphorically and literally. You've made me a mommy! For eight months you've been the single reason I look forward to the next day. In the beginning, because it was a day closer to seeing you again. And now, because it's another day I get to spend on this adventure through life with you. I know right now you may be a little upset with me, but please know that I'm always in your corner and I vow to never leave it. You're the man of my dreams (and thankfully my reality) and I'm so grateful that you've chosen me to love for the rest of your life. I'm so proud of you and I can't wait to see you in a week.

I miss you, I love you, and I'm thinking about you every second that you're gone.

Your Charley

I glance at the picture again, my eyes suddenly blurry after reading Charley's words. *Upset with her? Never.* The guilt takes over my mind as I think about what the last few days have meant for Charley. *What has she been doing? I hope she's gotten out and not stayed in the house sulking. Drew and Lauren better have checked in on her.* I can't wait to take her in my arms and hold her, touch her soft skin, pepper kisses all over her stomach.

Baby.

We made a baby. I left so quickly we barely had a chance to celebrate. I smile, thinking about the new life growing inside of her by the day. Something only I've given her. Something she's only wanted from me. I read over her words at least a dozen more times wishing they would transport me to her. I trace my fingertip over her face before I press the picture of her to my heart. I've long forgotten about the book, and clearly the insomnia, because within moments I'm asleep.

———

Saturday: Day Six

I run a hand over my jaw, feeling the new growth that's grown over the past week. I haven't been able to trim or do any landscaping on my beard. *They don't exactly let you come in with razors or clippers.* I scratch my jaw hoping that Charley won't hate it too much before I trim it back to its usual length.

It's only nine in the evening and I feel like a kid on the night before Christmas. I'm anxious to get into bed knowing what the next day will bring—*Charley.*

I press a kiss to the picture she gave me, like I have the last few nights since I discovered it, and slide into bed. I haven't masturbated at all since I've been here as I know it's something they advise you not to do in rehab, but the thought of seeing Charley tomorrow has the excitement coursing through my dick making it impossible to go down.

I turn on my side in a huff, ignoring the tingling sensation in my balls and the throbbing in my cock.

What I wouldn't give for Charley's mouth wrapped around my—No Will. Besides, think about how much better the release will be tomorrow inside of her. I put a pillow over my face and groan thinking about how I still have one final session tomorrow before I get to leave the facility.

I look at the clock on my nightstand. *Just sixteen more hours.* A smile finds my face as I think about how I plan to never be without her this long ever again.

No. More. Alcohol.

CHAPTER
Thirty

WILL

Sunday: Day Seven

I HAVEN'T TALKED TO ANYONE OUTSIDE OF THESE FOUR WALLS for the past week so I am unaware if anyone is coming with Charley to pick me up tonight. *Is Drew bringing her?* I shudder thinking about my parents bullying her into wanting to come as well; I had told Drew to let them know what has been going on.

I think about the conversations that needs to be had with both of my parents regarding their attitudes towards my future bride, especially now that she'll be giving them their first grand-child within the year. I pull my bag up over my shoulder as I walk through the halls for the last time.

"Montgomery," I hear from behind me, and I turn around to see him staring at me.

"Tuck." I nod.

"I'm proud of you, Will." He smiles. "You've come a long way this past week."

"You're not going to get me to agree that I couldn't talk to Charley this whole time," I tell him, raising an eyebrow.

"That's fair," he says holding his hands up in defeat.

"But…thank you."

"Call me next week…we'll play golf."

"Pass." I laugh. "I've spent enough time with you the past week to last me through the New Year."

"I'm hurt!" he says, putting a hand over his heart jokingly. "Tell me I still get a wedding invite?"

"To be determined." I give him a smug grin and he slaps my back as we make our way through the lobby. I'm surprised I don't see Charley inside, waiting for me, but maybe she isn't here yet. "You told her what time, right?"

"Yes, I called her personally."

"How did she sound?" I ask.

"Anxious. She really misses you."

I grab my phone from the exit station as I make my way into the lobby. I unlock my phone and the wind is almost knocked out of me as I find dozens of texts and emails from Charley, Drew, and both of my parents. I open the most recent text from Charley sent a few moments ago.

———

Charley: I'm outside! I was too worried I would cause a scene...I've yelled at a lot of people at this facility. I wasn't sure if I was banned haha. And didn't want a bunch of people watching our reunion!

I chuckle reading her words, before I push through the double doors and make my way out into the November sunset. I spot her Audi immediately, and smile when I see her bouncing excitedly next to the car. I move down the steps and when her eyes finally find me, she takes off for me. I jog toward her, meeting her halfway when she stops suddenly looking me over as if she's not sure that I'm really standing in front of her.

The tears are flowing down her cheeks. "Hi," she whispers.

"Hi, baby," I move towards her, closing the space between us.

She bites her bottom lip and looks me over again. "You look… really good," she says, the air leaving her lungs as she says it.

"I did a lot of running in there." She nods appreciatively and I feel a burst of pride the way she's looking at me. I've lost a few pounds but I've gotten more toned, something I know Charley can see even with my jacket on given how well acquainted she is with my body.

"I'm going to lose it the second I touch you," she tells me as she wipes her nose with the sleeve of her sweater.

"Same," I tell her.

She takes a step closer to me and I do the same. "I missed you…so much."

"I got your note," I tell her, the emotions of seeing her again building in my throat. "I didn't see it until Thursday and it was the turning point. You have no idea how much strength it gave me."

She puts her hand over her heart and smiles. "I'm so glad to hear that. I have a dozen more at home for you." She giggles.

"I wrote a bit while I was in there too…" I tell her. "My wedding vows are perfect." I smile and before I know it she's lunged for me, her arms and legs both wrapped completely around me and she's sobbing so hard she begins to shake in my arms.

"Oh my God," she cries. "I called and called and they wouldn't let me talk to you! They said I was a trigger and—I wasn't helping. I'm sorry! I just wanted to help, and make sure you were okay and—I can't ever do this again! Not talk to you or see you! Please, promise me!" She's borderline hysterical as she sobs against me, her tears wetting my neck and sliding down my torso underneath my sweater and coat.

I press my hand to the back of her head keeping her pressed to me protectively as I carry her to her car. "I know you tried to call. Baby, I tried to get them to let me talk to you. And you're not a trigger, this is not your fault. Don't apologize," I reassure her as I stroke her back. "And nothing like this ever again, I promise,"

I whisper into her ear. I'm fighting the tears myself hearing her plead with me to never have to be apart again. "Never again," I repeat. I open the door to place her in the passenger seat when she clings to me even harder, not wanting to let me go. "Let's just get in the car, okay?"

She nods and lets me slide her into the car. I've barely shut the door on the driver's side before she's climbed across the console and into my lap straddling me. *Let me get us off the premises at least if you're going to try and mount me.* I smile to myself.

"I was so worried when I couldn't get you on the phone. I thought they were doing something to you in there. Brainwashing you, telling you that I wasn't good for you...that I did this to you."

"No one could convince me that you aren't good for me." I grab her face making her look at me. "No one. And you can't blame yourself, alright?"

She nods before she continues. "Then I thought maybe they weren't telling you I was calling and you thought I didn't care... that I stood you up on Family Day...Tuck said he would tell you I was calling. Did he tell you?"

"Yes, baby. He told me. I knew you'd never forget me. I knew you cared from the beginning even before I realized they weren't letting us talk."

Her shoulders sag as if a weight has been lifted and she begins to strokes my jaw slowly, her eyes boring into mine. "What?" I ask her.

"I'm just...reacquainting myself with my favorite face. This is a little longer than usual." She says rubbing my facial hair, her fingertip tracing my jaw.

"They don't allow a whole lot of sharp objects in there."

"I like it." She smiles. "You are still the most gorgeous man I've ever laid eyes on." She smiles as she runs her fingers through my hair and brings her forehead to mine. "Once I kiss you I don't know that I'll be able to stop." She bites her lip before letting them graze across my cheek, towards my chin and across the other cheek. They move across my nose and along my eyelids and land on my forehead having completely skipped over my mouth.

My cock stirs in my pants feeling her lips on me and I move my face attempting to capture her lips with mine. "Charley," I murmur and she pulls back to look at me, her eyes full of lust. "Kiss me, baby."

She lets her tongue dart out to wet her lips and tucks a hair behind her ear nervously as if she'd never kissed me before. *God, she is so fucking sweet.* She lowers her lips to mine and places a gentle kiss on my lips. She lets out a tiny whimper as her soft lips find mine, and she opens her mouth immediately allowing my tongue to snake into hers without hesitation. I move in time with hers, our mouths doing their familiar dance that we haven't been able to do in seven days. I groan into her mouth as she pulls back slightly to nibble on my bottom lip. Her hands find the sides of my face and scratch gently as we continue to kiss like teenagers in a parking lot.

I don't know how long our lips are attached when we pull away, but hers are swollen and red and slightly glossy from my saliva, and the tears that leaked out of her eyes while we kissed. "I missed you so much," I tell her as I cup her cheek. "I'm sorry I did this to us."

"You got better for me…and our baby. You have nothing to apologize for…" She trails off. "Unless…"

I can hear her mind working overtime and I press a finger to her lips, silencing her, and hopefully her thoughts as well. "I'm better. The best I've ever felt. But we can talk about everything tomorrow."

"Sounds good. I'm sorry for making you feel that I abandoned you. I never want you to feel like that again. I'll help you with your baggage just like you've always helped with mine."

I'm unbelievably moved hearing her simple words.

She's in this with me, no matter what.

"How are you feeling?" I ask, still cupping her cheek with one hand and rub her belly gently with the other.

"Good." She smiles. "I've made an appointment with an OBGYN for two weeks from now. You'll come?"

"I'd follow you anywhere, but right now, I just want to go home, take a hot bath and climb into bed with you until tomorrow afternoon." The beds in the facility weren't particularly comfortable and coupled with not having Charley beside me made for some pretty shitty sleep.

"I think I like the sound of that." She blushes before rubbing her nose against mine.

I wrap my arms around her petite frame and bury my face in her neck. "I'm so happy to be home."

"Well, you're not home yet." She chuckles.

"Yes, I am," I whisper against her skin as I drag my lips up and lose myself in her kiss once more.

CHAPTER
Thirty-One

Charlotte

THE CAR RIDE HOME IS NO EASY FEAT, WITH WILL'S HAND permanently glued to some part of my body. I'm trying my best to keep my hands to myself as he needs to focus on the road, but the second his hand parted my thighs and began drawing lazy circles on the skin between them I figured all bets were off. I immediately unbuckle my seatbelt and lean over the console, taking his earlobe in my mouth, my breasts pressed against his shoulder. I trail my fingertips down his chest and find his crotch and grab him possessively, my fingers trying their best to make out the hard flesh underneath his jeans.

The car is quiet, just the gentle hum of my Audi as we make our way home and the sounds of my lips moving against his skin.

"Charlotte," he says, and I can hear the lustful strain in his voice. *He's going to lose it.* "Baby, I haven't had you in almost three weeks…" His sentence is cut off when I apply more pressure against him as I begin to rub his cock through his jeans. He's hard enough now for me to find him easily, and if I didn't think dragging the zipper down his hard shaft would kill him, I would.

"I wish you could feel how wet I am," I moan in his ear. "How many times I've come thinking about you this week." I know I'm goading him, but I want him to know how desperate I am for him, how much I need him. I want him to know I won't last a second past getting over the threshold of his townhouse.

He chances a glance at me and the wicked gleam in his eye does nothing but add to the moisture collecting in my panties. "You... touched yourself?"

"You didn't?" I ask as my lips trail down his neck. *God, I want to kiss his lips.* I'm somewhat cursing myself that I didn't have Drew come with me. *My guess is Drew nor Will would want that show though.*

"No, masturbation is something they want you to typically avoid when you're in rehab." His eyes find my wide ones. "Though I wanted to."

I drag my hand away from his crotch, somewhat stunned. In light of this new information, I'm led to believe he's probably only holding on by a thread. *This is probably tormenting him.*

"Well, that sucks."

He chuckles. "Don't I know it."

"Well, I can fix that... now?" I tell him as I reach for his dick, knowing that my mouth around him may take the edge off a little.

He grabs my jaw before I get too close and squeezes as he pulls my face back up. "No." I lean back, my confused eyes narrowing and he continues, "I want to take my time with you. I haven't had you in three weeks. I don't want a blow job while I have to focus on not crashing the car. I want you naked in our bed, coated with a layer of sweat, coming hard around my cock when I finally come. I want to taste your orgasm as you ride my face all the while my dick is down your throat. When I come, Charlotte, you're coming with me."

The wind is knocked out of me upon hearing his sinful description of what I assume to be the next twenty-four hours, and my hands find my thighs, the sexual frustration running through me as I dig my nails into them. "Well, can't you drive any faster?" I whimper as we pull up to yet another red light.

The tension between us crackles as we pull into his neighborhood. I'm trying my best not to make eye contact with him so that we don't consummate his homecoming right here in the car, but I can feel his gaze on the side of my face when he puts the car in park.

Don't look at him, Charley. Do not look at him, I chant as he opens the car door for me.

I've barely stepped two feet before I hear his bag hit the floor and I'm being pushed hard against the door in his garage, and his lips seal over mine. I open my mouth on instinct and his tongue finds mine. His hands have found their way to my face, his thumbs stroking my cheeks in time with his tongue moving with mine. This is the second time I've kissed him in a week and it's taking everything out of me not to cry again.

He's home. He's back. He's not going anywhere.

"Will," I moan.

"Mmm," he moans into my mouth as his hands move down my body and underneath my long sweater to cup my ass through my leggings. "I can't wait to run my lips over every inch of this," he growls. He moves his hands to the front of me and slides one under the waistband of my leggings and underwear, running two fingers through my folds. "And this."

I convulse feeling the light pressure on what I know is my very stimulated clitoris, and I grab his shoulders to steady myself. "I want you naked within thirty seconds. And grab some water from the fridge. You'll want to stay hydrated for what I have in store for you."

He places a final kiss on my lips before grabbing his bag. I nod, my eyes wide and my mouth suddenly dry. I wet my lips, and attempt to swallow some moisture down when I hear his keys letting us inside. The door has barely shut completely when I hear his bag hit the floor and I'm in his arms and pressed against the wall.

"Change of plans," he growls in my ear. "I want you naked *now.*" I'm hoisted into his arms, my legs around his back, his

hard cock pressing against the fabric of his jeans and now pushing against my core. The delicious friction pulls a moan out of me
so loud that I almost miss the faint sound of someone calling my
fiancé's name. *Almost.*

He pulls away from my lips, having heard the same thing and
narrows his eyes at me. "Did you hear something?"

I nod, but he still doesn't let me down until we hear it again.
Louder. "Will, honey!" I hear, and I almost groan for a whole completely different reason.

*Oh, what the fuck?! The wicked witch of Atlanta flew in on
her broom?*

"You invited my family?" Will asked, setting me on shaky
legs as the sexual haze we were just in is still affecting every bone
in my body.

"Oh, yeah right." I roll my eyes. "Of course, I didn't. Oh…
should I have?" My eyes widen as I remember that once upon a
time I did have stellar manners. "Oh, that would have been appropriate…like a welcome home thing? Shit, baby, I'm sorry." I
blanche. "I should have baked a cake or something. I'll make it up
to you. See this is what happens, when a woman thinks with her
vagina. All the years of good manners just—" I snap and point
towards the wall, "out the window!"

"Charley stop it. I didn't want a welcome home party…I had a
week-long stint in rehab. I didn't go off to war." He shakes his head.
"And there's nothing sweeter than what's between your legs, baby."
He growls in my ear. "But what the hell is my mother doing here?"

"I don't know!" I whisper in an exasperated voice. "You gave
her keys long before I came into the picture."

"Oh, there you are!" Diana appears before us looking as if
she just stepped off the runway of a Chanel fashion show. *If I
didn't hate her so much I might actually enjoy going shopping with
her. The woman can dress.* Her matching tweed jacket and skirt,
paired with this season's newest slingbacks suddenly make me

feel inadequate as I look down at my sweater, leggings, and riding boots. I didn't think it mattered what I wore given that Will would be ripping it off with his teeth the second we got home. *Which was the plan after all.*

"Mom, what are you doing here?"

"Honey," she says, linking her arm through his and away from me as they walk through the foyer with me trailing behind them, "you go to rehab for a week and you can't be bothered to call your mother and tell her ahead of time that you'll be unreachable? I was beside myself, until your brother came over for his weekly lunch on Tuesday and filled me in. How could you agree to go to rehab? You are fine, you are perfect!"

"I thought your weekly lunch is on Thursday?" Will asks.

"That's lunch at the club, silly. We have lunch at home on Tuesday. I know I've told you this. Lunches you know you have a standing invitation to." Diana pulls out of his grasp and sashays towards the living room.

"Yeah, as of late," he says under his breath, and I don't think he meant for me to hear that so I tuck that bit of information away for later. *She has lunch with Drew twice a week?* I wrack my brain for any small piece of information that would allude that Will also had lunch with his mother, but I come up empty. *So, she has lunch with Drew but not Will? And judging by his comment I don't think that's by his choice.* My hand finds his and I squeeze, letting him know that I'm still here and he gives me a small smile.

We make it to the living room to find J.R., with his hands crossed and his expression hostile, as well as Drew who looks nervous.

"Rehab Will, really?" J.R. asks, motioning for him to sit down between himself and Diana. I'm left standing by myself in the corner as I watch the scene unfold.

"And Charlotte really, I mean were you planning to starve my son after he's been eating God knows what for the past week? I mean look at him, he's skin and bones," Diana pinches Will's arm and I sigh. "I see you didn't have anything prepared. Drew darling, grab my purse, I suppose we can order something."

"Well, I—"

"Mom," Will snaps before he stands up and makes his way back over to me, "enough. What are you doing here?"

"I haven't talked to you…or seen you in a week!"

"That's not unheard of," Will retorts immediately and you would think that someone just smacked her across the face with the look she gives him.

"Well, maybe if you called your mother! Or returned my phone calls! But that is not the point. The point is you let someone convince you that there was a problem when there wasn't. I see why you didn't call us before you left; we would have talked you out of that pointless foolishness."

"It wasn't pointless, Mother."

"My son tells me that it was your idea." Her gaze narrows at me and the tears begin to flood my eyes.

"Drew!" Will growls at his brother and he winces.

"I didn't mean—"

"Jesus Christ, Drew cut the fucking cord already. Do you have to tell her everything?" Will barks. "Mother, Charley and I decided it was for the best, *together.*"

"Funny, that all of your bad ideas start with this young lady."

I'm torn between telling this bitch where she could stick her unsolicited opinion, and keeping quiet out of respect that this is Will's mother. *But she is testing me.*

"Di," J.R. says, the lawyer in him having picked up on my tense stance.

"J.R., you know our son is fine. I mean what is a drinking problem anyway? Who doesn't like a casual cocktail here and there? Speaking of which, is that why this house is drier than the Sahara now?"

Will glances at me and I haven't had a chance to tell him that I've purged the house of all alcohol. "I…I wasn't sure if it could be in the house? I just didn't want you to be tempted," I say, stumbling slightly out of nervousness. "I read that the constant stimulation isn't good. I know a lot of it was expensive so I didn't dump it…it's just not here."

He gives me a smile and presses a kiss to my forehead. "Thank you."

"Will!" Diana scolds and I see the familiar look in his eyes. *He's about to snap.*

"Mother!" he roars. "You need to leave. Actually, *all* of you need to leave. Now. I just got home, and I want to be with my fiancée. I don't know why you felt the need to show up here unannounced. But as you can see, I'm fine. And Mother, seeing as how you still haven't learned the appropriate way to speak to Charley, you have to go."

"Will, don't be like that! We just want what's best for you."

"Which is Charley."

"Until she does to you what she did to that poor unsuspecting ex-husband of hers."

"Mom, there's really a lot more to that story you don't know," Drew interjects, and I wonder just how much Will has shared with him.

"Enough!" Will yells, and I flinch beside him, although I know it's not directed at me. "All of you, OUT!"

"Oh, for Heaven's sake, Will."

"Wow, you can actually say that without turning into a pillar of salt?" I snap, and I immediately know I've gone too far when I feel Will tense next to me. Drew's eyes widen although I do notice a hint of amusement behind them, and J.R shakes his head.

She glares at me, her eyes almost penetrating my soul. "Excuse me but you can't—" she starts.

"Actually, I can," I interrupt. "I've sat and taken a lot from you, jumped through countless of your hoops in attempts to prove that I love your son and yet, you treat me as if I'm not good enough." I shake my head. "I guess that makes sense, given from what I've observed you treat him the same way."

The room is silent. "Charley." I hear his voice in my ear and I look up at the blue eyes that hold so much emotion.

"Sorry, I… I snapped," I whisper at him.

"Well," I hear as Diana moves to her feet sliding her gloves on her hands dramatically, "I have never been so insulted. You've been a part of his life for five minutes and you think you have the right to pass judgment on me?" She stops in front of me. "Hmm. Silly girl." She turns to Will and her demeanor changes instantly. "Goodbye, darling!" She gives him an air kiss before she heads out of the living room.

J.R. stands from the couch and follows her same course stopping before me. "You only get one of those in this family. So, I hope that felt good," he warns before he follows his wife into the foyer. I let out the breath I've been holding since Diana left the room once I hear the door close behind them, leaving us alone with Drew.

"You told Mom it was Charley's idea? You didn't tell her you supported it? Did you even bother to tell her everything? Or just enough to villainize the woman I love?" I can hear the anger in his voice and see it in his eyes.

Drew puts his hands up defensively. "I told her I thought it was a good idea…but I didn't think you wanted me explaining to her my reasoning for it. And lay off, will you? I'm sorry!"

"Sorry?! Do you think sorry is enough to fix what just happened here?"

"It's not—" I start when I see Will's gaze snap to mine. "Baby, it's not his fault."

"No, it is." He nods and stares at his brother with cold eyes. "Maybe he didn't make you say what you said, but he knew what to do to plant the seed with my mother. He knew your relationship was precarious, and yet he was in her ear telling her it was your idea!"

"Will—" Drew starts.

"This is so typical of you. And I thought after we talked last week, you'd be more mindful about this bullshit, but I guess not. You'll never change."

I see the look in Drew's eyes, and I wonder if his words are cutting him deeper than Will realizes. "Baby…" I grab his face and make him look at me, wondering if he's going to snap at me next, but his eyes soften dramatically. I search his face, trying to discover what's lying beneath the mask that he has on right now.

"You should go," he tells Drew finally as he turns his gaze back to him.

"Will, it wasn't my intention to turn anyone against Charley…I certainly never meant to hurt either of you." His expression looks so lost and hurt, I actually feel bad; I don't think he really meant any harm.

Will doesn't say anything and Drew nods. "Okay then, well…I guess call me when you're ready to talk?"

Will nods but still doesn't say anything as he walks out of his living room. The click of the door closing snaps Will out of his quiet seething and I feel myself being lifted off the ground and pushed hard against the wall. His lips find my neck as his erection grinds into my core once again though he's significantly less hard. His tongue starts at the bottom of my neck and drags upwards slowly towards my ear before he presses a kiss there causing me to shudder.

"I'm sorry," he says in my ear. "I'm sorry for how she speaks to you."

My hands find the back of his neck, as I play with the hair there. "Stop," I tell him as I pull his lips from my neck. "That's not your fault but…should we talk about what just happened?"

"I don't want to talk, I want to be inside of you."

"And we can do that too, I just…what was that with your brother?"

"Charley…can we not do this right now?"

I bite my bottom lip, and it's as if it doesn't have the same reaction as it always does because he sighs and sets me gently on my feet. He puts one hand on either side of my head boxing me against the wall. "We need to talk," he says, his voice so low it sends a chill through me.

"Okay?" I wince and his hand finds my face in response. He strokes my cheek a few times and he places a kiss on my lips. Before I know it, he's leading me to the couch and sits me down. He sits on his coffee table in front of me so that we are facing each other.

"When you said that my mother treated you a certain way because of how she treats me… what did you mean by that?" He narrows his eyes, and I realize now that in that simple comment, I may have unlocked a whole bunch of complex and painful memories. *God, maybe I really am a fucking trigger.*

"I'm sorry I said that, I—"

His finger finds my lips and he shakes his head. "Don't apologize if you don't mean it," he says, and I'm transported back to a time where I was sitting on a similar couch in front of Will Montgomery.

"I mean it this time. I shouldn't have said that."

"Why? You believe that."

"She was right, I shouldn't have passed judgment."

"As my future wife and the woman that promises to love me above all else, I would say that you're a little bit entitled to your opinion." He holds his thumb and index finger very close together.

I lick my lips, the tears forming in my eyes as I take a deep breath. "I believe it."

My heart is racing a mile a minute, there's a thin layer of sweat coating every inch of my body as I come down from what was probably my fourth orgasm in the last hour. The man in charge of giving me all four of them is still on top of me, giving my breasts lazy kisses, allowing his tongue to trace my hardened nipple.

Shortly after his parents left, he carried me to his bedroom kissing me the entire way there. I barely had a chance to think before my boots were thrown across the room and all of my clothes were flying off of me.

Will reacquainted himself with every inch of my body starting with my belly. He talked to it, telling the growing baby that he couldn't wait to meet them. How Daddy was sorry for everything and promised to be the best father ever. And most importantly how he loved us more than anything. He gave me kisses everywhere from the tips of my toes to the space behind my earlobes and gave special attention to my breasts and my aching pussy. Sure, enough he made good on his promise and our first orgasms came from me sitting on his face with his cock in my mouth.

I had barely come down from the orgasm before I was riding him, desperate for the connection that came from him shooting his seed into the place that had brought new life.

"I can't come again," I moan out as I feel his fingers rubbing my folds gently.

"Yes, you can," he mumbles against my breast as he bares his teeth and grazes the sensitive skin. I whimper in response as he bites down gently. "Just give me one more, baby."

I grab his head pulling him up my body so that we are nose to nose. "You're trying to kill me, Will."

"No, just your ability to walk tomorrow."

I chuckle as his lips find my neck and his cock finds my folds. I feel him draw his tongue across my neck and he groans in response. "Even your sweat tastes sweet."

He slides through my slightly abused pussy and begins to rock in and out of me gently. "Don't fall asleep," he whispers in my ear just as my eyes flutter closed.

"I'm not." I let my head fall to the side as I feel sleep and my orgasm coming at me at equal speeds letting me know that the tingly feeling shooting through me will lead me right to a peaceful slumber.

"I love you, Charley," he murmurs in my ear and his words feel like warm honey all over.

"I love—" I start as I feel my orgasm begin to move through me.

"There it is," he whispers in my ear. "Come for me, baby," he says as I feel like I'm shattering into a million pieces. I scream out his name as he continues to thrust into me chasing his own orgasm. I hear my name leave his lips as they find mine, gently leaving kisses all over my face before he slowly pulls out of me. The last thing I feel before sleep finds me is him spooning me from behind, his hand resting protectively over my belly.

CHAPTER
Thirty-Two

Charlotte

I T'S BEEN TWO WEEKS SINCE WILL'S WEEK IN REHAB, AND I HAVE to say that his mood has dramatically improved. Maybe it has something to do with my first trimester turning me into a horny, sex-crazed mess. If Will and I are in the same room, I'm on top of him, my hands down his pants and my lips on his neck. I don't think I've had so much sex in my life, and he seems happy to oblige. Last night, he actually told me he couldn't go again after three back to back rounds of sex. So, he brought me to a mind-numbing orgasm with his mouth instead. In short, things have been wonderful.

Will and I booked a month long Euro-trip for February and we are unbelievably excited for this adventure—and of course all of the pasta that Italy has to offer. Neither of us studied abroad in college or has done a lot of traveling for the sake of travel and exploration, so it'll be a new experience for both of us.

I'm about seven weeks along, and the baby is growing perfectly. You would think I'm ready to go into labor, though, with the way Will has been fussing over me. He's gone with me to every appointment and gotten up with me every time I've had morning sickness, and any time I even mention a food item, it's sitting in front of me before I can blink. *And I thought he was attentive to my needs before…*

We had an appointment earlier this week, and the second the

doctor "gave mom and dad a minute alone," the tears were sliding down my cheeks as I took in the image on the monitor of the tiny human growing inside of me.

"Wow," I hear his voice right at my ear as he squeezes my hand gently. "That's…our baby."

I turn my head slightly to look at him and his gaze is fixated on the monitor. I wipe the tears from my eyes and I nod. "So tiny," I say as I press my fingertips to the screen. "I love you so much," I say, talking to the screen before turning back to the equally emotional father next to me. "And you." He finally breaks his gaze from the monitor and looks at me, the love and adoration glowing in his eyes.

"You gave me the most precious gift, Charlotte." He cups my cheeks and brushes his lips against mine. "Thank you." He kisses me again, his tongue desperately seeking mine as it slides through my lips. I whimper in response as I feel the blood rushing through my veins. I was seconds from asking him if he could climb on top of the bed and have his way with me when the doctor returns.

She chuckles when she sees us break apart and I feel my cheeks get hot in response. "Nothing to be embarrassed about. First kid…I know the drill." She winks before settling in to tell us all about our baby's vitals.

I smile as I run my fingers over the small black and white picture and press a kiss to it before sliding it back into my wallet just as I feel Will's presence. I look up to see him strolling into our bedroom. He sits next to me on our bed and presses a kiss to my shoulder.

"Baby, we have to tell them."

"Now?" I ask as I think about the "them" in question.

Will had it out with his parents right after the last time they were here when Diana and I both shared our feelings. Will made it clear that I was here to stay and that we wanted nothing more to do with them. Since then, they'd both been calling non-stop wanting to "make amends" with both of us. I'm skeptical, but it appears as though my pregnancy has made Will more forgiving, loving, and accepting. His parents still don't know about my pregnancy, and he wants to share that with them. Somewhere deep inside I wonder if he's so anxious to tell them because it's one thing Will is doing before his brother—grandchildren.

But I suppose that's a conversation for another time.

"I just think they should know. Trust me, I know how they are, but…they're trying." He assures me. I know that they're trying *now. I guess, better late than never?*

I sigh. "I already agreed to go to dinner at your parents' house. I just don't see why we have to tell them about the baby *now.*"

"You really want to wait? You told your mom," he says quietly.

"Yes, the difference is my mom actually *likes* me," I tell him, and Will cocks his head to the side. "We aren't married…they probably don't even consider us really engaged, and I can just see your mom insinuating that I trapped you. All while your father is drafting our prenuptial agreement in his head." I shake my head as I think about the only thing that hasn't happened this month. I look down at my naked ring finger wondering when Will was planning to give me the ring that I know he has.

"Hey," he says as he pulls me into his lap. I wrap my legs around his back as he cups my face. "None of that is going to happen, alright? I've given my parents explicit instructions, and if they don't follow them, we're leaving. I won't let them hurt you, Charley. I'll protect you."

———

I wake the next morning to kisses on my face and one hand rubbing my naked belly which eventually snakes down lower and lower until I feel his hand rubbing my sex. My eyes flutter open with the biggest smile on my face as I see Will staring down at me. "Good morning, beautiful," he tells me before he presses a kiss to my lips. He moves the blanket off of me, exposing me to him and the cool air of the bedroom, and I whimper at the immediate loss of heat.

"Will, it's cold!" I giggle.

"I'll warm you," he says with a devilish smirk before he moves so that he's hovering on top of me and lines his cock up with my pussy. I feel my arousal forming as he coats his dick with my cum, dragging his dick through my folds, back and forth, grazing my clit each time. I feel the tingles in my core as I feel the orgasm building from the constant contact with my sensitive bundle of nerves. He strays away from my clit, much to my disappointment and begins to push inside as his hands find mine, lacing our fingers and pulling them above my head. He continues to thrust into me, his eyes boring into mine. It's so intense I don't dare look away, I can't even blink.

"Oh God!" I moan as I feel him hit my cervix lightly and I squeeze my eyes shut in response.

"Eyes on me, baby," he demands.

My eyes fly open, to find his piercing gaze staring at me. "Let my hands go," I beg. "Please! I need to touch you."

He frees my hands from his grip and within a second, my hands find the back of his head, my nails dragging along his scalp, through his hair. "Charley," he groans. "You. Feel. So. Good." I wrap my legs around him tighter and my arms around his neck.

"Kiss me," I plead, knowing that his lips on my neck is one way to push me over the edge when I'm this close.

He attaches his lips to my neck, his tongue darting out to lick the skin behind my ear. "Come for me, baby. Let me feel your pussy pulse around my cock," he whispers sinfully in my ear.

He says these things to me every time we're intimate, and his words never fail to make me blush just like the first time.

My mind drifts back to that *first time*. That first Monday in May that changed my entire life. It's hard to believe that was seven months ago. Seven months ago, I jumped down the rabbit hole and I haven't looked up since.

Seven months ago…

"Once I have a taste I don't know that I'll be able to stop."

I look down at this man, my marriage counselor, kneeling in front of me, staring at my pussy like a starving man in line at a buffet, and I do the only thing I can think of. I nod.

He smiles, a wicked gleam in his eye and I can't help but wonder if I just sold my soul to the devil. The deliciously sexy devil that is sliding my panties down my legs as we speak. "Sit." He points at the couch and I do as he says, my legs touching so as to not expose myself to him. "Open them," he tells me and I swallow, as I slowly open my legs showing him my completely bare pussy.

"You're bare," he says, his eyes never leaving the space between my legs.

"Yes," I croak out, the lust having taken over my voice completely.

"Why?" he asks, and I can see the wheels in his head turning. *If she's not having sex, why bother with the landscaping?*

"I…just prefer not to have hair. It…itches."

He chuckles at my response before pulling me toward him so that my butt is on the edge of the couch and pushes me back gently. I feel his hands on my thighs and I almost jump feeling his fingertip draw circles into my skin. "You're so wet for me."

I nod. *Do I tell him I've been fantasizing about this for months? That he's the star of every single one of my sexy fantasies? That I've named my favorite vibrator Dr. Montgomery? No Charley, shut the fuck up! Don't ruin this. He's going to give you an orgasm, you remember what those feel like when someone else gives them to you, right?*

"You're in your head," he tells me and words fail me instantly.

"I…I…" I stammer. "Sorry," I say weakly, and within a second, he's hovering over me, his mouth nowhere near my pussy, but dangerously close to my lips.

"Stop. With. The. Sorry," he growls and for a split second I'm slightly afraid of this much larger man, towering over me while I'm naked, with the exception of my bra—but I see the amusement in his eyes and instantly it calms me. "I'll break you of this one day."

"I look forward to it," I say and for the first time, I feel his lips against mine. It's not passionate or consuming. It's simple, and yet I feel the spark the second his lips touched mine. It was a kiss that held so much promise. It's as if he's saying, *this is the first kiss of many*. I don't feel his tongue, just his lips, pressed against mine gently. When he pulls back, all of the air has left my lungs, and I know the look in his eyes matches the one in mine. I think he's just as convinced that our lives just changed in that split second. "Wow," I say, and my eyes widen slightly as I hear what I just said. I press my hands to my cheeks trying to cool them because it feels like all my blood has rushed to them.

I feel his lips trail down my torso and belly until he's back between my spread legs. "Your body is phenomenal, Charley. I imagined it would be but…you are so beautiful."

Before I can respond I feel his lips on my pelvis, gently pressing a kiss to my pubic mound. I let out a breath I hadn't realized that I was holding as his tongue swirls around the same patch of skin. At this point, I wouldn't be surprised if my cum was leaking out of me and onto his leather couch as I clench nervously.

He must notice that I've tensed slightly and he chuckles. "Don't worry, Charlotte. I'll make sure not a drop of you goes to waste."

I feel like I could faint from his sexy words. He winks at me and then I feel it. His tongue. *There.*

"Oh my God!" I whimper as I feel his tongue take one long, slow lick through my folds. He looks up at me, his blue eyes staring into my soul, and just like that, I'm lost.

My hands find his hair as he begins to lick me aggressively, and I can safely say in all the times that Matt has done this—not that there had been a ton, it's never felt like this. It feels as if he's trying to climb inside of me through his tongue. He moves my legs to lift over his shoulders and opens me up further to him. He pulls away slightly and when I look down I see my arousal glistening all over the bottom of his face. We only make eye contact for a mere second before I feel his tongue on my clit again, his lips closing around it, and I *explode*.

I've been wound up tighter than a wind up doll and this is the first time that there's been a mouth between my legs in over a year. I'm actually surprised that I lasted this long.

I ride out my orgasm, panting and whimpering at the assault of his mouth and when I'm finished, I feel him place a tiny kiss on my pussy and I jolt, feeling overly sensitive.

"Your pussy is so sweet," he tells me before I feel his lips on mine, his lips and tongue that taste like my arousal. His tongue probes my closed lips begging for entry. When I let him in, I immediately taste the evidence of my orgasm.

Fuck. Me.

I'm brought back into the here and now by the orgasm wracking my body as the thoughts of my past come flooding back to me. "Will!" I moan. My body shakes violently as it rips through me.

A beat after I feel his orgasm shooting through me. "Fuck, Charley!" he growls as his thrusts slow and his lips press lazy kisses against my neck. "My beautiful girl." His hands move to my chest, his hands palming my breasts and rolling my nipples between his fingers. "I love you so much," he says as he pulls out of me gently.

"I love you too." I smile as I cuddle against him before I fall into a sex-induced sleep.

I'm not sure how long I've been asleep, but when I wake up, Will is staring down at me, with a lazy smile on his gorgeous face.

"Hi."

"Hello, beautiful," he murmurs before he presses a kiss to my forehead.

I move so that I'm resting on top of him before nuzzling my face into his neck. I breathe deeply, letting his scent calm me, and then kiss his jaw.

"We've come a long way, Charley."

I pull away from him and cock my head to the side. "I'd say so."

"We both did things that hurt other people for the sake of you and me." My brows furrow together wondering where he's going with this. "But I'm not sorry," he tells me. "I would do it again. All of it. If it meant that I was going to get you in the end. That we'd get here, together... with the new life we created. I wouldn't change any of what we did to get here. Maybe that makes me a terrible person—"

"It doesn't," I interrupt. "I understand what you're saying." I rub his face and give him a reassuring smile, letting him know that I feel the same.

"I'll never...not want this, Charley. I'll never take you for granted...ignore you..." he trails off before his hands find my face. "I never want to hurt you again."

My teeth find my bottom lip as I nod. "I never want to hurt you either."

———

His right hand finds my left as he drives us to his parents' house and he places a kiss on my knuckles. "It's going to be fine. Don't worry."

"I'm not," I lie.

"You know I know when you're lying to me, Charlotte."

I roll my eyes at the shrink coming out of my fiancé. "I know that you'll handle it if things get out of hand."

"Yes, I will."

This will be the first time I have been to Will's parents' house, and somewhere deep inside of me *that* makes me nervous. My eyes widen as I take in the size of Montgomery Manor. *Jesus Christ, he grew up here?* "This is your parents' house?"

"Yes."

"You grew up here?"

"Yes, and it was as lonely as you'd imagine," he says sadly.

I narrow my eyes at him sadly as he pulls up the long driveway and parks behind Drew's car. I grab his hand and squeeze; for the first time, I realize that Will may be as nervous as I am. "Hey, before we go in there…" I trail off. "Just know that you never have to feel lonely in that house ever again. I'm here." I kiss his knuckles one by one, and he pulls my face away from his hand before pressing his lips to mine. We kiss for what feels like ages, like teenagers as we make out in a car in front of his parent's house. After a while, I pull away, his lips now bright red from my lipstick, and I know it has to be all over my lips also. After a few minutes, we're presentable as we begin our trek up the long walkway into Montgomery Manor.

When we walk through the front door, I'm not sure what I expected, but it's not as cold as I thought it would be. It's actually quite the opposite.

"SON!" J.R. bellows as he pulls Will into a hug. "Charley." He squeezes me tight and lifts me slightly off the ground before setting me on my feet. "You look lovely as always," he tells me as he begins walking towards the kitchen. "Come, your mother is almost finished with dinner."

Will and I walk hand in hand to the kitchen to find Drew sitting at the bar talking to Diana. Diana has an apron wrapped around her waist, with slippers on her feet, and if I wasn't seeing it with my own two eyes I wouldn't have believed it. *She's so domestic. No heels?*

"Oh, honey!" Diana says as she makes her way over to us. "I'm so glad you came." She kisses Will's cheek and it's almost as if it's a completely different Diana. *They're trying, Charley.*

"Charley. You look lovely," she says, pressing a kiss to my cheek and I stiffen slightly. *This is so…awkward. Are we just pretending that nothing has happened between us?*

"Thank…you, Mrs. Montgomery."

"Please, Diana." *Diana? Really? I don't know what it is this woman is selling, but I'm not buying it.*

I look at Drew and he hasn't said anything to Will, and Will doesn't seem that interested in saying anything either.

"Hi, Drew." I give a small wave and he stands to make his way over to me.

"Charley," he says wrapping his arms around me and squeezing me.

The kitchen is silent, the awkwardness amongst five people, four immediate family members, and one transplant almost stifling. "Ummm, where's your bathroom?" I ask, wanting out of this completely tense situation, and knowing that Will can probably better diffuse the situation without me present.

"Down the hall to the left, baby. Do you want me to take you?"

"No, I can find it…I'm good." I smile before taking off down the hall. I close myself in the bathroom, locking the door behind me, and lean against the door. I press off the door and drop the lid to the toilet down so that I can sit, crossing my legs and putting my head in my hands.

Make the best of this situation, Charley. They're trying. I know it's weird, but they are trying to be nice. You have a baby on the way, and they are the grandparents. Play nice. For now.

I look down at my stomach. "I'm only doing this for you, little one," I whisper. After a few minutes, I figure it's time to get back out there. I open the door to see Will standing in front of the entrance, his eyes boring into me.

"Are you okay?" he whispers as his hands find my hair, tucking a group of strands behind one ear.

I nod. "Are you?"

"Yes, come. I want to tell them…are you okay with that?"

"Yes, I'm ready if you are."

We make it back to the kitchen to see the three of them talking. As soon as we enter the kitchen their attention turns to us.

"Before we sit down to dinner, we want to talk to you about a few things," Will announces.

"We should move into the living room while we wait for everything to be ready. Everything should be ready soon." Diana urges us as she removes her apron from her waist. Will pulls me through the kitchen and through a few rooms until we enter the living room. Everything is beige and tan and just so… *clean.* It makes me wonder what happens when anything is spilled. Room after room, everything is pristine and untouched like the space is for show and not for really for *living*. He sits down, pulling me as close as possible to him. Drew sits in the adjacent loveseat and his parents sit in the two chairs across from us.

"I hate that you've reduced us to this," he says after a moment. "You have my fiancée shaking like a leaf beside me because you make her so goddamn nervous." He turns to me and I'm slightly embarrassed to be put on the spot. "Baby, are you okay?" he whispers and I nod.

"I'm okay if you're okay," I whisper back and he smiles before kissing my lips.

"I'm not doing this bullshit with any of you," he says looking at his family. "I'm not bringing my family here ever again if you don't start putting in some effort. And I don't mean telling her she looks nice or faking pleasantries. I mean a real and valiant effort," he says. "Because…we are bringing a baby into the world, and I'm not doing it amidst tension and animosity."

Drew smiles, having known this all along. J.R.'s eyes widen as he chokes a little on his drink and Diana presses a hand to her chest.

"A… baby?" Diana asks, her eyes wide with an emotion I couldn't quite define.

"Yes, Charley is pregnant. We are having a baby."

"Oh my…a baby?" Diana asks again, and I nod as I see her attention has turned to me.

"Wow, son…congratulations!" J.R. says as he stands to his feet and pulls Will to his feet in response. "That is wonderful news. How far along are you?" he asks me. *Is he drunk? Who is this man?*

"About eight weeks," I say with a smile, my hand immediately going to my stomach.

"Well, I think this is the best news I've heard in a while," Drew says as he stands and hugs Will and then me. We are all standing, except for Diana whose eyes have now fixated on me. She must feel my gaze because she stands and gives me one of her signature smiles. *Fake.*

"That is…wonderful news. Congratulations." She hugs Will and gives me a cold kiss on my cheek. "I think the hens are finished, so let me just go check on them," she says before she disappears out of the room.

I purse my lips, trying to tell myself not to cry as the rejection from my future husband's mom cuts deeper than ever before. It's not just about me anymore. *She's rejecting my baby too.*

I. Have. Fucking. Had. It.

"One second," I tell Will, and I feel his hand on my arm stopping me.

"Baby…" he trails off and I shake my head.

"I'll be fine."

"Should I come—"

"No," I tell him. I press my lips to his, completely ignoring the fact that his father and brother's gazes are on me.

I make my way through the rooms, and when I make it to

the kitchen I am shocked to see that she isn't there. I see that the Cornish hens have been taken from the oven, but I don't see her anywhere. I make my way out of the kitchen, through the foyer and stare at the long staircase that leads to the second floor. I look around once before making my way up the stairs, knowing that there would be a long road ahead of me if I didn't end this tension between us once and for all.

I make it to the top and the sounds are unmistakable as I move closer to what I assume is the master suite. I'm frozen in place as I peek into the room, and spot Will's mother seated on a cream sofa in the corner of the room. Her face is buried in her hands as sobs wrack her body. I take a step into the room, holding my breath wondering now that I'm here, what on Earth am I going to say?

"D…Diana?" I stammer out and her eyes shoot up as if she's just been caught. She sweeps two fingers under her eyes and stands, wiping her hands on her apron.

She clears her throat. "I just needed a minute."

"I didn't mean to intrude I just wanted to—"

"To tell me about myself, I assume," she says.

"Well, that was the intention…" I trail off as I reluctantly move to the sofa by the window. She sits back down, and I sit next to her. I reach my hand out to touch her before yanking my hand back instantly like she's a stove…hot to the touch.

"Does my son hate me, Charley?" she asks, the tears in her eyes streaking down her cheeks. "Did I ruin him?"

The words hurt my heart, and I want nothing more than to tell her that she certainly didn't help. "Your son isn't ruined," I say softly. "He's brilliant, and kind, and wonderful. He's an amazing human. You should be proud of the man you raised," I tell her honestly.

"I'm a mother to a psychologist. I know what sidestepping a question looks like." She smiles sadly as she wipes her eyes. "This is all so very embarrassing. I shouldn't be asking you that."

"I think Will harbors some pain over things that have happened in the past but...Will doesn't hate you. Despite any issues, he adores you. He looks up to you."

"He does?" she asks, and I nod, knowing that deep down it's the truth, which is why I need everyone on the same team.

"I thought he hated me, and then..." she sniffles, "he'd never let me see my grandchild." The tears flood her eyes. "And how I've treated you...why would you want me around your baby? I wouldn't. I'd tell me to go straight to hell."

"I think I kind of already did that once." I smile and she gives me a small smile in return.

"I had a mother in law from hell too." She looks at me before she looks down at the ground. "I had the last word though," she says, and I can't help but chuckle at her morbid humor. "I don't expect you to want to get lunch or spend time together or...want me involved in your life but, if you could find it in your heart to forgive me for being my worst fear—*my* mother in law—I would really love that."

My thoughts go back to something that Lauren had said a few months back. "Children may not fix anything, but grandchildren fix everything." I guess she was right. All it took was the promise of new life to quiet the storm.

"I...I have sonograms...if you want one."

"I would love one." She smiles before she dabs at her eyes. "I am sorry, Charley. I know you don't think I was acting in my son's best interest, but I truly was. And now that you're a mother, I hope you can understand. I just—"

"I get it," I tell her, wondering how I'd react if my son were in a similar situation. *Would I trust the woman? Would I trust that her intentions were true?* "But I would just like you to know, that I would *never* hurt Will. I love him with everything I am. He's my soulmate...and I was powerless to stop what happened between us. Maybe you still need more time to trust me, that I'm not going to hurt him or leave him or whatever it is that you thought, but I'm just asking that you give me a chance."

"I'll give you one if you give me a chance to make this right."

I look away from Diana towards the door and smile. "You have to make it right with more than just me."

"I will. I'll fix everything."

"It won't happen overnight," I warn her. *There are years of pain that they need to work through.*

"I know." She nods in understanding.

I nod. "Then I think we will be just fine." We both stand and I wonder if she's going to hug me, but I don't think either of us are ready for that.

"I'm going to fix my face, and then I'll be right down."

"Of course, I'll give you some space," I say as I make my way out of the room.

"Charley?" she calls after me, and I turn to face her. "Welcome to the family." She gives me a small, genuine smile, and then she's gone.

———

"So, you're having lunch with my mother next week?" Will asks as he climbs into bed next to me.

Lord give me strength. "Indeed."

"You going to tell me what that's about?"

"We just had a…mother to mother talk."

He nods. "I'm supposed to have lunch with her and my brother on Monday."

"Ah, the weekly lunch."

"They both want to talk to me." He presses his lips to my temple. "Something tells me you had something to do with that."

I turn my head to look at him and pucker my lips allowing him to kiss me. "I don't know what you're talking about."

He chuckles. "It's funny, you came to me because you needed

help, you wanted change… and somehow you were the one to change me." I turn around in his arms so that I can face him. "I had years of issues built up, and you've somehow slowly broke down all of them."

"It's amazing what love can do." I smile, knowing that he did the same for me.

"Can you believe this time next year, we'll have a baby?"

A smile finds my face immediately. "Do you want to know if it's a boy or a girl?"

"Mmmm, no." He shakes his head.

"Me either." I giggle as I snuggle closer back to him.

"I can't wait to marry you," he whispers in my ear.

"So, no to eloping in Europe, right?"

"I suppose that's up to you, and how lunch with my mother goes." He raises an eyebrow at me and I roll my eyes.

"She seems to be coming around…" I trail off, "but I've got my eyes open."

———

Two months later

"Careful!" I point as Will and Drew move boxes into the house. We leave for Europe in three days and for some crazy, unknown reason, we decided to move out of his townhouse before we left.

"Baby, get inside, it's chilly out here." Despite the movers we hired, Will and Drew are still moving a fair share of our stuff as well. We'd been moving since yesterday morning, and it finally seemed like there was light at the end of the tunnel. I look around the living room and there is shit *everywhere.* I'd hired an interior decorator, that I'd be meeting with next month when we returned, to help furnish some of the rooms that I had no idea what to do with. Coming from a townhouse, to a large, five bedroom house, clearly called for much more furniture than we already had. *And now we needed a nursery.*

Hours later, Will and I are sitting on our bed, the only piece of furniture in the whole house that we assembled. "You know this is the only room of the house we didn't christen when we were here?" he growls in my ear as I remember that we wanted to leave something sacred.

I bounce excitedly on our new future marital bed and grin. "Are you suggesting that we change that?"

"Yes, I am," he says as he begins to peel my clothes off of me slowly.

I sigh as I think about the fact that I'm here, in a new house, with the love of my life, about to embark on a new chapter of life together. I'm starting a family, the new life inside of me growing stronger by the day.

Last week, I had lunch with Bree, Matt's best friend's wife, that he'd had an affair with a while back and I finally disclosed everything that Nathan didn't know like *who* exactly my affair was with. She was supportive, understanding, and begged me to let her know when the wedding would be. She also apologized for never telling me about her and Matt. *But that was the last thing I was concerned about.*

On top of everything, she had actually given me some interesting news. Matt was moving too. *To San Francisco.* His job had promoted him, and he'd jumped at the opportunity to relocate. *My guess is to get away from the drama of his failed marriage.* Nevertheless, I was happy for him. He deserved happiness. Happiness that he couldn't find with me. My hopes are that maybe he could find it elsewhere. As much as Matt hurt me—as much as we hurt each other—if it weren't for him, there's a chance I never would have met Will. *My happily ever after.*

Epilogue

Charlotte

I**T IS RARE THAT IT SNOWS IN ATLANTA, BUT EVERY ONCE IN A** while, when the North gets a crazy February snow storm, we are blessed with a few flakes, our streets covered with a thin sheet of white powder. Will and I are outside, the snowflakes falling all around us, and I can't help but feel that something magical is about to happen. I feel his hand laced with mine and, despite our gloves, I can feel the spark between us.

The sky has gotten darker since we've been walking around the park near our house, and it makes the air more gray and magical. The ground is completely covered, and the snow is already piling up on the branches making for a complete winter wonderland. I pull my hat further down over my ears as the snow begins to fall more heavily. We've been walking in silence for a few minutes when I feel his hands on me, prohibiting me from taking another step.

"Charlotte," he says, and my heart races out of lust hearing my name fall from his lips.

"Will." I can see the breath I let out, as well as his as he's breathing hard at this point.

"I don't want you to think that I'm…stealing your thunder." He smiles. "You've asked, I said yes… when we were naked." He teases.

My mouth drops open and I playfully hit him, until my brain realizes what's happening.

"I was in this spot a little under a year ago when I realized I was in love with you."

"Really?" My eyes light up. I look around trying to memorize the scenery before turning back to him. He pulls his gloves off his hands and cups my face, giving me a slow kiss on my lips and, despite the cold temperatures, I'm warm all over. His tongue massages mine gently and when he pulls away I can't stop the smile from spreading across my face.

"Charlotte Pierce," he starts, "my favorite patient. The one that got under my skin from the start and stayed there. For so long I thought you were just burrowing your way into my mind. I spent so many nights, trying to get you out of my head. So many times, I tried to stop thinking about you. But it was no use, because you had burrowed your way into my heart. You are the best person that I've ever met in my life, and I plan to spend the rest of my life proving to you that I'm worthy of you…that me and…this," he points between us and I get the point he's trying to make, "is worth…*everything*." At this point, I don't even try to stop the tears from streaming down my face. "For the first time in maybe my entire life, you've shown me what unconditional love feels like. You loved me even when I was at my lowest. You loved me even when the world was against us…when we were backed into a corner. You fought for me and for us, and I promise to do that with you for the rest of our lives. You and me against the world, baby." He pulls my gloves gently from my hands, before he brings them to his lips, kissing them gently before he lowers himself to one knee. "So, since you've already asked…" he smirks, "I'll ask you in a different way. Will you spend the rest of your life with me, Charlotte? Spend…forever with me?" He opens the ring box to reveal the most gorgeous, not to mention large, oval shaped diamond ring.

"Oh my God, yes!" I scream so loud I wonder if all of Georgia heard me.

He's immediately on his feet scooping me into his arms and spinning me around once before he sets me on his feet.

"I love you so much, Charlotte. I am going to make you so happy."

"You already do, Will. We are going to be so happy together." He slides the ring on my finger and I'm in awe at the beauty of this piece of jewelry. I don't know how long I've been staring at it when I feel his lips at my temple.

"Do you like it?"

"Like it?! Will I'm in awe, it's so beautiful," I tell him as fresh tears find my eyes.

"You're beautiful," he murmurs in my ear, and I look up to find his eyes shining with love and adoration.

I press my lips to his, and I'm lost in his kiss as the snowflakes surround us—a couple who fell in love against all odds.

During my divorce, I spent so much time regretting the time that I lost, but I've realized that without my failed marriage I wouldn't have been ready for the perfect one with Will—my marriage counselor.

The End.

Author's Note

Will and Charlotte's story is complete. It feels odd to type that, it was even more surreal typing the words "*The End.*" These two possessed and consumed me in a way that I feel like they're embedded deep in my soul somewhere. For all of you that joined me on their journey, a million thank yous! The shares and comments and kind words moved me more than you know. Although their story is complete, I can promise you'll see a glimpse of their life through someone else's eyes. Lauren's story is up next and as you can probably guess—hers is nothing like Charlotte's.

I hope you're ready for the next ride.

Acknowledgements

Carmel, Helen, Kristene and Erica: Thank you for being the most fantastic betas! Neither of the Bittersweet books would have been possible without you. Your love, support and friendship mean the world to me. Love you guys!

Liz: Thank you for making my books so beautiful! I can't to see what you come up with next!

Meli, Suzan, Christelle, Alexis, Melissa, Amanda, Jeanette, Kelly, Samantha, Kristina, Rachel, Harlipen, Paula, Leslie, Nani, Pat, Carol (x3), Kerri, Colleen, Gayle, Hope, Regina, Amber, Candice, Crissy, Aby, Kris, Karen (x2), Gloria, Julie (x2), Connie, Nichole, Tonya, Tatiane, Cindy, Lori, Shannon, Kim, Marie-Lyne and SO many more including Everyone in the Hive(s) and all of the Witches: Thank you for being on this ride with me. Thank you for your excitement. For making me laugh on the regular and making me believe in myself. For being the family I've made for myself. You're the best.

Also by
Q.B. TYLER

My Best Friend's Sister
Unconditional
Forget Me Not
Bittersweet Love
Love Unexpected
Unlawful Coming Soon

BITTERSWEET DUET

Bittersweet Surrender
Bittersweet Addiction

CAMPUS TALES SERIES

First Semester
Second Semester
Spring Semester
Summer Semester Coming Soon

ABOUT

the Author

Hailing from the Nation's Capital, Q.B. Tyler, spends her days constructing her "happily ever afters" with a twist, featuring sassy heroines and the heroes that worship them. But most importantly the love story that develops despite *inconvenient* circumstances.

Sign up for her newsletter to stay in touch!
eepurl.com/doT8EL

Qbtyler03@gmail.com

Website:
www.authorqbtyler.com

Facebook
www.facebook.com/author.qbtyler

Reader Group:
www.facebook.com/groups/784082448468154

Goodreads:
www.goodreads.com/author/show/17506935.Q_B_Tyler

Instagram;
www.instagram.com/qbtyler.author

Bookbub:
www.bookbub.com/profile/q-b-tyler

Twitter:
twitter.com/qbtyler

Printed in Great Britain
by Amazon

82612055R00202